Long Reach

Mike Lunnon-Wood was born in Africa and edu-
cated in Australia and New Zealand. Based in
the Middle East for ten years, he now lives in
West Sussex and has a young son.

MIKE LUNNON-WOOD

LONG REACH

HarperCollins*Publishers*

HarperCollins*Publishers*
77–85 Fulham Palace Road,
Hammersmith, London W6 8JB

The HarperCollins website address is:
www.**fire**and**water**.com

A Paperback Original 1999
1 3 5 7 9 8 6 4 2

A catalogue record for this book is
available from the British Library

ISBN 0 00 651163 5

Set in Meridien by
Rowland Phototypesetting Ltd,
Bury St Edmunds, Suffolk

Printed and bound in Great Britain by
Caledonian International Book Manufacturing Ltd, Glasgow

For Harry Maddison.
Thanks, Harry, this one's for you.

Acknowledgements

No book like this can be written by a civilian without immense help and support from those who know about warfare. I thank, again, the wardroom and crew of HMS *Richmond* for helping me understand modern naval action and I must acknowledge the sterling efforts of Michael Hill at PJHQ Northwood, without whom researching a book like this would be very difficult.

Here I thank publicly, but without naming them for obvious reasons, the many professional soldiers at Aldershot and Hereford, especially Mike and Harry, who gave so much of their time helping me understand soldiering, that oldest of professions. Any mistakes are mine, not theirs.

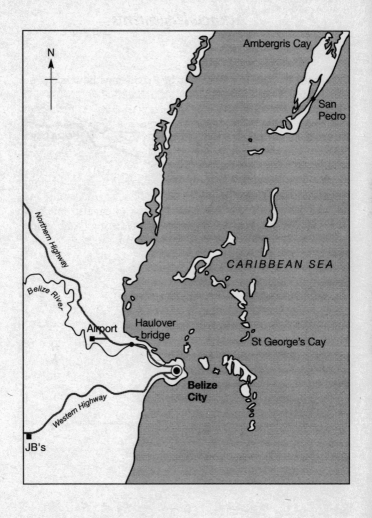

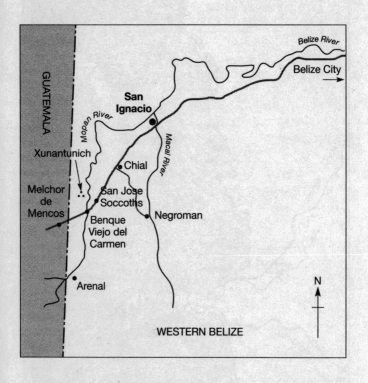

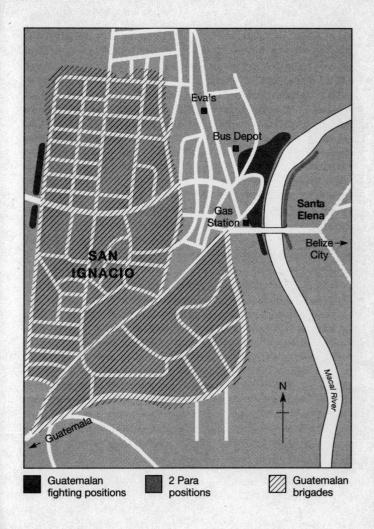

Eva's

Bus Depot

Gas
Station

**SAN
IGNACIO**

Santa
Elena

Belize →
City

Guatemala →

Macal River

N

| ■ | Guatemalan fighting positions | ▨ | 2 Para positions | ▩ | Guatemalan brigades |

Prologue

It was theirs: part of Guatemala. Always was, always had been. He looked out from his hilltop position, across the canopy of the rain-forest into Belize, and lifted the binoculars to his eyes, sweeping them north-east towards the river and the valley. His understanding of Central American history was flawed by his patriotically biased edu-cation and like many army officers he was more interested in his appearance than in things tactical. He liked clean, crisp creases, his splendid dress uniform, and the figure he cut in aviator Ray-Bans, his moustache perfectly trimmed.

The girls liked it too and there weren't many out here, which was why he was keen to get back to Guatemala City. Two more days and his patrol would be over; with luck he could return to the capital, give those who might ask about his absence a knowing smile, an I'm-sorry-but-I-can't-say look, develop the mystique a bit – but he wasn't sure. Lots of orders had been changed in the last month or so.

His patrol were out behind him, men of the crack 2nd Regiment. He really should get them out here more often, he thought, too much ceremonial duty wasn't good for elite troops; but his command didn't seem too worried about it, so why should he bother? He would rather be back in the city. He, Capitano José Biente, wasn't a lover of the forest or the rivers, but he was as vain and resplendent as any tropical bird. He had a new pair of Calvin Klein jeans and with the white shirt knocked up by his tailor worn open to show the spread of his chest, a cream linen jacket over his shoulders matinée-idol style, and his current girlfriend on his arm, he would look good on the plaza.

He had no idea, but within a week, down in the forest below, deep inside Belize, he would meet another professional soldier, Company Sergeant Major Nandu Goreng of the 7th Duke of Edinburgh's Own Gurkha Rifles, now C Company, 2nd Battalion, the Parachute Regiment. CSM Goreng with his heavy-bladed kukri, the traditional

11

curved fighting knife of the Gurkhas, would, with two blows, end the career and the life of Guatemalan Army Capitano José Biente. Which was just as well, because the first blow would remove his left cheek and shatter his lower jaw and he would not have looked much good on the plaza after that.

Some eighty miles away in a squalid flat on the first floor of a wooden clapboard house in Belize City, a fifty-eight-year-old man of very mixed origins waited and drank. His drink of choice was Gordon's Gin, but that was expensive, so he made do with a cheaper variant and early in the day he mixed it with water. By three o'clock he was drinking it neat and by sundown on most days he was stone drunk. Like many very heavy drinkers he hid it well; he could walk, talk, hold a conversation if anyone would listen, but he remembered nothing the following day, often waking fully clothed. From the window in the flat he had rented six weeks before he could see the port over the rooftops. The big grey bulk of the British ship was nowhere to be seen. She was scheduled in three days' time, but one could never tell. All he had to do was watch her loading and report her departure – then he would get the second half of the money.

Once he had been a professional man, an architect, working in the sprawling metropolis of Mexico City. He had even been up north once, to Los Angeles, but they had found him and thrown him out. In the last few years it had become worse – the drink. This money would give him a new start, back in Mexico, where he belonged. Maybe he could go back into his work, designing elegant buildings, not the electricity sub-stations and dreary local police headquarters he had worked on before. He looked out over the filthy narrow canal, past clapboard houses, peeling paint and corrugated iron rooftops at the harbour, in reality nothing more than a long concrete pier that jutted out into the shallow waters. Big ships, like those that carried the sugar northwards, had to wait out in the channel, but lighter ships with shallower draught could get all the way in and tie up at the jetty.

The heat and humidity were stifling, and his shirt was damp in spite of the shuttered, unglazed window openings. He lifted his grubby glass; just one more shot, he thought. After all, what was it they said? Something about the sun being over the arm yard?

12

Chapter One

It was hot on the crowded street, people jostling each other as they made their way out of the market. A black man, his hair in dreadlocks, was following two tourists, young women, hassling them to buy something. They refused again, but he was persistent, his demeanour now threatening. Harry Rees took it all in and against his better judgement increased his pace. Most of Belize City's population were courteous and decent God-fearing people, the traders just trying to scratch a living. There was sometimes, as anywhere, an unpleasant edge, and very often it was the Rastafarian peddlers and ganja dealers, who were common in Belize City, selling drugs and doing deals with the eco-tourists. That was fair enough, but they didn't like being refused and weren't above intimidation to get the sale made. Rees didn't like that sort of thing, particularly when English girls were being hassled. He was big, six-feet-five in his bare feet, with a fifty-two-inch chest; he had played competitive rugby, and two seasons before he had been capped for England.

The Rasta moved round in front of the two girls and held out his hands to stop them. They tried to brush past to one side and he sidestepped in front of them again; then Rees was there, towering over them.

'Eh! You hassling my friends?'

An ally, a bloke, English – the relief in the eyes of the two girls was evident.

'No ma'an, I just wanna –' the Rasta began.

'Fuck off!' Rees interjected, jerking a thumb. 'Jo'ear me ma'an?' He managed a credible impression of the Rastafarian's part-Jamaican, part-local patois.

The chap looked daggers at Rees and then shrugged and disappeared back into the market.

13

'Thanks,' one of the girls said. 'That was getting, um, uncomfortable.'

Rees looked at her closely for the first time. Tallish, chunky round the sarong-wrapped hips, a loose cotton sleeveless blouse, hair the colour of dark copper tied back and a pair of expensive sunglasses that she took off. She smiled, her green eyes taking him in; she was older than he had first thought. Not a kid – mid to late twenties perhaps. The other was blonde, svelte, little colourful plastic beads threaded through strands of hair over her ears and back into the rubber band that held it all together in a loose pony-tail.

'My pleasure, ladies. They can be a pain in the arse . . . Excuse my French.'

The dark girl smiled at the expression. Manners – he had manners.

'Do you know the town?' she asked. 'We were going to look for something long and cold.'

'No, Soph. Tea! Tea! I'm gagging for a decent cup of tea!' the blonde said.

'I've been here once or twice; often enough, I think, to please both of you.' He smiled, turned and pointed. 'Do you know the Fort Street Guest House, just up there on the right?'

The dark one smiled. 'Yes, we know it. We are staying there.'

'Ah. Well . . . that's the closest that I could recommend,' he replied.

'Can we buy you one?' the blonde asked. 'Come on, don't be a sad bastard,' she finished with a cheeky little grin.

'Helen!' the other said with mild reproach.

He grinned and flicked a look at his watch. 'I'd love to join you.' He held out a hand. 'I'm Harry.'

The dark girl took it. 'Sophie. This is Helen.'

They sat on the veranda, at a table in the shade, the breeze off the sea taking the heat from the air. Sophie and Harry were drinking fresh lime juice from pint mugs loaded with ice, and Helen had tea. They talked amiably as people do when they have discovered someone they like where they least expect it, Harry mildly flirting with both of them. They discovered they all lived within twenty miles of each other.

14

'Oh. Aldershot,' Sophie said. 'Are you a . . .'

'Squaddy?' Helen chimed in

'I am,' Harry replied with a grin. 'Crap job, but someone has to do it.'

'You're no squaddy,' Helen said, her eyes taking him in over her teacup. 'Bloody officer and gentleman written all over you.'

'Guilty. I'm with 2 Para,' he replied, with some pride in his regiment. 'What about you two?'

'We teach special-needs children,' Helen replied and the talk rambled on until Harry looked at his watch.

'I have to go. It was nice meeting you both,' he said, his eyes on Sophie's.

'Oh. How long are you here for? Will we . . . ?' She trailed off.

'Away tomorrow afternoon, I'm afraid,' he replied, thinking, I should get her number. Get her number, come on, dimwit. Opportunity is fading. 'Perhaps I can phone you when you get back?'

'Ah . . . sure. Yes,' Sophie said with a little confused smile, 'I don't have –'

'I do,' Helen said. She fished in her bag and passed Harry a small gold address label, one of the type people stick on envelopes. 'We share a house. Phone number's at the bottom.'

'Thanks. Well, enjoy the rest of your holiday, and mind the Rastas.'

He picked up the bags of vegetables and meat he had bought and took the steps two at a time. After he had gone Sophie looked at Helen.

'God! You were forward!'

'Oh bollocks,' Helen replied, pouring more tea, 'he is a drop-dead-gorgeous hunk and you are too bloody coy by half. Did you see the way he looked at you? He could slip his shoes under my bed anytime.'

'Well, then you –'

'He didn't fancy me. He fancied you.'

'You may have forgotten, but I am seeing someone,' Sophie responded, but she could feel herself weakening as she said it, a nice warm feeling flowing up through her.

15

'He is a bastard and you know it – so do his wife and kids. Give up on him.'

At that moment, a hundred miles to the south-west, Rob McKay finished shovelling his 'scoff' into his mouth and pushed the soft packaging into a plastic bag and back into his bergen. Leave nothing. Nothing to say you had passed, no sign – ever. The other three were doing the same. This was hard routine; they had been moving since leaving the observation post at midday, their 'gollocks', their machetes or kukris, sheathed, pushing their way slowly through the undergrowth, leaving no marks on trees, sidestepping spiders' webs, avoiding anything that would betray their passage. The last food had been wolfed down cold that morning. The day had passed in silence. No words had been spoken; all communication was by hand signals, everyone understanding exactly what they were to do if it went pear-shaped, the rendezvous agreed if they had a contact and had to scatter. This was not a fighting patrol, it was covert. Their task was to establish what was going on over the border, check out the rumours, learn what they could and return unseen. Two hours till nightfall and they had stopped to eat again, the last food this day, again cold from the packaging. Up this high with the wind direction as it was no one was going to smell anything downwind, if in fact anyone was there. This was the rain-forest, the jungle – the 'J'. The pleasure of hot food was wonderful, even the bland gunk that came out of the ratpacks, but they couldn't risk it. They had eaten in silence, one of them on stag thirty feet below where he could see any movement along the river's edge and on the track below them; anything moving in the secondary growth they would hear. They would get out the comms kit, set up the aerial and try for a contact with their base at Hereford. That was standard – comms always went back to Hereford. They would channel it back to Airport Camp. If that failed, then tab on and try later, then move on again, using the last two hours of light to clear the area before settling into a lying-up point, LUP, and selecting where they would put up their bashas. Stand to again until darkness fell, then get bashas up, the hammocks that would keep them above ground level while they rested, away from the mud, the snakes and creatures that bit and stung. Change into dry kit and sleep. This deep into the secondary 'J' nothing moved at night – sometimes even in broad daylight you couldn't see four feet in front of your face. They would be safe enough, even if they were still a mile inside Guatemala and only two miles from the army post they had watched that morning. McKay nodded to Jack Boyce who was humping the comms kit and without speaking, in almost absolute silence, they began to run out the aerial wires.

The patrol had been routine but covert. Air troop's sixteen members were in Belize as part of the British MoD training team on attachment to the Belize Defence Force. This was basic skills transfer: use, care and maintenance of weapons, basic section and platoon drills and tactics. But some of the troop were often deployed on patrol, their role more direct in the defence of the small nation so long threatened by its larger neighbour, Guatemala, who wanted better access to the Caribbean and the Atlantic, and claimed much of the southern half of Belize, once British Honduras, as their legitimate territory.

Every so often one of the patrols, in response to rumour and their own intelligence-gathering among the Maya people of the forest, would cross into Guatemala and check things out, actually see what was going on. This time there was plenty; a new vehicle track had been cut through a section of the jungle to link what was once a small Guatemalan army post with the main road. There was movement on the road, trucks of troops moving northwards, one vehicle broken down, its driver sitting in the cab asleep. He would never know how close he came to 'disappearing' – if he had woken up while one of the patrol was removing the paperwork, the vehicle records, clearances and orders from the seat beside him, he would have had to go.

There were recent repairs to bridges and culverts, fuel was being stored and so on, and this was way to the north-west of the Guatemalan military's usual concentrations around Punta Bario. This was the tenth day of the patrol and the third time they were calling in with intelligence. The previous two reports had offered nothing substantive; indications of troop build-ups, but nothing concrete. The talk among the Mayans, who respected no borders and crossed through the rain-forest at will, was that they had seen soldiers moving about, some times many, many of them and McKay's patrol had at last seen the evidence that morning. But how far did it go? Was there other movement along the border? This was one place – the Guatemalan–Belize border was a hundred miles long and there were at least three or four other points where there would be activity. The south? Possible, McKay thought, but unlikely. There was a crossing point down near Punta Bario, but it was more likely up on the road border post above San Ignacio at Melchor, and there were also the rivers either side of the post. The strip of relatively dry low ground was about ten miles wide at that point. The rest of the southern border had the best natural defence in the world. Thick rain-forest, primary and secondary jungle, steep ridges that climbed and fell without warning. In some places small expert patrols took days to cover a few kilometres, and there was no way you could move any number of men through the 'green'. Some of it was primary jungle, easy enough, the high rain-forest canopy shading the ground enough to prevent secondary growth. But much of it had been slashed and burned and the growth was now secondary, thick vegetation, wait-a-while thorn on almost vertical slopes.

Oddly, towards the river there were miles of pine trees where the topography changed. From there northwards the country was more similar to the northern Yucatan and Mexico: savannah grasslands, pines, mangrove swamps. But here the green was exhausting to move through and no com-mander in his right mind would try and manoeuvre any size-able tactical attacking force through it.

Down in the south the crossing was a bitch, a series of foot-trails down in the low-lying areas near Guatemala's little strip of Atlantic coast. On the Belize side the road ran out at Punta Gorda and from there on, even overt, it was on foot through the swamps or by helicopter, just to get to the border. That wasn't an option, which left only one, and you didn't have to be a tactical genius to work that out – straight down the road to San Ignacio. The river was a possible, but the two little dams would hinder progress. However, once below the dams men could be moved by boat, enough to make flank attacks. The rains had started, so the water level would be high enough to take inflatables over the rapids. He would, he reasoned, someone would need to recce the river, there would be indications on the Guats' side.

A patrol would have to be dropped somewhere and then tab in through the bush. Either way, things were looking interesting and the head sheds back at both Hereford and Airport Camp needed to know. The Guats had done this before, built up troops in a border area; in the sixties, the seventies and again in the eighties. Now in the nineties they seemed to be doing it again, but this time they were covering their tracks better, and according to the pre-patrol briefing there seemed to have been none of the diplomatic bluster or public challenges of the previous decades. It could be manoeuvres or training, but it also could be more and the head sheds might want to put a couple more patrols out.

Boyce shifted his end of the wire and checked the bearing with a compass. They had been in this valley ten days before and the east-sou'east line worked best. The aerial extended, Sergeant Robert McKay, B Squadron (Air Troop) of the Special Air Service Regiment, began entering the message on to the tiny keypad. Boyce left him to it and moved back to cover their rear. For him this was the fourth day without a cigarette and the thought of the smoke hitting the back of his throat when they cleared the area was wonderful. The ridge before them, the route back, was primary jungle. Compared with today it would be fast tabbing that and they would be back in Belize before dark and lie up back on their side of the border, maybe even come off the hard routine and get to light a smoke.

Oddly enough for a twenty-a-day man Boyce was phenomenally fit, a triathlete who had represented Britain and was also handy at what many in the Regiment called 'jap-slapping', the martial arts. Gibson, sitting a few feet from him, was better, international standard, and like Dozy Tupping, the

19

fourth man in the patrol, he didn't have any front teeth to prove it. Dozy had lost his in an attack outside a pub in Belfast, hit in the face with a section of angle-iron without warning. As he went down he saw a gun and kept rolling, drawing his own weapon and firing. He expended five rounds from his Browning and was then running like hell, his face masked in blood, his lower jaw broken. It was all over in under five seconds and the IRA were short three of their players.

Gibbo was the jungle expert; he had spent time as an instructor in the jungle training camps and was as at home in the 'J' as any westerner could be. He had led them on the tab and was now checking their position relative to the maps they used with a global positioning system. He looked up from his GPS and across at Boyce and mimed smoking a cigarette, knowing it would piss him off, a grin all over his face. Boyce from his position thirty feet away extended two fingers at him. McKay had finished entering the message and hit the fast burst transmit button. A confirmation flashed back at him and within a minute he was rolling up his end of the aerial. Time to go. He would report in again when they made their LUP.

At Airport Camp the D Coy offices were in a old prefab hut that had been temporary in the seventies. The door swung open and Captain Atlee looked up. Harry Rees, back from town, was still in civvy kit, carrying the essentials he had gone in for. Two cases of Heineken beer, salad stuff, some meat from one of the few decent butchers, big steaks, pork chops, some beef mince that he had watched them put through the machine and some sausages that had reputedly been made up in one of the Mennonite settlements, solid Germanic-looking things of some size. Atlee looked at them.

'They're organic,' Harry said drily. 'Made by the Mennonites.'

'I shall eat one with due reverence. All we need now is a steel band and some totty to brighten the place up a bit.'

'I don't know about a band,' Harry replied with a grin, 'but I did just meet two ladies. I know where they are staying. They might be busy though, it's very short notice.'

'What? And miss the chance of seeing us cook on an open-top tourer?' Be a dashing young sub and phone 'em – and let's ask the two at the consulate.'

This was their last night in Belize and the company officers were going to wind down. Someone, in return for a bottle of Scotch, had borrowed a barbecue from the engineers, a half forty-four-gallon oil drum upturned on legs, with a harrow disc that sat over half the surface area, forming a huge wok, and an open grill the other end for direct heat. The harrow disc had been the innovation of an SAS bloke who had seen them used in Zimbabwe, but below the half-drum the rest was REME through and through. They were not so much wheels on a frame as an undercarriage, with high-tensile steel axles beautifully machined on a lathe and small pneumatic tyres on lightweight wheels. The front axle was mounted on a vertical shaft, an aluminium bogey pylon that would have looked good on a Harrier, that allowed it to turn, and there was an A-frame tow-bar and seemingly enough bearings to require grease nipples. It had been towed over that morning behind a drab-painted quad bike, one of the machines going through tropical testing.

'Fuck me,' Atlee muttered, standing back and looking at it. 'It's a Bentley with a barbecue on it.'

'So much for defence cuts,' Harry had replied. ''Tis a wonder to behold.'

''Tis that,' Atlee agreed in the same tone.

'This requires more than a few bits of chicken. This needs – '

'Off you go then,' Atlee said.

Atlee watched Rees with a smile as he picked up the telephone book and looked up the number. Six weeks in Belize – this was a good way to spend the last night. The company was packed up and ready to go. He wasn't officially part of D Coy's strength, but attached for the exercise; tomorrow afternoon the Hercs that had brought in C Coy two hours before, for their training stint, would return to the UK with D Company and he would be going with them. The toms would be pleased to get back – real beer, families, girlfriends, Sunday lunches.

21

'I suppose we better invite Dickie Fox's chaps,' he said, thinking aloud.

Airport Camp was big, big enough for the battalion-sized garrison it had housed in the seventies and eighties. Back then the garrison was supported by Harriers and all the usual support elements to keep a battalion at readiness, but now most of the camp was empty, Britain's withdrawal slow but inexorable as the defence dividend bit deeper into a seemingly ever-smaller military capability.

At the other end of the camp, the quieter end further from the road and the airport buildings, where the SAS training detachment troop was billeted, Captain Chris Bonner was standing behind one of the signallers in the small hot room that housed the troop's comms gear. It was high-tech stuff, much of it satellite-linked, but still there were some serious radio masts out the back. Bonner was wearing only a pair of shorts and flip-flops; his bergen, webbing and weapons were, as always, packed and ready to go in his room. The signaller transcribed the message and handed it to him. His patrol had reported in, through Hereford as was standard operating procedure, and things were happening. His remaining men were scattered round the place: McKay's lads were in the 'J'; four of them were in the camp, another four were detached with the BDF on river crossing training and the last patrol were split, two of them in Belmopan with various local units doing weapons skills courses and two with the BDF's B Coy at the barracks opposite the Maritime Wing in Belize City. The Belize Defence Force was only six hundred strong and it was, as the military attaché at the embassy described it, 'a shit job'. Badly paid and poorly motivated, they surprisingly rose to the challenges laid down by their trainers, who using praise and encouragement found something in the men; but invariably, once the training team had departed, the standards slipped again and within weeks the weapons and kit were filthy and the pride had evaporated.

On the basis of what had come through from Regiment, Bonner made his decisions and the signallers went to work. Bleepers went off all over Belize as he recalled his troop from their various functions. Bonner would have made a first-class major in any line unit in the British army, but in the Regiment he wore a captain's pips. He was like many of his troop out of 2 Para, but unlike them he could not stay indefinitely and had only another eighteen months to run with the Regiment. Most officers had two years only but he had managed to extend for a second two because he was about to make major and take over as the Regiment's G-2. G-2 was Intelligence, an HQ function, but this for him was soldiering at its best. He walked to the door, pulled it open and looked out. Two of his blokes were sunning themselves in chairs by the door to their hut and he could see a third under the open-air shower, the door open as the man washed after a run. He whistled once and all three looked round. He jerked a thumb towards himself and went back into the comms room.

In London, it was late, but several short phone calls between senior people in Whitehall, some still in the MoD and the FCO buildings, and others at home had given the necessary authorizations. In Hereford things were stepped up a notch or two. The remaining three troops of B Squadron were being pulled together. Some were scattered as far as Botswana and as of half an hour before all were making their way to various RVs, most back to Hereford; others would meet up on route. Bonner was to expect the first of them by 0900 local the following day.

The Royal Fleet Auxiliary *Black Rover*, now almost a day out of Belize, was asked to turn around, and her helicopter, a Sea King crewed by the Royal Navy, was tasked and directed to fly to Airport Camp at Belize and await orders. She lifted off with every pound of fuel she could carry and two aircraft artificers for the three-hundred-and-fifty-mile over-water flight, the P1 not a happy man.

Six hundred miles away the Royal Navy's vessel on guardship duties in the Caribbean was HMS *Beaufort*. A Type 23 frigate, she had been on deployment for two months and was currently making passage between Grand Cayman and Jamaica for a goodwill visit and some shore leave for her company. None of them knew it, but there was to be no leave. Her Majesty's Government knew the value of big and visible signals, and there were few signals bigger and more visible than a warship if you wished to remind someone of your national interest. This tactic wasn't new – their Majesties and their governments had been putting their ships into situations as visible reminders of Great Britain's foreign policy for three hundred years. Various channels were being worked through, the decision process for any change of deployment. Northwood had responded and at that moment a coded signal was being prepared for HMS *Beaufort*, but owing to problems tracking down the necessary people, one of whom was in a gîte somewhere in France, and it now being 2100 Zulu (GMT), it would be another nine hours before Northwood were authorized and requested to redeploy *Beaufort*. It would be midnight local time before *Beaufort*'s complex comms gear began to hum with incoming through into her MCO, the main communications office. She would be ordered to proceed with all available speed to Belize. Further orders would be forthcoming.

At Airport Camp Captain Bonner pulled the big hardboard-mounted tactical maps away from the rack and selected four. Ordnance Survey had mapped Belize to hell and back. In this series there were some forty sheets mapping a country only a hundred and fifty miles long and seventy-odd miles wide. The 1:50,000 scale had houses, huts and walking paths marked. The ones he had pulled were mostly green with some scattered contour lines, only the thin strip of low-lying terrain with the twin ribbons of the road with its scattered settlements and the river varying the hue. Four men stood around the table, one of them rubbing a towel through his hair.

'McKay's patrol has called in – the scrotes are moving. Got a job for you,' Bonner said. He gave them their task, repeated it three times, finishing with, 'The other team will go in round the road border. Work out how you want to do it. I'll be back in half an hour. Find some transport, I want this patrol up there by 1900 hours. Do you want air?'

'Not initially,' the sergeant said, looking at the map, 'we'll take a Land-Rover. Might need it.'

'Take two. Tanner's team have called in, they will meet you

at the turn-off. Take enough kit for them. If you do want air there will be a Sea King here tonight, by 2000 hours.'

'Where you gonna be, boss?'

'Belmopan. I'll be back here by dawn, rest of the Squadron's coming in. A Gazelle will lift out McKay's team either tonight or at first light. Mark up an RV for noon tomorrow – if his team are there then form up with McKay as OC.' The sergeant nodded. He was new and McKay had more experience than most of the men in the Squadron.

'If you blokes want to be put in then say so now, because the pilots will need some sleep and they'll be working their arses off tomorrow.'

He looked at his watch. He had been invited across the camp to the Para lines for a barbecue but he would have to bin that. He wondered if they had been advised – probably not. Even if there was really something happening the warlords in Whitehall would wait for a further assessment from Squadron. 2 Para were rotating companies, one in, one out, routine training. If it all went pear-shaped there weren't many of them, he mused. His troop, RVing already; half a dozen techies from 148 battery-testing a remote reconnaissance vehicle, a little pilotless helicopter about the size of a rubbish bin with a serious television camera looking downward. There were about five REME – Royal Electrical and Mechanical Engineers – blokes maintaining the airstrips and the places the Harriers worked from, when they had them. There were the chaps on the two ancient AAC – the Army Air Corps – Gazelles, maybe ten of them. There was supposedly a troop of Comacchio marines down near Dangriga somewhere, but he hadn't come across them and just down the lines from them some 'loggies' were tropical-testing quad bikes, eight or nine of them. Word was that mobility troop were getting them and his blokes had borrowed a few of the quads for a thrash the weekend before. There were a few men out at St George's Cay at the training centre. Then there was the Para company, D Coy, of 2 Para. Bonner knew some of their officers from when he was with the battalion, and he had kept in touch as he would return to the unit at the end of his time with the Regiment.

Peter Tyson-Davis was the boss of D Company. Bonner had

heard the talk; Tyson-Davis was, they said, crash-hot. A tour with the Regiment under his belt, apparently he had pissed through selection, and was now reputedly the best line officer in the Parachute Reg and therefore arguably the best in the airborne. Tipped to make half-colonel on his return to the UK, his company shone at whatever they did, his ethos of nothing but excellence driven right down to the newest entrant. Even the crap-hats in P had heard of him and hoped, if they made the grade, they would be in his company. Known as 'Ted' by his toms, he was a lean, hard, superfit, focused individual on his way to the very top. They were out tomorrow, and Dickie Fox's C Company had come in and were at that moment sorting out their kit and getting squared away in the quarters they would operate from for the next six weeks. They wouldn't be there much; probably ten or twelve nights in Airport Camp in the entire time – the rest they would spend in the jungle. C Company were Gurkhas and he knew they took to the jungle training like they did to everything, committed and hardworking. This bunch had been through Brunei only two years before so they were familiar with the jungle.

One hundred and ninety-ish British army people, no RAF, no navy. If the scrote Guatemalans wanted to roll into Belize there wasn't much to stop them, certainly not the six-hundred-strong Belize Defence Force. The last strategic study estimated that the Guatemalans might use a force of some-thing between fifteen and twenty thousand troops, half of those they had available.

Whitehall – London

In the Foreign and Commonwealth Office in London two senior staff were manning the night desks. They had chased down the necessary people, one in the audience of a concert at the Royal Albert Hall and a second at home and advised them of the report from Belize. They in turn had spoken to the senior minister in the MoD who chaired the C3 standing committee and who authorized Hereford to step up their resources and ascertain what was happening. Now they were trying to get the necessary chain of decisions to authorize Northwood to re-task the RN's West Indies guardship. Now it was wait and see.

'That's that then,' one said. 'Let's hope it's all OK.'

'Probably nothing, they do this periodically. Lot of Latin-American sabre rattling,' the other responded. He was big, heavy, his waistcoat opened and his tie loosened. He was a double-first from Oxford, History and Modern languages, and had been in the FCO twelve years. His tone wasn't convincing.

'That's what we said about the Falklands.'

'Don't worry about it. Chaps from Hereford are going down to have a look. We will know soon enough.'

'And if?'

'God forbid,' the big man replied, taking his glasses from his nose. 'Then our lords and masters will be in a quandary. It's all very well having a defence obligation but most people in this country couldn't even spell Belize, let alone tell you where it was or why we would send troops.' He trailed off. The Falklands had been bad enough. A small place a long way away, but at least the Falklands flew the Union flag, had Brits living there, used British currency, spoke English; under any definition, historically and culturally part of Britain, if geographically distant. But Belize? An independent Central American nation in every way, the only link being historical and one of the Commonwealth.

The public opposition to a military solution for the Falklands had been real if limited, and the accusations that Prime Minister Margaret Thatcher had sent the task force south as an election-winning political gesture lived on. Aware of that, this first Labour government in almost twenty years may have different views, he thought. They had only been in office two months and had yet to define their foreign policy, or show their steel on anything significant beyond Britain's shores.

'The West Indies guardship will go there. Prudence I think, just in case we want to rattle our own cutlery. Tie up alongside, be seen.'

'Let's just bloody hope that's enough.'

'The Secretary is apparently seeking reassurance from the Guatemalans. They have said it's an internal security issue – anti-terrorist ops.'

'Believe 'em?'

The older man thought for a moment before speaking. 'You know, I don't believe I do.'

Airport Camp – Belize

Major Peter Tyson-Davis flicked a look out of the window and then back at his watch. Kick-off in thirty minutes and he wanted to finish his work, shower and change before his little band gathered round the barbecue. D Company's command structure was below strength; what should have been three infantry platoons and a support platoon each commanded by a lieutenant, was woefully short. Two lieutenants, platoon commanders, were away on courses leaving eleven platoon commanded by their sergeant and support platoon by the company sergeant major. This was somewhat made up for by an extra officer there from support company with his six mortars and four .50 calibre machine guns, and Captain Atlee, a jungle warfare specialist attached to them for the trip. Atlee had trained them all, but concentrated on the special group with the company, the small detachment of patrols from the battalion. Atlee had made a hell of a difference but as Tyson-Davis looked back at his work he thought how nice it would have been to have had his entire team there for the training deployment. He was pleased and had told his people; they had performed well, even when driven beyond what anyone had expected, even from him. Two platoons were on an almost constant war game with camp attacks, ambush after ambush, with the other two on live firing training, river crossing, jungle navigation and short survival courses with a local chap who had been training British troops in jungle survival for twenty years.

They had worked and reworked their mortar training and had practised both assault and defence backed up by the support company's M2 heavy machine guns. They were fit and jungle-conditioned, and the sick list wasn't too bad, with a handful of sprains, a soldier who had been bitten by a snake, and the inevitable parasitic infections. One tom, much to his mates' amusement, had a larva under the skin on his scalp and they were taking bets on when the fat white grub, the size of a cigarette butt, would break out.

The toms would be out on the town tonight, whatever 'town' Belize could offer. There was a Chinese restaurant that was ever-popular; it had a bar and a balcony and would be crowded with the lads on their last night before going home. Some would no doubt end up at 'the Garden'.

Raoul's Rose Garden was a ramshackle breeze-block nightclub and brothel on the road heading back from town, and had been infecting British soldiers with syphilis and every other known sexually-transmitted disease for the better part of twenty years. A skinful of beer, six weeks away from home and all the health warnings were forgotten as libido ruled. Visions of dusky lovelies that should have been shattered by the AIDS statistics for the country were simply blurred by alcohol; egged on by their mates, the sergeant's warnings to 'wear condoms' unheeded, they did what soldiers have done since the camp followers of biblical times. In ten days' time they would be dolefully appearing before the MO at Aldershot.

Tyson-Davis read steadily through the reports, looking up only when a Land-Rover hared past his hut down the road to the gate. There was a strict speed limit in the camp and whoever was in this vehicle had ignored it, but he kept on reading. Whoever it was, it wasn't one of his. He finished his work, put the papers back into a large brown manila envelope, and picking up his towel and his one luxury, a proper toilet bag, he headed for the showers.

He was of medium height, five-tennish, and lean with it. His hair was dark, his skin olive and his eyes were brown. He had his mother's looks; she was a girl from the valleys, a schoolteacher who had met and married his father when he was still a medical student and they now lived near his father's general practice in Bath. Tyson-Davis had decided on the army early, and entered with a clutch of A levels as an officer cadet

29

at Sandhurst in 1976. Now thirty-eight, he had pursued a classic fast-track career. In his time with 2 Para he had the usual secondments and courses. He had served in the Falklands, a two-pip looey, made captain, done a two-year tour with 22 SAS at Hereford, a two-year attachment to the US Defense department, made major and completed the first phases of staff college. As well as the Falklands, he had two tours of Northern Ireland under his belt, and a short four-month stint in Bosnia. His reports were exemplary; he was gifted, bright, a fine leader and an outstanding tactician. He was being groomed for the top, and many saw him as the next battalion commander. Only his subordinates saw failings – to them he seemed driven, a man totally focused on excellence at the expense of all else. His self-control was legendary and they wished that sometimes, even just once, he would relax, get pissed with them, let his hair down – be normal.

He did relax occasionally, but they didn't see it. Once a year for a week and on the odd weekend he would drive down to his parents' place, take down an old fly rod, pull on waders and stand in the water alongside his father. They would spend hours there, his father in an old battered hat, his pipe packed with tobacco but unlit – he hadn't lit it for years, he was a doctor after all – and cast their flies over the water, sometimes saying nothing to each other for an hour or more. If they caught something it was returned alive.

Millie would charge around the country with the boys, doing things, and just let him get on with it. This was when he rested, 'chilled out' as his little sister called it. Some evenings he would put the boys to bed and he wouldn't come down. She would go up and find him asleep between their beds, lying on the floor, the book he was reading to them over his face.

On the most recent occasion, he cast a fly, put his rod down, lay on the riverbank and closed his eyes. His father left him to doze in the sun, knowing this was what his son needed. He reeled in the line, put the rod on the bank and took his place back in the water. A week down on the river once a year and he could hack the rest, go back to work with his batteries charged, his famous focus like a laser beam. That

30

was him sorted. Ten days with Millie and the boys bucket-and-spading somewhere later in the summer was a mission like any other, max deliverables, meet and exceed the objectives, like the training deployment in Belize.

He turned on the taps and the water, lukewarm, thundered out.

Fort Street Guest House – Belize City

'Come on, he'll be here soon,' Helen said, brushing her hair and looking over at Sophie, who was drying hers with a towel. Sophie stopped for a moment and moved directly in line with the window. Like most older buildings in Belize, the guest house, built in 1927 for a Spanish doctor, didn't have glass in its windows. Instead louvred shutters kept out the direct sunlight, but allowed the sea breeze through, and for the nights when the breeze was gentle and the mosquitoes would be flying, screens were fitted over the inside. In line with the window, and under the overhead fan that turned lazily, even on full power, it was as cool as it was going to get at six in the evening.

'I'm hot,' Sophie said. She pulled on a light skirt and a thin cotton top, the only one she had packed that had sleeves. 'I'm not using the bloody drier.' She attacked her damp hair with a brush. The shower had been lukewarm. No one wanted really hot water, but the pressure was low and it had taken ages to get the shampoo out of her hair.

'It'll be fine,' Helen said. 'Don't be grumpy. Just think, all those scrummy men. Not that top. Too hippyish,' she said, looking over, 'wear my green one.'

Sophie smiled, and changed the blouse. Helen was for ever on the lookout for men, for herself and for everyone else. She put on a smear of lipstick and walked out into the sitting room where white-painted wicker chairs surrounded a small coffee table. The small bedrooms either side of the sitting room were empty, their doors open, and the breeze blew straight through. She flopped into a chair and waited, her light batik wrap-around skirt riding up over tanned legs. They had four days

31

in Belize City and were planning on hiring a car the following day and over the next few days intended to drive up to see the Mayan ruins at Xunantunich, then the northern highway to Corozal, crossing into Mexico and, if they had the time and the energy, southwards to Placencia. Belize was small; each of these trips was driveable in a day. Then they were going out to Cay Caulker for a week, living in a little clapboard shack on stilts by the beach, vegging out, doing a dive or two, and just letting the warm wind of the Caribbean blow their troubles away.

Sophie took the newspaper from the wicker coffee table and flicked through it. The local rag, she realized, before dipping into it. Poorly printed, it was nevertheless surprisingly outspoken for Central America, blatantly supporting the opposition, lambasting the government for lack of spending on education. A story caught her eye, the headline short; 'Spate of Slashings'. It dealt with a series of incidents over the previous weekend where people had used machetes on each other. Now that doesn't happen much in Hampshire, she thought; another story about incestuous rape ran alongside – that does. She tossed the paper back down on the table; she was on holiday, she didn't want to read about that sort of thing. It had been a good day. They had spent the morning wandering the streets, taking in the noise and smells and jostle. A man outside a shelter for the homeless had played a banjo for them and told them a tale. The shelter had been named after Mr Parks, a homeless man who would place himself at the head of funeral processions and bang a bucket to clear the way ahead. No one, he said, should go to their grave in silence. He became something of an institution; no funeral was complete without him and when he eventually died people realized that a little piece of Belize had gone with him. But who would bang the bucket for him? Everyone did – without prior arrangement they came. The police band turned out unpaid, as did another civic band, and individuals brought instruments and banged tubs and buckets and hub-caps. They marched at the head of his procession, a funeral like Belize had never seen, and a few years later the first shelter for the homeless was named after him.

When the man had told them the tale he said, 'So I play 'ere for 'eem . . . and collect a dalla or two,' he finished, holding out his hand with a smile. The girls loved it and gave him some money, not sure whether to believe the story but charmed by it anyway. The rest of the beggars and hustlers some not so charming, they ignored, and hence their meeting with Harry. He would be here soon, she thought.

She swung her feet up on to the tabletop, pulled the skirt up her legs and looked down at herself critically. The tan was coming along, but she was putting on weight, she thought. The emerald-green top was stretched across her boobs, normal when she wore Helen's clothes, but her jeans were getting tight, that was for sure.

'I'm fat!' she shouted.

'No you're not,' a voice replied.

She looked round; it was Harry. He had come up the stairs, missed every one that creaked and caught her, hair still damp, splayed like a tart in the chair, engaging in girl talk with no one in sight. She blushed.

'Good evening,' he said with a grin.

Behind him a middle-aged American woman crossed the hall to the bathroom, her tight pink shorts cutting into massive cellulite thighs, her husband following, his vast bulk covered by a yellow poly-cotton shirt the size of a small tent. Both clutched toilet bag and towels. Harry turned, nodded a greeting, and then looked back at Sophie, the expression on his face as legible as words. As the bathroom door closed behind the couple he grinned and said softly, 'If I ever get that big talk me through it, OK? That or shoot me.'

Sophie laughed softly and stood up, brushing down the folds of her skirt, and Helen appeared from their room, hair up and looking stunning. Two or three minutes later they were in the small unmarked car and heading towards the airport road, through the narrow streets busy with people, bicycles, playing children and badly-driven cars. Sophie rolled her window down, and took it all in. Clapboard shops and houses were crammed either side of the street and washing and hammocks hung on balconies. Music blared from various windows, hand-painted signs adorned shops and once-brightly-coloured paint peeled everywhere. A scruffy mongrel sniffing in the gutters darted to one side to avoid being hit by a fellow on a bicycle and in front of them a taxi lurched along, its driver sounding the horn every few seconds and waving to people he knew.

London

It was about then that a fellow employed in the Foreign and Commonwealth Office in London decided to repay a favour to his sister's ex-boyfriend. He dialled a number in Venezuela, chatted for a few minutes and then asked, 'Central America still part of your patch, Leo?' The reply was affirmative. 'I can't answer any questions, but just do yourself a favour and get up there. Might be something happening in our prime interest there.' He listened for a moment or two. 'Yes. Yes. The old problem. Debt paid, mmm?'

The sister's ex-boyfriend, Leo Scobey, was ITN's correspondent in Latin America.

Belize

Sally Moretto looked across as the people came through the door. She was sitting at a table with her friend Miss Jenny, a position chosen so she could see the whole place. She loved JB's. Set off the western highway on the thirty-two-mile marker, JB's was a café-restaurant, its high poles carrying a palm-thatched roof. It was mostly open on two sides; people could leave the bar area, move down one step and sit at tables and look out over the orange groves towards the mountains in the distance. She had been a regular for years, driving the twenty-six miles with her husband from their place at the crossing to spend an evening of convivial conversation over ice-cold beers, and when it came up for sale she couldn't stand the thought of someone buying it and making changes. A canny business woman, she went to the auction and forty-five minutes later she was the new owner. Part of JB's' fame

34

came from the unusual ambience created by the decor. British troops moving back to Airport Camp from their jungle training areas were allowed one stop on the road for refreshments. They uniformly chose JB's, where they were always welcome, and over the years the relationship between the staff and the troops grew and now it was almost an institution. Regimental crests and mottoes from virtually every unit in the British army were painted on to boards which hung on every available surface. Presented by grateful squaddies over the years, they were now part of the place – and not just crests. At one end, high up in the thatch, there were several pairs of underpants, thrown high by revellers, and caught on the rough underside of the palm thatching. No one bothered to take them down and they too were now part of JB's.

Sally watched her staff serve the new customers and turned back to Miss Jenny. Once the place had Brit troops there most nights, but since the last garrison battalion had moved on they weren't around so much anymore. Nowadays there was usually a much smaller unit on training visits, but the numbers of tourists had picked up, so the place was doing well, and the restaurant wasn't her only business. On the site she had also bought other buildings, a low once-temporary place that she used as an office and a small warehouse a few hundred yards across the lot nearer the road. From there she supplied hotel equipment to the growing eco-tourism industry, everything from knives and forks to good American mattresses, but JB's was her favourite. She still drank there, sang what she thought of as terrible karaoke on Sunday afternoons with the customers, her light skirt short enough to show off the legs that had won her Miss Legs of New Orleans twenty years before. Her voice was actually very good in a gravelly, bluesy sort of way that reminded people of Janis Joplin or Elkie Brooks.

Heavier now, she was sexy in an earthy sort of way, dark hair and flashing dark eyes, tanned, laughing, relaxed; the customers loved both her and the best homemade burgers south of the Rio Grande. Miss Jenny was her friend, an Alabaman nurse who had come south ten years before to help build and commission hospitals in Mexico. She now had fledgeling business interests in Belize, and regularly drove through the border from Mexico to push things along and see Sally and her husband, who was currently in the States on a buying trip. Older than Sally, she was nearing fifty, single, but still attracted men, usually the wrong sort, as she would admit with a rough, throaty smoker's laugh. Together they were going to diversify the hotel supply side of the business, move into hospital supplies, and start tendering for health department work. Miss Jenny knew the minister, he often called into JB's, and although the small Belize health market would never make them rich, it was an opportunity. Belize was a nice place to live as an expatriate entrepreneur; only an hour and a half from Miami, it was a little Wild West, a little Caribbean. It was democratic, interesting, relatively relaxed about individual freedoms, and attracted colourful characters. It could be frustrating in the extreme, driving normally patient people to distraction, but they put up with that because the best thing about it, unusually for Central America, was that it was peaceful. Miss Jenny liked that; after spending years dealing with the much more volatile Latinos in Mexico, Belize seemed to her a sleepy backwater where people chilled out, smoked some weed, went to church, got on with their lives in an almost fatalistic way. If Mexico was *mañana*, then Belize was *mañana* on ganja.

Both Sally and Miss Jenny turned as the familiar road-whine of a Land-Rover moving fast reached them from the highway, but they flashed past, two of them in the drab green of the British army, without stopping. They did get a wave from the driver of the first.

'Those boys sure are in a hurry,' Sally said.

The family were gathering. The house was bigger than most, a clapboard building six feet off the ground on pillars, that Edwardo Sanchez had extended after the birth of his seventh child. He knew he shouldn't have had that many, they were expensive, but he would ask ruefully, what were you to do when a woman was beside you in the night and you felt the need? The American influence was strong in Belize; he spoke English with their accent, used their vernacular, some of it learned from the tourists, some from the pirated television signals all Belizeans could receive. He liked to be known as Eddie, made a living driving a big Chevrolet Caprice as a taxi, and called anything other than American cars 'foreign'. He was from the melting pot that is modern Belize; Creole, that wonderful primary mix of Spanish and black African blood, spiced with some Mayan and English genes way back. He spoke Spanish as well as English but was happiest in Creole, the patois of the people. Broadminded, mildly Catholic, he was politically aware, but not active. Gregarious, noisy, he was a hard drinker, smoked the odd bit of ganja and caroused in Raoul's with the pretty El Salvadorian hookers when someone was paying. He worked long hours, hitting the horn at the pretty girls and leering out of the window, and he was convivial and popular with his customers. He took money home to his family. The children were clothed, fed, went to church with their mother, did well at school and as long as things were satisfactory at home then he could be himself. Eddie Sanchez was fairly typical of the average red-blooded Belizean male. He had had a good day; a tourist had taken one of his guided tours, all the way up to Xunantunich, and he had 200 US dollars in his pocket.

'We need more tourists,' he said to his wife, thinking about the American who had been with him all day. He had money to spend, and wanted to see things that Eddie could show him. Tomorrow maybe he would want to go down to Placencia.

Dion Manuelez was a Hollywood vision of a Mayan. In his late thirties, taller than most, he wore his hair long, shoulder-length, and brushed it back from his face. He had the wide, high cheekbones of his people, flashing dark eyes and perfect white teeth. He was a mariner, unusual for a Mayan; most of them lived and worked up-country, but he loved the sea and the reefs and for twenty years had worked the charter boats, the last few years as skipper on a big hundred-and-fifty-foot live-aboard dive boat. Tired of that, of the demands of the divers, mostly wealthy Americans, who were never pleased with anything, he had just taken a job running a day-boat for the owner of the Fort Street Guest House. Together they would build a dive business running a pair of twenty-foot boats out to the reefs. The day-divers were different – paying less, they weren't expecting chilled champagne and canapés, and to be dropped directly on to dolphins every time. They were happy to go over the side wherever he stopped the boat, appreciative of Dion's local knowledge. He had a wealth of that; he understood the reefs, the fish, the tides and the currents, he knew where it was safe to dive and where it wasn't and he knew when to respect the creatures of the water and lead his party back to the boat. A long jagged scar down his left leg, the result of an encounter with a tiger shark after going down to check the anchor one night, helped him demonstrate the point when he needed to.

He was dry-humoured and smiled easily; his natural, unaffected sexual appeal seemed sometimes to bemuse him. A bachelor, he had a steady girlfriend and gently rejected the overtures of the tourists and dive groupies. She was a receptionist at the Ramada. He would be seeing her later, when she finished work and so this evening he had accepted Dave's offer of a meal with him and Ruthie. Dave and Ruthie had bought the guest house three years before, building on its solid reputation as the 'cool' place to stay in Belize City. They had been in and out of Belize for years and when the guest house had come up for sale they had snapped it up and moved down from Florida. The old house was steeped in atmosphere, with overhead fans and shutters; the staff were informal but well trained and nothing was too much trouble. The dining room was surrounded on three sides by a veranda where tables were full most of the time. Diners could eat inside or out and the guest house consistently had the best food in the city. Dave was something of an entrepreneur and he was also a dive-master, and it was he who approached Dion with the idea of a dive business; two boats, and a shop on the Radisson Jetty. The guest house's reputation would enhance the business – the guests would visit the shop.

Dave and Ruthie lived on the ground floor of the house, but unlike the upper floors their place was air-conditioned, and Dion sat nursing a beer while Ruthie finished off the cooking – roast beef the English way, with gravy, roast potatoes and the trimmings.

'Busy upstairs?' Dion asked.

'Doin' OK,' Dave answered, dropping into a chair. He was big, six-feet-two in bare feet and heavy like a linebacker, which he once had been. Now in his mid-forties, he was in his element, doing what he wanted to do. He hadn't worn a pair of long trousers or socks for a month now and loved it. 'Six in the house, did twenty-two lunches, and we are pretty much full for the season.'

'The group tomorrow, still seven?'

'Eight. One comin' over from the Ramada. Two non-divers.'

Dion nodded. 'It's three to four from the east. I thought maybe Goff's Cay, leave the non-divers and then run out from there. Be a bit rough to try for Rendezvous.'

Eighty-three miles away in San Ignacio, Eva's was humming. Its owner was also expatriate – Pete Collins had spent seventeen years in Belize with the British army and fell in love with it. When he left the army, he went back, married the local girl he had met and bought a dreary eating-house on the main street of the picturesque hill town. San Ignacio was different to Belize City; it was cooler for starters, up in the hills, and the ambience was different. Where the city was Creole and Caribbean, the average fellow on the street looking like he could be from Jamaica, San Ignacio was Central American. Within spitting distance of Guatemala, its influences were Spanish. It felt more like Mexico, and refugees from El Salvador and Guatemala were common. You could see horses on the street, and men with machetes and sacks of mangoes and other fruits; many of the people were light-skinned and slightly built, *mestizos*. The town moved with a different rhythm, and these days it was the local centre for eco-tourism: the famous Mayan ruin of Xunantunich was a few miles up the road, there was river-rafting, riding, caves and jungle walks. Pete knew San Ignacio well, he had spent time there while with the army, watching the Guatemalans on the other side of the border, and he had seen the potential for tourism and bought wisely. He slowly turned the place into something

39

unusual, attracting both residents and tourists, with good local food and cold beers. It became something of a hang-out for the visitors, be they the New Age hippie throwbacks, backpackers, or the more mainstream couple dragging their teenage kids somewhere other than Florida.

Pete was a convivial host; his arms covered in tattoos, his misspent youth on show, he stood out in a country that attracted colourful characters. He was lean and slightly built, with hair cropped short, a smile wide and fast, always ready with a joke. Like many of the foreigners who lived in Belize, he loved it there. He ran a tight business, working the bar himself, the atmosphere more that of a surf or beach club than a remote hill town restaurant in the middle of Central America. The real surprise as people walked in was not the Hertfordshire English accent of the man behind the bar, but the space to the right. Modern personal computers lined the wall – Eva's was an online cyber-café. People sat at the keyboards, drank a beer or two, cleared their e-mails and sent messages out, cyber-surfing while they waited for beans and rice with something. A visiting woman had captured it once, described it perfectly. 'This is Rick's Café in Casablanca,' she said with a grin, 'moved to another continent and fifty years later, but all it needs is a piano man. There's Humphrey Bogart,' she finished, pointing at Pete. Pete had smiled. Crazy fuckin' Americans, he had thought – but she was right. Like Casablanca back then, San Ignacio attracted all kinds and inevitably those running away from something. They all went through here eventually and the embassies knew it. The US Embassy routinely passed Pete wanted notices, people on the run from the law. They all thought they could hide out in Central America, but not any more, not in a country that went straight from no telephones to mobiles, where remote hill towns were on the World Wide Web.

Pete served another round of drinks and watched food come from the kitchen. There was a plate of plantains for an English girl who had asked if she could taste them. He had said no, explaining they were quite hard to get and were reserved as an accompaniment to main courses, but weakened as he usually did and sent over a plate, on the house. People remembered things like that and came back and consequently most nights, like tonight, the tables were full. Over on the computers three Americans were on the keyboards. One of his staff had taken off the local ragga tape and put on some vintage Jimmy Hendrix, the mellow vibes of 'Hey Joe' filling the background above the laughter and conversation. He'd take a break soon, tuck his little angels into bed. They had two daughters now, two little mop-tops with huge dark eyes like their mother, and he adored them. Life was pretty good. But, he mused, when things were this good, fate had a wonderful way of kicking you right in the bollocks.

Airport Camp

The handful of men, with Sophie and Helen at the centre, were gathered round the table that had been set up with the drinks. The hi-tech barbecue was alight off to one side, but no one stood over it, it was too hot. Where they were in the channel between the huts, the buildings created a wind-tunnel and the sea breeze that had managed the two miles from the beach was funnelled to best effect. The two girls from the consulate hadn't arrived yet, so it was just Sophie and Helen, with the four officers of D Coy.

Major Fox was ambling over with his men, the officers from C Coy, the newly-arrived Gurkhas, and Tyson-Davis intercepted them as he left his quarters. Major Fox, stocky, blond, with a wonderful handlebar moustache, was on jocular form and obviously looking forward to the deployment. Together they wandered down to the barbecue.

'The boss,' Harry said softly to Sophie, 'in the blue chinos on the left.'

'I'll be wonderfully respectful,' she said drily, sipping her drink. It was a gin and tonic in a long glass, but strong enough for her to notice.

He ignored her gentle sarcasm with a smile. 'The one with him is Dickie Fox, OC of C Company. They are taking over from us.'

'The others are of no consequence,' Atlee joined in. 'Mere

41

subbies, except for Brock, who plays golf. Say no more, shall we?' Atlee hated golf, and the battalion's officer in charge of the assault pioneers and he were old sparring partners in the mess. Ian Brock, also a captain, had come up the hard way, through the ranks, what everyone called a 'retread'. It wasn't unusual in the Parachute Regiment, and Brock, who took the piss out of everyone and everything, was fast-witted, the perfect foil for Atlee's studied nonchalance.

'Ah! It's Bridges Atlee. Is it safe to approach?' Brock called. Atlee smothered a smile. Bastard – he was on to it already, and he's only been here a few hours. Four days before Atlee had crossed a temporary bridge over a river with a section; shouting 'Let's go,' he led the way and promptly fell into the river, to the wild amusement of the watching platoon. The Reg was a family – there was no hiding an event like that.

'Of course. As safe as crossing a fairway when you are driving,' he countered. The others grinned; it would be a good night with these two at it.

Tyson-Davis moved forward, looking at the two ladies. 'I see we have company this evening.'

'We do, sir.' Harry stepped forward. 'This is Sophie and Helen. Ladies, Major Tyson-Davis.'

He shook their hands, made eye contact, nodding slightly. 'Call me Peter, please. I must thank you for coming. You can see the level of the humour I normally have to put up with. You will raise the game for all of us with your presence.'

'Sir, you are gallant. In the far-flung reaches of the Commonwealth, it is surely our duty,' Helen replied, with a matching mock-Edwardian formality.

Good, Harry thought. She can entertain Ted and that'll leave Sophie to me. He turned to her and headed off two of C Coy's subbies intent on breaking his monopoly. Behind them on the pan a helicopter was coming in. He turned for a second, listening to the engine note; it wasn't one of the Gazelles. It was big, a different sound altogether. He looked up and could see it, its A/C beacon flashing. He was wondering where it had come from and why, when Sophie said something and he looked back at her and smiled.

'Is this it then? Us two girls and all you men?'

'No,' he replied. 'Two other ladies from the consulate will be here any minute and,' he looked around, 'there's another chap from . . . down the camp.' Bonner – where's Bonner, he thought. 'Let me get you another drink.'

'Who's cooking?'

'Cap' Atlee,' he replied with a grin. 'A globally renowned expert on barbecue sauce. I am his humble assistant, but I do make probably the best burgers in the known world. Believe me, this evening there is nowhere you would rather be.'

She smiled back, thinking, you got that spot on, soldier. Helen was right, you really are rather scrummy.

2100 hours

Two of Captain Bonner's air troop patrols had crossed over and were now inside Guatemala and on hard routine. Air troop were parachute specialists, they were trained to jump into the theatre and could land exactly on target, carrying enormous loads, enough to re-supply the Squadron on the ground. They could opt for HALO, high altitude low opening, free-falling thousands of feet so no one on the ground would hear the aircraft, or HAHO, high altitude high opening, where they would jump breathing oxygen up to fifty miles away and glide in on the new high-performance canopies. But they didn't have the luxury of time or the resources to do anything exotic about getting in and did it the old-fashioned way, the way soldiers have done it since time began. They walked.

To the south of the border post roads cut into the bush, the thickening vegetation that would become jungle further south. They turned off at Benque Viejo del Carmen, just a mile from the border. Benque, pronounced 'Benk', was a small town, with the usual school, churches, houses; but it was new, laid out by planners and so had a rather characterless, spacious sleepiness about it. They took the road that ran down to Arenal, a tiny village on the border two miles from Benque. Halfway in they did a hard right turn and moved off the road and then stopped. They hid their vehicle and simply tabbed over the border under the cover of darkness, moving slowly,

43

like ghosts, silent shadows in the darkness. There had been movement reported up here over time, Guatemalan loggers crossing over to steal Belizean mahogany, and there were a few vehicle tracks to prove it. A mile in, the bush began to thicken and they silently came to a halt and laid up for the night. No bashas, no fire, no hot food. Dressed in their 'wet' kit, they sat back to back, dozed in turns, one always on stag twenty feet away where he could see any approaching movement.

The second team had crossed in to the north of the post. They had forded the river, not using the chain ferry, but six hundred yards above it, driving their four-wheel-drive across the flat rapids. Timed well, no one would have seen them from the road and the water was manageable, just, the engine's snorkel air intake doing its job. They picked up the rough track, and moved north-west before parking up and camouflaging the Land-Rover.

Behind them they could see the massive bulk of Xunantunich against the moon through scudding clouds. The border was only a mile or so away and they moved fast, just below a trot, their bergens heavy. This was a recce patrol, but they were equipped to fight their way out if it came down to it and the bulk of the weight in the bergens and draped over their shoulders was in the form of ammunition, 66s and explosives. A quarter of a mile from the frontier they slowed and one man moved ahead, to recce at the point where they wanted to cross. By nine o'clock local time they were in and laid up for the night. At first light they would move on, find somewhere to stash the heavy gear, set up in effect a mini forward supply dump. Then if the role changed and they were ordered to stay put or go on to the offensive, they had the necessary kit.

The rest of the Squadron were on the move. The chain of command for deployment decision was different to the 'green' army. One of the subordinates of the Deputy Chief of the Defence Staff is a one-star general who is Director Special Forces and wears a second hat, that of Director SAS. It is he, in assessing intelligence needs direct with people in Hereford, who is authorized to deploy the Regiment's resources and, on the basis of what they were learning, he did so.

There were C-130s available, but a transit time of seventeen hours was too long. The Royal Air Force could also offer a VC10, or a Tristar, both much faster, but Hereford had said no thanks. It was difficult doing a discreet arrival in a bloody great jet in air force colours, so the RAF produced something else, an ageing DC8 freighter they had on lease for the Falklands supply runs. It was ideal. Airborne out of Brize Norton, thirty-eight members of the Squadron whose bleepers had gone off less than three hours before were in the long narrow fuselage, sorting their kit, repacking bergens and making preparations. The P1 would have been most unhappy if he had known about some of the work going on down the back. In among the various teams, all busy, there were three men stripping detonators out of packaging, cutting C4 plastic explosive into easily packed chunks and moulding them into bits of clingfilm. Others unpacked ammunition, pored over maps, cleaned weapons, checked equipment. Those finished with their tasks were smoking or eating, spooning cold rations from foil bags. One, better equipped, was wading through a packet of chocolate Hobnobs, his mates helping themselves as they saw fit. Open food was open season.

The Squadron was experienced; the average age of the soldiers was thirty and on the aircraft there were eleven sergeants, a lieutenant, two captains and the Squadron commanding officer, a major. Between them they had over four hundred and fifty years of direct experience, three hundred of those as special forces, trained in every possible scenario. They were confident, relaxed and going about their business the way they usually did. ETA was 0830 local. The boss, Major Chard, due to return to the Royal Green Jackets in six weeks' time, was born in Rhodesia and his accent still betrayed his upbringing. He had first seen action in the nasty little bush war in that country, doing his National Service as a foot soldier. Fresh out of the School of Infantry in Gwelo he had been thrown into the thick of it, into the elite Rhodesian Light Infantry, and loved it. A natural soldier, he had stayed in until Independence; then he had used his British parentage and passport to emigrate. Chard was a keen mountain-biker; scars and missing teeth were testimony to his competitiveness. His wife, the daughter of a Cheshire landowner, who patched him up each time he came a cropper, thought him a complete lunatic.

He called the three troop officers together and with maps spread out on a pile of gear, they began to work out tasks. The last six men coming from other directions would be some five hours after them on a commercial flight out of Miami. Four wouldn't make it. Coming from a team job in Botswana, they would be too late.

Chapter Two

Raoul's Rose Garden was jumping. In the tacky interior, where the working girls moved among the customers, and the floor show teetered between awful and appalling, the drinks were expensive, but no one seemed to care. There was the usual mix of girls, local Creole, some black as ebony, and a good number of Spanish girls, all of them needing to make a living doing what they could. Many of them were refugees from El Salvador and Nicaragua.

The punters were there in force. American tourists, men looking for some action, for the seamier side of Central America, delivered there by taxi drivers. There was a handful of local Belizeans and the rest were British soldiers, the establishment's raison d'être. A full thirty per cent of D Coy's fighting strength was scattered round the main room and propping up the bar. Many of them weren't there for the ladies. They were there egged on by their mates, to take in a piece of tradition. You couldn't spend time in Belize with the British army and not go to 'the Garden' at least once, and apart from four days on St George's, adventure-training, Ted had kept them busy for the last six weeks. Some were there for the girls, and others who had gone simply to have a look and get a couple of beers in would succumb to the temptation.

Boys will be boys, and they were slipping out the back to the rooms with ladies on their arms as regular as clockwork. When they did the girls wanted them to wear 'skins'. The CSM wanted them to wear seven and the MO wanted them to just not risk it at all.

Dave Cutter sipped his beer. It wasn't bad, he had to admit; he wasn't a lager drinker, he preferred real ale, but as lagers went this local stuff wasn't bad. 'Belikin, the beer of Belize' the poster on the wall proclaimed. He burped. Jesus, I'm pissed, he thought. How many of these? Seven, maybe eight at the

Chinese. What's the ABV? He lifted the bottle, looking for the information on the label. It wasn't there.

'Watcha doing, mun?' Plonker asked.

'How strong is this stuff?'

'Who fookin' cares, mun?' Plonker answered. He was from 'up north', a Geordie.

'There's loadsa totty in here, any of which will shag your brains out for thirty quid, and you wanna know that! 'Ere, check that one there,' Plonker pointed, 'that tall dark one. I fookin' fancy shaggin' her, mun.'

'Well go and talk to her then,' Cutter said.

'Aye, I will, mun. You coming?'

Cutter shook his head. He had a girlfriend at home, and he had really missed her. Up in the 'J' it was worst. Lying in his basha, sweating, aching all over, he thought about her in her little flat in Guildford, the softness of her skin, the warmth in her eyes, the way she looked after a bath, soft and slippery. He didn't like the tattoo very much, but she had that done before she met him, a butterfly on her shoulder. She had to keep it covered at work, at the Halifax on the counter – a good job. They had their hassles but she was good for him. She hated the deployments – she put up with them, but didn't like him being away as much as he was. He had been thinking about getting out lately, taking a civvy job. It was just that firing a mortar wasn't a skill that they wanted, and he didn't fancy being out the back at Tesco's.

Trouble was, no one appreciated them, no one valued them. There were pubs within five miles of the camp at Aldershot where they were unwelcome – bastards. Aldershot was a garrison town, the home of the British army. Aldershot *was* the army, and yet these bastards treat us like shit. They talked about it often, the lads. One of them, Rhah, their philosopher, had quoted Kipling. It was a problem as old as the army – no one wants a tom in peacetime. They don't spend much, they get rowdy, frighten away the family punters. But wait till the shit starts, then they want us. As they tuck themselves into their nice warm beds, safe and sound, they forget just why they are safe and sound – because there's lads like us, and there's no bastard coming over the wall, not while we have the watch.

48

'Come on, mun,' Plonker urged. He was well pissed, his black hair matted and wet where someone had let go some beer, the gap in his teeth stark in the tan of his face. 'You'll never have the chance again, not for foreign gash, mun. Look at that one, mun. A fookin' cracker, looks like Grace Jones.'

Cutter grinned. He could imagine nothing worse, but Plonker loved Grace Jones, and kept getting out the James Bond video, where she did her thing.

'I'm getting out, Plonker.'

'Wha?'

'I'm getting out. Pissed off with it, I'm gonna jack in.'

'Don't be fuckin' stupid, mun, you'll be 'ome tomorra. Everything will look better.'

'Naa. Had it,' Cutter replied. 'No fucker wants us, we just get slagged off. I'm going back, gonna jack in, move in with Debbie, get a job.'

'Fook off! You're a squaddy! Aye, airborne, but a fookin' squaddy, mun. Who wants to employ shite like us?'

'Dorsey did,' Cutter challenged, 'he got out, got a job.'

Plonker moved closer, all thoughts of shagging a Grace Jones look-alike gone. Grace wasn't a mate. 'Yeah, driving a van. Look, you get paid, right?'

'Yeah.'

'Badly?'

'No,' Cutter said on reflection.

'You get to travel. How many countries you been paid to go to?'

'That's not the point.'

'Fookin' is!' Plonker paused. 'Elias, listen, mun. You got a good job, now. Think about it. Corporal at twenty-six. You'll make sergeant. Travelled to places you would never have got to. You can get quarters – you want Debbie, marry 'er, she's a good lass. But don't jack in, son. You think they don't appreciate us – you're right. But I'll tell you something else, they don't appreciate each other out there, they appreciate no fooker. Here in the Reg it's different. So get another beer down you and stop being a daft cunt.' He ordered two more beers.

'I thought you were after some of that?' Cutter asked,

49

nodding back at the girls, who were having a very lucrative evening.

'Later, son. The night is young.'

Rhah Bundy staggered over. 'Bastards. Elias? Why didn't you stop me?' he slurred.

'Stop you doing what?'

'I can't believe what I just did,' he replied. Bundy was the deep thinker. Lithe and quick, he played semi-professional football when he could. He was their moralist, their conscience, their philosopher on the section. He was nicknamed Rhah after the character in *Platoon* – soldiers love war movies and the characters in them. The all-time towering icon was Steiner, the corporal in *Cross of Iron*. One tom, on the edge of promotion, had changed his name by deed poll to Steiner so he could be Corporal Steiner. He lived it for years and was gutted when he made sergeant. The lads in the section had tagged Bundy with the nickname of Rhah, and that night, presented him with a face veil to wrap round his head like a pirate and a wooden staff with barbed wire round the top, the final memorable image in *Platoon*.

The same film had tagged Cutter with Elias. The decent half of the warring pair of Barnes and Elias, the man who, without losing his professionalism as a soldier, stood up to the brutality of others around him. It was the highest compliment they could pay him.

Cutter looked at Rhah. A lance corporal, he was never happier than when out sailing. He had charge of one of the section's two fire teams, had applied for Sandhurst, and was awaiting news; if he went they would all miss him. He'd be a good retread.

'I just paid for some other bastard to get a shag, dip his horrible appendage into a little Guatemalan angel. I must have risen in Maslow's hierarchy of needs or something. That or I need counselling.'

'What the fook you on about?' Plonker asked, shaking his head. Cutter grinned; his section – good lads. He looked round for the others. Spud and Jonesy were down the bar. Jonesy was a Brummie lad, gentle, some thought too gentle for the Reg; he was the one who offered to do things, carried his load, never shirked, never complained, and for some reason Plonker disliked him. Maybe, Elias thought, because he was everything Plonker wasn't. Plonker was abrasive at times, selfish, and his behaviour was so laddish that he could be thoroughly unpopular for days after an episode. He used to disappear up to Newcastle every time he had leave, but for the last year he had stayed local.

Spud Murphy was a scouse git; more accurately, Liverpudlian Irish. He had the patter, smooth as silk, and Cutter could see him further down the bar with the company sergeant major. If Cutter was Elias, then some saw CSM Jennings as Barnes. He wasn't brutal, but he was committed, totally. At thirty-five he was the oldest non-commissioned man in the company, its backbone. He ran the company, administering its affairs from day to day, was responsible for discipline, and as long as the support platoon's usual commander, a lieutenant, was away on a course, Jennings was platoon commander. The toms reckoned he had a maroon spine, that he 'lobbed out' from his mother's womb with a parachute, that he wasn't mortal. He could run further, carry more, endure longer than any of them. And he loved the Regiment – woe betide anyone who let standards slip. He was a non-com version of Ted, driven to excel. Some called him Barnes but for most he was 'Robo'. He was further down the bar and Spud, by the look of it, was trying for a free pint with a match trick. The lambs to the slaughter were four of the patrols, the special forces type trained Paras, part of support company and attached to D Coy for this exercise. Robo watched Spud take yet another pint off them and nursed his own beer. He wasn't here for the ladies, Cutter knew. He had an old-fashioned view of things and while he gave absolute loyalty he expected the same. In sixteen years of marriage he had never looked at another woman. Some said it was because there was only one thing on earth he feared – his wife. That was true, but not in the way they thought. He feared losing her.

Cutter looked at his watch – 2330. The lads had to be back in camp by midnight. Better start rounding them up, he thought. At the bar Robo had put down his drink and was beginning to remind others of the time. He wouldn't get heavy here, just point it out and then he would leave, but anyone who fucked up would be up before him at 0800.

Aldershot

Madeline Jennings pulled on a dressing-gown, looked into one of the other bedrooms and went downstairs. She yawned and ran a hand through her hair. She hadn't slept much; she had listened for every sound in the night, hoping for a key in the door and Tom back. The clock on the kitchen wall showed the time as just after six and as she waited for the kettle to boil she thought about what she had to do that day – plenty. Bob would be home tomorrow. Get down to Sainsbury's, do the big shop. Both boys needed jeans and Ian also wanted a new baseball cap. He had lost his other, playing 'silly buggers', as his father would say, on the train. Maybe have a barbecue this weekend, she thought; hope it's sunny. She poured the hot water into the pot. She never used teabags, always leaf tea and always in the old china pot they had bought when they married. She carried her cup through to the sitting room and enjoyed the silence of the early morning, giving her time to think. Tom had been gone a week now. She had checked his room each morning hoping he had returned, but so far nothing – no word. Bob was back tomorrow, he would know what to do, but it was going to be tough, because he would see himself as the cause.

Her Bob; she was the only woman he had ever loved, he said. She was his wife, his lover, his friend, she was the only person he confided in, ever, and she was the mother of his children. He told her he thought sometimes that she could have done better than him, married an officer, or a business-man, someone who wasn't away all the time, someone with a decent salary. Often when he came home from a deployment and she was still there, he marvelled at his good fortune. So he met her halfway. He paid his salary into their joint account, supported her every way he could. He remembered birthdays, bought her flowers sometimes; and occasionally, feeling

52

momentarily inarticulate, because it didn't seem enough, he told her he loved her and he meant it. Once, years before, he had not treated her so well and she had done what everyone expected; she had thrown him out. Until she took him back they were the worst weeks of his life and he admitted that to her. He was a good man, a decent man and she loved him. Her parents took a long time to like him; they never wanted her to go out with a soldier. 'Bloody squaddies' her father called them. Bloody snob, she mused. A small business-man, he owned his own garage and used-car yard, and the way he behaved you would have thought he was the chairman of Rover plc. She smiled at the thought, and pushed her toes through the thick shag pile of the Chinese rug they had bought at Alders, their joint Christmas present to each other.

Yes, she thought, a barbecue. Get some nice meat, some beer for the blokes. They had some good New Zealand white in at Gateway, get some of that. She smiled again, a little secret smile. Her man was coming home and she had missed him; she had felt randy as anything lately, she acknowledged to herself, until Tom left.

She looked at her watch; yesterday there still, she thought. They leave mid-afternoon of today. Seven hours' time differ-ence, seventeen in the air, back to camp, an hour or so back at Arnhem. He would be getting to the house late tomorrow night, in the wee hours really. Ian would be asleep for a while yet and she wondered where Tom was. Was he asleep somewhere, warm and fed? For Maddie, at fourteen and six-teen they were past the perfect age for boys. She sometimes wished they were ten again; big enough to have conver-sations, still have wide-eyed wonder at the things they learnt and saw, to be funny, to help a little, a joy to have around. Then the metamorphosis; the teenage years that she wasn't looking forward to had so far been what she had expected and been warned about. What was it about teenagers? Angst, rebellion, grunting truculence. What was it about them? A once articulate, confident young fellow changes into a sour uncommunicative hulking thing the moment his balls drop. Hormones – a friend had warned her about it and reassured her they grew through it. Tom, the eldest, was the problem. Rebelling against his father and all his father stood for: decency, order, consideration. He had never seen his father at work. If he had he would have realized that, in comparison to his work and dealing with fellows only two years older than Tom, he was an absolute pussycat at home. But no, they had clashed in the days before his deployment. It began with the usual – who was not pulling their weight in the home? Tom eventually took out the rubbish, sullen and sulky. It escalated that night when news came of a friend of the boys who was now in hospital after taking Ecstasy. Bob had gone straight upstairs and searched their rooms, and found a small plastic coin bag, the type used by banks. In it was a black sticky substance wrapped in tin foil. He knew what it was – hash. When Tom came home he presented the find.

'What's this?' he asked.

Tom ignored him.

'I asked you a question!'

'You know what it is.'

Bob snapped then. 'What's it doin' –'

'I don't go through your stuff!' Tom shouted back.

'Your friend is in bloody hospital!'

'From E!' Tom shouted, the frustration welling out of him. 'From E! I don't do E! Never have.'

'How do I know that? You –'

'You wouldn't, would you,' Tom interrupted again, 'you wouldn't fucking notice if I was on fire. We don't have maroon berets so we don't bloody exist!'

The accusation hit like a blow and Bob reeled for a moment, before taking refuge in, 'Don't use that kind of language in front of your mother.'

The row ran on for a good twenty minutes before Tom stormed out and he hadn't been there the following morning when Bob left for the deployment. One night about ten days ago he had said he was not going to be home when his father came back and she thought he meant he just wouldn't be there on the doorstep.

'But we have always been here when he comes home.'

'What? So he can have a go again?'

'He's your dad, he's concerned about you,' she said. 'He loves you and he loves Ian.'

'Funny way of showing it,' he said, walking out.

My God, they are so alike, she thought; strong, independent. Please come home, Tom, it won't be the same without you here when your dad gets back. She took the positive approach. He'll be back, so what do we need? We need food. Eat? These two could eat through the entire fridge, she thought with a smile. She began to make a shopping list and thought about the morning a week ago when Tom left. It had been early, this early at least. Ian had wandered in. She had looked up, surprised he was out of bed at this hour.

'Morning, Ian,' she said. 'You're up early. This is the middle of the night for you. Do you want a cup of tea?' Then she noticed – he didn't have that sleepy look. He shook his head and looked at her for a moment.

'Mum, Tom's gone.'

'Gone? Gone where?'

Ian shrugged. 'Dunno. He's not in his room and his bag is gone.'

'How do you . . .' she faded, then gathered again. 'His bag?'

'You know, his Adidas holdall. I saw him putting stuff in it last night.'

I want him back she thought. He's only sixteen.

The police had been pragmatic. They had talked with her and then advised that as a streetwise youngster, topping six feet in height, he wasn't in grave danger. He would turn up, they said, and even if they found him somewhere, maybe at one of the drop-ins, they couldn't make him come home.

Belize

In Belmopan, capital of Belize, it was midnight. Rain hammered on the rooftops; it was heavy and had been falling for two hours. At the British diplomatic mission Her Majesty's Ambassador James Constance was still up and at his desk. Across the other side in one of the chairs was his military attaché, a captain from the Hampshire Regiment.

The attaché's role varied from post to post and here in Belize it was relatively simple. The captain's role was the ongoing liaison between the MoD and the Belize authorities. Once a colonel's job, since the standing battalion had left in the early eighties it had dropped a couple of tiers and the captain made sure that everything worked and everyone was happy. In addition to the resident SAS troop attached to train the BDF, there was normally a small force in-country jungle training, a skeleton team at Airport Camp, the adventure-training facility on St George's Cay and a few specialists in and out. Standing orders required that the attaché be informed if the SAS troop altered their posture so he could discreetly clamp it down and head off the inevitable enquiries the following day when training schedules were altered. Bonner had just left.

'What do we make of it?' the ambassador asked. He was still marvelling at the sheer audacity of the SAS officer, who, with a grin, had made an outrageous request that he suddenly felt bound to agree to.

'Not sure, sir. They have obviously found something they don't like the look of, but he wouldn't elucidate. Probably nothing; we'll have to wait and see. Presumably there have been no grumbles from our friends over the border?'

'No,' Constance answered. 'It's been quiet, since, God, it must be four or five months now – before your time. Their last whinge was back in January.' Too quiet? he thought. No. They haven't seriously rattled their sabre since the late seventies. This government was new and tackling the usual problems, exacerbated in recent years by serious unemployment and growing debt to the World Bank. There was some civil unrest, with the guerrillas in the east the most visible issue. They periodically stopped vehicles on the road, stole a token amount as a road toll, and then lectured the occupants on their political aims. Every now and then they actually kept a four-wheel-drive they liked the look of and consequently Belizean car-hire operators weren't keen on their vehicles going over into Guatemala. But the guerrillas hadn't actually harmed a foreigner for about two years now.

The new President was a hard-liner, very right-wing; the Americans, who preferred him to the communists, were walking a delicate line after being embarrassed by their support of almost every right-wing group in Central America in turn. Groups in Nicaragua, El Salvador, Panama, all had bitten the hand that had fed them, supplied arms, advisers and aid, invariably because the Americans chose to support the wrong side; ideology in the face of common sense. The Americans thankfully had taken no stance on Guatemala's territorial ambition, for three reasons: their special relationship with Britain, the fact that they actually liked Belize, and its real time democracy. They saw it as very stable and friendly to the USA and in fact the American diplomatic mission in Belize City was the only US mission in the world without a marine guard detail – it was considered unnecessary. The last reason was historical fact.

The Guatemalan claim to southern Belize was fatuous. The last shot officially fired in anger was back in 1786 at St George's Cay when the loggers and slavers, with British support, had thrown the Spanish out. Guatemala didn't exist then. But it did now, and was much bigger and more powerful than little Belize and was short of access to the Caribbean and the Atlantic. When British Honduras became independent Belize back in 1981, after three Guatemalan military build-ups on the border in the last twenty years, the deal brokered by the UN was that Britain continue to be responsible for her security until such time as she could provide her own defences. There were also claims that Britain had agreed to build a road linking Guatemala City with the east coast and this had never happened. Rather like the Argentines and their 'Malvinas', Guatemala had never relinquished the claim but no one thought they were likely to try and enforce it.

'Anyway, sir,' the attaché said, standing up, 'as you are breakfasting with the minister of defence, and tomorrow he is due to visit the unit we are changing arrangements for, I thought you might want to know.'

'Quite right. Thanks,' Constance said.

'Then I'll bid you goodnight.'

Up in the highlands it was still raining, and although over
Belize City the sky had cleared, the runway was still wet as
the chartered DC8 carrying the remainder of B Squadron
touched down. It taxied straight to the military pan opposite
the civilian terminal, nosing itself alongside the narrow entry
taxi way so the occupants could deplane out of the portside
doors without the world watching. A set of stairs had been
towed across earlier and as the men came down they carried
their bergens, weapons and other equipment. The unloading
was fast with Squadron kit shared out and carried back into
the hangar and dumped with the personal gear. There were
two trucks waiting and the first troop due away were quickly
checking their kit and packing extra ordnance that they had
been unable to get to on the aircraft. The boss wanted the
first of them away within the hour on the RN Sea King that
was waiting. That would be a full troop and a patrol from a
second. They would be on recce posture, but with all the kit
they needed close to hand if the task changed and they became
fighting patrols. Mobility troop had already stashed their gear,
and leaving one bloke to stop anyone nicking their stuff, they
pushed off to see what other transport Bonner had managed
to organize.

The boss was already planning for worst-case and he wanted
enough vehicles to have the bulk of the Squadron mobile as
four- or eight-man patrols. Bonner had been working; he had
called in his last two blokes still in Belize City and they had
come up trumps. They had purloined four Land-Rovers and
a newish truck from round the camp and in addition had
hired the last six available four-wheel-drives from various
agencies around the city, one flashing a Visa card like a
millionaire. The colours weren't perfect – two were white and
one red, but that could be fixed. A mixture of oil, water and
fine dark soil sprayed all over and then liberally daubed-in
mud to flatten reflection would be enough. By the time they
had gone halfway up the highway the oily film would have
the entire vehicle coated in dust and make them merge into
whatever backgrounds they were operating in. The final coup,

one which delighted the lads, was the last vehicle in the line-up. A six-month-old Range Rover, the personal vehicle of the ambassador. The 4.2 litre engine powered among other things a CD player, an air-conditioner and a big chunky winch on the front.

'How the fuck did you get that?' one of them asked Bonner, grinning.

'It's the ambassador's. He thinks I just borrowed it to run around in for the next couple of days,' he replied, 'so don't bloody dent it!'

'Leather seats, air-conditioning – fuckin' magic. This is me sorted,' the soldier replied. 'Don't worry, we'll bring it back.'

None of them were to know it, but when the ambassador eventually got his Range Rover back he would barely recognize it.

Further down the camp, unaware of what was happening at air ops, D Coy were almost ready to move with only a few final preparations remaining. The camp had been handed over the day before. The men had all packed their gear and it was laid out platoon by platoon, the support equipment off to one side. Outside the silent officers' mess area the barbecue stood where it had been left. Someone would be through a little later to take in the glasses and clear up the mess, but for now it sat in the increasingly hot sun, steam rising from the wet grass and soggy paper napkins.

CSM Jennings had taken strips off four toms who had staggered back in the gate after midnight, roaring drunk. The gate guard detail had dragged them in after finding them playing football with a coconut up the road towards the gate. Two of them were so hungover that as he pointed them at the first fatigues job of the morning, cleaning toilets, they both knew they would throw up before it was done. The clean-up before handing their lines back would be thorough, the place spotless. Every toilet, every corner, every path, every light bulb cleaned. Most of it had been done yesterday, but even with the few odd jobs left it would take the fatigues parties till lunchtime to meet Jennings' standards before he would invite the OC down for his inspection.

Cutter's section were taking it easy doing the last little spit and polish on their hut, the other two on other tasks. The platoon sergeant, Norris, was new and none of them knew him that well, as before his promotion he had been with B Coy, prior to a two-year stint with ATR Lichfield. He was haggling with the REME sergeant who ran their QM stores over some lost kit, cutting a deal for his lads. In spite of hang-overs and everyone feeling a little rough, spirits were high. They were heading home, back to wives and girlfriends, some with leave booked.

'What's the first thing you're gonna do when clear of the gate?' Rhah asked.

'Get a fookin' decent pint in,' Plonker responded instantly.

'No, I mean what are you looking forward to?'

'A pint, mun,' Plonker replied. 'Decent beer, not this lager shite.'

'You always were a deep thinker,' Rhah responded.

Suddenly CSM Jennings was there. 'You cunts having a fucking lovely little chat then? Get this shithole finished. Where's Sar' Norris?'

'With the QM, O Great One,' Spud answered. He was still pleased he had taken two pints off the CSM the night before with his match game.

'Don't take the piss or I'll fucking drop you,' Jennings responded. 'Right, when you have done this, last check at your area cleaning of yesterday. Your hut, and down three. Got it?'

A few of them made positive noises, but there were also a few groans. No one took his threat to 'drop' them seriously. He had never done it, except to a civilian who had swung one at him, but he had gone down like a sack of shit after Robo had let go a punch.

'Don't overdo the fucking enthusiasm,' Jennings said drily and moved off.

'That's our man. Dial 1-800-SENSITIVE,' Jonesy mut-tered. He had spent a holiday in the USA the year before and had been fascinated and amused by the Americans' use of catchy little phrases for telephone numbers, predictably the sex lines, and could remember the best ones. Now he used the theme to describe others as if each person had their own number.

'I want a meal that isn't out of a mess tin,' Spud said, picking up the conversation, bending over and reaching under an iron bedframe with a mop, swishing it back and forth in the time-honoured way. 'Not deep and meaningful, just a nice meal. I want salmon in pastry – *en croûte* I think it is, you get it at Sainsbury's. Mashed potatoes, broccoli done just right. I know a girl who does that.'

'All they need is a cunt to keep me happy,' Plonker muttered.

'Na, not salmon,' from someone else. 'Cumberland sausages, with onion gravy, and I'll 'ave some of your mash, only wi' onion, grated fine like,' he qualified, 'mixed in the potato, and cayenne pepper on top. My Tracy does that. Got one of them Delia whatsername cookbooks.'

'I fookin' 'ate broccoli,' from Plonker. 'What about yowa,' he asked Rhah, 'what do you want?'

Rhah looked at them with a little smile. The lads; soldiers, simple tastes. If you can't eat it, drink it or fuck it there's no pleasure.

'My uncle has a boat. I want to go sailing, stand at the helm. Stand at the wheel and feel it, feel the sea, look out as far as the horizon with the wind in my face.'

There was a pause as they took that in and then Plonker spoke. 'Aye, but you'll take some beers, right?'

Fifty yards away the C Coy lads were out for their first morning, acclimatizing gently. Stripped down to shorts and T-shirts they were about to run the perimeter as platoons, work up a real sweat, rather than put up with the one they had already. These were Gurkhas, the tough little mountain men of Nepal. They were very fit, their CSM, Nandu Goreng, made sure of that and sometimes he would slow down the run so their officer, who occasionally ran with them, wouldn't be embarrassed as he began to flag, his entire platoon watching him. Goreng was old-school Gurkha; originally in the Duke of Edinburgh's Regiment he was now attached to 2 Para with his men. As CSM he was allowed his little eccentricities and he still wore his campaign hat, the wide brim up on one side like an Aussie slouch hat, his Para wings above the eye as they would have been on a beret. When everyone was in from the run they would split up and begin their various training tasks with the company up to Guacamole Bridge and into the jungle in two days' time. Goreng ran alongside the platoon sergeant from seven platoon, his hat on his head, breathing easily, and then turned and ran backwards, looking at them. They were not only running but they were running in step, in belt-kit and rifles. Tomorrow they would add light day-packs with just one brick and the following day increase the weight a little to three.

Twenty minutes later Cutter watched them go past his hut on the second circuit, not even breathing hard yet.

'Fuckin' 'ell,' Plonker said, looking up at them. 'Fit little bastids 'n' all.'

Cutter looked over. A shadow signalled someone's approach from round the corner and there was only one this size, their platoon commander, Lieutenant Rees. He was pale and looked like he hadn't had much sleep.

'Morning, sir,' Cutter said cheerfully.

'Morning, Corp'l Cutter.'

'Morning, sir,' Plonker added. 'May I say summat, sir?'

'If you are going to tell me I look like shite, I know.'

'That's all right then, sir.' Plonker grinned at him.

'Big Harry?' Jones said as he walked away. '1-800-'

'Fook Big Harry. What am I?' Plonker interrupted, trying to needle Jones or maybe get a WARRIOR or HARD MAN number.

'1-800-DUMB CUNT.'

The others burst out laughing, but Jones had struck home. 'Aye, and what are yowa, ya fat shit?' Plonker responded.

Jonesy just ignored him.

Across in the admin area Major Fox had C Coy's tiny command element settled in. The core team was just two men. The CSM and his radio operator, with other tasks, clerical in nature, carried out by men of the support platoon, rifle-toting, mortar-humping soldiers, who surprisingly quite enjoyed the break from routine, be it sorting and handing out mail, a prized job for a Gurkha, when one might sight a letter for oneself from home, or handling the inevitable paperwork of army life. There were no adjutant general's staff out here, no paymaster.

Major Fox listened with half an ear through the door as the OC support briefed the platoon sergeant on the tasks that needed handling as he read through the training plan. C Coy, as D had been, was beefed up for the deployment, but where D had patrols and a fifty section from HQ Company, he had a pioneers team but he was also saddled with mortar and anti-tank detachments. He had interrupted the CO during his closed-door hour and lobbied for the same, saying his toms were going to be jungle training, and lugging anti-tank kit that needed a mile of straight-line visibility on jungle exercise was about as much use as snowsuits. Colonel Wallace had listened, then looked up. 'Dickie, I want your blokes as familiar with anti-tank as they clearly are with rifle elements.' And then he looked back at the paper he was working on.

'Yes sir. With all due respect – '

Wallace looked up again. His expression said it – JFDI. Just fucking do it.

Although youthful, Fox was a classic officer of Gurkhas from the old school. Into the Gurkha's mess straight from Sandhurst, the Gurkhali language hammered into him, he had worked his way up quickly and when the company had moved across and parachute-trained for the indefinite attachment to the Parachute Regiment he had gone with them. His soldiers loved him; he was gifted with languages and his Gurkhali was absolutely fluent, his accent so good that he could talk to his lads through the canvas of a tent and they thought he was one of them. Scrupulously fair in his dealings with his men, he met the Gurkhas' ideal of an officer. He had no favourites and was absolutely consistent, measured and respectful of their traditions; he was everything they needed. Within the company, now estranged from their parent brigade, he was fiercely loyal, looking after their welfare, their needs in a regimental structure where they were the minority. In return they didn't disappoint him.

Fox was also slightly eccentric; a passionate hill walker, he had dragged his wife on Himalayan trekking holidays twice in two years, sometimes stopping to visit families of men in his company. He knew Nepal as well as anyone, and turning his fascination on northern India he was now teaching himself Urdu and Hindi. Of average height, he was solidly built, with short, powerfully muscular legs, very like the Gurkhas he commanded. He wore his hair longer than he should have, and above the wide handlebar moustache, his eyes were the most piercing blue. His men, many of whose fathers and grandfathers had fought under commanders like General Slim and Orde Wingate, thought the eccentricity absolutely normal, and found other OCs like D Company's Tyson-Davis almost colourless.

Fox put down the training schedule, walked across and looked out of the window in time to see the CSM running alongside a platoon of men. They looked the business; lean, fit, ready to go. The day after tomorrow they would head into the rain-forest, the environment where the Gurkhas had earned and consolidated their fearsome reputation over the last century.

Outside the guest house the day was bright and the sun already gathering its heat. From their table the girls could look out over the veranda wall and into the back garden of the adjoining house. It had once been elegant, a reminder of the colonial past, a piece of the old British Honduras, two storeys high, clapboard with the shuttered windows of the era. Now the paint was peeling, the corrugated iron roof showed rust through the patches of exposed primer, applied three decades before. Huge lush trees dominated the garden, banana, coconut, fan palms, flame trees, hibiscus and flamboyants. A wooden water butt twenty feet in diameter was fed by a pipe from the gutters round the roof, a legacy of the days before mains water supplies. On the low wall, wish-willies, the small local iguanas, bathed in the sunlight, and in the alley between the two buildings sand crabs pushed up mud from their holes. The entire area had been reclaimed from mangrove swamps, and here, a good city block from the nearest seawater, they were only twelve inches above sea level, the whole city just eighteen inches above the high tide.

Inside the open dining room Sophie and Helen were eating breakfast, mosquito toast and black coffee. Helen watched Sophie eat, marvelling at how she could after the night before. She groaned, 'How can you?'

'Serves you right,' Sophie said. 'If I hadn't been with you, you would still be there, asleep under a table – or worse.'

Helen smiled weakly through the dull thud of her headache, and sipped her coffee. 'It would have been "or worse" I'm afraid. That chap was very persistent and very charming, and I was weakening by the minute.' She looked up at Sophie. 'I left you two talking. What time did you come to bed?'

'Late,' Sophie said obliquely. It had been – they found the coffee pot downstairs and heated it up and they sat up in the sitting room, the lights off, talking softly. The two small bedrooms off the sitting room were thankfully both empty and with the doors open, the wind blew through the open shutters and helped the fan that slowly swished overhead.

'You didn't . . . did you?' Helen grinned.

'Mind your own business,' Sophie replied, dipping her mouth towards her fork as she lifted a piece of the mosquito toast dripping in maple syrup.

'You did!' Helen challenged.

'Shh,' Sophie said softly, her mouth full.

'You tart!'

'We didn't, for your information,' Sophie responded, looking round to see if anyone could overhear them. 'So there.'

But nearly, she thought, oh so nearly. He had been with her on the little wicker sofa, his hand lazily stroking her thigh through the cotton sarong she had changed into, talking about home, childhood, music, books and everything as they learned about each other, and then he leant forward and kissed her. It was sweet, gentle, unthreatening, his massive bulk simply reassuring. When he held her the world went away and then he rose and effortlessly lifted her in his arms and carried her to the room on the seaward side and laid her on the bed. Her heart was pounding and she was wet between her legs, very wet, and she wanted him. But knew she shouldn't; her pussy seemed to have a mind of its own – I'm wet and ready and open and want it and it's hard, I can feel it, that's what it's for, that's what I'm for. Her common sense told her, I've known this man less than twenty-four hours. Her common sense won and she whispered, 'No,' into his kiss, 'it's too soon.'

He smiled and kissed her again and whispered, 'I know,' and he lifted his bulk above her to let the breeze blow between them and cool her, the moonlight coming through the shutters making stripes down him. She could taste the saltiness of his sweat, and as he lowered himself to kiss her again she thought she was falling in love – or was she merely infatuated? Finally, after what seemed like hours of kissing and as she was about to give in to her libido's demands, he rose one last time.

'I have to go,' he whispered. 'Promise you'll go out with me when you get home.'

She nodded quickly. 'I promise.' She rose, splaying her thighs for balance and kissed him again. 'Don't meet anyone till then, please?'

'I'll wait,' he said and then he dropped, quickly like a big cat, his face dipping into the junction of her thighs. He licked once, then twice, and she shuddered as the pleasure rolled through her. Another kiss and he was gone.

'I'll bet,' Helen said sarcastically.

'It's true.'

Helen smiled at her. She knew Sophie was telling the truth, but she also knew her well enough to read the look in her eyes. She was smitten, slammed, head over heels.

'It may be. But you now wish you had, don't you?'

Sophie nodded.

'You're going to see him when we get back?'

'Yes, but there's Terry. I'll –'

'You will dump bloody Terry,' Helen said firmly, 'or I will do it for you. These two don't even compete on the same continent. One's everything you could want, the other's a deceitful married bastard.'

'Oh, while I think of it, the rental car people were on. They wanted to know if they could have the car back. Did we really want a four-wheel-drive, they could give us a lovely something or other. I told them we wanted to keep it.'

Helen looked out the windows at the big beast that had been delivered the evening before, a Toyota Land Cruiser.

'Absolutely right. That's going to be fun! And anyway, if the guidebooks are right we won't make Placencia without it. By the look of it the rains have begun.'

Sophie looked out at the sky and didn't argue. Helen's degree was geography and she knew about that sort of thing.

'C'mon. Let's get moving. Xunantunich beckons.'

The patrols' callsigns ran sequentially. Bravo for B Squadron, Two for air troop, and then the patrol designation one through to four. Bravo Two-Two, the SAS patrol that had crossed into Guatemala north of the border post, was now relatively deep inside hostile territory. Not deep in geographical terms, it was only four miles back to Belize, but deep into the area they wanted to recce. They were due to RV with Two-One, Sergeant McKay's patrol, who had been airlifted out of the 'J' down south last night. The head sheds and Bonner had stepped up the posture and had a Gazelle go in the dark. The moon had been out early so it wasn't too bad. Back inside Belize McKay's patrol had given the pilot their GPS reference, a clearing by a camp the pilots knew, and illuminating the LZ with Cyalume markers, they had been lifted out. They were dropped at the Belmopan airstrip where Bonner, on his way back from the embassy, had met them. He handed over fresh ration packs, extra ordnance, and issued new task orders. He left McKay alone with his team for half an hour and then listened to their plan. Happy with it, they piled into the Range Rover and he drove them northwards, turning off at roughly the same point as the previous patrol had, but this time using the chain ferry – the water level was up already and this vehicle didn't have a snorkel – to cross the Mopan river. With lights off in case the vehicle was being observed, he took them to within a mile of the border. They dumped their bergens on to the ground, piled out of the doors, and a moment or two later as he drove away they disappeared into the trees making for their incursion point and their rendezvous with Two-Two.

It was now 0900 hours and Two-Two had moved some miles from their overnight LUP. McKay knew he was still three hours behind them. He stopped briefly and looked back at his tail-end charlie. Weapon to the shoulder, moving very slowly, silently, Gibbo was the scout. Out ahead of the other three, far enough ahead that any noise they made wouldn't interfere with his hearing, he would be the first to contact the enemy. Gibbo wasn't typical; usually the best scouts were village or farm boys, and he was about as urban as they come, but he didn't smoke, didn't chew gum, didn't eat anything that would affect his sense of smell. Even as an SAS jungle warfare instructor, among the best fifteen jungle soldiers in the world, the stress of being out front was exhausting and at night he did a shorter time on stag than the others. They would rather he was rested and alert when he moved off as scout. If he was fully vigilant, then he would see the enemy before they spotted him and that was what it was all about. McKay as patrol leader was in the middle with Boyce, their medic and radio man, and Dozy was behind covering their rear. This was stressful. They were good at what they did, but they could have a contact at any moment, front, side or rear, and that wasn't what they were there for. Boyce had taken off his floppy hat and was now wearing his face veil as a headband keeping the sweat out of his eyes. This wasn't Rambo shit – the sweat mixed with cam cream stung like a bastard and a soldier with watering eyes was no good.

The loads were not bad. Personal ammo, rifle and hand-grenades and they had three 66s, Boyce carrying the minimi, the section weapon. At least they weren't humping mortar bombs. Their route was more direct than Two-Two, who with the luxury of time had made a wide circular track. He focused his mind and moved on. With less than an hour's sleep last night, they were moving well, alert, aware, silently through the bush. He thought of it as bush – much of it had been thinned by logging, but the secondary growth hadn't had time to come through, and there were odd clearings where someone not so long ago had cultivated something, ganja maybe. At other points the trees were old, with thick gnarled latan vines dropping to the ground, and progress slowed to a chameleon-like advance. It was drier here than in the south. The jungle looked the same, but the ground underfoot was firmer in spite of the heavy overnight rain.

They would RV at midday, when the heat was oppressive and the locals, if there were any out here, would be least likely to be out and about. They would check in with the troop commander and then get on with it. Their task was to get a view of the area west of Melchor. If any build-ups had taken place then this was where they would be. The two patrols would break apart again, each cover an area and RV back at a predetermined point one hour before dusk. The other team in at the south would watch the road route in.

Further south the other team was already on to game. With the luck that good soldiers always seem to generate they had come across movement, '*beaucoup* movement' as the scout, a Vietnam war movie aficionado, reported grinning from ear to ear to the rest of the patrol. Trucks were moving forward, mechanized infantry, some in APCs but the bulk in soft-skinned transports, some heavies with bridging gear.

The patrol went forward to verify and try to establish a pattern. Had their mate seen just a mixed make-up unit, a small battle-group, moving along the road, or was this bigger, a brigade or larger on the move?

The int, 'humint', the most valuable kind, that actually seen by expert observers, was flashed to Hereford through a satellite link in a half-second coded burst. They said what they had seen and would report again once they had a pattern.

At PJHQ Northwood, a small team, a mixture of Joint Intelligence J2 and Army G2, was trying to find out exactly what was going on on the Guatemala–Belize border. Permanent Joint Headquarters was just that, a tri-service facility, there to monitor and anticipate developments affecting Britain's interests and if necessary strategically direct the conduct of operations. Next door was the NATO facility, full of US staff, with direct access to the Pentagon and US Department of Defense and under normal circumstances a request for assistance would run through set channels, but there was not time for that.

In Whitehall in a small office towards the back of the MoD building a serving intelligence officer waited for the man who spent little time in this, his official office. Bertram Conway was a civil servant but with a difference. Moving as he wished between the MoD, MI5 at Century House, MI6, and PJHQ at Northwood, his role was liaison, specifically with the Americans. He spent a lot of time in the USA and knew the machinations of the Department of Defense and the Pentagon as well as anyone. He was good at his work. Convivial, yet with a mind like a scientist, he was also a natural networker, a man who used relationships as others used tools. Rotund and in his early fifties, he was mildly eccentric in that he wore bright bow-ties and vivid yellow or crimson cashmere sweaters in the staid environment of the Ministry of Defence, but that was where the eccentricity stopped. His job was getting things done, facilitating action where the natural barriers in the system foiled conventional attempts, and he achieved success where others failed.

'Hello, Don,' he said, coming through the door. His secretary followed him in, catching a pile of papers that was about to slide off the corner of his desk in the wake of his passing.

'Hello, Bertie.' The officer let him move his bulk past. 'Sorry to badger you like this.'

'No problem. Always delighted.' Conway beamed. 'Now then, to what do I owe this pleasure?'

'Need some help, Bertie,' Don said. He was a Lieutenant

Colonel spending two years at PJHQ Northwood before returning, he hoped, to command his regiment. He was with the Assistant Chief of Staff (J2), Intelligence. He had another man, an oppo who was the G2 at Hereford, waiting for a result, so he got straight down to it. 'Need a bird's eye view. My contact has moved on and we don't have time for official channels.'

'Go on.'

'Hereford have put some chaps in on the ground, but we are rather concerned.' He pulled a set of maps from his briefcase, computer-generated images that overlaid what SHAPE and PJHQ Northwood could normally request as areas scanned by US satellites. He turned straight to the second section, the area not usually needed by SHAPE or NATO because it was out of their theatre of operations. Page twenty-four was the top eastern end of the Yucatan peninsula down as far as Honduras, sweeping up north-eastern Mexico, Belize and eastern Guatemala.

He pointed to a strip along the border. 'We need to see last night's infra-red images of this area. Can they be sent to us down an ISDN line?'

'When?'

'As soon as possible,' he replied. 'It's important.'

Conway looked at his watch – mid-morning in Washington, they might even catch the routine processing. 'Give me a number where I can find you and the number of the secure ISDN line you want it on.'

The colonel passed over a card. 'I'm on my mobile for the next couple of hours, then I'm contactable at Northwood. Humint is coming in.'

'With luck the images will be there before you,' Conway said.

'Appreciate it, Bertie.'

'Oh, don't mention it. You know the price,' he said, reaching for a telephone, one of several on his desk. 'They will call in the favour sooner or later.'

Dion, lean and tanned the colour of teak, lifted the third fuel tank and shook it – half full. He had two full tanks, enough for the run out to Goff's Cay, but the big hundred and fifty horse outboards, two of them, drank plenty and he always had enough for an alternative landfall, in this case enough to go all the way to Rendezvous Point, out on Turneffe, and back in to the mainland. He had the gear, plenty of bottles, and the guest house staff had been down with the packed lunches for the dive party. They would be waiting round at the Radisson Jetty. He was happy with the loading and trim; weight belts were fore and aft, bottles amidships, fuel tanks aft. He wanted minimal weight up the front end, the bow riding high over the waves. Out to Goff's Cay, leave the non-divers on the most beautiful little island God ever made to swim and sunbathe, and then run the dive party out to the reef from there. Do a dive, bring everyone back to Goff's for lunch, then run over to Soldier Cay for the second tank each, back in by four-thirty. It would be a good day for them.

At JB's up at the thirty-two-mile marker, Sally Moretto had opened up the back areas so the early staff could start work. She glanced around, a sweeping look to check that all was well. There were two of her team in the kitchen doing prep work, slicing tomatoes, onions and lettuces for their famous burgers, and another was pushing oranges into the squeezer. A tub of limes was awaiting the same fate. Ribs were already marinating in honey and lemon juice and the baker should arrive any minute, to deliver the rolls and long torpedo-shaped loaves they used by the dozen. She moved through into the front of house where old Jed was sweeping out the bar and public areas. He had been working there as long as she could remember and he had seemed old back when she first met him, when she was just a drinker here and not the owner.

'How you doing, Jed?' she asked. 'Melanie OK?'

Melanie was his wife, a good solid woman; she had borne him nine children who had all grown up and moved on.

'She fine, Miss Sally,' Jed replied with a grin. The gaps in his teeth were substantial. She had offered to get him some false teeth once, from a good dentist in Belize City, but he just shook his head. The good Lord had meant his to fall out and that was that. Besides, he had said, he still had four in the front and they would do just fine. The rain that had rolled through overnight had left the ground smelling sweet as honeysuckle and as she walked back to the warehouse across the lot she looked out over her orange groves at the mountains in the distance.

Sure is beautiful, she thought.

In San Ignacio Pete Collins was also opening up. His wife, a local girl, was chatting to the cleaning lady in fast bursts of Creole, interlaced with Spanish. They both broke into gales of laughter about something but he ignored them and watched his youngest daughter pad over to him. Her hair was a shock of sumptuous black curls and waves, her eyes huge and dark and she clutched a teddy bear tightly to her chest with one hand, the other holding her juice bottle. This was his time of the day; seventeen years in the British army had conditioned him to early mornings and he loved to see the first light of day. It happened less now, running Eva's meant staying up late, but the three-hour siesta in the afternoon made the difference. They would be open in an hour or so, but he had time to fire up one of the computers and check their Web site and respond to any e-mails that had come in. His little cyber-café in the middle of nowhere was doing well and although it was down to many things, good food, good service, it was the technology that made the difference, the bank of four computers that people came in to use. Eva's became a meeting place for everyone and when they met they ate and drank – it was money in the till and a future for everyone on the payroll. The landlines had gone down for three days last month and he had got the satellite link installed. It wasn't really a sat link so much as a seriously expensive mobile phone setup that meant they could run the e-mails out regardless of whether some drunk had driven into a telephone pole on the highway.

He began clearing his mail, an odd collection of messages from people who had visited, friends and some business associates. His daughter climbed up on to his knee. He wrapped a lean tattooed arm around her and with a smile he shut down the e-mail and crossed over on to a commercial Web site and scrolled down till he found what he knew she wanted. Winnie the Pooh. A bright graphic of the bear filled the screen and he began to read the words along the bottom.

Back in Belize City Edwardo Sanchez pulled up and parked his car on the side of the road outside the guest house. He knew the people there and could wander in and pass his card around the guests, chat to them, try and hustle up some business. The American who had hired the car the day before had decided against the long drive down to Placencia so Edwardo needed another good fare. He opened the boot, took out a bucket and a sponge and half-filling the bucket from a big plastic two-gallon container he walked round the car, sponging the surfaces clean of mud and dust. His Chevrolet Caprice was a good car: maroon velour upholstery, air-conditioning, tinted windows. You couldn't ask wealthy tourists to drive round in an old wreck, and with this car he could command top dollar.

Two girls came down the steps from the guest house, laughing and giggling, small day-bags in their hands.

'Taxi, ladies?' he called. 'Got air-con,' he added, going for the fully differentiated sales proposition.

'No thanks,' one called back. 'We hired a car.'

'How long you here for? I do tours. Best value around – Mayan ruins, jungle.'

'No thanks, we're fine.'

He turned back to his cleaning.

Up in the dining room an American sitting at one of the side tables watched the interplay. He was flirting with the waitresses while he waited for his buddy to come down. They were salesmen, in Belize to sell machinery for their Chicago-based company. This hadn't been their choice; their hotel had double-booked and moved them over to the guest house, but now they were pleased. This was the cool place to stay and they had done the deal and could take the day off. His buddy came down the stairs; big, unshaven, wearing just a pair of shorts and a T-shirt, he ambled over to the table, catching the eye of the waitress.

'Mornin' darlin'. How about some coffee? Huh, damn, you look sweet. You comin' home with me?'

She scuttled off smiling and he laughed, lighting a cigarette and coughing, and slumped into the seat opposite his friend, looking out at the lushness of the gardens, the colours vibrant in the bright sunlight. He took another drag, coughing less this time, and blew out the smoke looking at the view.

'Sonofabitch, eh? Another day in paradise.'

Some twelve hours later he would change his view considerably.

Chapter Three

Major Chard, OC B Squadron, was bending over the map table, from where Captain Bonner had deployed his troop the night before. The Squadron was out, deployed on the various tasks they had been set. Only Bonner, four signallers, the soldiers manning the hi-tech communications gear, and the Squadron sergeant major were left in the admin area. Chard was leaning over the map looking down at the square that covered the border post and the road back towards Benque. He pointed at a turning off the road. 'What's this in here?'

'Grass. Grazing. Some trees where they couldn't clear it, but no cover.'

Chard was uncomfortable. Long stretches of the road from the border ran through farmland, open country. You could drive armour through it at thirty miles an hour. If they were right and the Guats were going to cross over, then this was the place they would do it. Two lanes of respectable blacktop, bordered for at least half the distance by farmland, at some points both sides of the road. Grazing – not even soft ploughed earth that would slow down wheeled vehicles. There were choke-points, but not many. There was a brisk knock and a man came into the hut, a sergeant that Bonner knew, one of the logistics corps people. He looked straight at Bonner.

'Your blokes have helped themselves to my kit . . . sir! It's not on!'

'How do you –'

'They were seen, sir. Only one bunch looks like yours. Nicked five wheels off a vehicle we had in the shop and loaded them on to a truck, and that's not all. They also fucked off with four of my quads. Now wheels I can live with, but not the prototype equipment that –'

'I'll look into it,' Bonner said, thinking, mobility troop getting themselves and the Squadron mobile. That's their job; when the boys were going to go to work, in their view any bit of kit that wasn't nailed down was fair game. But quads? Nicking ammo, food, clothing, comms kit was fair enough. But whole quads? That was pushing it a bit. Then he remembered the porky he had told the ambassador to get hold of his Range Rover. 'If my people have borrowed something you'll get it back.'

'They will have needed it,' Chard muttered, still bent over the map board.

'I don't give a fuck!' the sergeant snapped. 'I signed for the fucking things.'

Chard stood up and looked him in the eye. 'You say fuck to me and you better say sir or major in the same sentence. Captain Bonner said you'll get 'em back, and you will. Now piss off!'

The sergeant paled for a second. He had developed enough of a relationship with Bonner to speak his mind freely, but he had no idea that Bonner's OC was there.

'Sir,' he said and left the hut.

Chard turned back and looked at the map. 'Don't like this. Not one bit.' He was one of those men who trusted his instincts, felt the hairs on his neck rise, and took heed. One of the signallers came back in balancing a pile of dishes on a tray. There were cold sausages, chops and cold steaks, hard-boiled eggs, cold baked beans, some limp coleslaw, a couple of loaves of bread, butter and other odds and ends. In his pockets he had several cold bottles of Belikin beer.

'You want some scoff, boss?' he asked.

Chard looked up. He hadn't eaten in a while; last time had been in Hereford. He nodded. 'Thanks.'

The soldier went to work with the knife and a few minutes later passed his major a doorstep sized sandwich of cold meat, sliced eggs, salad and pickles. He cracked the top of a bottle of beer and passed that across. Chard took them both. He made no comment about the beer, knowing that it would be one each and no more. He bit into the sandwich, realizing he was hungry. It was delicious.

77

'Where did you purloin this from?'

'Your mess kitchen, sir.' The man grinned back, explaining, '2 Para Ruperts had a barby last night. It would only go to waste.'

'It's good,' Chard said. 'Thanks.' He looked back at Bonner who was reaching for a sandwich from the signaller. 'Your patrols,' he pointed at the map. 'One here,' he moved his finger a few inches to the right, noticed something, lifted it to his mouth, licked off some salad cream and again pointed to the map. 'And two about to RV in here.'

'Correct,' Bonner replied.

Chard was thinking quickly. He had deployed his troops on various tasks, with five patrols on recce, but the int coming through from the one team south of the border post was compelling. He wanted to change his posture. As senior officer on the ground he could do that, providing he could justify his actions later should that be required.

He looked at Bonner. 'Recall Two-Two and Two-One. Get them lifted out under those Gazelles. No excuses from them either, I want them back.' Bonner nodded. 'Any of those Land-Rovers you got Wolf?' he went on.

The Land-Rover Wolf version, now standard for much of the British army, were designed with a built-in Milan firing position on the back. Not all units had them.

'Three of the four from the camp are. The others are all civvy vehicles.'

Chard nodded and looked across at the signallers. 'One of you blokes nip out and find that loggy sergeant and ask him if we can have a minute. Also, grab whoever runs the stores. Let's see what kit they have got here.' He looked over at the Squadron sergeant major who was listening in on the radio traffic, and eating a cold lamb chop. 'Listen up, Bob, here's what we are going to do.'

He began outlining his thoughts, the SSM and Captain Bonner listening, chipping in, making suggestions, challenging the thinking as equals. Three or four minutes later the signaller was back with the logistics corps sergeant. Chard swallowed the last of his sandwich and drank deeply from the beer bottle, finishing the contents.

'Your quads – any of them capable of being Milan-equipped?'

'Why?' the sergeant asked with an edge to his voice.

'Never mind that,' Chard replied gently. 'Are they?'

'No. Well, not as they are. We have the conversion kits; easy enough to change them over. Three of the ones your blokes "borrowed" will take a fifty. You lift the load rack and under that are the mountings.'

Chard smiled. They'd had them at Hereford for about four years now, quads that could carry a heavy machine gun on the back, one driver, one gunner, and could fire on the move. The rest of the army was catching up and they could be useful.

'How many others have you got?'

'So your blokes can go and play? Sorry, sir, I have a schedule to finish or my arse is –'

'This isn't play,' Chard said softly.

The room went quiet and the sergeant took it all in – the new signals people bent over their equipment, the faint sound of signals traffic, heavy traffic in the background, the fact that a 22 SAS major was now on the ground, the tension; the comings and goings that morning, the jet arriving. Oh fuck.

'What's happening?' he asked quietly.

'Hopefully nothing,' Chard replied.

'And that's why you're here, sir. That's why your blokes have taken four Land-Rovers, the wheels of a fifth, four of my quads, that's why you want the others, Milan launch-equipped. That's why you smiled when I said you can mount a fifty on the back of these – because hopefully nothing is happening.' There was an awkward pause. 'The Guatemalans,' he said.

Chard just raised an eyebrow.

'Fucking marvellous,' he said, as if the Guatemalans were behaving like arseholes just to ruin his day.

'So how many have you got?'

'You sign?'

Chard nodded.

'Another six. Your blokes missed the best. Big ones, twelve hundred cc, four-by-fours. Got trailers too – you can whack three hundred pounds of ordnance on to 'em before the

79

engine struggles. Go through anything, pure fucking magic they are.'

'I'll take 'em,' Chard said. 'What else can you help us with?'

'Not much. I have two heavies, but if you think you will need re-supply, I'll need those – not that there's much I can re-supply you with. Everything that's just come in is for the Paras. You're still on recce right?'

Chard didn't answer, but the fact he didn't deny it was enough.

'Then there's something you might want to look at. Not mine, I might add, so I don't care if you nick it,' the logistics sergeant said with a grin and looked across at Bonner. 'You seen the Beadle?'

Bonner shook his head.

'There's six blokes from RA with a couple of pointy heads from BAe. They are trialling a thing that looks like a flying rubbish bin.'

'A remote flying camera,' Chard said softly, his eyes displaying his new interest. 'Saw a briefing on it.'

'The lads call it Beadle for obvious reasons.'

'Because it's fucking irritating and every time you see it you just want to punch it?' the Squadron sergeant major offered.

The loggy sergeant grinned. 'The pointy heads call it Hi-Eye. Get your hands on that and it will save you some sweat.'

'Where are they?'

Leo Scobey, the ITN correspondent who had been tipped off by his ex-girlfriend's brother in the FCO, was on the American Airlines flight coming in from Miami. This was the only way in – Caracas to Miami and then down again. He was up the sharp end. The seats weren't much bigger, but that didn't matter on a sector as short as this, he wanted the leg-room, but with the 'shitholes' he routinely travelled in and out of in central and southern America he had argued and got business or first-class travel in his contract.

He was tall, well over six feet, dark-haired and lean, skinny almost. His face was brown from the sun, but a scar that ran from his earlobe around to the base of his hairline was white. It was the legacy of a shrapnel wound picked up when he had covered East Africa and had been a little too close to an Eritrean 'technical' when it was hit and exploded, its own ammunition cooking off.

Chubby Morton, sitting alongside him, had put on a dressing and got him back to a clinic. Chubby, an award-winning cameraman, who had given up fighting his weight problem at school, rarely wore anything but a T-shirt and jeans. He was one of life's slobs and Leo's only demand was that he shave before they went to work. It was difficult enough to gain the cooperation and retain the respect of the interviewee, he thought, without your crew looking like they were sleeping rough. There hadn't been another seat up the front, so the rest of the crew, the soundman and the satellite technician, were at the back. Neither objected – both were light, small, and barely noticed their environment, caught up in their technical worlds, the sat tech like a real nerd. Their cases of equipment were down in the hold; only Chubby's camera and the sound man's basic recorder and two microphones were in the cabin. Neither went anywhere without them, ever.

'What we gonna do on arrival? Get a hotel or hit the road?' Chubby asked.

'Get a room, I think,' Scobey answered.

At the back of the aircraft, in fact in the last six seats opposite the galley were six men travelling together. Four of them were wearing bad-taste Hawaiian shirts, and anywhere else they would have been very conspicuous indeed, but on a flight out of Miami, the world's capital of bad taste, no one seemed to notice. In fact, further towards the front there was a tourist wearing an even worse example of the genre and this slightly irritated one of the men who took pride in his shirts as being about as bad as one could get.

'Bastard,' he muttered. 'Wonder where he got that?'

The fellow next to him nodded. 'Fucking awful, isn't it,' he said in wonder. 'Not even you would wear that.'

The four men in the shirts were members of B Squadron boat troop on their way in from a team job in Peru and the other two were coming in off a training deployment with anti-drugs teams in the Bahamas. They bumped into each other in Miami airport. Their gear, in civvy tote bags, was in the hold and they were travelling unarmed. Squadron had carried their kit in, and it would be waiting for them.

'This better be worth it,' one of the Bahamian blokes, Jock Edwards, said. 'I was on to game.'

'What, the big redhead?' his mate asked.

Edwards nodded.

'You're a sick man,' the other responded, 'she would have killed you. You need to see someone.'

'Na, she was lubbly-jubbly.' Edwards yawned and scratched his face. 'I'm gagging for a smoke. When do we get in?'

'Half an hour,' the other replied and pointed out the window, 'thar she blows.'

Out on the starboard side was land, miles of swamp and savannah, the mangrove lagoons, beyond fast-flow tidal reach, black like crude oil against the yellow and red earth. Further out he could see the bush; this was Mexico, the Yucatan peninsula, with Belize just ahead. A few minutes later he saw a landmark he recognized. He knew Belize, knew it well, had felt sometimes that he had hacked his way through every snake, wait-a-bit thorn and mosquito-infested acre of it. There you are, you stinking, humid, sweaty old slut.

'Honey,' he called softly, looking out the window, 'Daddy's home.'

Belize

Sophie was driving, Helen sitting alongside her in the passenger seat, her feet up on the dashboard, her hair billowing in the wind through the open windows. The road was straight most of the way up to the western border, but here in the last few miles there were curves and bends as it followed the contours of the landscape and the river, the Mopan that snaked its way along the left-hand side. Small settlements and dwellings were dotted along the roadside; ramshackle wooden houses, some no more than shacks, stood on stilts, some garishly painted bright pink or green, others not having seen a paint brush in forty years. In almost every one a hammock hung either on the veranda or underneath the house and a fan blew air on the sleeping occupant. Banana trees and flamboyants dotted the gardens. The landscape was different up here; there were fewer coconut palms, they had noticed, and on the other side of the river a few miles past San Ignacio back towards Belize City there was a ranch that could have been in the USA or Australia, with wide, open paddocks and blue gum trees.

Xunantunich had been, in Helen's word, awesome. At the turn-off for the ruin, opposite a collection of small houses, the river flowed within ten feet of the road and they simply pulled off and dropped down the steep track. No queue and no waiting – they drove straight on to the chain ferry, big enough to take two cars, and stood out on the deck as the old man had cranked them across. The Mopan was up he had said because of the rain. He pointed further up and showed them where the rapids were visible just the day before.

'There will be more tonight.'

'Oh, I heard it was going to dry up, be fine,' Sophie said.

'It will rain,' the old man said. 'I am Mayan. I know,' he finished with a little smile, a twinkle in his eye.

They tipped him, left the ferry and the kids hawking carvings on the bank and drove the mile or two up to the Mayan ruin, feeling lazy, and then parked and walked the last few hundred yards, the massive edifice of the largest temple visible from the main road now towering above them.

They had spent an hour there, wandering through the site, excavated and funded by an American programme. It was large, covering some acres, and finally they climbed to the top of the main dominant structure, passing ancient bas-relief carvings of sacrifice and nobles and looked out over the jungle to the north and west, the green-clad hills stretching away as far as the eye could see.

'God. Look at it,' Sophie had said. 'You know why they built it here. You can see for ever. Look at it,' she enthused, glad they had made the effort, pleased to be looking out over Central America, an ambition first aroused by Huey, Dewey and Louie cartoons as they found lost cities in the jungle with

83

their uncle, Scrooge McDuck, and reinforced years later by leafing through *National Geographic* in her own uncle's house on wet afternoons.

'That's Guatemala,' Helen, ever the geographer, pointed. 'About where that hill is over there.'

'It's close. Shall we try and go over?' Sophie suggested.

'I don't think we can. We would need papers for the car and stuff.'

They decided they were hungry then and couldn't face the thought of fish-heads, rice and beans and were now heading east again back towards San Ignacio, a few miles down the road.

'Got the guide book?' Helen asked.

Sophie nodded and dug round in her big woven string bag, and a few minutes later she said, 'Here's a place that sounds interesting.'

Airport Camp

On the pan at Airport Camp things were busy. The Gazelle maintenance crews were preparing their sturdy little helicopters for various tasks, two of them being fitted with cables that hung underneath to which were attached four loops of bungee cord. The fitters weren't sure of what was going on; there were regular requests from the training troop for helicopters so the resident SAS men could practise their skills and all this seemed to be was an increase in activity. They knew not to ask questions and when they had finished they ambled over to the RN Sea King and had a good poke around its innards, chatting to the two RN artificers who had flown in from the Royal Fleet Auxiliary ship. Compared to their little Gazelles this was a monster, although smaller than the RAF's heavy-lift twin-rotored Chinooks. As they were chatting two men in flight suits left the hangar office where a grubby tray of cups and teabags sat on a table with a kettle. Both were carrying helmets. They were followed by two army blokes with huge bergens, pulling a small trolley with other gear on it.

'Aye aye,' one of the artificers said. 'Off we go into the fucking wild blue yonder then.'

He fired up the start-up unit, its cable already plugged into the Sea King, and pulled his ear protectors from his pocket, turning as he did so to look out at the main civilian runway where a commercial flight, an American Airlines stretch 737, was on short finals. Behind them a Land-Rover drove past the pan and accelerated on to the runway perimeter road. As the two army flight engineers walked away from the Sea King one turned to the other.

'Fookin' 'ell,' he said softly. 'See what was on that trolley?'

'No. What?'

'Belt ammo and loadsa bang-bang stuff. Someone is going to get a fucking snotty.'

'Glad it ain't me,' the other replied. 'As long as they are taking it all somewhere else I don't mind. I like being miles away from aggressive people with guns.'

Seven and a half hours later he would be in the thick of it and his view would be reinforced, for the remaining four minutes of his life.

Across the other side of the runway was the civilian terminal. The American Airlines flight in from Miami had just come to a halt at its usual position, on the extreme right as people looked out of the departure lounge. The steps were drawn up to the front portside door and passengers began coming down, Leo Scobey and his cameraman in the first five or six. When they arrived at the bottom of the steps they stood to one side and waited for the other two guys in the crew.

They were chatting, people moving past them, when the six B Squadron men came down the stairs, Scobey only noticing them because instead of following the rest into the arrivals hall, they moved round to the other side of the aircraft. He saw them again a few moments later, carrying their own luggage. Escorted by an airport security type they moved quickly to the edge of the apron, where a waiting green army Land-Rover was parked discreetly behind a tanker truck. The engine started and it drove away immediately. Peculiar, he thought, very peculiar. Who can get away with that? Who has the influence to break all the procedures? Who, wearing civilian gear, climbs into army vehicles like that? Only one bunch. He was right – the bugger was right. Scobey hadn't doubted the source, just the magnitude of the possible story. Something was going on all right, something big.

A few minutes later, standing in the immigration queue in the arrivals hall, he turned to his cameraman. 'Changed my mind. We'll get on the road, I think.'

'Where?' Chubby asked.

Scobey, standing on the left, looked over Chubby's shoulder and out of the window across the airport to where he knew the British troops based themselves. There were two C-130s parked on the pan. Limited presence? Training only? There seemed to be a lot of very expensive aeroplanes for a limited training presence. As he watched a heavy helicopter, a Sea King, its Royal Navy markings visible, lifted off and began to fly away. He guessed who it was carrying. Get official, he thought, get accredited, play the game. He pointed out the helicopter to Chubby with a little grin.

'Belmopan – the High Commission. Let's go and introduce ourselves.'

Across the other side of the airport in the camp Lieutenant Rees and Captain Atlee were ambling down towards the officers' mess for lunch. Everything was ready, packing complete, the place clean. The toms were now lying about, some still nursing hangovers, smoking, eating, chatting to each other, waiting for orders to load the trucks that would transport their heavy kit across to the two waiting C-130s that would take them home. Ahead of them another figure entered the mess. Harry recognized him with a grin. It was Toby Estelle, a C Coy subby, and he was sweating like a pig. Acclimatized after six weeks here, Harry was getting used to it, but he remembered how it was for the first few days. He was about to say something to Atlee when the noise of a helicopter made him think again. Both men turned and looked up and to the left. Obviously the same heavy helicopter they had heard come in the night before, it was gathering speed and height, an RN Sea King with its side doors open.

Atlee looked up at it and as he did so a figure wearing a

colourful shirt leant out of the door and threw up two fingers at him. He recognized the face, the beaming grin, a man he had spent three months instructing with in the jungles of Brunei and Sarawak. The face disappeared and the helicopter clattered away.

'Bloody peculiar,' Atlee muttered.

'What?' Harry asked.

'That bloke in the chopper . . .' he replied, thinking aloud. Jock Edwards. The last time he had seen Jock, a corporal in B Squadron, was in Brunei. Now here he was flying out over Airport Camp in an RN Sea King, wearing one of his horrible shirts. Small world – or was it? Team job? But in such a hurry that they weren't even changing into something sensible? Whatever, it was bad form to talk about them so he muttered, 'Never mind. Presumably you got your two young ladies safely back home last night?'

'I did,' Rees said with a smile. He had thought about little else all morning. Even when he should have been concentrating on the job at hand he found his mind wandering, thinking about her, what she was doing, imagining her, the way she walked, spoke, brushed her hair back behind her ear.

'I think you ruined young Toby's evening. He thought he had cracked it with the blonde one.'

'C Coy – bloody Gurkhas can find their own totty,' Harry replied with a smile. Five days, they would be back in five days. He had already thought about where he would take her – the Hotel du Vin in Winchester. He would make a reservation the moment they were back. Not something you could afford to do too often on a lieutenant's pay, but worth it. The best food within an hour of Aldershot, and as good as anywhere of its genre.

San Ignacio is a hill town. Set in the highlands of the Cayo district, it sprawls either side of the Macal river, the western side the higher with houses and shacks dotted up the hillsides. The main commercial area is also on the western side, a handful of streets that run parallel to the river, the main thoroughfare running off a roundabout where the bridge, the town's raison d'être, crosses the river. In the centre of the roundabout is a small concreted area with benches painted garish colours and a couple of trees that offer shade to the old-timers who sit there. It's a little cooler up in the hills, but still hot, and people walk down to the river and swim, cool their horses, wash fruit and clothing, smoke a little weed.

The approach from the west brings vehicles down the hill, the town laid out below them, tin roofs baking in the hot sun, past the electricity generator station, its two huge diesel engines roaring away within sight of the road, and on to a wide street above the roundabout.

The girls came down the hill and eased round the park with its painted concrete benches and into the main street, ignoring the fork that ran down to the bus station and the river. Hawkers and street-sellers lined the thoroughfare and in front of them a man walked his horse across the road, with two huge sacks of fruit over the saddle and a machete dangling from the saddle-horn. It was an ethnic rainbow and the street corners were active, in a sleepy mañana kind of way, with vendors selling mangoes, oranges and watermelons. There were plastic goods from Guatemala, hammocks, T-shirts and machetes for the tourists and incongruously an ice-cream van still sporting the original owner's name and address in Huddersfield. From him you could apparently still buy a snow-freeze ice-cream complete with a Cadbury's flake for ninety-nine pence.

You could also buy some cheap rum, or casual sex down by the river provided by *café con leche* Guatemalan or Nicaraguan girls, refugees who had run from fighting in their own homelands. For them life was tough and sex felt good and if a man was prepared to pay for what you had given away since puberty then you could get by. Besides, one might really like you and take you away. You could buy some ganja, although for tourists it was a risky business as the local police earned a bonus if they caught a tourist in possession. There was no point trying to arrest locals for smoking ganja, everyone did it, but the authorities didn't want to attract the wrong kind of tourists. They wanted the ones with money to spend, not those with nothing but a spare T-shirt and trendy sandals who were looking for a relaxed society where they could remain stoned twenty-four hours a day.

For Sophie and Helen it was very different to Belize City. Where the city was impoverished Caribbean, this was more Mexico, a real taste of Central America.

'There's a place up there on the left,' Helen said. She had seen westerners sitting at tables on the sidewalk, young backpacker types with sensible hiking boots, and tie-dyed T-shirts. 'That might be it.'

Sophie eased the big four-wheel-drive forward. She was still unsure of exactly where the front of the vehicle ended and it seemed very wide. As they came up the street, they both looked across and saw the name on the wall.

'It is,' Sophie said.

'There's a space,' Helen said.

A huge, battered pickup, loaded with sacks of produce and what looked like two derelict washing machines, was pulling out on to the street, its moustached driver wearing a straw hat like many of the locals. A few minutes later they had parked, and walked past the three plastic tables outside on the pavement and into Eva's Restaurant where Pete Collins was behind the bar. The place was all blues and greens; there were eight or nine tables in the main dining area and a bar ran down the back wall as far as the kitchen and back door. Posters and messages left by people covered one wall and in the corner a cat slept on a cushion. In the opposite corner a small shop took up most of the space. The tables were mostly full with eco-tourists and backpackers, there for the caves, the rafting, the jungle walks. There were also one or two archaeology students from the various digs in and around the area. Sophie was threading her way through to take a stool at the bar when she heard Helen laugh. 'I don't believe it,' she said. 'Look,' she pointed to the right. There on a raised area was a bank of computers. 'A cyber-café here in the middle of nowhere.' To complete the incongruous scene two kittens played on the floor at the feet of an American girl who was busy typing an e-mail message on to her screen. Sophie took it in with a smile and then turned to the scrawny, tough-looking tattooed man behind the bar who had enjoyed Helen's reaction to the computer setup.

'Hello. Have you got a table we can have?'

He pointed to the full room. 'Not at the moment, but take a seat. By the time you've had a drink someone will have finished, or,' he said with a grin, 'you can eat at the bar.' She was not the sort of girl who sat at a bar and thought quickly. He could see the process.

'Chill out,' he said, a cheeky little smile crossing his face. He flicked his bar towel over his shoulder with a much-tattooed arm. 'This is Eva's and you're on Belize time.'

He pulled two cold bottles of Belikin from a chest-chiller to his right, whipped the caps off and a waitress swept them away. 'What ya say? Couple of cold ones then?'

'Why not?' she weakened.

'That's my girl. I'm Pete. What'll it be?'

'Beers,' Helen said, arriving alongside. 'Cold beers.'

Another couple of people arrived at the bar, students working on a dig somewhere, and they got chatting. Both of them were seriously knowledgeable about the Mayan civilization.

Sophie pounced. 'Xunantunich. Tell me . . .' and she launched into her question. Very quickly they were in a happy little group at the bar, the time ticking by. The two students were working on a new dig not far away and were delighted at Sophie's interest. The young man, a born-again Pennsylvanian, finally said, 'We're going back after a bite to eat. You gotta four-by-four? Follow us in and we'll show you around a bit.'

'We'd love to, but we have to get back to Belize City this –'

'No we don't,' Helen challenged. 'Why?'

'We just –'

'Plenty of places to stay,' Pete said from behind the bar. 'Not the Marriott, but clean and reasonable.'

'I've got a pair of knickers. We get you a pair, buy toothbrushes and a T-shirt. Come on, don't be a sad bastard all your life,' Helen pleaded.

HMS *Beaufort* was heading towards Belize. Not flat out over the safety line of 190 revolutions of her propeller a minute, but at a solid 160, giving her just over twenty-five knots through the water. The navigator had laid off the course and she was powering her way due west. Her captain, Commander Bennett, was thinking through what needed to be done; this was a change in her deployment, a reactive posture to a political situation. The orders had come through just after midnight and he had been woken by the officer of the watch. He had issued new orders and changed course directly and they were now one hundred and ten miles from Belize. *Beaufort* was a Type 23 frigate and the newest ship on the navy's active list, not counting a couple of brand spanking new GRP minehunters that few regarded as real fighting ships. A general-purpose warship, her prime role was that of a sub hunter and she had state of the art electronics deep in the ops room that could seek out submarines through incredibly sensitive hydrophonic sensor equipment on her hull and towed array. Above the water she had the most sophisticated radars available and she could seek out a threat and destroy it with torpedoes, Sea Wolf anti-aircraft missiles, Harpoon anti-ship missiles, or her prime weapons platform, the Lynx helicopter in the hangar aft. The Lynx could reach out hundreds of miles and depending on her weapons load could dip sonar buoys into the water to listen for her prey, deliver depth charges, or Sea Skua missiles that were ship-killers. In addition, mounted on the foredeck was a rapid-firing self-loading automatic 4.5 inch gun that could fire a round every second and a half. It could be aimed with radar, lasers, or by TDS, an optical sight if the target was near enough, and in theory was sufficiently accurate enough to shoot down attacking aircraft, although the ship's prime defence system was the silos of Sea Wolf directly in front of the bridge. The crew, one hundred and seventy of them, of both sexes, would have to be briefed. They were understandably disappointed at the Jamaican port leave being cancelled, but the prospect of something active to do rather than just patrolling the Caribbean had eased the mood.

Beaufort was a formidable warship, and her crew were proven, only the year before evacuating foreign nationals out of Liberia under fire, but Bennett suspected that where they were going she was just intended to be seen – big, grey, powerful. As the junior marine engineering officer had subtly explained to someone within earshot, it was 'Don't fuck with us' – old-fashioned gunboat diplomacy. Even so, Bennett had the various departments working up in case they were moved up a notch by Northwood when the situation clarified. That could mean defence watches, a higher state of readiness, or the Lynx on stand-by.

1400 – Guatemala

The two air troop callsigns were in position. The two teams had rendezvoused on time, in fact four minutes early, just before noon, the second team arriving at the bend in the stream, settling into a defensive position before working their 'cricket', a small plastic case enclosing a metal band that when squeezed made a noise like a cricket. They had a response immediately and one man from each patrol moved forward, covered by his colleagues, to make visual contact. The two patrols gathered, posted stags, and a few minutes later were setting up their aerial. Bonner's message came through and was unequivocal. It told them where to be by 1400 hours to be lifted out. 'Fucking hell, we just got here,' was Dozy's response. 'Wish the cunts would make their minds up.'

'Stand down?' Boyce asked.

'Na,' Sergeant McKay replied softly, wiping the sweat from his forehead. 'More likely it's going pear-shaped quicker than anyone thought. This is Chard's recall.'

Had they been observing the enemy, or in a position that would offer real benefit later, someone might have suggested sitting tight and making the 'bad comms' excuse, but they could have been miles and hours from the nearest decent intelligence-gathering opportunity and they were too disciplined to do anything but get on the move. Major Chard wasn't a bloke to ignore either, without sound tactical reasons.

The two four-man recce patrols now joined up and formed an eight-man patrol, equipped to fight if they had to. They had the firepower and skills to take on anything less than a company of this particular potential enemy and there wasn't much likelihood that there would be a formation that size out here north of the road. They teamed up and moved on to the exfiltration point, still silently, but much faster than on their way in. On the point was a stocky Fijian called Snowy by one and all. When he had arrived at the Squadron after selection he had walked into a room where some of the air troop lads were gathered and introduced himself, finishing with, 'Any cunt who calls me Snowy gets dropped.'

Of course they all called him Snowy in the next five seconds, some in chorus, led by Dave Ransley, a New Zealander and half-Maori who was now back in New Zealand. In truth he had been called Snowy since childhood because of a fascination with the white stuff in pictures at school. This was his reverse psychology to ensure that he was tagged with something that he could live with.

Snowy was like a cat in the 'J'. He could carry huge loads, move fast in absolute silence; he had an almost animal instinct for danger, and his weapon of choice was the light section weapon. He habitually carried a shotgun too – loaded with SSG shot it was inaccurate at anything over thirty yards, but up close in bush it was a terrifying weapon and some of them had seen him use it to devastating effect. He led them safely to their pickup point in good time.

Each Gazelle could lift out four men and their kit. It was a fast way of moving people out of hostile territory but it wasn't comfortable. As the helicopter came in, trailing a cable with four bungee loops hanging from the bottom, then slowed overhead, the men grabbed a loop each and pulled it over their heads and under their arms. If they were lucky and their bergens were packed just right, the loop would run round underneath the back of the pack and take the weight directly and they would be plucked up from the ground. If not, when the machine gathered height and speed the entire weight of the man's body and his bergen was taken on the bungee line under his arms. Not pleasant for the next half an hour or however long it took to reach friendly territory where the machine could land and the men could pile into the cabin. This would be short, ten minutes max, but nevertheless all but three of them were hurriedly shifting stuff in their packs so the shape would catch the line; the last three were on stag, on guard.

'Fucking red marks for weeks last time,' Boyce muttered almost to himself.

'Beats fucking tabbing,' someone muttered in response.

'Helo inbound,' Snowy called softly. He had seen it, obviously, because no one had heard it. Suddenly they were there, two Gazelles, one two hundred yards behind the other, cables down, bleeding off airspeed. McKay's team would go second and they quickly took up a defensive position to cover Two-Two's departure.

'Go!' he said.

Two-Two broke from cover, the four men running hunched over through the chest-high brush and new growth, arriving at the precise moment the cable bungees swung into reach. Three seconds later the pitch changed, the power came on, the disc dropped and the helicopter was gathering height and speed. The second was almost upon them.

'Let's go.'

The bulk of the Squadron were gathered at an old ruined church a mile up a dirt track off the highway just east of San Ignacio. Chard had decided against using the facility at Holdfast Camp at Esperanza. They would be watching that one. This was Belize Defence Ministry property, but yet to be developed in any way and Chard had chosen it rather than the old BDF post near Benque, as that was, like Holdfast, likely in the current circumstances to be under observation for any change or movements. There were three four-man patrols out already, one reconnoitring the road from the border post back into Benque, sizing it up in defensive terms. A boat troop patrol was out on the river at the same point, and a third was in San Ignacio looking at the approaches to the town.

Major Chard had a mass of intelligence already; polaroid pictures and video footage of the route were all now available to support the maps. The patrols had been given their tasks. Some were four-man, some were eight-man, but all were setting up as fighting patrols, a fundamentally different posture from that of reconnaissance. They were scattered round the old church hall, preparing their equipment, repacking bergens, breaking ammunition, explosives and ordnance from their containers into lighter loads, some carrying matériel out to the vehicles. One man was walking round the hall handing out LAWs, the disposable anti-tank weapon. Each team had one or two sighting rifles, and most teams had Addermine kits. The Addermine was a leave-behind anti-vehicle device that fired a LAW missile from a hidden position as the target crossed a certain point. It was a terrible weapon, because not only could it take out an armoured vehicle, but those following didn't know if it was a mine or fired by an attacking force. One mine could slow an advance for as long as it took for a tactical decision to be made.

In and around these individual preparations the men from mobility troop were doing their best at very short notice to prepare the vehicles as fighting platforms, and they weren't happy. Preparations of this nature normally took days rather than hours and then the individual patrols were given time to train with the equipment. Other than being four-wheel-drive, the hired vehicles bore no resemblance to the Regiment's fighting vehicles. On Land-Rover chassis, they were modified in the extreme, with extra fuel tanks, mine protection and pedestal mounts for weapons. The hired four-by-fours were left alone except for any extraneous weight being removed, and the rear canopies being unbolted and lifted from two of them. The army Land-Rovers were a different story. Those that were Wolf versions were stripped down, the doors, windscreens and roof coming off. Mounts for machine guns were installed, racks for jerry cans attached, camo netting rolled over the bonnets. On the back tray Milan launchers were mounted on the in-built positions, missiles loaded in makeshift racks either side. The standard Land-Rovers were also stripped down, except for the canopy left in place held by two small bolts. This would hide the contents until they were needed and could then be binned wherever the patrol was, allowing the men to fight from an open position.

When the helicopters landed in the clearing the men from air troop's Two-One and Two-Two jumped clear and moved away so the machines could lift off, and then walked the fifty yards to the church, smiling at faces they hadn't seen in months. This was a rare occasion, the entire Squadron working together. Other than the four blokes still on their way from Botswana, and three still in Belize City, they were all here; Jock Edwards was still in his Hawaiian shirt, sweating now, carrying Milan missiles over his shoulder and a heavy ammunition box out to his team's four-wheel-drive.

'Snowy,' he called. 'You look horrible. Been sleeping rough?'

He looked over and winked at McKay and Boyce. 'Yeah, in your wife's bed. She likes my big black snake.'

Edwards grinned back – the thought was absolutely improbable. Snowy was something of a novelty in Hereford. Five-feet-ten tall and almost as wide, black as pitch, there were local girls who found him rather exotic and would try to catch his eye when the boys got him out to one of the local discos. But as confident as he was as a soldier, he was a gibbering wreck whenever he addressed a woman. Stumbling, awkward, shy, he was also a devout Christian, a product of a Methodist mission education. Adultery was a no-no, absolutely. Snowy had strict morals that amazed his mates, most of whom would have shagged anything that walked given the chance.

Three others were sitting on the steps wolfing down food, each man's spoon, like everything else, tied to his person. This was their way – it was practical and expedient, if everything you needed was attached you couldn't lose it. In a tactical environment every piece of equipment was necessary or you wouldn't be carrying it, and in that same environment where you kept moving, leaving no trace of your presence, you might have to get going in seconds. A piece of kit left behind was not only a bloody nuisance but it could betray your presence. There was another practical reason for having everything tied on; it wouldn't fall out, be left lying around for someone to nick.

One by one the patrols were ready and vehicles began leaving the clearing, most laden down with equipment, but all of it covered, the men in the hired vehicles dressed in civilian kit. Chard didn't want his blokes in uniform charging round the place, there was no point letting everyone know they were there. For the time being they were still covert. The mobility blokes who, to jeering and hoots, had stressed the extensive nature of their training and the complexity of a modern Range Rover, had managed to hang on to it and they drove away, the big vehicle down on its springs, the 4.2 litre engine working to move them around in air-conditioned splendour. The only change had been the obscuring of its number plates with mud, and a light spray of the oil compound that would have dust sticking to it, as someone said, 'like shit to a blanket'. In an hour its shiny clean British racing green paint job would be olive drab. The doors would be removed later, windows in the body taken out, with a boot if necessary, if it came down to it.

The new arrivals walked across to Major Chard. 'Glad you could make it,' he said with a grin. 'No problems?'

'No, no problems. Seems a wasted entry though,' McKay replied honestly.

'That can't be helped. You have work here,' Chard answered. 'Captain Bonner will brief you.'

D Coy were gathered, lounging around with their kit, which was laid out in rows on the pan by the aircraft. Most of the men had taken shelter in whatever shade was available and Rhah and Plonker were sitting on the ground leaning back against the hangar wall. Spud was a few feet away with Cutter. It was hot and they were all sweating.

'Fookin' 'ell,' Plonker muttered. 'It's 'ot. Why can't we fookin' mount and go, eh? Plane's here. We're here.' Mail had come in on the Herc with the C Coy lads and a support platoon bloke was walking down handing out letters. He stopped and slung two at Plonker, who stuffed them inside his shirt unopened.

'Because that would be too easy, too sensible and this, this, my Geordie mate, is the army. If you wanted easy and sensible, you should have joined the marines.'

Rhah looked at his watch. '1500 mounting. Five minutes to go.'

'We'll be late,' Plonker muttered.

As he said it, as if on cue, C S M Jennings moved down the

line. 'On your feet. We will mount in platoon order. Support, then eleven.' He stopped by Rhah and Plonker. 'And then you shower of shite in twelve. Goddit?'

'Sar' Major,' Spud replied, 'look around you. These stalwart men, these hearts of oak. Twelve platoon, D Coy of 2 Para. We are the pride of the airborne.'

'Yeah. We are mobile, hostile, agile,' Rhah cut in, mimicking an American accent. 'We are life-takers and heart-breakers.'

'Aye,' Plonker added, 'a fookin' lean mean fighting machine, thas us.'

'Bollocks,' Jennings replied, moving on.

They moved towards their gear, pleased to be leaving at last. Lieutenant Rees was also moving down the line and behind him they could see the OC.

'Aye aye, and here's Big Harry and Ted,' Spud muttered softly. 'I ask you,' he began, rolling out an old joke, 'would you follow those men into battle.'

'I wouldn't follow them into a pub,' someone replied with a groan and he lifted his bergen.

'I wouldn't follow them into a pub with a whorehouse out back.'

'I wouldn't follow them into a whorehouse pub where the drinks and the women were free.'

'Home-time, lads. I can taste the beer already,' Plonker said, swinging his bergen up effortlessly. 'Seventeen hours and it's Blighty.'

Chapter Four

Plonker looked down the aircraft. The men were sitting in four rows, two along each side facing inward and two down the middle facing outward. It was tightly packed, each man leaning back against his bergen, their knees almost touching. To move down the fuselage was almost impossible. The heat was incredible, and the men were wishing the aircraft would take-off and climb to where the air was cooler. A combat jump, lobbing out over a landing zone, required much more space, as each man had his parachute, stores, ammunition and everything to hand. This was a simple transport job and they were crammed in. Defence cuts meant fewer transport aircraft than ever, and every one was used to maximum capacity, unlike the Americans who had built-in redundancy of upwards of thirty per cent on every level.

'Fookin' 'ell,' Plonker muttered. The sweat was streaming down his face. The engines were running, so no one heard him, and the tail-ramp was coming up. It was time to go. 'Thank fook for that,' he finished miserably.

The platoon officers were scattered down the aircraft with their men, sharing their discomfort in the egalitarian way of the airborne, but Major Tyson-Davis was up in the cockpit in the jumpseat. This was Alpha's seat, the boss. From there, within reach of the secure comms panel and the navigator's station, he could carry out his tasks. The C-130 rolled forward; turning on to the runway, it halted briefly as the pilot lined up and with his feet hard on the brakes, ran up the power on all four engines. This would be a tactical take-off, as required very close to the theatre of operations where there was threat of an enemy anti-aircraft capability, something they liked to practise whenever they could. Using the aircraft's short-field capability they would get off the ground as soon as they could, either with full flap down and maximum power on the engines for a maximum rate climb in a close spiral above the airfield, or as they would today, fly extremely low indeed, tree-top height away from the landing strip and the direction of the threat.

The pilot released brakes and the huge aircraft lumbered forward, gathering speed. He hit take-off speed, lifted the plane off the ground and slowly raised the flaps, allowing it to gather speed, but he held the nose down, and trimmed for straight and level flight, skimming the tree-tops, shacks and houses flashing past below them. Suddenly they were out over the water, above the muted hues of the sand and reefs, in stark contrast to the mangroves that formed huge green marine forests for the next ten miles until the reef wall dropped into the deep of the Caribbean. Four miles clear of the beach he raised the nose and began to climb, pleased with the take-off. The second aircraft was one minute behind them.

Seventy miles away at the long-deserted BDF site where B Squadron had set up their forward base Chard was inspecting the strange new arrival.

'What's its range?' he asked, looking up at it. It was waist-high, sitting in a travelling cradle strapped on the lorry floor. Behind in the gloom there were things under covers, and stainless steel travelling cases, obviously for the ground station.

'Seventy miles round trip,' the civilian replied, pushing his glasses up his nose. He was sweating gently, his shirt damp. 'That's a flight duration issue, fuel limitation rather than technical problems over the signal.'

He was the expert, one of two people supplied by the manufacturers to the Royal Artillery test team of six. They had been in Belize three weeks, tropical-testing the pilotless drone. This was a new concept in unmanned aircraft, a hybrid derivative of an executive toy, a miniature remote-control helicopter and the latest in surveillance cameras. The size and shape of a kitchen swing-top rubbish bin, the top half was the engine and fuel tank, coupled to a pair of stubby rotors. The bottom half held the electronics, the remote receivers, the camera and the transmitter that sent the pictures back to where the base station was set up. Chard had seen the Americans' version in Bosnia. Theirs was different – with proper fixed wings it was a perfect miniature aeroplane, and it looked the business – not a flying rubbish bin like this.

'Does it work?' Chard asked bluntly.

The civilian looked at him. 'Well, we have had a few problems with humidity but those are pretty well sorted out, I think.' He took his glasses off and cleaned them on his shirt, before slipping them on again, no clearer than before. 'Can I ask why we have been . . .' he sought for a word, 'summoned? The chap at the High Commission wasn't forthcoming.'

'We . . . we may want you to use it for us.'

'Use it?' He looked up into the lorry, as if the Hi-Eye might have heard. 'What? A demonstration? You could have come down to the site for that. We test most days.'

'Not a simple demo, no,' Chard responded, 'more like a live trial.'

'A live trial? Sorry, I'm not with you.'

'What's your security clearance?'

'What? Oh . . . oh, pretty high I suppose, I do this MoD stuff all the time. Chap over there is MoD.'

Chard nodded. 'I want you to operate your camera over an area that we need to see.'

'Oh . . . yes, of course. Actually we are encouraged to help where we can, make our tests as real as possible. What is it you want a look at?' he finished, thinking a possible landing site for a helicopter, a piece of jungle somewhere, the height of a river over a ford, perhaps.

Chard paused for a second. 'An area of road and the forest edge, just over the border in Guatemala.'

'Guatemala? Oh, I'm afraid we aren't cleared for that sort of thing. Loads of hassle – need the permission of the civil aviation authorities in the area, you see. No. Belize is fine. Got them used to it,' he finished brightly as if offering sufficient compensation. 'Just phone in a flight plan.'

'No phone calls, no permissions. This will need to be covert.'

'Covert? Oh, I see. This is official?' he replied, catching on. As he said it, as if to underline the point one of the troopers walked out of the hall, a brace of LAW rockets over his

101

shoulder and humping a box of link ammunition to the last vehicle that was still parked in the clearing.

Chard gave a brief nod.

'Aah . . .' He looked at the man from the MoD chatting to the RA observers. 'Can you get him on board?'

'No problem,' Chard replied.

'Then I might just be able to have her stray off course,' he said, with a twinkle in his eye. 'Dreadful wind drift round here. When? We will need to set up. We haven't got a genny. We only have one and that's bolted to a concrete plinth at our site. We need 240 volts for the base station equipment.'

Chard jerked a thumb into the church building. 'In there.'

'How far away is this place?'

'No more than twenty miles max.'

'Give us an hour.'

'What do you need from us?'

'Lat and longs of the area you want to beat. GPS will do the rest.'

Beat, Chard thought. The artilleryman's expression for an area to come under fire, or that one moved through to throw up game birds for the guns on a shoot. How appropriate.

Sophie and Helen followed the young archaeologist up the narrow, muddy path. 'The main structure is just up ahead,' he said. Behind them was the camp, where they had left their vehicles. It was well established, two months into the dig. There were tents, tarpaulin stretched over pole frames for communal areas, a few people gathered in one tent where trestle-tables were laid out. The drive had been forty minutes of slow going down the track from the main road. Not demanding on the vehicle or the driver's skills, it would still have been too much for an ordinary car and they were both pleased they had something more appropriate. Sophie was excited. Xunantunich had been one thing – fully excavated, it was all there for the eye, but the mowed grass and national park look detracted from the mood. This was different, a new site, possibly as big as Xunantunich, but virgin, untouched by anyone in two thousand years. A small team of archaeologists were moving slowly and painstakingly to begin plotting the site. This was the Central America of her childish imaginings, of *National Geographic* and Huey Dewey and Louie on wild adventures to lost worlds. Suddenly there was the sound of a little motor running, a two-stroke overhead, fading almost as soon as she heard it. How odd, she thought, it sounded like a model aeroplane. Her grandfather had owned one and he flew it for her when she was a child. No, can't be, she thought. She pushed on up the path, her mind wandering back to the man she had met the night before, as it had done about fifty times that day.

The little machine, its go-kart engine muffled down, its rotors beating, lifted hesitantly off the ground; as the operator took full control, it climbed straight up and began to move northwards over the tree-tops, gaining height all the while till it disappeared into the cloud base.

Chard watched it fly away and then moved back into the old church hall where the Royal Artillery men had established their observers' station. They had purloined a trestle-table and set up their equipment on its surface: a console like a computer game with a joystick allowed the operator to fly the craft and work the camera; above the console were screens, a large one showing the images from the main camera, and a second for the smaller forward view. On the second view the GPS coordinates flashed as figures at the foot of the screen. On a third small screen was a grid showing the courses that were being overflown, the area flown in yellow, that ahead in green, the whole in a red box that outlined the limits of the sortie.

'It's a bit slow. Be overhead the first area in about fifteen minutes,' the civilian explained. 'We are trying to work out ways of speeding it up without making it any bigger.'

'Give me a shout the moment you cross the border,' Chard responded. Outside a helicopter was approaching, and knowing what it was, he went out to meet it. He had asked for one of the Gazelles to be put at his disposal, in case he wanted to move any of his men about in light teams, and had also requested some forward comms. Two of his people jumped clear of the doors. They were signallers, and would form the end of the downlink. From here they could channel messages either through Airport Camp or, once they had the aerials sussed, straight through to Hereford. Before the rotors had finished turning the two signallers were unpacking their kit. They would set up an aerial, run it back to the radios, and then begin to rotate it slowly, looking for the best orientation. Chard briefed them quickly and just as he was finished the SQM gave a low whistle from the church door. He moved back to the hall and within a few moments was standing looking over the civilian operator's shoulder at the screens. On the large screen was the view from the main look-down camera, a canopy of trees interspersed with clearings and tracks. Suddenly there was a depressed ribbon across the screen, where the trees had been cleared.

'That's a road,' the operator said. Suddenly the screen went blank, a murky white.

'Oops, sorry. Back into the cloud there. Is that recorder running?'

'Yeah,' from one of the RA men.

'Stay close to the cloud so you can climb back into it if needed,' Chard said. 'I'd rather they didn't see it – they might just have a go at it.'

The civilian flicked a look at him. 'Right, we are on the first sweep of the area you asked for, flying on a north-easterly heading.'

'Can you get nearer the road?' Chard asked.

'What am I looking for? And what do you mean, have a go at it?' He moved the little control column and the picture began to change as the remote drone swung towards the road.

'There has been a troop build-up. They will be positioned in there somewhere, maybe under the trees. Trucks, vehicles parked or moving, camps maybe, tents, churned-up mud on intersections, any indication that they are in this area.'

'You didn't answer my other question.'

'The people we are looking for won't want some little helicopter flying around. Stay close to the cloud.'

'That's why it's grey-blue,' the civvy replied, 'quite difficult to see looking up at it. Look, if it gets shot and damaged I'll have some explaining to do.'

'If it gets shot and damaged it will be the least of everyone's worries,' Chard responded drily.

They were all quiet for the next minute or so, watching the scene through the camera lens. It was Chard who broke the silence.

'Hold it. Can we look at that bit again?'

'Hang on, we're doing thirty miles an hour. Let's go round again.' The civvy swung the drone in a long elliptical loop, watching the compass graphic swing a full three-sixty degrees and bring them back on the original course.

'Closer?' Chard asked, leaning forward over the man's shoulder. 'Can we get down closer?'

'I'll zoom in a bit.'

'That's . . . fuckeroo,' Chard muttered. The screen showed armoured vehicles and trucks, casting long shadows in the afternoon sun. Tiny figures of men were moving around.

'Mark it!' the civvy called.

'Four, five, six, no five, that's an APC . . .' Chard was counting aloud. 'Keep flying this course. Someone get me a map!' One of the Royal Artillery men, a lieutenant, had heard the commotion and moved over. He thrust a map at Chard and almost pushed him out of the way of the screens.

'Is that smoke?' someone asked.

'Yeah and that's a tent it's coming from. Field kitchens,' the RA lieutenant muttered.

'More heavies, sir,' from the SQM.

Chard looked back from the map. On the screen there were more of the familiar shapes, and some were just peeping out from under trees, backed in to keep them in the shade or hidden from view perhaps.

'Fucking hell,' softly from someone. 'That must be an armoured regiment?'

'No. It's a brigade position,' the lieutenant said, taking it in. 'Less than ten bloody miles away.'

The SQM nodded. 'There's probably another two or so we haven't seen yet.'

'Sweep it again please,' the lieutenant said. 'Sarn't, recorder?' He held out a hand and was passed a Dictaphone. Chard let him get on with it; this was the guy's job.

The Royal Artillery produced highly specialized observers, analysts almost. They could identify any equipment in general use anywhere in the world from almost any angle or distance.

'1608 hours. Cambry. GPS ref . . .' he began speaking into the recorder, Chard looking over every few moments.

One of the civilians, the MoD man, looked up from the screen. 'This was designed for remote forward use in the theatre.' He wasn't very happy about this; he was a civil servant, not a soldier, and here they were in a Central American country where, it seemed, war was dreadfully close to breaking out.

'That's all right then,' the SQM replied softly, sipping at a bottle of water, 'we are forward, and by the look of it we will be getting forwarder by the hour.'

'Forwarder by the hour?' He sounded appalled at the prospect. 'What I meant was, that it allows a battlefield commander or forward observers to see deep into an enemy's position from a safe location. This isn't our problem. Should we not be prudent and withdraw?'

'In fact,' the civilian at the controls said, 'there's nowhere to withdraw to. If they choose to roll, in a couple of hours we could be flying back towards Belmopan to see the same chaps.'

'What's your point?' the MoD man snapped.

'Get a grip,' the civilian responded. 'That's tanks and trucks and APCs. Seen anything that will stop them in this country? Christ, by midnight they could be in Belize City.'

'Well said,' the RA lieutenant came in with a smile. 'Now if I can have some quiet, we'll get on with it.' The MoD man fell silent.

'Log SR 2.01 six, and another, seven M-41 light tanks. Possibly A3s. Refueller tanker there alongside that one. We have, aah, a recovery vehicle, one, now two M-8 recce vehicles. Canvas. We now have canvas. Troops in small number visible on the ground. Field kitchens, two fifty-by-twenties for two battalions. Standard Guatemalan Brigade size. Smoke rising.' He fell silent as the view changed back to jungle. 'Smoke from the trees SR 2.03, cooking fires by the look of it.' A cloud covered the jungle here, smoke rising from the canopy in many places and merging into a light haze as the sluggish air dispersed it.

'A battle group?' Chard asked. The question was important. An armoured unit might just be camped alongside an infantry unit, or it could be a true battle group, a mixed force, worked up and trained together, as in the West, a much more formidable foe.

'Didn't see any arty or triple-A. You would expect that even in an army like this. This is basic American doctrine, but it's not a battle group as you and I understand it, not on the basis of what we have seen,' the RA lieutenant replied. 'No, thrown together by the look of it. A battle group would have been more integrated, the armour spread wider, interspersed and integrated with the mounted units they would be fighting with.' He never took his eyes off the screen so when the view changed again he was ready. 'Here we go . . .'

The drone flew over another encampment and for two minutes the lieutenant spoke quietly and steadily into the microphone of the little recorder. The screen showed vehicles moving, activity on the ground.

'That's the limit of the run,' the civvy said. 'All rather exciting actually. Right, where next?'

'Work the box we agreed,' Chard replied. 'Sar' Major?' He nodded over to where the two signallers were setting up their radios. 'See if the scaleys have got comms yet.'

Four minutes later he was with them, rapidly encoding a message that they would push straight through to Hereford.

England

The signal came through, and in Hereford at the 22 SAS camp things went ballistic. They had pulled out the stops and in advance of any word from Northwood had begun recalling members of A Squadron who were scattered round the UK. The message was simple – as they reacted to bleepers and phoned in they were told to return to the camp immediately. The signal was flashed through to PJHQ at Northwood and simultaneously into Whitehall to the liaison officer in the Ministry of Defence.

At Northwood, coincidentally, the satellite images requested from the Americans had just arrived down the ISDN line. It had taken longer than originally thought, and Bertie Conway, the liaison officer, had needed to call in a couple of favours, but now the pictures were in and the intelligence people were starting to look through them as they came off the printer. The evidence was there – thermal images in what should have been empty jungle by the side of what was obviously the road.

At the MoD the officer who took the message flashed through from Hereford, via Northwood, made one phone call and grabbed a colleague from UK Land at Wilton, who he knew was in the building just leaving a late meeting. 'Stick around, we may want you in a minute.'

'I was just going home.'

'Well don't, or you'll probably have to drive straight back. Grab a cup of tea.'

He watched as his staff began making calls, following an established procedure. Since the first intelligence had come in, various senior people on a standing committee had been making their way back to London and into the MoD. They had been there most of the day, and had left only an hour before. Now they were being called back in. Each of the three services had established roles, but they could all be boiled down to three: aiding the civil power in times of unrest or natural disaster, limited regional conflict, or the big one, general war. There were two other groups that each shouldered the other prime roles of Her Majesty's armed forces, but this group was charged with overseeing the formulation and updating of various contingency plans covering everything from further involvement in Bosnia to the response options to support the UN in Rwanda – what was termed Limited Regional Conflict.

For this group, which met in committee room C3, there were various plans in place, but the Belize planning had not been updated in recent years. It just hadn't been a prime issue in a world where there were other priorities. There were individual plans: there was one by an RAF wing commander on what was required from whom to move a squadron of Harriers back into Belize; there were Royal Engineers' papers on the work they had done maintaining landing areas for the aircraft and years of planning on response scenarios from the garrison at Airport Camp. But the garrison battalion was no longer there. The massive files of plans and supporting documents for Britain to meet her defence obligation to the tiny free nation of Belize all depended on the garrison force and its support elements at the far end. The only original element still in place was the training team from 22 SAS, a handful of people.

The three men had taken seats in the office of the Secretary of State for Defence. It was a large, gracious room with high ceilings and panelled walls. There was a Persian carpet on the floor, one of a pair presented to Douglas Hurd when he was Minister for Foreign Affairs. The other was in his old office at the FCO. The men were seated in old leather wingback chairs in front of the fireplace, and two senior MoD people had dragged over chairs from the meeting table to complete the circle.

'Large force, estimate two to three brigades. How many soldiers is that?' The minister looked up from the message, over the tops of his half-lenses. He was wearing evening dress and had been on his way home from a reception when his staff advised him of the news.

'Their structure has smaller brigades, but our people will be using our definition to prevent confusion. About five thousand men to a brigade – reckon on something between ten to fifteen thousand.'

'Large force, estimate two to three brigades,' he read out again, the message slip in his hand, 'offensive posture concealed three miles from Melchor. Melchor is . . . ?'

'The border town, Minister. It's actually on the border. Bits of it sometimes infringe into Belizean territory,' one of the MoD men answered. He was one of the standing committee and rapidly familiarizing himself with the geography.

'Believe attack imminent, repeat attack imminent. Have

video evidence,' the minister finished, looking up. 'You say the material from the US supports this?'

'Yes, Minister. Definite infra-red traces.'

'Not the sort of thing we would expect if they were conducting anti-terrorist operations, as they say?'

'No, sir. This is concentrated force, an aggressive posture. For anti-terrorist ops we would see widely deployed units, fewer vehicles and certainly not this level of armour.'

The minister nodded. 'Who have we got on the ground there?' he asked, looking at the serving officers present.

They were two of the joint chiefs, both having just arrived a few minutes before, and a brigadier from UK Land at Wilton who answered, 'Other than Squadron, not much, Minister. A company from 5 A/B jungle training, arrived yesterday. A Gazelle flight, some logistics types, eight or ten of them, another handful from RA. Twenty-odd marines. But another Para company has just left, what, no more than a couple of hours ago. Shall we turn them around?'

The minister thought quickly. Every minute they would be flying further away. 'Suggestion?'

'This is classic Joint Rapid Deployment Force,' one of the joint chiefs replied. 'The company in the air, they are part of JRDF. This could be quite fortuitous. Advise them and change orders, contact the Americans, see if we can turn them round there. Move them back in, redeploy them, very visibly, up on the border with the rest of JRDF moved up in posture with a view to deployment. Hereford are recalling now. HMS *Beaufort* is on her way. I think we should get on to High Wycombe, get some air worked up and out there asap. We can be very obvious and very visible within forty-eight hours. JRDF can, if we so wish, be there in five days.'

The minister looked up at the ceiling and thought about that. Ordering the West Indies guardship closer and getting half a dozen Harriers down there was one thing. Moving in the Joint Rapid Deployment Force was another entirely. JRDF was currently 5 Airborne Brigade. The effort was huge. Five thousand men, their equipment, support units – a logistical nightmare. And that was just the beginning; the implications were vast. One brigade going in against a potential of three or maybe more – unacceptable odds. They would only be the lead element; there would need to be plans in place to support them, feed them, supply them with a logistics chain that crossed the Atlantic and the Caribbean. This wasn't British territory, and there would be those who would argue that it wasn't even a British problem. But the defence obligation was real and ratified under an agreement in the United Nations, no doubt by men who hoped like hell it would never be needed – and now it looked like it just might. This called for dialogue with the Guatemalans, and bloody soon.

He stood up, walked across the elegant room to his desk, picked up one of three telephones and dialled three digits.

'Prime Minister please ... Disturb him, please.' A few moments later he spoke again. 'It's David, we have a problem. No, no it's Belize. I'd like to bring three people over with me right now. Be there in ten minutes. You'll want Jim Hildon now, and follow with whatever cabinet we can muster first thing.'

The officers were asked to leave the meeting room and wait outside. Left in the room were four men: the Prime Minister, the Secretary of State for Defence, a senior defence adviser, and a younger man, one of the political breed that the media termed spin doctors, who was now speaking.

'But if it's our people fired upon, then –'

'That's a terrible thing to suggest,' the Prime Minister challenged. He was not going to put his people into a position where they would be fired at simply to justify an armed response, certainly not with a longstanding obligation to the UN anyway. 'The commitment is real and it stands. In the eyes of the world we are expected to honour that obligation.'

'Prime Minister, let's cut to the quick. What are our options? Immediate withdrawal of all British forces in Belize. Their problem. Or we morally honour the United Nations resolution that requires us to defend the Independent State of Belize, the old state of British Honduras, until such time as they can build up their own defensive capability.'

'It could be argued they have had long enough to do that.'

'Agreed, but against Guatemala? Forty-thousand-strong

armed forces? They would never match that and everyone knew it. But it's a matter of how we do it. You put British forces into action in Central America without bloody good reason, and by that I mean better than some outdated agreement we never wanted anyway, and you can kiss goodbye to the next election. Thatcher got away with it – but there were Union flags flying in the Falklands, English settlers, English language, they use our bloody currency for Christ's sake. She could justify that. This? No way. The public is too tired, too jaded. The Third World has its hand out for aid, for compensation for our colonial past, for every bloody thing they can think of and we must defend them as well? Our sons?' He presented the average voter's thinking perfectly, in a regional accent, the way he had done all through the strategy sessions in the election campaign. He leaned forward on the table. 'They will say no, they wanted to be independent, let 'em be. When we broke Enigma, Churchill knew that the Germans were going to bomb Coventry twenty-four hours before they did it. But to protect the secret, to save even more lives, he took a decision. You and I aren't arguing about whether we should go to Belize's aid – we know we must. But there's a way to present it that makes it more palatable.' He stood back, his hands in his pockets. 'Now you are right, it's a terrible thing to do, but the end justifies the means. We could word something.'

'I agree,' James Hildon added, the Secretary of State at the Foreign and Commonwealth Office. This venture needed his full support. 'Our credibility rests on our reaction to events like this. If we withdraw, what's next? Gibraltar? The Falklands again? And anyway, this sticks in my craw; I don't like bully nations. There's enough of them already. Appeasement leads to further aggression.'

Half an hour later after a flurry of activity, including a phone call between the Prime Minister and the White House, a directive from Downing Street to PJHQ at Northwood started a chain of events.

They began to issue orders, the first of which went via UK Land, through 3rd UK Division at Bulford Camp, to 5 Airborne Brigade at Aldershot. D Coy 2 Para, airborne out of

Belize and returning home after six weeks' jungle training, was diverted to Fort Bragg, North Carolina.

At about the same time Hildon attempted to summon the Guatemalan Ambassador to the court of St James's to his office. Repeated attempts by the ambassador's staff to locate him failed. They were most apologetic but Hildon, a no-nonsense plain-speaking northerner, wasn't fooled for a second.

'The buggers are giving us the run around. Let me talk to 'em.' Ten seconds later he was put through and as he expected he hit the same barrier. 'I know the ambassador is unavailable. Let me speak to the chargé d'affaires. Oh, he is unavailable too. What a surprise . . . I know it is late, I know exactly what time it is. Who is the most senior person there?'

On board the lead RAF C-130 Major Tyson-Davis was relaxing as best he could in the jumpseat. There were six crew on this aircraft, three on duty and three crammed in with the lads, who would take over after they had refuelled – seventeen hours in the air needed two crews. The P1, a squadron leader, was sitting in front of him and to the right, relaxing back into his seat, his earphones down round his neck. The other pilot tapped him on the arm to get his attention and then tapped his own headset. The squadron leader pulled his headset up on to his ears and as he did so he leant forward and looked at the panel of lights and indicators in front of him. He listened for a moment and then turned his head and looked at Tyson-Davis, and motioned for him to put his headphones on.

'There's traffic coming in on secure comms for you. The printer is there.' The pilot pointed at the engineer's station.

Tyson-Davis nodded. 'Thanks.'

About ten seconds later, the decoder having changed the message into plaintext, a page began to slide out of the small printer, and the engineer handed it to him without looking at it. Tyson-Davis read it, then read it again. He looked up as a second page was being handed to the P1. They were being diverted – Fort Bragg, North Carolina, to await official orders to return and deploy in Belize. There were no other details, just the broad intelligence.

'Right, gentlemen,' the P1 said, 'a change of plan.' He handed his message to Tyson-Davis. 'We divert to Fort Bragg, North Carolina.'

He began to issue his instructions. They had no flight plan for the USA, no maps, none of the pilot notes or procedural handbooks they would normally have brought for an American destination. They would have to take what they needed over the air from US air force and in the message there were instructions on when to make contact and on what frequency.

When he had finished he looked round at Tyson-Davis who was rising in his seat. 'I'll give you an ETA in a few minutes. What's your feel?'

'Looks like you might be taking us back,' Tyson-Davis answered. He moved away and dropped down the steep ladder into the main load area, his eyes sweeping the crowded deck. There were a few card schools, some of the men were reading or chatting, but most were asleep.

He bent down to the nearest soldier. 'Pass the word, please. Officers and CSM up here.' Elbows nudged and the order was passed down, and a few moments later two lieutenants, one of them Harry Rees, Captain Atlee and CSM 'Robo' Jennings were making their way forward. It hadn't been missed by the toms – the boss calling all officers forward on a crammed transport flight? The aircraft began to make a left turn, long and gentle, but it was very obvious to everyone that they had changed course.

'Maybe there's a problem, like wi' the engines or summat?' the man sitting opposite Elias Cutter said loudly over the engine noise.

Elias shook his head encouragingly, but he was wondering the same thing. Know soon enough, he thought. He looked up the body of the aircraft; Ted was talking animatedly, counting things off on his fingers, the others nodding. Two hours out – they must be over Florida he thought, or the southern bit, the Keys. Now they had turned left. He was still watching Ted who then looked at his watch and said something to the others, who began to move back down the aircraft as Tyson-Davis took the steps up to the flight deck.

Major Fox, the OC C Coy, was in his company command area, his corporal still getting organized in a room with one of the few working air-conditioners running, when a lean, wiry individual wearing uniform but without badges of rank or other identifying insignia knocked once and walked in.

'You must be Alpha C. I'm Dave Chard, B Squadron.'

'Hello,' Fox responded, somewhat taken aback.

'We need to talk.' Chard looked at the corporal. 'Excuse us, please.'

The Gurkha nodded and left the room immediately. Fox bridled slightly; like most Gurkha officers he was quite sensitive about chain of command.

'Have you had comms from your command in the last half an hour?'

'No,' Fox replied. 'Should I?'

'It won't be long. I'll bring you into the loop as quickly as I can, then I must get back.' He pulled a map from his pocket and spread it out on the desk. 'You are the senior regular forces officer in the theatre. We share a rank,' Chard gave a bleak grin, 'but I've got my own job.' His use of the word 'theatre' was ominous and Fox looked down at the map he was spreading out.

'We came in early this morning to support one of my troops in some recce. This is the sitrep. Here,' he pointed at Melchor, 'and here,' his finger moved slightly, 'we have found major Guatemalan troop concentrations. Two, maybe three brigades. The posture is offensive.'

'They have done this before,' Fox challenged, 'moved forces up.'

'All the indications are that this time the scrotes are going to do it. There's too many of them for it to be a bluff like last time.' Chard began to brief the 2 Para officer in detail. Ten minutes later Fox had everything the SAS major could give him.

'What's happening at the other end?'

'Lots of lights burning late in Whitehall, I would think. This

115

thing is moving faster than they are set up to respond to. Your blokes? How long?'

'JRDF, midweek recall? Five days, maybe four at a push. Spearhead sooner, airmount in forty-eight hours.'

'This thing might go pear-shaped sooner than that – maybe even tonight or tomorrow. This is in-theatre and tactical. Expect orders any minute.' Chard looked him in the eye. 'Now it's your call, but if you can deploy some of your blokes up with my mob, then, if it goes off, and rules of engagement allow we can slow 'em down a little.'

'Airhead,' Fox answered. 'If it goes off we have to hold the airhead.'

Five minutes later, Chard was on his way back to his forward base in the Gazelle, and Fox called for his two senior platoon commanders. There had been nothing from Battalion or Brigade other than a carefully worded statement that had arrived minutes earlier, the body copy reading, 'Int suggests Guatemalan offensive imminent. Three mobile brigades, mixed armour, mounted infantry deployed Melchor. Support unknown. Efforts for diplomatic resolution underway. In the event of full-scale hostilities initiated against hosts GB's defence obligation may be met in a form appropriate to size of forces in theatre and with regard to tactical limitations. In interim suggest full defensive posture in applied tactical judgement. In the case of limited hostilities meet with commensurate limited response. Do not initiate hostilities but return fire if fired upon.'

Jesus, Fox thought. He read the signal again. '. . . may be met in a form appropriate to size of forces in theatre . . .' Up to me – my judgement. Fight if we can. He had already made a decision; the airhead was critical, absolutely critical, the strategic imperative. The elements up towards the border would be forced back, but whatever happened they had to hold the airhead for incoming support. Therefore that was where he would position his headquarters. But he also had to support Major Chard; engage the enemy, slow him down, and that meant splitting his resources, something no commander liked to do whatever his force size.

He looked at Toby Estelle, his senior platoon commander.

'Don't like this, Toby, but you and James, get yourselves and your men up to San Ignacio. Major Chard will command up there. Toby, you are the senior platoon commander. You are in charge, till you are back here, OK?'

The lieutenant nodded, swallowing.

'Take the Milan and mortar teams. Link up with Squadron. Chard will show you where he wants you. I've met him, he's a good man. It will be dark when you get there so you will be able to get quite close, but I suggest you park your vehicles somewhere back and out of sight. Take some civvy kit, change, and you two go forward and see the lay of it, mark out your defensive positions. Chard's people have been there all afternoon so they can talk you through whatever you can't see, then when you move your lads up you know exactly where you want them. If it starts, God forbid, but if it does, slow 'em down, any way you can, then fall back as you have to and rally back here where we will defend the airhead.'

Both men nodded.

'Questions?'

'Sir, if it goes off, the whole area is going to be crawling with civilians,' Estelle said. 'They will be clogging the roads, panicking.'

'And if they are, what is your intention?'

Estelle thought quickly. 'Let 'em through – less to worry about later. We will have two or three minutes warning at least, we can move them off the roads then, set up some sort of roadblock point. And anyone still in the immediate vicinity, well, once we have engaged they will get out of the way quickly enough.'

Fox nodded. 'Sounds pragmatic enough to me. Do your jobs the way you have been trained and you'll be fine. Off you go now. QM is waiting with every bit of 5.56 ammunition in Belize. There isn't a lot, but it will have to do. I'm seeing if I can raid the BDF arsenal.'

'What do the scrotes use, sir?'

'It's all American kit. You can expect they will have M16s, mortars, some mounted heavy automatic weapons, maybe some artillery.'

'How many of them, sir?' James asked.

'Estimates in the seventies and eighties said they would throw half their forces at this, fifteen to seventeen thousand men. There's no reason to think it's changed.'

Estelle's expression said it all. Jesus – three brigades, mobile and armed with American kit.

'The good news is, there is only one way through and you can bet it will be everything you would expect in Latin America. Loads of officers with shoulder-boards like planks, festooned in medals, seeking glory from miles behind the action. They will have the combined tactical ability of a bunch of schoolgirls and they will cock it up. There is only one road they can advance along and there are choke-points on that road, half a dozen at least. If they roll tonight, it will be dark, they won't be expecting you and they won't know what size force they are up against. Slow them down and RV back here. But once here, we stand. We will defend the airhead until we know what's happening, and if they are smart, they will leave us alone. There is a small detachment of marines in Dangriga. I'm going to ask that navy helicopter to go down and pick them up. They are bugger-all use down there and we will consolidate here. On your way, chaps.'

Slow 'em down, Estelle thought. For how long? Then what? Fall back here. To what? With two platoons to defend an entire airfield from a possible direct attack?

'Make a suggestion, sir?' Estelle said. 'Why don't you hang on to a couple of the mortars?'

''Cos if it goes off you will need 'em.'

'Sir, the difference between six and four is not going to slow them down much but it could make a hell of a difference to the situation here. If it's all the same to you, sir,' Estelle smiled, not feeling like smiling, 'we'd like an airhead to fall back to.'

Fox returned the smile bleakly. 'Fair enough.'

118

Lieutenant Rees had moved back down and pointed to his platoon sergeant, and the four section leaders. Corporal Cutter stood up and made his way up to Rees, stepping over the legs of his comrades.

'Right,' Rees said, 'Listen up. Sitrep is as follows. It looks like the Guat scrotes are going to have a go at Belize. They have moved troops up to the border. We are on active footing as of now. Got it?' They nodded. 'We are diverting to Fort Bragg. That's in North Carolina, where we will await orders to redeploy. If that happens, we will draw kit and ammunition from their QM. I want you to get round your sections, find out what each of your men will need. There will be general issues but we need to know about anything particular. OK?'

There were many things that they would want. The first thing Paras did when faced with the prospect of going on to an active deployment where there might be fighting was review everything in their bergen, day-bag and belt-kit. Would they be lobbing in or running off the ramp on to the ground? Hot or cold? Wet or dry? How long before re-supply? The Paras were essentially light infantry who were trained to be delivered into battle from the air. Their formidable reputation was based round three things: their parachute entry into the theatre, their ability to land on the ground and then march, maybe many miles, carrying huge loads to where they were to fight, and lastly the sheer aggression they displayed once they engaged. As well as their bergens, belt-kit and personal weapon, they would jump with extra ordnance for the platoon or company. They might be carrying belt ammunition, Milans, mortar tubes or bombs, mines, a variety of things, all uncomfortable, awkward and heavy, with a total jump weight of 130 pounds. That meant they were sparing with electives; personal items other than their medical kit, rations and water could be as minimal as a toothbrush, toothpaste, T-shirt, maybe a bar of chocolate and a bivvy bag. Choices were intensely personal and most toms spent many hours working out exactly what they would want to carry if it came down to it. Others were more lenient on themselves and always took a few comforts.

Tabasco sauce was popular, it could spice up dreary rations, and ounce for ounce there was more bang for one's buck than anything else. Cigarettes were popular – the risk of getting lung cancer sometime, maybe fifty years out in the future, wasn't much of a deterrent to a soldier about to go into action. In the Falklands all sorts of odd things appeared from bergens: hip flasks, puppets, Walkman personal stereos; one fellow even had a laughing machine from a joke shop, and on one memorable occasion while under sniper fire, every time the sniper fired he pulled the string on the little machine and the canned laugh emanated from the side pocket of his bergen.

One of the lads in the section had two Teletubbies, Po and Laa-Laa. Plonker kidnapped them once and was found teaching them to head-butt each other. Spud had a Buzz Lightyear. If he had batteries, something he usually failed to remember, he would pull the string at odd times and the doll's cry, 'To infinity and beyond,' would come from the little speaker. There were also the superstitious, who had talismans and lucky charms, and many toms carried something intensely personal, usually from their wives or girlfriends; a scarf, a photo perhaps. Cutter himself carried a credit-card-sized map of the London Underground on which, now faded, was the lipstick kiss of his girlfriend. Even Plonker, hard as nails Plonker, had something. In his wallet, always empty of money, was a photo of a girl now married who lived in Newcastle. Around his neck on a leather thong was a single suspender clip she had pulled off and given him in a pub one night. But what would they need to fight and sustain themselves till re-supply?

'Right, back to me in thirty minutes.'

Belmopan

Leo Scobey was waiting in the comfortable lobby for his meeting with the high commissioner. He was fidgety. He had been here well over two hours and there was much scurrying around, doors opening and closing. Every so often a woman, a local girl, pretty with her hair tied back, appeared and apologized for the delay.

Scobey knew something was on. British diplomatic posts in the far-flung corners of the earth were usually quiet, sleepy places of predictable routine. Flies buzzed round faded photos of the Queen and British Council posters advertised courses while others offered clichéd images of England; London taxis, red double-decker buses, beefeaters and bobbies smiling down from the latest tourist board promotion. They smelled the same too, of flyspray, teabags, ink pads and old paper as tired air-conditioning hummed and blustered away and people complained about the photocopier breaking down again. But not here, not today – this place was buzzing.

Through the security door and down the passage the high commissioner was a busy man. 'Is he still there?' he asked.

'Yes, sir,' his secretary answered.

'Shit. OK, one more call. Then let's see him.'

He placed a call to the Belize minister of defence, with whom he had just eaten lunch, and came straight to the point. 'The Foreign and Commonwealth Office will be contacting the minister for foreign affairs directly, but I thought I'd come straight through to you. Up to you of course, sir, but our people think it fairly urgent. You might like to consider the level of threat with your colleagues. We would be pleased to brief you on what we know.' He listened for a moment or two. 'Tomorrow?'

Hereford

At Hereford ten members of A Squadron's air troop were back and being briefed in the Squadron's interest room. The walls were covered in maps and photographs, everything they could pull on Belize. There was frantic activity all over the camp but these men were listening intently. Their task would be twofold: to drop into the theatre and deliver ammunition and supplies to the Squadron already on the ground, and then as a ten-man fighting patrol attach themselves to B Squadron till further notice. They would go down in an RAF Tristar;

that would cut the journey time down to twelve hours. They were to jump in with man-portable air defence. If the Guatemalans attacked they would use their air if they possibly could and the tiny British force on the ground had no means of defending themselves from air attack. Javelin was the answer. They would also jump in with Milan missiles, and push out of the door ahead of them loads of 5.56, .50 calibre, and LAW anti-tank missiles; there were other odd things going. Almost the entire Regiment's non-badged people had turned out to get B Squadron away, but there were things that were forgotten, or simply weren't available in the timeframe.

This ordnance would not be mounted on a wedge, the special pallet used for parachute operations. It would have to fit through the narrower load door of a jet so it would be mounted on small pallets. They would also be escorting a field surgical team who would jump with them, none of whom had ever lobbed out of the door of a jet, even with its engines powered right back. For this reason six of the team would jump with the medics, the rest would worry about the loads, following them in.

The other half of air troop would have a different task and would be leaving later. They would be free-falling into Guatemala, south of the border post, there to attack and harry the Guatemalan supply lines, take out bridges, culverts, anything to stop re-supply of their soldiers. There was only one road all the way to Melchor and that made it very vulnerable.

North Carolina

At Fort Bragg, a huge sprawling military base, and the home of the US special forces, the base commander, a two-star general, had just taken a call from the Pentagon. He immediately summoned his OC supply (special ops), a colonel.

'Listen carefully. We have been asked to lay on some help with the situation down in Belize. Ever been there? No? I have, did a fishing trip there two years back. Wonderful place. Brit intelligence reckons half the Guatemalan army is about to roll over the border there. Sat Int confirms that view.

Motherfuckers. Any more than that I don't have, but there's a Brit Para company just left there a few hours ago and they are turning round and going back in. They will want to be loaded for bear. Orders are any and all assistance to be offered. Get your stores people back in; they will need T-10s, rations, expendable ordnance and then some. Get some chow laid on and people down there to help.'

'Jesus, General. One company?'

'There's another there at the airhead, and a few special forces, but the odds are bad. Even so these boys are going back in anyway.'

'Brit airborne,' the colonel said, thinking aloud, as if that were reason enough to defy such odds. 'Crazy mothers.'

'Balls that clang, that's for sure. Be advised, I want these people to have whatever they want.'

'Yessir. What about air ops?'

'They are on to it. The turnaround is organized. They have two C-130s, we will supply a third if they need it. We will provide wedges, so get some rolled into place for loading.'

Belize

At Airport Camp darkness was falling. Major Fox had deployed his two platoons of Gurkhas, but there wasn't much he could do. With sixty-eight men he couldn't cover the whole perimeter, so he concentrated his force at the eastern end, and had them begin to dig defensive positions. Traffic was moving along the airport road but those that noticed kept driving. Belizeans were used to seeing British soldiers around the airport.

They were hard at it when a big Chevrolet that had driven round the airport perimeter road without lights drew up beside them, and a man jumped out.

'Major Fox?'

He nodded.

'Corp'l Garvey. I'm with the training team,' he said obliquely.

'I thought all you chaps were up-country.'

'No, there's two of us still here, we've been working a BDF company for a few months. Anyway, I spoke to Cap't Bonner a few minutes ago and we have just liberated some stuff from the armoury. Hagan is staying in town, he's got half the lads in case they have a go at the Maritime Wing. I have the other half with me, fifty-four of Belize's finest, B Company, motto, "Shoot to kill".' He grinned. 'Thought you might be able to use us.'

'Certainly can,' Fox said, returning the grin. 'What are they like?'

'Crap,' Garvey answered. 'But they have basic skills, and a few of them can shoot straight.'

'Officers?'

'I have one, a real rookie, but dead keen. He is in the picture and will be here in a few minutes. I didn't wait for the others, but the lads will work for me and I'll be with them.'

'Excellent. Do they know what is going on?'

'No, they think this is an exercise. I'll get them into position and set up and then issue live rounds and brief them. There were three 81 mill mortar tubes so I grabbed those and sixty bombs. Fuck knows what state they are in and my blokes have never used them, but I'll fire 'em if we have to.'

'Not necessary. My trained mortar teams are on their way up the highway, but all my men have done basic on 81s.'

'Right, they are yours. We also have a couple of gimmpys,' Garvey lied. They had three, but the big 7.62 sustained-fire GPMG was his weapon of choice and he was holding one back for his personal use. With the correct converging fields of fire, GPMGs could at their optimum range of 500 metres create a twenty-metre-deep zone, where nothing should survive. 'Where do you want us?'

Cayo District – Western Belize

Up in San Ignacio and further west B Squadron, now under the cover of darkness, were working at a furious pace. Usually they were able to work up to a job, practise it again and again, use the equipment, fire thousands of rounds in mock-ups of

124

the area until they had it down perfect. No time on this job – this was where sheer professionalism would carry the day. There were three small teams in San Ignacio itself. One was placing explosives at the bridge so it could be dropped if the attack happened, small charges at various critical points.

Another team was setting explosives at the petrol station on the western side and at various points up the hill on the road towards Benque and the border. They had surveyed the ground, measured exactly the distances. The third team was on the river, mining the western bank, putting out range markers, setting explosive charges along the track that led down to the water. They would then move upriver and wait in case the attackers used the waterway.

The boat troop lads were out, further up the river, setting up trip-lines and booby-traps on the water, marine mines in the rapids, floaters and bottom mines, whose upward blast would blow a boat to pieces. The river was up, so exact positions were difficult to measure, but each mine was secured to the bank on a line.

Civilian cooperation had been easy to establish. One of Bonner's training team had walked into the police station, shown his BDF identification and asked to see the officer in charge. He was out, hadn't been seen all day. Someone thought that maybe he had gone to see his sister at Spanish Lookout. The SAS man then spoke to the next senior man, telling him that they thought they had found an old explosive device on the riverbank and could the local police keep the townspeople away from the river tonight? They would sort it out tomorrow in daylight. Two cars were sent down and that was that.

The people already there were asked to move. On the northern bank, two or three young men, with the dreadlocks of the Rasta, were enjoying their version of sundowners, passing round a joint the size of a Havana cigar. On the southern bank in a little eddy beside what was the ford in the dry season, a couple were making love in the water; the woman, copper-skinned, her hair in ringlets, voluptuous in her wet T-shirt, had her legs around the man's waist. The movements were subtle but unmistakable.

'Ethel, come out de water and go home,' the policeman

said, his torch on them. 'To your husband,' he added drily.

'What de problem, ma?' the man said, his black skin shining like a seal's. He hadn't let Ethel go.

'No one allow on de river tonight. On ya wey now, boat uv ya.'

Five miles to the west, just short of the small town of Benque, at the turn-off at Chial, four Land-Rovers and the quad bikes were dispersed and parked up, the teams working at a frantic pace. In a field on the southern side of the highway they were burying explosives, some almost at the road and the last actually in a culvert under the road. The small C5 charges were laid out carefully, just east of the turn-off that led by an unmade road to Negroman. The explosives when detonated in sequence would replicate exactly the fall of mortar bombs, and any half-decent enemy officer would count the fall, and know what size mortar force he was up against. They dug in enough for the 'mortar' fire in that quantity to come from nothing less than a battalion, a minimum of six tubes. He would know not to try and proceed through the fire from a battery that size, he would try to go round it. If he faltered, there was a back-up option, intended to channel the attack, move it off the highway. The only place to go would be to turn right off the road and hope to work through that way. The maps were confusing; the British army maps produced by Ordnance Survey were astonishingly accurate, but even those suggested that the narrow dirt road, track more properly, led to a crossing point at Negroman and round back on to the main Western Highway east of San Ignacio. There was no easy crossing point, and in fact the two roads either side of the river did not actually meet up – it was a dead end. A four- or five-mile cul-de-sac, and if they could swing it, B Squadron would turn it into a killing ground.

The first crews were finished. Eight men, with two quads and one of the Wolf Land-Rovers, would then be ready to help the Guats make that decision. They would move up to Benque and wait; the absolute forward point would be up at the border itself. One of the men had 'borrowed' a motorbike from an agricultural dealership in San Ignacio. He wanted a trial ride and the salesman, moved to help with a pair of US fifty-dollar bills, agreed to an overnight test. The machine, a 450cc Honda off-road bike, would allow one of them to get right up to the border. If it went off, he had comms; nothing sophisticated, just a powerful transmitter that could throw a pre-programmed signal much further than the small tactical radio he held. Everyone would hear it: the Squadron base, each of the teams, Airport Camp.

Both of the quads now had their Milan posts on the rear cargo area. It looked, as one of the mobility troop men said, 'like shit', but it worked. The launcher post was secured to the little luggage rack and, through two holes, under the fibreglass body with a nylon load strop, the tension taken up with a ratchet. Centre of gravity would be the problem, and the second man on the machine would have to counterbalance the weight problem like a racing sidecar rider. The quad trailers were lightly loaded to allow for top end speed so the three vehicles had to operate together as the Land-Rover was carrying the patrol's spare missiles.

One vehicle was working back towards San Ignacio, laying charges. This was highly dangerous stuff, not only to the men from the Squadron, but to the local population. As the men laid their bar-mines and charges they were fervently hoping that no one would be venturing out after dark, or be foolish enough to get into culverts, where the massive mines were being hidden.

Many of the rest of the Squadron were on the road to Negroman. Assuming the channelling worked they now had to prepare to harry and skirmish the attacking force, never revealing their own size, seeking to wound, taking out officers, killing vehicles on the narrow muddy road. With luck and a fair wind they could slow down the momentum of an attack until the confusion was eliminated by a decent enemy commander.

They were using a mixture of high and low tech. At the hi-tech end, teams were setting up bar-mines with remote triggers, anti-vehicle mines and Addermines, which fired a LAW anti-tank missile by a trip-wire or electronic sensor. The troopers settled on trip-wires for the first followed by laser for the rest. Landmines were dug into the road surface and around fords and culverts. The low-tech end was simple; a chainsaw used to weaken the twin log wheeltracks over a ditch could slow down the progress of the attacking force; anti-personnel Claymore mines on trip-wires would take out the soldiers who went for cover on the roadside after an Addermine strike ahead. The first defensive measures were two miles in, enough to drag two mechanized battalions into the cul-de-sac before they were engaged and realized they had been channelled. Addermines, nearer the road, in effect behind the attacking force, where the laser triggers were activated by radio signal, would block any hasty retreat, leaving bewildered, frightened troops, in the darkness with rain falling, unable to move forward or backward without triggering something.

Two of the four-wheel-drives and the truck were driven into the area from the east down the road on the other side of the river, the egress route. The drivers debussed, laid booby-traps and then crossed the river and made their way up the trail to assist in the ambush. The teams started in the middle and splitting, worked backwards towards the dead end and the main road so when they finished, three of the Land-Rovers were back on the highway and ready in time.

The vehicles on the eastern side of the river would get the last eight-man fighting patrol away. They would work the ambush, moving ahead of the enemy column harrying them, arming devices, with one vehicle and two quads, and then abandon them at the end of the road. By then a three-man team with the truck, now with four 81 mill mortar tubes on the flatbed, would be firing. The mortars could be dropped anything up to six kilometres away and with GPS references on the mine positions they could drop bombs on the column as it halted each time there was an attack.

Northwood had issued orders to RAF Strike Command at High Wycombe and the Royal Air Force was about to break all records to put a mixed detachment on an active deployment. The mission was clear and unambiguous, to provide immediate air cover, air defence and offensive support to a small force of British troops who might be about to engage a numerically superior enemy.

The detachment was mixed. The first aircraft scrambled was a Nimrod from 206 Squadron out of RAF Kinloss; with its 'long legs' it could get all the way down to the theatre before needing refuelling. The second aircraft airborne was a tanker, who would top up her vast tanks at the Pensacola Naval Air Station in Florida. Another Nimrod would be leaving six hours later and until further notice one of the pair of hunters would be in the sky, her ears and eyes seeking out hundreds of miles around her, able to identify any threat on the sea or in the air.

Two more VC10s loaded with aircrews, engineers, ground staff, armourers, technicians and the various bits of equipment needed to keep aircraft operational, would be leaving Wittering, and a VC10 freighter would be outbound from RAF Brize Norton carrying ordnance: the bombs, missiles, and belt munitions for the offensive package. A BAe 125 from the Royal Flight would leave at the same time. Her mission would be as a ferry aircraft to move personnel and equipment forward as she was able. The fighting wing was six Harrier VTOL jets, GR7s from 1 Squadron at RAF Wittering. The activity at the airbases was frantic, but Strike Command had committed to cover the British forces on the ground with the first aircraft in strike range in thirty-two hours.

The Harriers would initially operate from St George's Cay and the small British detachment resident there, who ran the adventure training centre were advised of probable hostilities on the mainland and to expect VTOL support aircraft. Heavy-lift fuel transporters in the form of C-130s loaded with drums of aviation spirit would go into Ambergris Cay where there was a civilian runway. Once they had a secured area just behind the FLOT, the forward line own troops, they could be moved up to shorten the distance between take-off and attack, which meant less fuel was needed and consequently more payload could be carried on the hardpoints before the aircraft's operating limits were reached, delivering more bang in the right place much faster.

San Ignacio

Lieutenant Estelle had left his men in their trucks and moved forward in the Land-Rover to find the SAS man who would show them in. He was where he was expected, looking a little out of place at the clapboard Coke shack at the eastern end of the bridge. He waved and as Estelle slowed the vehicle he climbed into the front passenger seat.

'Down there,' he said, pointing to the track that fell away down from the bridge towards the river. A few yards down the track a policeman stood guard, stopping anyone going down, but the SAS man just waved at him as they went past.

'They in the loop?' Estelle asked.

'They think there's a suspect package in the river. Keeping people away till daylight.'

They drove on for two or three hundred yards until the slope levelled out and the road did a sharp left-hander.

'Pull over here.'

They climbed out and the SAS man began his briefing. 'This is the shallowest point. Before the rains you can wade across without a problem – in fact, when they are doing bridge repairs, this is the main east-west ford point. The water's up now, as you can see.'

Estelle looked left down the bank at the bridge and swept his eyes slowly left to right, looking across at the opposite side. San Ignacio was laid out before them, pretty in the lights that ran up the hill. He wasn't looking at the pretty lights, he was looking at cover, concealment, ways in towards the water.

'If we drop the centre span then this is the way they will come – the *only* way they can come.'

'There's a lot of cover over there,' Estelle said.

The SAS man smiled tiredly. He was now into his thirtieth hour without sleep. 'Say that again. We have mined that bank, set charges in the buildings there,' he pointed. 'But there's too much dead ground and it drops away above the bank. There's a depression there you could hide a couple of companies in if they were lying down. We got a GPS position on it, as we have most of the landmarks over there.'

'How deep's the water?' Estelle asked.

'Five feet or so in the middle there.'

'Their tanks got snorkels?'

'How the fuck would I know?' the SAS man snapped back. 'Sorry, I'm tired. I doubt it.'

'Right, where's our position?'

'From the other side of the bridge, through past here. If you can set up so you can cover up the river with one gun,' he pointed to the right, 'that should take care of it.' Estelle was appalled. It was a three-hundred-yard stretch of the riverbank, much of it a tangle of undergrowth, levelling out here, where it was cleared for twenty yards back, then thickening again. Can't be done, he thought, not with two platoons. Eight sections, eight section weapons, two GPMGs; one section up there somewhere with the mortars, another with the Milans. Down to six sections, one section every fifty yards. Concentrate our defence here at the crossing point, with what? Half? That left twenty-four men to cover the rest of the area. At least we will have silhouettes, but no night vision – flares, I want flares.

'There will be Squadron teams around about. The boss will fill you in later but get dug in. There's only fifteen thousand of the cunts. Oh,' the SAS man said as he turned to leave, 'we did see something on the video – bridging sections and rafts.'

'Fucking marvellous,' Estelle replied.

The SAS man laughed. 'Fucking lovely way to fight a war, innit.' He was still laughing as he walked back up to the Land-Rover.

131

Chapter Five

His men were digging in, defensive positions with interlocking fields of fire. Dickie Fox was moving up and down between the positions and had heard the helicopter returning a few minutes before so when a group of men loomed out of the dark, he was expecting them. 'Ah, the marines. What commando?'

'Comacchio,' one of them responded. 'What's all the drama . . . sir?' The man, a sergeant, sounded pissed off. They had just been told to get themselves and their gear on to the chopper quicksmart, this from the naval lieutenant P1, after a hard three-day exercise. They were tired, their kit was dirty; they wanted a shower, clean rig and then debrief in that order. Now this, a major in a maroon beret, Paras no less, the arch-rivals. Another man moved forward from the rear and Fox saw the two pips on his shoulders. This was getting better and better; if he could only have a few marines for this job then there was no better unit, the Royal Marines Comacchio group were defensive specialists. They defended nuclear installations, secret facilities; they weren't assault specialists, they trained to be attacked.

'Major Fox? Lieutenant Murray. Jack.'

Fox took the proffered hand. 'How many men have you got?'

'Twenty,' Murray replied. 'Major, why have we been dragged off our ex?'

'I'll brief you.'

Ten minutes later, Murray, his beret in his pocket, his shock of blond hair a stark contrast to the cam cream on his face, lit a cigarette. His sergeant was to his right, silent, listening. Murray was thinking fast. To properly defend an airfield you needed a battalion, with mortars and heavy support. You put your defensive positions away from the airfield itself, where you had room to fight and could prevent the enemy getting anywhere near the actual runway. Fox knew it, he knew it – but with this few men?

'We're Comacchio, this is what we do. But given the small resource, best use of my chaps is probably as first contact.' He looked up as another man walked up. Fox introduced him.

'This is Corporal Garvey, B Squadron. Corporal, join us please.' Garvey squatted down on his haunches. This was normal in the Squadron – the Chinese parliament, when everyone had their say – but he was mildly surprised at a green army major inviting it. Although Fox was wearing a maroon beret, he was Brigade of Gurkhas through and through. 'Garvey has fifty-odd Belize Defence Force,' Fox explained.

Murray nodded at Garvey and continued. 'My blokes as a recce troop. Then once we have a feel for what we're up against, their calibre, strength, fall back into set positions.' He was looking at a map of the airfield and surrounding area. 'You're pretty sure, sir, that they aren't jumping in?'

'No, I'm not. They have airborne and special forces, trained by the Israelis, called the "Kaibiles". They have two battalions of them, but they don't have the uplift. I'm told that if they can get half their transports up then they are doing well. Current assessments,' he nodded towards Garvey, meaning assessments from Hereford, 'reckon it may be under half. So I think they could use airborne, but because they are limited in numbers, they will be used to get at the other strategic targets. Drop into Belmopan perhaps, take out the radio station, maybe try and secure government buildings.' He looked up at the sky. 'However, the weather may preclude that.'

'What's your view, sir?'

'I think that given we are so close to the sea that's where our threat will come from. The surrounding area is hard going. Mangroves, swamp, bush; this is the only road. They won't be expecting a reception committee.'

'Most likely?'

Fox pointed east. 'I think they will either come in at the port, or the beach, maybe both. The beach is what, two miles away? I'm not a marine, but it's what I'd do.'

Me too, thought Murray, with a contingent big enough to take and hold the only long hard runway in the country and sit on it till the main force arrives. He nodded. 'Sir, what I suggest is that I move my men up to the crossroads. That will give us a view of all three ways in. Can we put OPs out on the flanks and the rear?'

'Done,' Garvey replied. 'Five-man sections, with VHF comms. I'll be up there with them.' Murray nodded; it made sense with their limited strength. He would be on the eastern approach with his troop, the main force at the eastern end of the airport proper, with the SAS corporal and some of the local people at the far end in case they came that way. 'What stores have we got? I need ammunition, grenades. Have we got any Claymores?'

Fox shook his head. 'Four Claymores and they are in already. I can let you have two grenades each, and two hundred rounds of 5.56. Garvey, can you . . . ?'

Murray's face dropped. Two grenades and two hundred rounds wasn't enough, not nearly enough to dig in and defend a position. He looked at the SAS corporal.

Garvey grinned. 'Don't worry, I raided the pantry. My blokes are using 5.56. Not sure what state it's in but there's plenty of it. We have even got a few old L7 Bren guns . . .' He paused for a moment and then issued his gentle jibe at the arch-rivals, 'If your crap-hat sailors can adapt.'

Murray looked at him and raised an eyebrow. The SAS corporal was obviously out of the airborne and the marine sergeant, silent thus far, a man who had done a tour in the Special Boat Squadron, couldn't let that one go. 'Marines have been fuckin' adapting for three hundred years, Corporal. We take arms off the enemy dead if we have to. Stand back and watch real men fight. We might even save your soft little maroon arses.' His grin was wolflike in the darkness. Garvey chuckled softly.

Eva's was rocking and it was still early. The diners were mostly Americans, who, Pete knew, ate early rather than late. No self-respecting Brit would order food before eight, and by then there wouldn't be an American left at the tables. That was fine by him, he got two sittings in. The people at the tables were eco-tourists, in sensible boots, the baggy shorts Americans wore, with their ubiquitous trendy little day-packs. None of the women wore make-up, and too many of the men had beards for Pete's liking. There was a small gaggle of people by the bar, and a few scattered round the PCs. He walked over to the CD player, and torn for a second or two between Jimi Hendrix and Eric Clapton, he opted for the black guitarist. He was a rhythm section man himself, a bass guitarist, but he loved to hear a master play. He slipped the CD on and a few seconds later the mellow tones of 'Hey Joe' were filling the background. He looked around; things were fine, and he could take his constitutional. Each evening, once the early diners were in and eating, he would go for a short walk down the street, maybe chat with others who ran businesses. He took off his apron and the tea towel that was habitually over his shoulder and ambled out on to the street, one of the waitresses slipping in behind the bar.

He walked down Burns Street towards the intersection, taking his time, waving to people he knew, an orange-seller still out under a streetlight, the old lady from the hardware shop, now heading home to prepare her family's evening meal. A car drove up towards him and the driver hit the horn. Pete smiled. Eddie Sanchez, taxi driver, bullshitter, man about town. Pete found Eddie likeable enough, but only in small doses; the ebullient bonhomie was all a bit forced at times, like a fairground barker, or a snake-oil salesman. It was odd to see him up here in the evenings. Eddie liked to be back in Belize City at night; that was where the money was, taking tourists out to the Garden.

'Hey, Pete my buddy! What's happening?'

'You're a long way from your patch.'

'Eh, what can I say, man? Got a fare up this afternoon. Know anyone heading back who needs a ride?'

Pete thought about it quickly. They all survived on each other's work. Eddie often brought customers to Eva's, and he in turn would direct Eddie towards people he thought might be looking to go back down to the coast, but within reason. Eddie could be a bit too familiar and noisy, so Pete chose the punters carefully. There were the two English girls but they were staying, had their own wheels anyway.

'Na.'

'What's happening down da riva?'

'Dunno. Why?'

'Police close it, marn. I was just gonna go down, blow some weed, reelux and dey sent me away.'

A car behind him hooted and Eddie returned the hoot with one of his own. 'Fuckers, man. I see you roun', man.'

Pete waved and he drove away. Closed the river? The police? He thought about it for a moment or two. The police in San Ignacio were a pretty sleepy lot and they wouldn't do it without someone telling them to. He wandered down the street.

Four hundred yards away the Gurkhas were digging in. Company Sergeant Major Nandu Goreng and a four-man section were thirty yards away from the bridge at the southern end of the company position with a section weapon and they were digging themselves in deep – four holes, each with a field of fire and large enough for four men. The ground was soft and they had dug holes in harder earth, but four was a lot and because the ground was soft they had to go deeper. They scraped back the humus and the rotting leaves, then dug, shovelling the earth they removed into sandbags. They were also digging in under cover, trying not to disturb the vegetation on the bank. Once in and sighting their weapons they could carefully cut away bits of it, but the intention was to remain hidden from the far bank of the river and be able to move between sangars unseen.

The Gurkhas were working stripped to the waist, not because of the heat but to avoid their shirts getting dirty; they worked in silence, each knowing exactly what he had to do and each doing his share. They were proud – the CSM had chosen them, hand-picked them from the two platoons to form the left flank with him. If fighting began, and some of them secretly doubted that it would, then no enemy was coming past them. This was their job and they were professionals.

Two miles up the river, Jock Edwards, the jungle warfare instructor whom Captain Atlee had last seen in Brunei, was with three other men from boat troop. They had 'borrowed' a pair of rigid inflatable boats, Ribs, from the shed of one of the river touring companies. Two troopers were working their way downriver, setting mines in the water, hooking other devices into the trees on the bank. Their task was to discourage use of the water, channel any effort there back on to the road, make the first few miles of the river so dangerous and so well defended that it ceased to be an option and by stopping any enemy crossing to the western bank, prevent a flanking attack on the bridge positions. They were on the Mopan, the branch that flowed parallel to the main road down from the border. The eastern branch, called the Macal, flowed north, widening as it went, under the bridge at San Ignacio, and just about a mile from the bridge and the town it met the Mopan and turned east, becoming the Belize river and flowing eventually down to the sea.

Edwards and his oppo in the second boat were at the confluence of the two rivers. On the western bank of the confluence, known to locals as Branch Mouth, was clear ground, and a huge tree drooped its branches into the water. An old rusty mooring ring in the trunk was there from the days of river transport. Opposite in the jungle on the other bank was where they would set up their final position to cover the river, Branch Mouth, the landing and the path back into San Ignacio.

They set about reconnoitring the immediate area. The plan was that the two four-man fighting patrols would fight the river, darting ahead, drawing the enemy into the pre-set ambush areas, wearing them down, until if necessary they would eventually race ahead again and set up their GPMG on the bank where the two rivers joined. To move further downstream towards Belize City, or move up the eastern branch, any remaining enemy would have to get past their position and they had enough LAW rockets to make that difficult. The problem was that there was a resort camp close by; Las Casitas had tents and cabañas, some very close to the water.

'Do we tell 'em?'

'No,' Edwards replied. 'It might not happen. If it does, then they'll hear it coming.'

That recce finished, they would move back upstream, join the other pair and then, until it either went off or they were stood down, they would block the waterway and defend the outer northern flank.

Edwards, still in his Hawaiian shirt, was digging a flare launcher into the bank, in the bush just up from the landing. From where they would make their stand, it was far enough from them that the inevitable fire it would attract wouldn't matter. The launcher could take six flares into its magazine and fire them on remote command. He was filthy, wet, covered in red mud, digging into the stinking damp earth of a Central American riverbank in complete darkness – and thoroughly enjoying himself. They had plenty of bang-bang stuff. The Squadron had come in heavy and they had the absolute luxury of plenty of everything they needed. Explosives, marine mines, Claymore, anti-tank rockets, and enough armour-piercing ammunition to rip boats to pieces. They were confident; they had enough kit to take care of anything up to and including fast river patrol craft. If the scrotes had anything bigger than that and it all went pear-shaped, they would just withdraw quicksmart, meet up at an emergency RV they would agree and move back to the bridge.

A few minutes later, when the flare launcher was in position and ready, the boat stooged in and Edwards jumped aboard.

'Done?'

'Like a kipper,' he replied. They moved one hundred yards, stopped again, and left the boat, each carrying a Claymore mine. Both men were wearing head lamps, but with red filters.

This meant they could see to set the mines without ruining their night-sight, and within ten minutes they were back in the boat, this time Edwards at the small outboard, while the other trooper was taking care of the remote arming kits. Because they had a variety of weapon systems they actually had four different remote arming systems and they had to be kept dry, and in the correct order for use through a transmitter. The Claymore used Shrike pads, a device with three buttons the size of a cigarette packet which could control three mines each. But instead of sending a signal down electric detonator cords, they were hooked into transmitters that would blast a signal at a receiver on the weapon's detonators. The transmitters had ten frequencies each and each boat had two transmitters, although one was a back-up. Even so, it allowed the two boats to set up to twenty remote devices on twelve miles of river. That was in addition to the other measures. Keeping the gear dry was the problem; even sealed in plastic containers they went the belt and braces route and the containers were themselves inside a see-through polythene bag. Each of the pre-set devices was coded and its position marked on a map. They moved on again, this time stopping at a rock in the middle of the river.

'Oooh yes!' Edwards' oppo said. 'One each side! That'll make their fuckin' eyes water.'

Edwards grinned. A Claymore mine set each side of the rock, but pointing off at forty-five degrees upriver would have a devastating effect. A hundred-metre killing ground. 'Lubbly jubbly,' he agreed.

In San Ignacio Pete was down below the intersection at the bus station when a four-wheel-drive, loaded down, came haring up from the river. It stopped briefly to allow a chicken bus through and for a moment he saw the people inside. Three men, whites, the one in the front passenger seat looking at something with a small torch. Then it took off again.

Odd, he thought, Eddie said they had closed off the river. He looked down the track. A police car was down there. He looked back at the four-by-four, as it accelerated round the corner. They are in a hurry, he thought, not the laid-back tourists one usually found up here; they seemed purposeful, familiar almost. He ambled back up towards Burns Street and perhaps it was because he had spent seventeen years in the British army, or because the last time it looked like going wrong here he was here in uniform, the pieces fell into place. That's the mob, he thought, tooling round in civvies. What the fuck's going on? He turned again, this time heading back towards the gas station and the bridge. Twenty minutes later he was back at the restaurant. He knew what he was looking for and had seen enough to know something was going down. He went upstairs to the flat and phoned his brother-in-law who lived a few miles up the road towards the border, just north of Benque opposite the chain ferry. He was out, so he slipped across the road to another restaurant-bar owned by another ex-Brit army bloke. He was out too, down in Belize City, trying for a new chip fryer at an auction. He slipped back in behind his bar, donned his apron and went to work. A few minutes later the two English girls walked in. Showered and in clean T-shirts they had bought somewhere; refreshingly after the Americans, both were wearing lipstick and had bothered to do something with their hair.

'Ladies! Good evening. How was it? Mud up to your knees, I'll bet.'

'It was wonderful,' Sophie said.

While Pete finished the round he was working on Sophie and Helen settled themselves on stools at the bar. Sophie looked down at her watch. 'Seventeen hours, he said. They left at three, they'll be home at –'

'Oh, for God's sake,' Helen muttered. 'Can't you think of anything else? You'll be seeing him in a week.'

'What can I get you girls?' Pete asked, turning to them.

'What have you got for someone who's lovesick?' Helen quipped. Sophie hit her under the level of the bar and smiled sweetly at Pete, who had a big grin spreading across his face.

'Just the thing,' he said and pulled a couple of bottles of cold beer from the fridge.

'Always worked for me. Quaff on that and I'll make you something more exotic in a minute. A real Del Boy drink, wiv an umbrella if you like. How's the hotel?'

'Fine, thanks,' Helen replied. 'For ten quid a night . . .' She shrugged. Pete turned away to serve one of the waitresses and Sophie sipped her beer and then looked at Helen.

'Do you think he'll phone? Really? I mean tell me honestly. Then I'll shut up about it.'

Major Chard had swung by the bridge, not to check his men had completed their task, that was a given, but to meet and brief the young lieutenant with his Gurkhas. Chard rated the Nepalese fighting men very highly. They were tough, resilient, resourceful, highly disciplined and had proven themselves over and over again. They were as demanding on their officers as they were on themselves and expected consistency and fairness. Chard liked what he saw in their young officer and the sections were well positioned. He finished his briefing and asked, 'All right. Any questions?'

'What do we do with the civvies? They will be pouring back over the bridge.' Chard knew that. He also knew it was their only way out.

'Hopefully we will slow them down, but you can expect people coming across the moment it starts. You might have a couple of hours even. In theory you could empty this town in that time. We'll be falling back ahead of their advance, how many of us and in what state, I can't say, but you'll get some warning, time enough to close the western end and get your patrol back across. You've been shown the arming device and the initiator?'

Estelle nodded. 'Yes, I have.'

'If I'm not around then it's your call. Drop the bridge.' Chard smiled. 'I'd like to see that mother go. Defend till it's untenable, withdraw and, if you can, get your men back to the airhead. What the roads back will be like Christ only knows.'

'Your lads, sir?'

'We'll be staying here,' Chard said, shaking his head.

'Sir, honestly? What odds they will try something tonight?'

Chard looked at him in the darkness. Normally as a Squadron commander he treated everything on a need-to-know basis and the Regiment prided itself on its own internal management of information. If you weren't directly involved, you weren't to know – less risk for everyone. This dropped right down to teams and individuals, and as an individual Estelle needed to know this, as did every one of his handful of men.

'My view only, from what we have seen, the int, better than sixty per cent. In fact I'll be surprised if they don't. The politicos are hard at it, so they know we know. If they don't move tonight or tomorrow then they lose the initiative. They know they can roll through here any time in the next few days without much to stop 'em.' Chard flipped back the leather cover and looked at his watch. 'Gotta go.'

Estelle nodded and watched the major walk away, the rain now falling harder than before.

St George's Cay

On St George's Cay, five or so miles off the coast, where the British Army had their adventure training camp, the small team were busy. There were twelve full-time MoD staff: five instructors, four cooks, a mechanic, a storeman and the senior man, a staff sergeant. They had four local chaps, Belizeans, on the payroll and they were all out on the task at hand. They had taken the message by telephone from the signallers at Airport Camp and were now following a set of instructions last consulted in the late eighties. The two-page document was entitled, 'Preparations to receive VTOL aircraft on St George's Cay – an aide-mémoire'.

The landing area wasn't in bad nick; helicopters used it frequently, but not all of the steel-matted area was clear. The Gazelle never used more than one corner. The excess sand would have to be cleared, the matting swept regularly. The new Harriers were more tolerant of sand, but even so, if you could sweep it away then you did so. Someone once suggested spraying it with oil to stop it flying around, fine for rotary wing ops, but not much good for the superheated exhaust gases channelled downwards from the VTOLs' jet engines which were hot enough to ignite the oily sand.

'What about us, Sarge,' one of the cooks asked miserably,

his Birmingham accent nasal and flat. He was only here to save money. The posting was sunny, warm, with good pay and nothing to spend it on, but he hadn't counted on ever actually having to be a soldier, a target for bullets. That's why he chose to be a cook. 'Will we be attacked?'

'Don't be a fucking plonker, Smallboy,' came the response. "'Oo the fuck would want this bloody place? A handful of buildings and a palm tree or two.'

'Club Med?' someone chimed in from the darkness.

'But we're strategic,' Smallboy, the cook, who was six-feet-four and weighed in at eighteen stone, responded, ignoring the interruption. 'You said so yourself once.'

You're right there, china, the sergeant thought. The closest point to the mainland equipped to operate VTOL offensive aircraft and all we have is a few non-combatants and a guard-room with two rifles and two pistols in it.

'What would you know about what was strategic?' one of the instructors challenged. 'Stick to making French toast, right, and get that fucking shite moved.'

'I haven't got stores you know,' Smallboy went on, pulling back on some four-by-twos they were using to repair a boat shed. 'Like, if they arrive and want feeding, I just don't have enough stores. Those Paras cleaned me out. Boat's not in till – '

'Smallboy, stop whingeing,' the sergeant said tiredly. 'We gotta do this tonight, right? In the dark, where no one can see us. So let's just get on with it.'

'See us? Who's going to see us?' Smallboy persisted. 'We're on an atoll in the middle of the ocean.'

'Shut the fuck up!'

Less than a kilometre away, on what looked like a local fishing boat overnighting like any other, her anchor down in the coral, a man was watching them. With PNG rig on his head, passive night vision, he watched the movements on the small British base. He wasn't a very good spy – he had put the boat in the wrong place, and from where he was there was no activity visible, because the facility buildings were between him and the landing area. There was nothing to report. He had been in the area three days now and the bat-teries on the PNG unit he had been given were fading. He was also bored and had run out of Cokes; even warm they were better than nothing. He was an officer in Guatemalan naval intelligence and fairly typical of the calibre of junior officers in the corps which is perhaps why they were totally unaware that HMS *Beaufort* was heading towards the area and in just over two hours her remote weapons platform, her state-of-the-art ship-killing Lynx helicopter would be in range.

Fort Bragg – North Carolina

The two British aircraft taxied in, following a jeep across the vast military base. Finally they were guided round the front of a hangar by a man with light-wands and the engines shut down. A lieutenant arrived in a second jeep and Tyson-Davis jumped down to the ground through the small hatch in the C-130's forward fuselage.

'Major Tyson-Davis? Sir, as soon as you are ready, if you'd like to follow me, General MacLennan is expecting you.'

'Have I got a few minutes? I'd like to brief my men.'

'Sure, sir. General Mac said you might do that.'

The men piled out on to the pan, stretching their legs and looking around.

Tyson-Davis wasted no time. 'Gather round, lads.' They did so and he stood on the upper end of the lowered ramp so he could see them all. 'Right, God knows how much of what is happening filtered back to you; I think I'm deaf after that noise.' He put a finger to his ear and there was some laughter. 'But this ain't Brize Norton.' He filled them in as quickly as he could, finishing with, '. . . so we're gonna re-equip and go back, be a very visible presence while the politicians get it sorted. It may be a few days or a week or so before we are homeward bound again.' A groan rolled through the group. 'Questions?'

'Sir,' someone called from the back, 'does this mean we have to take real bullets, 'cos my mum says they are dangerous.' There was a burst of laughter. Tyson-Davis grinned.

'Stretch your legs, but don't move away from the aircraft till ordered.'

Fifteen minutes later the men were escorted into the hangar. A supply sergeant moved across to meet them. He identified Tyson-Davis.

'Sir, if you have someone who could let me know what you'd like . . .' he pointed to his left. There, laid out as in a supermarket, were pallet-loads of ordnance and equipment, and wedges were ready in front of the line-up. Tyson-Davis walked over to the stockpile; it looked enough to equip a small country. Jesus, he said to himself under his breath. There was ball ammunition of differing calibres, tracer, mortar rounds, anti-tank rockets. There were mines of every size and type, racks of weapons and alongside those, ration packs and medical supplies. Round to the right clothing and packs were laid out and across the other side stood a parachute table; T-10s, the US airborne forces' parachutes, ready for issue and repacking.

'Excellent,' he said. 'Sar' Major?'

'Sir?'

'A QM section from your platoon to lend a hand please.'

Twenty minutes later the issue had begun. Support platoon and Captain Atlee's patrols group were first.

'Eighty-one and fifty-one mill. Got any?'

'Got any fifty calibre?' It was pointed at. 'Ooh yes! Come to Daddy!'

One of the patrols men moved up, thinking, Fort Bragg, special forces base – they must have some. 'Seven-point-six-two long. As new as you can, please.' He held up his weapon, a sniper's rifle. 'Fifty should do it.'

The US serviceman looked at the rifle and crooked his finger. 'Come with me.' He led the soldier away to a room behind the issue area. Its shelves were piled high with a wide range of exotic ammunition, much of it commercially made for the hunting market. 'Second bay, middle shelf. Write down a list of what you might take if you were allowed – I'm not saying you will get it – and then forget you ever came in here, OK?'

The soldier nodded. It was like an Aladdin's cave: soft point, hollow point, full metal jacket, differing weights and grains,

145

expanding rounds, explosive rounds, armour-piercing. Much of it was banned under the Geneva Convention.

'It's, aah, the personal property of some of the folks round here.'

'There's two of us.'

'Then, if you were allowed, you might think about enough for two.'

'I will.' The soldier was elated; he would never be the first to use an illegal round, but if the enemy fired them, if his mates had just one hit with an illegal bullet, then he would retaliate. When snipers were at work, shooting over distances up to a thousand yards, often the only thing to use against an enemy sniper was one of your own. If all you could see was a foot or a limb then you wanted to hit it hard enough to disable the other marksman, and if he was using hollow points then he would get one back. Any strike on the human body with an expanding round of any kind would incapacitate the victim, totally.

Captain Atlee, with the privilege of rank, was walking down the back of the block of weapons behind the QM section. Often during exercises equipment was damaged; rifles were no different and there were rifles in racks in case anyone needed a replacement. Behind these were disposable anti-tank rockets and hand-held portable grenade launchers, but it was something else that caught Atlee's eye. He bent down and looked. It was a Mk 19 automatic grenade launcher; a big, bulky weapon, it could fire grenades a thousand yards, one every second. The trouble was, it was heavy, and designed to be mounted on a plinth or a baseplate. He knew 22 SAS mobility people used them mounted on vehicles. He looked more closely; there was a mount for it. They could find a use for it, he knew – with mortars able to drop their bombs anything up to three or four kilometres away, and the fifties and GPMGs covering the short range, under eight hundred yards and down to one hundred, a Mk 19 could cover the middle ground. If things went badly and they were likely to have to defend an airhead, this weapon could be invaluable. He signalled to two of his patrols team and pointed downwards. They came over.

146

'Ever used one of these?'

'What is it?'

Oh well, he thought, I've had a go with one. 'Looks like it's me then. Somewhere around here is a weapons specialist – grab him. I need a ten-minute refresher course. You two listen in.'

On the other side of the hangar Plonker, Rhah, Spud, Elias Cutter and the rest of his section were repacking their bergens, now called containers, trying to find space for everything they would be taking back. There was plenty; each man would carry an extra sixty pounds or more. Plonker had found Jonesy's Teletubbies again and they were now on his bergen, one bent over, the other standing behind, the position positively sexual.

'Aye aye, give it one yer booger,' he laughed to himself. He looked back down at the pile at his feet. 'Two fookin' mortar bombs each. Fookin' 'ell, mun, I was really lookin' forard to a decent pint. Now we're going back into the fookin' J. I fookin' 'ate jungle. 'Ave I tol' yowa 'ow I fookin' 'ate jungle?'

'Over and over again,' Elias muttered.

'I 'ate fookin' jungle like I 'ate fookin' Arsenal supporters.'

Rhah looked over and grinned. He was an Arsenal man, a Gunners supporter since he could walk into a match. 'You love us really.'

'Oh aye? Yowa cunts are shite. Canna score a . . .' He trailed off, looking down at his bergen. 'Where the fook ama gonna put two bombs, mun?'

'In yer gob, yer northern git, it's big enough,' someone threw back.

'Or up yer arse, yer fat bastid,' Spud offered.

Plonker, tall, rangy, with a face that a woman had once described as 'battered about a bit' wasn't impressed, and his look said it all.

'Oh aye? Well fook yowa lot. Fookin' woofta Arsenal supporters, yowa lot.'

'Making friends again are we?' Lieutenant Rees had loomed out of nowhere.

'Sir, I wanna transfer to a platoon of men. Real men,' Plonker responded.

'Transfer him to the air force,' someone yelled.

'Or the Falklands,' from someone else.

'Or the nursing corps.'

Rees just smiled and moved on down his platoon.

'Yowa cunts, the lotta ya,' Plonker muttered and looked over at his platoon commander's substantial bulk moving away. 'And how does a bastid that fookin' big move so quietly?'

'Who?' asked Rhah, looking up.

''Im. Big Harry. Fooksakes . . .' Plonker was in a world of fools. 'Two bombs, mun,' he muttered to himself.

CSM 'Robo' Jennings was moving ceaselessly from one group to the next. He had his own platoon, his own support and administrative functions, but even so, there was a very junior lieutenant with eleven platoon so he was keeping an eye on them too. As he moved past twelve platoon he overheard Plonker's complaining.

'Find 'em a good home because you will be carrying link ammo as well,' Jennings said. 'Go and draw 200 rounds each. All of you.'

Guatemala

In Guatemala City Her Majesty's Ambassador to Guatemala had been trying to see their Minister for Foreign Affairs for three hours. He had three of his staff on the telephones trying various numbers and he himself had driven down to the ministry and was waiting in the vaulted lobby outside the minister's office reception area. For the fourth time a minor functionary came out.

'I regret the minister is not available. If the ambassador would care to make an appointment?'

'No, I would not. I insist that he sees me.'

'But he is not here,' the man lied again, for the fourth time.

'Well find him. Tell him that I am here and waiting for him. The ambassador of Great Britain, a permanent member of the security council of the United Nations. I'm not leaving,' he said firmly, 'so you go back in there and tell him that.'

It was 0315 when the Guatemalan Ambassador to the Court of St James's was finally 'located', now back at the mission after a late dinner party with friends. In truth he had been back for three hours, but had only just received permission from his own people in Guatemala to return Hildon's calls. He telephoned the secretary of state and began with apologies and pleasantries, but Hildon cut him off.

'Let's come to the point, Ambassador. You know why I am calling.'

'I do not, sir, but if you wish I shall call upon you tomorrow at your convenience.'

'You shall call on me now. This is official. In your capacity as the representative of the government of Guatemala I expect you here in my office in half an hour.'

'I protest, sir! It is the middle of the night. I shall need . . .' The ambassador was looking across at another man, ostensibly the attaché, but in fact much nearer the top of the Guatemalan Interior Ministry. He was listening on a second line. He held up one finger. 'I shall need at least an hour!'

'Your residence is fifteen minutes from my office. If your driver is unavailable, the police car on the street will bring you over. Be here!' Hildon hung up.

The ambassador walked back to his desk, careful not to let the other man see his expression. What were these lunatics playing at? He had been kept in the dark, his own people using what the Americans termed 'plausible deniability'. Madness, sheer madness, whatever it was. He suspected he knew, it was an old trick; when things get tough, find a scapegoat, blame them and then give people something else to think about. Despots and juntas the world over did it. History was full of it, from the Jews and the Sudetenland, to the Malvinas, to the Iraqi people being told that all their problems were caused by the Americans. And what do we get if we take Belize? A few months of national pride, a few months of 'unification'? A Greater Guatemala spreading from east to west across Central America. And then what? Huge costs, more civil insurrection. We can't even control the FAR guerrillas in the Peten highlands; why create another 'province' where the entire population will be hostile?

Madness. They must be mad, he thought, and now the British know – they must do. They have no one there, none of their army anymore, but they didn't in the Malvinas either and look what happened there. Will they do it again? With luck, maybe they will just protest, and look for diplomatic solutions. They must support the United Nations mandates, but they won't want to. Yes, he had to admit it, there was a strong chance that the junta might just get away with this. But at what price? A high one for him personally, he thought. A momentary feeling of sadness washed over him; he liked living in London. He had had good postings and bad in his career, but this was the best. It was also in the top five senior posts: Washington, Mexico City, Paris, Bonn and London, and of those cities for him this was the best. Now there was every chance it was all over, and it would be back to Guatemala City. What a way to end a lifelong career as a diplomat, with a summons. He was to retire in three years, his family grown and moved on and only his wife now living with him. She hated Guatemala City; the poverty, the violence, the brutality, the street children, most of them *resistoleros*, glue-sniffers. He went to change his clothes. There was no protocol for meetings in the middle of the night, but clearly the evening dress he was wearing would not be appropriate.

In Washington DC, the National Security Adviser was finishing his late briefing to the President; as usual there were aides present and other parties. There were updates on Bosnia, Liberia and Sierra Leone, but it was the one in their backyard that was saved till last – Guatemala. The briefing was running late because the Adviser wanted three other people present, one of them the CIA ex-head of station at the embassy in Guatemala, the other two men from the Central American desks at the Department of State. All three were experts on the region and none of them had met the President before. There were in total twelve people in the situation room.

'So summarize, please, someone,' the President said. He was

getting irritated. So far the meeting had been split on views; some said the threat was real, others thought it merely more of the old sabre-rattling. There was no consensus view.

'It's possible, Mr President. With what they have moved up, they could do it. But I don't believe they will,' one of the men from State said. 'They understand what our view would be. They know what they get from us in aid and assistance.'

The CIA man shook his head.

'You disagree?' queried the President.

'I do, sir. They have gone beyond the long view on our reaction. They see aid from us as a given. As long as they remain right-wing, it will keep coming, even if they displease this administration. I think they will do it.'

'Well, the British seem to think they will.' He remembered something and looked across at the Adviser. 'That group going back – we taking good care of them?'

'Yes, Mr President.'

'I think they ought to be in no doubt as to our views on this development. I'll ask State to get a message to them first thing in the morning. In the meantime – ' He was interrupted by an aide who opened the door and passed a message across to him. 'Excuse me, gentlemen. John, join me please,' he said to the Adviser, rising from his seat. 'We'll be back presently.' They left the room and as he did the man from State looked at the CIA officer, his expression clear. He didn't like being contradicted.

'You are forgetting that much of this supposition is based on the thinking of a single individual on the ground there. Not even an American. Other than some – ' the man from State argued.

'You asshole. ''Not even an American'',' the CIA man repeated with a laugh. 'Jesus! What planet are you from? It's that kind of arrogance that gets us into trouble. You think that Americans have the monopoly on intelligence-gathering and assessment? You ever met anyone from his organization?'

'No, I haven't. I didn't mean that anyway. And there have been movements of the military in the Peten for the last two years; this might well be no different.'

'I know what you meant. A single individual? Let me

remind you it may have begun with one man's view of things, but it's corroborated by satellite int. And this man is highly qualified to make this assessment, he is a special forces officer from an outfit that can teach our people a thing or two any day of the week.'

'That's enough, gentlemen,' a senior aide muttered.

In Belize City, Dion was cleaned up and ready to spend an evening out. The day's dive trip had been good. The party had seen plenty, including a couple of decent-sized hammerheads, and the non-divers had just idled around on Goff's Cay, sunbathing, swimming in the warm shallow water, on Belize time. They had lunched, done a second dive, and then headed in at three, sweeping back to stooge slowly through the mangroves of Drowned Cay looking for manatees, and he had them back at the Radisson pier at five on the nail. The Americans had tipped well, and with a couple of fifties on top of his salary it had been a good day. He drove over to the guest house to wander around. This was part of it, Dave had said, seeing the guests, chatting to those who had been out that day with him, and because the Fort Street house was a small friendly place where people introduced themselves to each other and took time to talk, it paid off. They would be on a big high about the day and in no time, from just a couple of people interested, you could have a full boat and maybe, with people from the Radisson, even need a second boat.

Dave was downstairs in his flat and he would look in there first, see what was booked for tomorrow before he went upstairs and did the rounds. He parked his old car just up the street, and walked in. Across the road at the Belize Defence Force Maritime Wing things were in darkness as usual, and he noticed that the barracks behind him, Militia Hall, seemed pretty quiet too. His cousin's boyfriend was in the BDF, in fact with B Company, who were based here at the Hall. Usually it was noisier, music and laughing from the men. Maybe they were out. He thought no more about it and walked in through the gate.

* * *

In San Ignacio, Helen and Sophie were settled in at Eva's, eating at one of the tables. Pete Collins was at work behind the bar. He had eventually spoken to his brother-in-law and was now serving drinks, running the till, and personally supervising things as he usually did.

A quarter of a mile away, on the eastern side of the river, Edwardo Sanchez was eating his evening meal in a cheap and cheerful roadside diner. There was no fare back to Belize, but a man he knew had bought a small fridge and wanted a lift back to Belmopan. He would pay for the fuel and that would almost get Edwardo back home without cost, so it was worth waiting for the guy.

Between them in the thick jungle vegetation on the bank of the river Lieutenant Estelle and his Gurkhas were dug in and now making the final preparations. Firing steps, covers of logs and dirt making foxholes into sangars. Most had eaten, heating their rations with hexy blocks, and had returned to the task.

Out ahead of them the Squadron were also still hard at it. The base defences were in, and now it was time to refine things with grenade necklaces and flare trip-wires. Within sight of the border post was the lone member of mobility troop with his motorbike. He was settled in with a passive night vision headset. He didn't need it – the post was illuminated like a Christmas tree. At the Squadron base camp the Hi-Eye was flying again. The pointy heads didn't like night flying, but they had a thermal imaging camera and Chard had insisted it was loaded and the machine sent up again. The pictures were very telling indeed, bright spots showing heat emissions for miles around the border town of Melchor, where in daylight there had been only jungle. The bright heat emissions were engines and exhausts, hundreds of them clustered in groups, some of them moving.

Seventy miles away at the airport outside Belize City Major Fox was on schedule with his men, and Corporal Garvey was working stripped to the waist alongside his BDF fellows. They had been told what was possibly going to happen and amazingly they now understood the need for good deep foxholes and were digging them like men possessed. Murray was with his troop of marines at the crossroads, settled in and waiting and back in Belize City the last SAS trooper in the town had deployed his fifty BDF people in and around the Maritime Wing. There wasn't much more he could do; just await the attack or the dawn, whichever came first. It was three minutes to nine in the evening.

Chapter Six

The B Squadron mobility troop soldier was just three hundred metres from the long eight-foot-high gate that formed the border post. Ordinarily, after a driver and passengers had completed their exit formalities in the drab, shabby building on the left, the gate was opened and they drove through the thirty or so yards to the Guatemalan immigration post to begin entry formalities on the other side. At this hour of the night things were quiet. Some trucks were parked on the Belize side and a few people ambled about, but there was little activity, although the border was officially open twenty-four hours a day.

A lone guard sat on a chair outside his sentry box, bored and scuffing the ground with the edge of his boot. The SAS man lifted his binoculars and looked across at him. There would be another one with a corporal inside the building, he knew. It began to rain again, heavily, thunder rumbling through the sky, the lights picking out the raindrops as they fell. The guard outside rose languidly and picking up the chair, carried it inside the sentry box, disappearing from sight.

Then almost without drama it began. A small group of men appeared from the left, two stopping at the sentry box, four running across the road into the offices where the other two guards were.

Gotcha, you fuckers, the watching soldier thought, swinging his glasses back to the sentry box in time to see the guard there step out with his hands up, two weapons trained on him. A second group of men came from the shadows on the left, one of them wielding bolt-cutters, and within moments they were at the latch that locked the gate. An old American M-8 armoured recce vehicle suddenly appeared from the other side, but the driver didn't wait for the gate to be swung back for him. The men with the bolt-cutters jumped clear and the M-8 just kept rolling, hitting the gate; its tubular frame buckled for a moment, then it sprang open as the latch gave. Another shape loomed up behind it, this one a main armoured piece, a tank. The SAS man recognized it as an M-41 A3, an American-designed medium tank, and it rolled into Belize like an ancient monster. They were in, and not a shot had been fired. Here we fucking go, he thought. It's showtime.

He mounted the bike, kicked it into life and with the engine running, he took out the small transmitter, lifted the cover and hit the send button.

At Airport Camp, at the forward operating base in the old church hall and in the team vehicles small receivers all emitted simultaneously a high-pitched bleeping sound. At the camp one of the signallers reached across to let the Para major out on the eastern perimeter know that it had started, while the other flashed a pre-coded message back to Hereford. That done he raised Major Chard, just to make sure that his receiver had worked.

In Chard's vehicle the receiver, sitting on the dashboard, began its shrill signal. The driver, a mobility troop man, reached over and turned it off.

'That's just fucking wonderful.'

'Why?' Chard asked.

'I've got tickets for a show in Bristol on Tuesday night.'

One of the pair in the back, a signaller, laughed softly. The other man pulled out two pins and kicked the back door off its hinges and down on to the muddy ground. Three nuts followed and he stood and lifted the lightweight aluminium roof section and dropped it over the side. He now had a clear field of fire for the Milan.

Chard looked down at his watch. It was 2103 exactly. The border was three miles away. With nothing in their way they could be here in eight or nine minutes, but he had his first two teams in Benque, both Milan-equipped, and the flatbed with the pair of mortars mounted on the back. That would slow them. Then fall back here to the junction. He hoped it would be enough. Most modern armies trained against this sort of tactic and could manage their way out of or around the problem quickly and efficiently. But the Guatemalans, while looking like a conventional army, were in fact largely set up and trained for COIN operations, counter-insurgency, a fundamentally different proposition. These troops facing his men were used to chasing small bands of guerrillas, not being attacked – certainly not by professional soldiers.

He reached back for a handset and as it was passed to him the radio crackled into life. Airport Camp had received the signal, and asked him to confirm they had too. He did so, then began to contact his people.

In Benque the men crewing the three vehicles were ready. Halfway through the town the road dropped into a long gentle dip alongside the football ground. At the far end in the cover of some roadside buildings the first Land-Rover was set and waiting. Three hundred yards past it was the flatbed with the two mortar tubes, and round to their left, the second Wolf waited. Its firing position would put in a missile at forty-five degrees to the first and confuse any return fire long enough to have the first mortar rounds dropping among them.

The motorcyclist roared over the rise, flashed his headlights twice, then overtook two civilian vehicles that were meandering along and turned to the right, crossing the football pitch, before stopping on the far side, now to the right of the Wolf on the road. The Milan crews would be too busy to do much else, so his job would be to spot for the mortar crew, correct their fire so they were dropping rounds directly on to the road, at the brow of the hill, a bottleneck, and then fall back. They were a few minutes behind him.

Ten miles away at the bridge at San Ignacio Lieutenant Estelle, who had been given a receiver by Major Chard, immediately called the other platoon commander, the CSM and the two platoon sergeants together and advised them that the incursion had begun. As he was speaking lightning forked across the sky and a peal of thunder rolled overhead, ominously.

At Belize international airport Major Fox saw the same lightning and smiled bleakly. The gods of the weather were on their side tonight – there would be no parachute entry through this lot. A major electrical storm would keep most aircraft on the ground; any already in the air would stay well away. He looked back to where one of Brock's pioneers was in the cab of a JCB, digging long narrow trenches. The machine had been purloined from the construction site at the far end of the terminal building. The soft earth was piled up in the right places and now they had some useful defensive positions.

England

At Hereford the coded flash was decrypted by the machine, the message coming up on the screen in plaintext.

'Belize! It's on!' the signaller snapped. 'Get this over to the boss.' He ripped the page from the printer and following standard operating procedures, he hit the forward button and sent the message straight on to PJHQ Northwood, with a top-urgent prefix.

At Northwood they were waiting for it; hoping it wouldn't happen, but waiting nevertheless. They would react to instructions from Whitehall that came down the chain of command, and once the go was received, work to the instructions of the Chief of Joint Operations. Below him was his Chief of Staff with service or functional deputies who would be sleeves rolled up and hands-on. Drawing together would be the Assistant Chief of Staff, the ACOS, J2, Intelligence, ACOS J3, Operations, and the linchpin, Chief of Joint Rapid Deployment Force Operations, CJRDFO. If the situation required specialist skills or equipment, armour, uplift, air defence, the ACOS J3, who had direct lines into the three services, would provide it.

In Whitehall at the MoD, although it was four in the morning, the C3 group earlier gathered in committee room three were recalled. Some had not gone home, but opted rather to stay in central London at a club that offered the MoD preferential rates, in this case the RAF Club on Piccadilly. A car was sent to collect them. The defence secretary, and the FCO man James Hildon, still in his office awaiting the arrival of the Guatemalan ambassador, were advised, as was the Prime Minister.

Chief of the Defence Staff was telephoned at home, and in sequence so were his immediate senior staff officers, the Chief of the Naval Staff and First Sea Lord, Chief of the General Staff, and Chief of the Air Staff. None of the three would have direct involvement as this was not General War, but the development had implications for all three fighting arms and as the heads of the services they were to be appraised on a prioritized basis of any development that might require their services' involvement. PJHQ Northwood had dropped into its second role, the direction of strategic and tactical response. The earlier orders had been timely and fortuitous. The RAF, already putting together the offensive support detachment, moved the pace up and began to cut corners. The admin could wait.

ACOS J3 Sea, the Royal Navy's senior hands-on man at Northwood was in first and without waiting for his colleagues, he obtained permission from the Chief of Staff over the telephone and sent a message to HMS *Beaufort*, now seventy miles from Belize and powering her way westward. She was advised of the invasion and ordered to proceed at maximum speed to be able to deploy her weapons systems to seek out and if necessary engage any Guatemalan naval or invasion forces in the theatre. In particular her role would be to defend Belize City and the international airport against an attack from the sea.

HMS Beaufort

Her captain read the message, called for increased revolutions, and picked up the main broadcast system microphone. Just seventy miles from Belize, they were in range of many modern weapons, and certainly able to deploy their own from this distance. The waters they were in had just become hostile.

'Do you hear there, this is the captain. Assume condition Zulu. Assume condition Zulu. XO and navigator to the bridge. XO and navigator to the bridge. Starboard watch will close up. I say again, starboard watch will close up. WEO and helo crew to the bridge immediately. Aviation ops special duty seamen close up in the hangar immediately. All officers to the bridge in five minutes. The ship will go to action stations. This is not a drill. This is not a drill. I shall brief you all in fifteen minutes.' The captain replaced the microphone. 'Sound action stations, please.'

'Aye aye, sir, sound action stations.'

The Lynx was ready and had been most of the day; all she would need was her stores loaded. As the klaxon began to sound and people ran for their stations, the crew of the helicopter, both in the wardroom watching a video, rose together. The senior of the two, the observer, a lieutenant commander, looked at the pilot who grimaced slightly. 'Don't like the weather much,' he said.

On the bridge Commander Bennett was thinking fast. They had received an intelligence summary suggesting that Guatemala's only blue-water ship was unserviceable. The old US *Broadsword*-class ship was only a hundred feet long but mounted a 75 millimetre gun and could be racked out to carry anti-ship missiles. If she was out of the picture then they were down to fast patrol craft, which weren't up to much in open water – but close to the shore with a good brave skipper, they could be lethal. If the Guatemalans were going to mount an attack from the sea, then it would be merchantmen as troop carriers with patrol craft as escort.

'Someone get me *Jane's*. Let's see what these people can float.'

'Yes sir,' replied the yeoman as he darted back into the navigator's station for the book.

'Ops, Captain.'

'Captain, Ops.'

'Anything on the screens?'

'Yes, Captain. One contact heading north, bearing red one zero. Thirty miles off. She will cross our track in the next hour or so. One large contact off Belize City. That one is stationary. Then two clusters, one to the south of the city and one to the north.'

'Right. I'm coming down. Passive only please. Let's not let anyone know we are here just yet.'

Milan 2 is a second-generation anti-tank weapon. The original Milan, the Mark 1, had a three-hundred metre minimum range, but the 2 had a minimum of twenty-five metres, almost point-blank. Not that anyone would want to fire an anti-tank missile with three and a half pounds of high explosive to detonate that close. That capability was, the SAS men knew, most effective when this weapon was used as a remote mine. So they would engage at a tactically sound distance, when the lead vehicle was seventy yards away. Letting it get that close would mean that there would also be between ten and twelve visible behind it. The second team would take out the rear vehicle, bottling up the others with nowhere to go, and the mortars would do the rest, while the Wolfs withdrew.

Sergeant McKay, with his original air troop team and a mobility troop driver, was in the second Wolf. He was in the commander's seat, Dozy Tupping was in the back with Boyce on the Milan and Gibbo was on the GPMG mounted on the roll frame. It was high enough that he could fire over the heads of the Milan team, but that wouldn't be necessary because the vehicle was side on and parked behind a low breeze-block wall. The boys were tired. After a ten-day patrol sleeping in hammocks and three nights sitting on the ground, and then no sleep at all last night it seemed an age since they had last rested properly. Like many professional soldiers they had taught themselves to grab sleep when they could and over the last hour they had managed to snatch a few minutes here and there. Dozy was the master – he could sleep anywhere.

McKay saw the motorcyclist cross the football field and sat up and stretched. An absolute professional, he checked the drum on the Mk 19 grenade launcher mounted in front of him. They wouldn't use it here, it was an area defence weapon that could drop grenades over a thousand yards away; this was too close and there were too many civilians in homes in the town. But the moment they were on the road the weapon would come into its own – this was his responsibility and the check was made.

He turned to the driver. 'Start up.' The engine caught immediately. 'Dozy, Boycey, you ready?' Dozy opened his eyes and nodded. 'Stand to then, lads.'

Belize International Airport

Lieutenant Murray, the Royal Marines officer, was positioned in the bush on the airport side of the intersection. Out ahead was a lone Belizean soldier, a sergeant, who had volunteered to go forward to where the road down towards the mangroves and the waterfront petered out. He had 'borrowed' a pickup truck from the airport car park; Garvey had been pleased when the fellow displayed signs of a misspent youth and hot-wired the ignition. The road heading down to the beach wasn't up to much, not even appearing on the map. It was just a few hundred yards of track lined by houses, but given the hard going either side of it, anyone but the most disciplined troops expecting to encounter resistance would use it.

Murray had his men either side of the two-lane blacktop that came left off the highway leading to the airport, directly opposite the track down to the sea. With a GPMG and two light section weapons they were well armed for a small detachment, but he wished he had a couple of Claymore mines. His men were hidden, not only from any attacking force, but also from the traffic on the highway. An old chicken bus loaded with baggage and people chugged past, fumes belching from its exhausts. A heavy lorry came the other way, followed by two or three cars. This was the main road from Corozal and Orange Walk through to Belize City and access from there south to Dangriga or where they had come from, Punta Gorda, or to the west, the highlands and the border. There would be traffic twenty-four hours a day, and tactically this was a worry. If an attack became a reality, then the traffic on the road would be driving right through the first contact, with all the risks to civilians that that entailed. Murray shook off the problem – this was the critical point, the first defensive line.

Milan is a tank-killer. The missile flies at 742 kilometres an hour and can hit a target two kilometres away in just over twelve seconds, punching through 350mm of armour, its 1.76 kilogram high-explosive warhead detonating inside the vehicle, turning the interior into a superheated inferno. In a few milliseconds the ammunition inside the tank will explode, with enough energy to blast the heavy turret into the air. Nothing will survive – the occupants will be smeared over the inside walls and then turned into charred ash. There are military experts who see Milan and its generation of anti-tank weapons as the final Nemesis of the traditional main battle tank. Chadian irregulars with Milan mounted on twelve Toyota pickups accounted for over sixty Russian-built Libyan T-55s and T-62s as early as 1987.

Smart tanks with stealth surfaces and anti-missile blast screens were, for most armies, a generation away. Certainly the Guatemalans had nothing that would hinder the missiles' effectiveness, so as the first armoured vehicle came over the rise and Dozy Tupping settled in behind the sight he knew it was as good as dead. He counted, waiting for it to reach the dip, his eyes flicking back to the sight so he could target the last armoured vehicle in view and close the escape route. Visibility was not great with the driving rain, but it was good enough. There were soft skins, trucks with soldiers, a four-wheel-drive command vehicle, its radio antennae whipping in the wind and rain. He knew Gibbo would be sighting the command vehicle with the GPMG. Two tanks now visible, an armoured personnel carrier on the rise, another tank rumbling over; they were careless, too close to each other, cocky and over-confident. Whoever was running this was not a student of tactics; they were bunching up, breaking the most elementary rules.

A flare of light to his right – first missile away.

'Hit it!' McKay snapped.

Tupping sighted and pressed the trigger. There was a blast and a whoosh as the missile seared away from the post but he remained lying down, holding the target vehicle in the sight; the missile, guided by wire, would hit whatever was in the centre of the sighting reticle. There was a massive blast and a flash lit the night but he ignored it. Beside him Boycey was reloading. His missile hit, and the tank shuddered and in the next half-second exploded like something on a movie set, the turret thrown into the air as a white flash blazed outward. There were more explosions as ammunition began to go off, shaking the ground and leaves on the trees. There was another blast to his right.

'Ready! Tank one hundred metres to the right.'

He swung the launcher, found the target. Its turret was traversing towards them. He fired. Overhead the GPMG opened up as Gibbo poured rounds into the four-wheel-drive command vehicle. The Milan hit and immediately McKay shouted 'Let's go' to the driver and they were moving, Gibbo turning his weapon on the soft skins as they rolled away. As they took the bend, the Land-Rover accelerating, the mortar rounds began to fall, first on the lead elements of the column that had already been hit, then, once the angle was right, they 'walked' down the straight road out of sight over the hill, into the vehicles that were full of panicked troops, reversing and crashing into each other, looking for a way out of the killing ground.

The attack had been swift – the SAS teams were rolling within fifty seconds – and it had been brutally efficient. Front and rear vehicles destroyed, both tanks, another tank knocked out with an M-113 armoured personnel carrier, the command vehicle raked with fire, its occupants dead or wounded and many, many wounded in the attack on the soft-skinned troop-carrying trucks by the GPMG. That was Gibbo's intention, to take out the officers and then to wound, not to kill. Every wounded man absorbed the efforts of seven others to deal with his injuries. One focused attack on a company-size force that killed or incapacitated its officers and then inflicted serious injuries on ten per cent of its strength would take it out of the fight until it managed to reorganize and regroup. Nothing hit morale like an attack from nowhere, without warning, that left you stunned, knowing that your officers were dead and your comrades screaming in pain, some of them dying.

It was brutal in the extreme. It was warfare.

Belize City

Dion, working through the diners at the Fort Street Guest House, had just stopped at a table when all hell broke loose. There was a nasty flat crack, then another, and then gunfire, automatic weapons, very close. There were thumps on the wall, and windows in the dining room shattered as people came running in screaming from the veranda on the Fort Street side. The barracks – someone has gone crazy with a gun at the barracks, he thought.

'On the floor!' he shouted. 'Get down.' There was more shooting, sustained now, from a heavier gun of some kind. People were dropping to the floor, screaming, crying. A woman, an American with greying hair, staggered in from the veranda, her hand to her neck, a glazed look in her eyes, blood pulsing from a neck wound. She fell forward.

'Everyone this side. Move this way!' Dion shouted. 'Stay down!' A waitress, a pretty girl called Caprice, was down on the floor in a pool of blood by the door to the veranda. She was twitching, the nerves' reflex action. Dion had hunted enough to know it – the death throes. Jesus no, please. No. He crawled forward towards her, pulling terrified people out of his way. There was a blast, a flash of light, more glass blowing in. Not the barracks, he thought, the Maritime Wing. An American man was wedged in, his back to the concrete wall below the windows. He still had a cigarette in his fingers, and seemed calm, stoical even, but it was the dulling effect of alcohol and he was sobering up, fast.

'Dion?' a voice called over the screaming. He looked over. It was Dave, at the head of the stairs up from his flat. 'Douse the lights and move 'em this way.'

Shouting came from the street, yells, more shots, closer now; footsteps running on the path, a burst of firing, a cry. Dion turned. A figure came up the stairs, a soldier, panting, bleeding from somewhere, wet, dripping, his eyes wild. He turned, two shots snapped off from somewhere and he fell backwards. Another figure mounted the stairs, a white man, armed. His eyes swept the room in a second, his weapon trained on the man who had fallen.

'Any more?' he shouted. No one spoke, but there were sobs and moans and one woman continued screaming.

'QUIET!' The room fell silent. 'Was there only this one?'

'Yeah,' Dion replied. He recognized the man, had seen him training the B Coy lads. British army, he realized. He normally saw him wearing shorts and a T-shirt running with the men, but now he was in full kit. The soldier moved forward and kicked the gun from the downed man's hands.

'Sar' Morris!' he shouted. An excited call came from the dark in acknowledgement. 'Secure your area!' He looked round the room, lowering his weapon. 'Someone call for ambulances. How many hurt?'

'What the fuck's going on?' Dave bellowed, crossing the room, his bulk imposing.

'We came under attack,' the British soldier explained. He nodded down at the dead man at his feet. 'Guatemalan. There were ten or so of them. We got them all, I think.'

'Guatemalans? Jesus! You sure?'

'We're sure. I have a medic, I'll send him over – but get some ambulances here.' He crossed to where a man was holding his wife. She was moaning, wounded. 'Put your hand there, over the wound. Press down gently. That's it.' His radio crackled and he turned his head to listen and then began to speak into it. Outside there was shouting, cheering, whistles; the B Coy Belize Defence Force men, adrenaline still surging through their bloodstreams, letting off steam after their first contact and first victory. It was important to them – their first engagement with the bully next door and they had won. They were also the first shots fired in anger in Belize by Belizeans since the eighteenth century.

The fast-sobering American who had been under the window stood up. He looked across at Caprice, the waitress with whom he had flirted at breakfast. She lay still. Dead. He looked out on the veranda. There were two others out there, one of them certainly dead. He crossed to where the woman was still holding her neck, blood running down her hands.

'OK, darling, let me help you here. My name is Dave. I was a medic in the Marine Corps. We gonna get you fixed up,' he lied. She was losing it as he spoke. Pale, clammy, shaking softly, going into deep traumatic shock. She died a few moments later in his arms. He released her and ran his hand over her eyes to close them.

'So much for another day in paradise,' he said softly.

The Airport

The confirmation of the incursion at the border had been relayed to Murray by Major Fox and there now seemed no doubt that they could expect an attack on the airfield. It was just a matter of timing. Tactically they should have hit the airport simultaneously, if not in the minutes before the main border invasion. Murray looked at his watch – ten-past-nine.

The marine sergeant tapped Murray's arm and pointed. The traffic was still crisscrossing along the highway in front of them, but the old pickup truck taken by the Belizean soldier was coming back up the track opposite them. It hit a rut and bounced, its engine revving, and then without stopping, risking an appalling accident it crossed straight over the road and screeched to a halt on the blacktop beside them. Murray grimaced. The plan was that he should just flash his lights, not stop, not draw attention to them.

'Dey comin',' he called out of the window, gunned the engine and drove away. Murray lifted his radio.

'Three Alpha, Three Alpha, Mike One.'

'Go Mike One.'

'Three Alpha, Golf, Golf, Golf. I say again Golf, Golf, Golf. Oscar Papa on his way in.'

'Roger that One, be advised maritime division just repelled limited attack.'

Repelled? Jesus. How did fifty local BDF guys with one Hereford hooligan repel an attack so quickly? They fucked up, he thought delightedly, too few men, seen coming in, bad planning, something. He grinned for a moment, taking comfort from the good omen. He clicked the handset once in acknowledgement. They were ready: two section weapons and a GPMG, plenty of ammo and some grenades; four vehicles, enough to let them get away and back over the mile to the airport perimeter, were parked in the trees round a bend in the road.

'Sir,' a corporal said, 'there's a bloke in a hammock over there. Second house along.'

'He'll move,' Murray said with some certainty.

'Lucky bastard. Wish I was in my fucking rack,' someone muttered softly.

Traffic was still moving on the highway; a bus loaded with people rattled past. This is surreal, Murray thought. Garvey had given up two of his blokes, one to go north up the highway a kilometre or so, and the other to go down it the same distance. The moment they heard a contact they were to stop traffic, but for the time being all was as normal. Please, he thought, no more buses, no more people.

'They're here. Enemy dead ahead. Right of the houses,' the sergeant said. 'One hundred metres.'

Murray looked across, lifting his binoculars. There in the half-dark, on the track, a group of armed men were advancing, an officer in front. They were moving quickly, confidently. This was it. There would be more – this was either the lead element, or simply the enemy to the front of their position, with others either side in an extended advance through the bush and houses to the road.

'Got 'em. On your way.'

The sergeant looked at the team beside him. 'Enemy beside the houses to your front, one hundred metres. Wait for the command to fire. Sight your targets, aim low. Conserve your rounds.' The men settled in, looking over sights, their hearts pounding and as another truck rumbled past, the sergeant darted across the road in its cover to command the half-troop on the other side.

'Wait for it,' Murray said. 'Gunner, take the centre group. Corporal Chaffey?'

'Sir?'

'Take the officer. Rest of you take the right.'

The sergeant's section would take the left, their side. The Guatemalans were almost at the road, more men behind them, some staying in cover, others on the track. The officer's radio operator was beside him. Sloppy, very sloppy, Murray found himself thinking, he deserves to get revved.

'Corp Chaffey. Hit him!' he hissed.

The Royal Marines corporal, the best rifle shot in Comacchio group, fired; two rounds, snapped off. The officer's head flicked back and as he was falling the corporal shot his radio operator and the GPMG, the queen of the infantry battle, opened up, cutting into the centre group of men on the road. Everyone was firing now and fire was coming back at them, the Guatemalans having dropped into cover. The shooting continued and a few moments later, just for an instant, the situation became farcical.

'Car!' someone yelled. Everyone ceased firing as the vehicle with its bewildered but heavenly-blessed driver went past and then they all opened up again.

Murray swung his eyes right, then left. For the moment they had halted the advance, but the enemy would be bringing forward more weapons. Rockets perhaps, grenade launchers, something to take out his gun positions. His men could put fire either way on the highway for some two hundred yards to the left and one hundred to the right, but they would be flanked sooner or later. Another minute or so and they would fall back to the next positions, back off the edge of the highway and nearer the airport itself.

Belmopan

The British High Commissioner swung the door back and looked at Leo Scobey. The ITN journalist was back. He had been brief at their first meeting, cagey, saying very little, letting Scobey introduce himself, present his credentials, and he had agreed to an interview that evening, but now the news was in the open anyway, and it was time to use the media to advantage. 'I'm sorry, I will have to postpone our meeting. Something has come up and your presence here is fortuitous,' he said. 'You are the only journalist here that I know of, and there won't be any others for the time being, for reasons I will explain, so I'll give you a quick statement, then ask you to stay out of the way, to cooperate when asked, the usual? All right?'

Scobey nodded, smothering his grin. Something was going down and he was on to it. Being the only broadcast journalist on a breaking worldwide story was something everyone dreamed of, but it was also an awesome responsibility, with no one covering the other angles, feeding the machine, the checks and balances that big stories needed. He had been in this position before: the Sudan, Eritrea, Chad, but others had been there within hours.

'Guatemala has invaded this country. There have been three incursions, the first,' he looked at his watch, 'twenty minutes ago. Great Britain deplores this hostile action and under United Nations resolution . . .'

Ten minutes later Scobey was running for the car and his satellite phone.

The Airport

At the airport turn-off the fire arcing back at them was now intense and thankfully the traffic had stopped. One vehicle had driven into the firefight; the driver had ignored the Belizean soldier's warning and had driven round the line of stationary cars, and he had paid the price for his arrogance and impatience. His car had left the road, hit a pillar under a house and was now on fire, flames licking up into the ground floor. The driver had not emerged.

The marines were pouring fire into the Guatemalans opposite, but it couldn't last long and Murray gave the order for the first team, the GPMG gunner and his oppo, to fall back. The officers on the other side would be trying to work out a way round them. They would be pissed off; their own int would have told them they would have a clear approach to the airport, little or no resistance – not this. Not only was the element of surprise gone, but they had hit a well-prepared

170

defensive position with machine guns and they were still a mile from their objective.

A rocket-propelled grenade of some sort blasted overhead and exploded in the trees behind Murray's men.

'Fuck me!' someone snapped.

'Anyone see where it came from?' Murray asked.

'The centre right. Under the pink house,' a marine answered. 'There he is . . .'

'Hit 'em!' snapped Murray. Four or five rifles opened up and the Guatemalan, who had ducked back, died as the bullets ripped through the planking wall like it was tissue paper.

'Well done. Corp'l Chaffey, prepare to move your section.'

Back at the eastern end of the airport perimeter Fox listened to the engagement. His men were in their positions, four of them back some way with the pair of mortars, Belize's only two that Corporal Garvey had arrived with. The light mortars, the two 51 mills that were C Coy's were also back there, fifty yards to the side in their own pit. He looked across. A section of his men were in the concrete sangar on the road, built for just this eventuality. It could cover the approach, its thick walls protecting the men inside from anything but an anti-tank weapon. The section would fight from sandbagged firing points along the top wall; up there a GPMG would have a two hundred and sixty degree firing arc, from well up the road almost to the airport terminal, round to the approaching enemy, and nearly to the eastern fence of Airport Camp. They wouldn't need that arc, there were other guns, but Fox had been pleased to see the sangar. It would be the southern flank, and crucial because that was the only road in.

C Coy was under strength in officers – with two platoons up at San Ignacio, apart from Captain Brock, with his section of assault pioneers, Major Fox was it. Like every regiment his was short of officers and since coming into 2 Para with his company he had been one platoon commander short. The other was on a course at Shrivenham. He had elected to send both his platoons with commanders to support Chard, knowing there would be just the two of them, and relying on the calibre of the two platoon sergeants. Murray, the Royal

Marines officer, would make a welcome addition to the strength, even without his detachment, and Garvey, the SAS corporal, would, he knew, be worth any junior officer he might have been lucky enough to have had. His thoughts were interrupted by a blast, then a second off to the left. He looked across; mortars, he thought, bloody mortars, big ones, 81 millimetre. A third landed, this one inside the lines of Airport Camp. A fourth came in on the same spot. They had ranged, they had a spotter, someone who could see the fall of the bombs. That meant they had either rushed an observer party forward through the bush down there, or worse, swung their advance line round with Murray's defence at the cross-roads as the southern pivot. If this was so then a force would just swing across to secure their left flank and in so doing make the road and cut the marines' withdrawal. He had to assume the worst case. He scooped the handset from his radio operator's chest-clip.

'Mike One, Mike One. Three Alpha.'

'Go, Alpha.'

'Mike One, suggest you retire forthwith. We have mortars incoming and believe they might have moved up to the left of your position. Your egress route is now under threat, over.'

'Aah, roger that, Alpha.'

Shit! Shit! Shit! Murray thought quickly. The longer they held the road the better, but if the Guats had moved forward and crossed further up, then getting cut off was a real risk and to let that happen with fully twenty-five per cent of the proper 'strength' was stupid in the extreme.

'Right, gentlemen, we are withdrawing,' he called calmly. 'As we planned it. Corporal Chaffey, your team first, on your way. Gun team, prepare to go. Smoke on my call.'

The smoke was also the signal for the sergeant's team across the road. The wind was perfect, coming off the sea, but gently, shifting and billowing round the trees and houses on the other side.

'Go smoke.'

Three men laid down heavy fire and a fourth marine threw two canisters off and to their right, grinning as they hit where he intended them to go. The wind would blow the smoke down across their front and for about thirty seconds or maybe a minute no one would see jack shit.

The marines began to move, running back towards where they had left the cars, leapfrogging each other, one team always facing backward, firing into the smoke to discourage any enemy advance. The Guatemalans fired back, long raking bursts through the smoke, partly out of frustration, fire discipline having broken down, and partly in case the smoke was to cover a counter-attack. In the billowing confusion, the smoke and the dark, one Guatemalan marine managed to shoot his comrade, and another with a lucky burst hit one of the British soldiers withdrawing seventy yards away, his 5.56 bullet hitting the marine's water-bottle clip and deflecting downward and inward. It entered the skin, travelled down five inches through the bulk of the muscle at the top of his thigh and exited six inches below his groin at the front. He was lucky. The wound was not life-threatening and he was scooped up by his comrades and carried bodily to the vehicles. In the cars he called out for someone to look at it.

'Wait till we're there,' someone replied. 'Two minutes.'

He was struggling with his belt-kit, trying to get to the wound. 'No, now. Someone look now,' he pleaded, the pain starting, coming in waves. 'Jesus, they shot me. The cunts shot me.'

The sergeant, in the back seat with him and one other, suddenly understood the marine's concern, a very masculine one at that. He took out his knife and slit the buttons away, pulling the man's trousers down. He flicked on his torch and wiped away blood with his face veil. The sergeant looked up quickly as a car raced past them from the airport, then back to what he was doing.

'Flesh wound, upper thigh. You'll be OK.'

'Sure, Sarge? Sure? You –'

'I'm sure, you'll be fine. Your tackle is intact. Missed it by miles.'

'Sure?' the marine asked, feeling better. It hurt like hell, but if his dick was OK then the rest could sort itself out. But was it? 'Sure, Sarge?' he asked again.

'Course I'm fucking sure!' He grabbed the marine's shell

dressing from his belt-kit and ripping the cover off he pressed it on to the exit wound. 'Here. Press down on this and stop fucking whingeing.'

The vehicles drew to a halt and they parked them as planned, broadside on across the road twenty feet up from the sangar, forming a roadblock. Two blokes carried out the casualty and they crossed the wire at the sangar, the mortar bombs still falling in Airport Camp. The first British fatality that night was technically a non-combatant. A warrant officer in charge of the army's flying corps engineers maintaining the Gazelles, he was running from his billet in the camp back towards the hangar, where he knew there was a trench that dated back to the eighties, when the fifth mortar bomb exploded against the hangar wall. It went off fifteen feet to his front as it struck the concrete foundation for the structure's external framework. The right angle of concrete formed a hard surface deflecting the energy outward, and the blast tore him to pieces.

Thirty feet behind him, one of his engineers took shrapnel in a series of wounds which left him lying under one of the palm trees that dotted the camp. He wasn't aware of much for the remaining minutes of his life, certainly not of the fluid dripping down on to his head and face from above. Up in the fronds of the tree were various parts of the warrant officer, the largest being a piece of his torso, heart and one lung still in place, dripping blood on to the whitewashed base of the tree and the young man dying there.

At the airport terminal bewildered workers and night staff, who had come to the windows or out on to the pan to see what was happening, realized that the airport was being attacked and could guess who was responsible. Some hid, some ran for the bush; two tried to drive out of it, passing the cars carrying the Royal Marines back in and dying when they drove into a hail of gunfire at the intersection with the highway.

The SAS team on the flatbed were sitting just over a rise where they could see their bombs fall a mile back down the road. Their mortars, 81 millimetres, had a much longer range and to drop them this short meant the barrels were virtually pointing straight up. The bombs would be aimed at the ground just this side of the turn-off. The explosive charges dug into the ground earlier, with the addition of their real mortar bombs, would give the enemy the impression that they were under fire from at least a battalion mortar battery, six tubes, and that in turn would suggest that the battalion itself was waiting to engage as soon as they were in range. This deception would be supported by the two Milan-equipped Land-Rovers; although only one of them had a sophisticated thermal imaging night-sight, it would be enough. The enemy, unable to advance into the prepared 'battalion front', would be forced off the main road. The only place to go was down the road to the right, the road to Negroman.

One of the men was watching through a pair of binoculars, looking for the signal from the lone mobility trooper out there on the motorcycle. He would flash his lights at them once, douse them, and make his escape in the dark. They would then begin dropping rounds behind him, and one of the Land-Rover teams nearer the turn-off would hit the first Shrike pad. The pad was connected to the explosives with electric detonator cord and each of the three buttons would set off three blasts a thirtieth of a second apart. There were four pads, ready and connected, in a plastic bag as protection from the rain. A light flashed weakly three times through the murk.

'Got it. Fire!'

The first mortar bomb was dropped down the tube and was blasted out with the weapon's distinctive 'whump'. The second tube let go and they dropped into a rhythm, one man passing the bomb to the other who dropped it down the barrel and bent down, covering his ears. As it fired he came up, took the next bomb and repeated the manoeuvre. A fifth man, between the two tubes, cranked a small wheel in tiny increments, altering the elevation, 'walking' the barrage forward.

A good mortar team could have five or six bombs in the air before the first hit the ground and these men, with two tubes, had eleven bombs on the way when the first landed eighty yards in front of the advancing column fifteen feet to the right of the highway and exploded. One of the Land-Rover teams, hidden in some bush just over a rise, was acting as the MFC, the mortar fire controller, calling back to the flatbed and directing their fire.

'Left twenty, left twenty, left twenty. Forward fifty, forward fifty, forward fifty.' Each instruction was given three times to ensure that it would be heard by the man sitting between the tubes, with earphones on his head and a radio between his knees.

The night was split by the bright white-orange flashes and concussion waves, followed by the sound of the blast a second or so later. Armour would have closed up and anyone trying to drive through the barrage in a soft-skinned vehicle would be risking almost certain injury and possible death. The Land-Rover with the thermal sight on its Milan found the leading armoured vehicle. There was some difficulty because the sight was flaring each time a mortar hit, but the soldier managed to get a fix and fired. The missile hit the armoured personnel carrier fifty yards past the turn-off, the vehicle grinding to a halt, smoke billowing from its hatches, effectively blocking the road. There was now no going forward for the column. They had to get out of the mortar barrage and the only way out was down the road to the right.

'I don't fucking believe it. They fell for it,' the driver of the command vehicle muttered. He was amazed – for him, a professional soldier, it had 'channel' written all over it. Chard, sitting beside him, nodded grimly; that was training, or rather the lack of it. People did amazingly stupid things under pressure, and officers trained for COIN operations, under fire in a 'real' engagement for the first time, could be almost guaranteed to miss the obvious and make a wrong decision.

Another Milan launched from the back of the Wolf concealed forty yards along the rise, and Chard and his three colleagues watched its deadly flight, its rocket motor spewing out a white-orange trail behind it, like a huge firework. Chard counted; seven, eight, nine, and it hit.

Belize International Airport

Corporal Garvey had done the Regiment's medic's course and took over the treatment of the Royal Marine with the gunshot wound. It was elementary stuff, and Garvey, who had spent four months in the A&E unit of a major Birmingham hospital, being taught to manage trauma, had the man stabilized very quickly. The wound dressed, a saline drip taking care of fluid loss and a syrette of morphine doing its job, the marine was sitting up smoking a cigarette, in the shelter of a waist-high pre-formed concrete bollard fifty yards back from the men who were dug in.

The mortars were still falling on the camp half a mile behind them and to the right. The two officers, one airborne and one marine, watched the bombardment come in. Neither man said much; as long as the Guatemalans thought that was where any resistance would come from and pounded it, they would have respite. Murray turned to face his front and then looked across at Major Fox. He had briefed the airborne officer on what he had established, the calibre of the attacking force, the quality of their front-line officers and leadership and now there was nothing to do but wait for the main attack.

Major Fox had shown them where he wanted them. With thick low cloud masking any moon, it was dark, very dark, and rain was falling. That would work in the attackers' favour. The site was a bitch – once outside the sandbagged foxholes and short trenches, there had been no cover for thirty yards until a wide but open storm ditch which was a foot deep in flowing rainwater, but Brock's pioneers, the nearest thing to assault engineers the battalion could muster, had been busy and used their initiative. From the rear of the position to the

177

right they had moved forward baggage trailers, the kind towed out to the aircraft by small tractors, and these were now tipped up on their sides, with earth, rocks and bits of concrete piled up on the forward side. At this centre point the rear had been dug out; this would be the company command area and aid post. A shallow trench, just deep enough to crawl down, but complete with zig-zag, ran back from the forward positions. Murray was impressed. 'Got any illumination rounds, sir?' he asked, looking at Fox.

Fox shook his head. 'No. Just a few flares. We have rigged some on to trip-wires out there at two hundred yards, and we have paced out and marked at one hundred.' Murray looked out again. His marines were consolidated at two points behind the line, there to support any breach in the Gurkha's defences. With thirty metres between their holes their positions were too widely spaced; you could drive a motorway through them, he thought. But they had no choice; they would have to rely on interlocking fields of fire to control the ground between the holes.

But this would only last so long. Once the Guatemalans had tested the defensive line here they would shift round, probe for a weaker point. The defenders could only cover so much ground and the enemy could come in through the camp, or approach and attack from the western end of the airport. Out there were just the Belize Defence Force people, ten or so, to raise the alarm, Garvey with them, and Murray knew his marines would have to support any breach, or meet an attack from the rear. Somewhere back there Murray could hear the JCB working, Brock's people still hard at it. They had built pipe bombs too, Fox had said, and cobbled together massive anti-personnel mines filled with C5 and hundreds of pounds of shrapnel that could cut a swath through anything.

A flare burst down on the right. Figures were caught in the glare, some dropping to their knees, looking round for their officer, some breaking into a run, going for cover. 'Now we earn our money,' Fox growled.

As he did so his section nearest that point opened fire, as did the machine gun in the sangar, the bullets cutting into the attackers, their bodies pirouetting, jerking as the murderous fire tore into them. There were screams, and fire was returned now from other points along the eastern perimeter, tracer rounds from an automatic gun off to the left, bright green and orange in the darkness.

Fox flicked on his tiny red-filtered torch, looked at a grid system he had worked out and mapped on a piece of paper, and picked up the radio handset. 'Three-Four, Three-Four. Three Alpha actual. Commence firing position Delta, position Delta.'

One hundred yards back, his three-man mortar team began dropping bombs into the tubes, to lay down a barrage in the bush between the perimeter fence and the road. The first bomb landed three or four hundred yards off into the bush – it was difficult to tell in the dark – but dead centre of the area behind where the fire was coming from.

'Back one hundred.'

HMS *Beaufort*'s Lynx was on the deck, her engines running, the rotors turning. She had been loaded with her max weight of ordnance, four lightweight Sea Skua anti-ship missiles in the racks, two either side.

Int was pouring through on secure comms into the main communications office from Northwood. The three SAS signallers still at Airport Camp had shifted their equipment into an old bunker, a dugout that dated back to the tense days in the seventies. With mortar rounds coming in they were safe from anything but a direct hit and so sat back and did what they did best, what they were trained for, the absolutely critical task of keeping the communications open. British army tactical communications comprises up-links and down-links; normally the up-link began with platoon, communicating with company, up to battalion, to brigade, to division, to corps and onwards. This was slightly different; short, punchy, very direct. The messages that began in the Squadron vehicles and with the split parachute company positions came up the link through them, and direct to command at Hereford and Northwood. From there they could be turned round for virtually anywhere, so HMS *Beaufort*'s captain knew that the

179

Guatemalans had crossed the border, that the airport attack had begun and that heavy mortar fire was coming in. He could see a cluster of vessels, five of them off the coast near the airport and knew that that must be the invasion fleet, albeit small. He was still on the bridge. Bennett disliked being down in the gloom of the ops room, his battle station, and so would remain on the bridge until they had to fight.

'I want to offer NGS. Pilot, how close can you get me?' Bennett asked. Naval gunfire support was one of the roles they trained for, using the Vickers rapid-firing 4.5 inch automatic gun to pound enemy positions that threatened friendly troops ashore. In effect artillery support, but from the deck of a ship. The gun had a range of ten miles.

'Captain, Ops.' Bennett was still on the bridge when the call came through.

'Ops, Captain. Go.'

'Sir, helo is ready to launch.'

'Right, ship coming into wind now,' Bennett replied. 'Officer of the watch, bring her head into wind.'

'Captain,' the navigator said, 'there are no depth markings on the charts in that close. The main channel is marked, but up there? If you want us close enough for NGS, we will be inside the barrier reef. It could be any depth, from a few inches over a coral head, to thirty feet.'

'See how close you can get me without going aground.' The navigator nodded. That meant going into the area where the contacts were. Even in the main channel they would be between the two clusters, the one off the airport and the one approaching from the south up the coast. Inside the reef, they would be in shallow water, with the potential of enemy both sides.

'Sir, I must caution on the depth again. We will have no room for manoeuvre.'

'Noted,' Bennett replied.

'Head's into wind, sir,' from the officer of the watch.

'Very well,' Bennett replied. He was wearing a mobile comms set and pressed the microphone switch on his belt. 'Ops, Captain.'

'Captain, Ops,' his operations officer came back.

'Ship is into wind. Launch helo.'

Down in the ops room, the officer, number three on the ship, was uncomfortable. They were in an almost stealth mode, using only the most basic of their radars, equipment which would appear to anyone being illuminated as little more than the sweep of a commercial rig, the kind on any merchant ship. The big powerful area defence and search systems were passive, the captain unwilling to broadcast their presence. In addition, the ship's stealth design gave her a radar signature the same as a fishing boat, so anyone seeing her on a radar screen would not know her for what she was. But without her big area radar 'eyes' she was also very myopic, and he didn't like that. Covers were off the point defence 30 mills and gunners were closed up; the Harpoon and Sea Wolf systems were humming, the main gun's feed ring was loaded. He knew the Guatemalans had nothing of any size on the east coast, but fast patrol boats with missiles could be a problem for the arrogant, and he was ready to power up the main defensive and targeting radar systems, designate targets, and launch any of the ship's formidable weapons in under ten seconds. He looked back down over a rating's shoulder and found some comfort; the moment a threat appeared they were ready.

On the aft deck the Lynx's rotors increased speed and pitch, she rose into the air and gently slipped sideways. Dropping her nose and gathering speed, she moved off into the night, collision beacons off, showing no lights, her P1 and observer wearing night-vision goggles. Her systems were damped down, offering no signature with active radar, making ELINT eavesdropping as difficult as they could. She flew in at 'wave-top' height, just over thirty feet above the water, her pilot concentrating intently on the task, flying a bearing from the international airport's still-active approach system, the broken water helping to give him some perspective. At this height they could close on the cluster of vessels below their radar height, approaching from the sea almost hiding behind the mangroves as they neared the coast.

The first Guatemalan vehicles in the column breaking off the killing ground on the main highway east were now three miles in on the unmade track to Negroman. The graded surface was now rutted, narrower, and muddy, the heavy vehicles having broken through the compacted top layer and churned up the soil beneath. Another half an hour and it would be a driver's nightmare and the rain was still falling.

Three vehicles back from the front a colonel was priding himself on his smart thinking. The lead elements through the border, the coveted role that would be covered in glory in tomorrow's Guatemala City papers, had been pulverized into a series of smoking wrecks in two ambushes and he was now very pleased that his battalion hadn't been given that job. The arrogant bastard who had seen himself as the all-conquering hero and had begged for the lead position was now dead like many of his men. The colonel flicked on his torch again, looking down at the map on his knees. It was good quality, British, from their Ordnance Survey and showed the road leading round in a curve to the south before crossing the river to end up back on the highway. Well, it didn't show a crossing, but that didn't mean there wasn't one. Would the British show everything on their maps? No, no one did; even the Guatemalans were nervous about showing every bridge and crossing. There would be a crossing – why have a road to one side and a road from the other if there was no ford or bridge to join them? In a classic denial of the indicators he did what many have done, ignored the intelligence and believed what he wanted to believe. He saw himself leading the column that broke through the resistance on the highway. After all, what else could be in front of them? That was a battalion mortar position, which meant the entire Belize Defence Force must have been lying in wait for them. We will show them, he thought.

But they had been ready. Obviously the British soldiers had helped them, the training team that was always here. But, he rationalized, there were only sixteen of them and they would have been leading the resistance on the road. The main column might be through now, he thought. He might be late, he suddenly realized, actually arrive back on the highway after them.

'Tell the lead vehicle to speed up,' he said to his radio operator.

The answer came back. The lieutenant, young and bright, who had listened to their Israeli instructors during training and commanded the light tank at the front of the column challenged the radio operator, saying he was wary of an ambush or mines and he was moving at the recommended speed for armour to advance through unknown country.

The colonel, who had stopped studying tactics when he made major, took the radio microphone personally and rebuked the lieutenant. Just because he had been in a staff position for the last five years these young ones considered he was out of touch and thought they knew everything. He ordered the second vehicle to take the point at the next widening in the track – that would show him. A minute or so later the vehicle in front of the colonel's increased speed and the gap widened in front of them. He told his driver to do the same. Speed was everything, whether in counter-insurgency operations or real warfare like this.

He knew that once momentum was lost it was difficult to regain and every time they stopped or slowed, they were vulnerable to attack and gave any opposing forces time to regroup. He had moved slowly down jungle roads before and been shot at for his caution. Besides, he wanted to be the first element to break through and if he was back on the highway when the others arrived through San Ignacio then he would lead all the way to Belize City, only two hours away.

Back at the road, the mortaring was continuing but the rate of fire had slowed, and the general in command of the 3rd Brigade had moved forward to find out what the hold-up was. The 2nd Brigade's command vehicle had been hit and their commander, also a one-star, was wounded, bleeding internally from a crush injury to his chest. His number two was dead. The lead element of a battalion with its tank support had been knocked out by fierce resistance and casualties were so high in the dark and the rain that the advance had stalled. The next group had used their initiative and got the hell off the road, but where were they? He looked across. Vehicles were still turning off the highway, following each other like sheep. Command? There was no command.

'Where the fuck are they going?' he snapped at one of his people. 'Find out and bloody stop them.' He looked at his watch. Shit! We should have been through San Ignacio by now. He looked up at the black sky, at the rain, and just then the clouds were brilliantly backlit by lightning. *Bastardo*! We should advance like we planned, he was thinking, up the highway, the old-fashioned way. Blitzkrieg. General Mondragon was youthful, fit, the new-look Guatemalan army. Rightwing, he was from a middle-class family but had done well, moving up the ranks with commitment and professionalism, unlike many of his contemporaries who were more interested in the parades and the uniform than the training and the reality. He was hard, drove his men remorselessly, and cared for little except success. Now they were here, stopped on the highway; the Kaibiles had been held up, and had not taken the bridges at San Ignacio and Roaring Creek – it was up to him to get there before they could be defended. Which idiot at General Command ordered this attack to go ahead without the Kaibiles?

'This is a fuck-up! Get some recovery vehicles up here, have Colonel Morales move up. We are going to make a flank attack on that position, clean it out and move on.'

'Sir, judging by the rate of fire, that is a battalion position. Shouldn't we –'

'Battalion? Battalion?' he yelled. 'There isn't a bloody battalion in this whole shithole country,' he bellowed. 'How can there be one here in front of us?' He pulled some papers from the hands of an aide and looked at them with a torch, studying the order of advance. The 2nd Brigade was here in smoking ruin; next was the 4th. The old adage was true, he realized with a clarity that surprised him. You can plan till you are blue in the face, but the moment the battle starts, the dynamics of chaos render the plans useless.

'Where is the 4th motorized?'

'They turned off, sir,' someone said. The general looked at the speaker. He wasn't one of his, a young corporal; bloody and filthy, his dazed eyes said it all. 'When the bombs were coming. It was lucky the road was there.'

He realized then, and his guts churned for a second. Lucky the road was there – no, not luck: channel. They have been channelled. The tactics were coming from the British advisers, that was sure. They had done this before, galvanized and led local troops, in Oman and on anti-drug operations in the south.

'Stop them! Quickly, get a message to O C –' He stopped and looked at the young corporal. 'Are you sure? Are you sure it was the 4th that drove off the highway first? Think about it, I need to know. Who commands the lead?'

'Yes it was the 4th.' The general tried to remember who commanded them. It wasn't his brigade and he knew few of their cadre, but he remembered it was a recent change, a colonel who moved back to a line battalion from support.

'And who followed? Did you see them?'

'Yes, General, the 9th. The tiger.' The general nodded. The 9th had the panther emblem on their equipment. He knew their battalion commander, who was steady if un-imaginative.

'Get a message to them both,' he snapped to his signals officer. 'They are to stop. Go no further. Tell them to expect an attack, to break into company formations, assume defensive positions and then one at a time turn round. Doesn't matter how he does it but he is to turn around and come back the way he went. OK? Go!'

They heard the first explosion in between the blasts of the falling mortars ahead of them. It was different to the mortars, and some way away, but they heard it, and he knew. They had the fourth and the ninth. He looked at his map quickly, at the contour lines, the topography. No way off and no way out except to push on or turn around. They had them bottled up on a jungle track. If the enemy fought like they did here, if they were led with this panache, this skill, it would be a killing ground. Holy Mary, Mother of God. He crossed himself.

Chapter Seven

The team were settled in just over a rise at the end of one of the few straight stretches of the track half a mile from the river. In here were patches of primary jungle, but mostly it was secondary, the results of years of logging operations and attempts at agriculture. Hidden in the undergrowth, their firing positions atop the rise allowed them to see two hundred metres along the track, but with the low cloud and falling rain visibility was appalling, even with passive night vision goggles, so they didn't use them. They would rely on night-fighting technology that had been around since the First World War – trip flares. Just round the bend was a bar-mine, the only one of the surprise packages that was set with its original pressure detonator. The area back from the bar-mine and the trip flares was heavily mined. Like the other mines, all the way back to the highway, these were only armed after a remote command signal activated the detonators or sensors. Forward from here they would be manually armed.

Their vehicle, the last on this side of the river, was just round the bend. It would be abandoned eventually, but it would serve to move them forward with their heavy equipment, ahead of the column, arming their traps as they went along, leaving the stay-behind teams. The plan was like all the best plans, very simple, with lots of 'flex' for circumstance. There were twenty-four SAS soldiers, in three eight-man fighting patrols, between the team at the end of the track and the start of the bush just off the highway, where the last set of mines and traps sealed the exit route. Those patrols, broken down into smaller four-man teams were lying in wait above the track ready with the arming devices for their concealed ordnance, and their own portable weapons. They waited for the team at the head of the line to initiate the contact, and block the way forward. The rear team would then close the way out. The central teams would then engage and when they had done their job, melt away into the jungle to RV points. Two patrols would make their way back to San Ignacio as best they could. The remaining patrol would stay in the area, re-equip themselves from caches and then provide intelligence reports, harry the enemy, exploit opportunities, create fear and confusion.

They could hear the column approaching, the low throaty rumble of the tank and armoured personnel carrier engines below the higher-pitched whine of the truck engines struggling in the mud. Reflections of lights, dimmed by the rain, flashed off the wet leaves of trees.

'They've got their lights on,' Snowy, the big Fijian, muttered incredulously. He was sixty yards down the hillside from a Milan post settled in with a machine gun where he could cover the track as far as the bend. He and his oppo also had the arming devices and five LAW rockets as well as their personal weapons, their 203s.

'Not for much longer,' the other muttered ominously. The first vehicle, an APC, crawled past them. It was followed by a light tank and a recce vehicle, then the first of the trucks, grinding and slithering past. The APC tripped the flare wire and half a second later rolled on to the bar-mine. There was a flash of orange-white and a deafening blast, the ground and trees shaking, and as the concussion wave blew over them the flare burst high above. A streak of orange sparks and a roaring, tearing sound followed and a Milan missile hit the tank. As it exploded, dirt, mud and leaves rained down on them from the bar-mine explosion; the B Squadron soldier remotely armed the four Addermines in their sector and Snowy opened fire on the trucks with the machine gun, the bullets ripping through the canvas sides.

Above them the flare slowly fell, swinging festively under its little parachute, illuminating the scene with an eerie blue-white light that threw harsh shadows. The track was carnage, a Dantean horror: the APC and tank were on fire, and the young lieutenant who had wanted a more cautious advance no longer existed, smeared all over the inside of the burning hulk. Ammunition began to cook off and behind them in the recce vehicle, the colonel was shrieking at the driver to reverse. He did, straight into the truck behind them. Snowy's oppo was at that moment sighting it with a LAW rocket through the hunting spotting rifle attachment and opened fire. The missile hit the recce vehicle, its shaped-charge warhead penetrating the M-8's light armour like paper. It exploded with enough force to blow the doors off the back, one of them flying into the bush by the roadside. No one inside the vehicle ever knew what happened. They ceased to exist, vaporized in the superheated milliseconds of the warhead's detonation.

Further down the column the Guatemalan soldiers did what they were trained to do. Counter-insurgency veterans, they knew all about ambush and their trucks were rigged so that the men sat facing outwards, able to jump off, get into cover and return fire instantly. They were jumping clear of the trucks and dropping down into the bush at the roadside, seeking an enemy, looking for where the fire was coming from, finding cover, hoping for command from someone. In the dark it was terrifying. The column was being attacked, but not at all points. For stretches of several hundred yards there was nothing, but they could hear their comrades under machine gun and anti-tank fire either side of their positions.

One group, off the track and in the bush at the roadside, were being mustered by their sergeant. A few vehicles down, a truck, its driver panicking, tried to do a reversing turn and crossed into the sensors of an Addermine. From the trees there was a flash, sparks, roaring and a massive blast as the remote LAW missile booby-trap blew the truck to pieces. Some of the men fired at the place the thing came from but the launch was so close that the sergeant knew it was a booby-trap. 'Down, down, cease firing!' he shouted. Further along another non-com was shouting, 'Mines! Beware! Mines!'

His men settled and he tried to think what to do. They weren't under fire, but everyone else seemed to be. How long till it was their turn? He looked up into the jungle. There was no muzzleflash, no light, no movement, nothing to indicate where the Belizeans were. They hadn't expected this, the briefing had said they would roll straight into this area that was rightfully a part of Guatemala, that the pitifully small

189

Belizean army wasn't prepared or expecting them; and yet here they were waiting, and with modern bombs and traps. The sergeant looked back at his men. They had watched an American war film a few weeks before, on video; the *muchachos* liked those, Vietnam movies especially. In this one the sergeant had said his job was bringing everyone back alive – he had thought about that at the time and he thought about it again now. Tracer fire was arcing up from places down the track, and explosions ripped the darkness apart, concussion waves rolling over them. This was a place for the dead and the dying, there would be no order here till daybreak. They should get away, somewhere where they could see what was coming at them, see trip-wires.

'Get your stuff, we are moving out,' he ordered, and pointed into the trees. A couple of them complained, argued, but he shouted them down. He was frightened too he said, but if they stayed here they would die. A flare went up, everyone in the group froze, and then as if to illustrate his point, somewhere just up the track someone triggered a mine. The Claymore, an anti-personnel mine, its shaped-charge packed with seven hundred ball bearings, exploded and cut a swath through trees, bush and flesh alike. Men were screaming, wounded and dying in the dark and the rain and the mud. As the flare died he signalled them back to the ground and cover – it wasn't safe to move either. He set them in a circle, a defensive position, as best he could without unnecessary movement and then settled down to wait for daylight. He wasn't to know but their attackers at this point on the track had moved already, melted away into the pitch-black of the jungle darkness.

The SAS patrol were making their way back to the vehicle, each pair in sequence, each holding a length of paracord so they would not become separated in the darkness. All that was left of them was their legacy, the mines and booby-traps. Further down the track the firefight continued, the B Squadron men dropping grenades from their 203s into the bush either side of the road, raking the areas with gunfire, then moving quickly on to the next attack position above the road.

Phase One objective had been met. They had channelled

the column off the highway, bottled them up and their limited armour was mostly knocked out. The attrition had begun, their objective simply to keep the enemy column locked in and taking fire, seeking to take out their officers and wound enough of their men to eliminate the unit as an effective force. This rolling firefight up and down the column would go on till the hour before dawn and then the patrols would break off their attack and put some territory between them and the enemy. Even with an all-night action there would still be the better part of two battalions, some fifteen hundred soldiers, ready to be rallied when it was light so the SAS men knew the fewer officers left the better. British troops losing their officer wouldn't matter a jot. An ethos of mission flexibility and a command style where everyone could fill the position of the man above-and-below, and understood the objective meant you could take casualties but the unit would continue to function. The brutal reality was that developing-world armies lacked that culture and ethos, and if you removed their officer corps they very quickly ceased to operate as a cohesive unit, and the SAS exploited this.

Gulf of Mexico

The Lynx was approaching fast, skimming the waves, buffeted by the winds of the thunderstorm over the land ahead of them.

The observer, a lieutenant commander and the senior officer in the aircraft, wanted to pop up and illuminate with his targeting radar for a few seconds, see what they were flying into. Ahead of them were mangroves, a dark smudge on the sea, the trees rising ten or fifteen feet from the water. They could come up over the mangroves, pop up, illuminate the targets and drop down again, below the fifty feet of conventional radar scanners. Their radar was military; sensitive enough to pick up a periscope, it would see everything metallic or of any size on the water surface and upwards, and a two-second sweep through the forward area would be enough.

'Here we go,' the pilot said. 'Illuminate now!'

The observer made the sweep and as they dropped down to their ultra-low level, he was looking at his screens. There were large contacts. He looked out ahead and saw flashes in the darkness. 'They are firing something from that vessel,' he said, wishing his radars were better than they were. The new kit on *Beaufort* could pick up a shell in flight, but on this there was jack shit.

'They said that they were being mortared. Could they be firing mortars from a ship?' the pilot asked, feeling the adrenaline in his blood.

'Must be,' the observer replied. 'Let's do it.' He sounded businesslike, but the tension showed in his voice.

The Guatemalan invasion fleet was peculiarly Central American, a mix of civilian and ageing secondhand military craft. The first wave, to put their marines ashore and provide fire support, comprised four vessels. Of the four, one was a merchantman, a coaster co-opted for the job because of its shallow draught, the troop carrier. There was a barge for carrying landing craft, towed by a tug. The landing craft were back from the beach but still in the water awaiting the second wave of marines, and now the barge switched to her secondary role as a platform for the ten mortars mounted aft. Finally there was a patrol craft, their escort, mounting a pair of 20 mill cannons, but the forward deck mounting for a missile-launcher stood empty.

On the barge, stern on to the beach half a mile away, sailors from the Guatemalan navy were watching army crews manning the mortar tubes. Their officers were behind them, one calling fire-control commands, next to their signaller, another marking the positions on a map. This had been an innovation of which they were proud. This was going to be a very small marine assault; first wave, followed by a second. They would need some sort of fire support, and the Guatemalan navy had no naval gunfire support capability. Then a junior engineer suggested that the barge carrying the landing craft be used as a platform to fire mortars. The deck of the barge was thick enough, there would be no buckling of plates and mounts were welded on in a matter of hours. It was simple and it worked. The second wave of marines would, on arrival, transfer to the landing craft and be taken ashore, while the barge and her escort remained on station.

They never saw the helicopter, never heard her, never knew she was there. The Lynx swung round to the north to gain a better radar view of the small group of ships and the barge. The lieutenant commander also wanted a visual, or more of a visual than he had. There would be no profile recognition, none of the usual enemy vessel identification methods, but if they could approach close enough to see mortars being fired they could satisfy themselves that they weren't about to sink a Belizean workboat or sugar barge. They both wanted that peace of mind.

The pilot thought that if he skimmed down the coast from the north his radar image would be minimalized by the terrain and the massive stormcloud over the land. They could move inland enough to see the airport off to the right. If mortar bombs were coming from these vessels then they would see the bombs leave the large contact on their radar screens and then actually see the detonation flashes as they hit the ground three or four miles away.

Racing down the coast they passed the trigonometrical station on Hicks Cay out to the left and swung round, max knots now in full attack posture. Off out of the right centre of the canopy was the airport and even with the falling rain they could see the flashes on the ground. The observer looked out at the night. 'More flashes, four, no, five.'

'Roger,' the pilot responded. The bombs would be a while in flight, and they waited. 'I have detonations. Three, four, five. Confirmed?' the pilot asked.

'Roger, I confirm five flashes.'

'That's good enough for me,' said the pilot. 'Ground speed one-fifty knots. Altitude sixty feet. The helo is yours.'

The observer quickly ran through a set of procedures, weapons lights on his control panels glowing, changing colour as he armed the systems. He then lifted a guard panel with his gloved thumb and pressed a switch downwards and dropped the panel again.

'Sea Skua activated.'

The Lynx popped up to ninety feet, and the pilot held it as steady as he could in the increased wind. Come on, come on, he was thinking, every second they were up and visible they were on every radar in miles. The observer was running through his procedures, his voice thick with tension. Finally, in reality only seconds later, he said, 'Stores away.'

There was a thump and the helicopter lifted slightly as the pair of Sea Skua missiles dropped away from the hardpoints, their activators locked on to the target, the data fed to them from the helicopter's battle-management systems. The rocket motors fired into life and they seared away, hugging the sea, skimming the wave-tops, increasing speed to close on the target at three hundred knots. Sea Skua was not a fire-and-forget system and as good as it was as a ship-killer, one of its limitations was that the helicopter's radars had to keep illuminating the target and feeding data to the missile. Against a warship this was a very dangerous practice; her defence systems would be throwing up chaff, flares, jamming ELINT, firing anti-missile missiles and anti-aircraft missiles at the attacking helicopter. The crew in the Lynx didn't know what these ships were. They knew the Guatemalans had nothing big this side, but even patrol craft were large enough to mount air-defence systems and they were up and visible and vulnerable, so all their counter-measures were active.

On the barge the Guatemalans never saw the incoming missiles. Streaking in just feet above the waves in the dark they were leaving no glow on the water, just the odd reflection of light from the rocket motor on a white wave-top every few seconds, and the noise from the mortar tubes masked every other sound. On the patrol boat they did see them – two sailors on lookout saw them but didn't recognize what they were, and with forks of lightning flashing across the sky they had impaired night vision.

The two missiles hit. One struck the barge in the centre of the waterline, the other further aft, both detonating. The explosion from the first ripped away a swath of deck twelve feet wide, killing the signaller and the officer with him. The second hit a main deck support girder and was deflected downwards and detonated lower, holing the far side of the hull. The barge shuddered and began to take on water and settle lower on the far side. There was mayhem on the deck. Four men died and others were wounded, either from flying steel shrapnel or with flash burns. There was no engine in the barge so it had no bunkers of fuel oil and with little else that was flammable there was no fire. Miraculously, and luckily for the men who survived the missile strike, the stores of mortar bombs didn't explode.

The Lynx passed by two miles out to sea and continued south. Her crew saw the missiles impact, advised *Beaufort* ops and were immediately tasked to head southwards while the confusion reigned. Sooner or later someone would figure out what had happened, and the small flotilla moving up the coast would be alerted. Speed and surprise were everything now.

2200 hours – San Ignacio

Helen was mellow – two beers before supper, wine with the meal, and life was great. A lean American ageing cowboy type had been making eyes at her and she found his scrawny, slightly debauched look mildly appealing. Long hair, once blonde but now prematurely grey, and a goatee beard made him look a little like images of General Custer. He had come over, introduced himself, and settled on a stool beside Helen. His name was Sean and he was a software writer, from the deep south, Georgia.

Eva's was busy. The rain was tipping down outside, thunder pealing loud enough to be heard over the music every now and then, but inside it was cosy and dry. Sophie seemed pre-occupied; Helen supposed she was thinking of where she had been at this time the previous night. She sat alongside her on a stool, occasionally chatting to the owner, Pete, who was behind the bar. Both of them now felt familiar and at ease enough with him to have totally relaxed. Pete, appreciative of someone at his bar with an English sense of humour, was having gentle digs at the Americans, popping the caps off bottles, serving drinks and dispensing advice.

The phone rang. Pete scooped up the handset, and then,

195

having trouble hearing, reached over and turned down the music a little and covered his other ear with his hand. He turned at one point, speaking quickly in Spanish, and then replaced the phone, and in three or four strides was at the back door, listening. Nothing unusual – music, the sounds from the kitchen, the babble from the bar, the sound of rain falling on tin roofs. He walked quickly through to the front and stepped on to the street. Someone called from the back but he ignored them. Jesus, I was right, he thought. The lads in the four-wheel-drive – if there was a punch-up going on this side of Benque then this would be the next def‗sive line; that was in the plan years ago. The bridge – they would hold at the bridge; Christ, they could drop the bridge! Either way you didn't want to be on this side if you could help it. He strained his ears again. You could hear a battle miles away, but he couldn't hear a thing over the sound of the rain and the storm. He had to assume his brother-in-law was right. He moved back inside, and called over his number two, Dave, an English guy who had drifted into Cayo a year or so before and stayed.

'Listen carefully; that was Cassie's brother. Something's happening up in Benque. He said he saw tanks and soldiers and there is a battle going on this side of the town. Get your car out, I want you to get Cassie and the girls over to your place and then wait and see. I'll get the two Brit girls and whoever else can fit in the truck and take them over the other side.'

'The Guatemalans?'

'Who else?'

'Fuckin' 'ell,' he muttered. 'OK. Just over to the other side?'

'The bridge,' Pete explained. 'The bridge is a choke-point. Your place is far enough back. Then wait and see and if you have to keep moving, get on the highway and drive to Spanish Lookout. Cassie has family there. OK?'

'You?'

'I've got too much sunk in here to leave it. Fuck 'em.'

Dave nodded. Pete's Spanish was outstanding, his accent local in the extreme and with his dark eyes and swarthy lean-ness he could pass for a Belizean.

196

'I'd better phone the Rooster and the Bel, let the guys know.' The Red Rooster and the Bel-Brit were two other expatriate-run bars, the owners both friends.

'Do that, but be moving in five minutes. The word's out, and that bridge will be clogged to shit in no time.'

Pete moved over to where the girls were sitting. Both were looking at him and the atmosphere was already tense. He handed some keys to Sophie. 'That's my truck over there.' He pointed out the door. 'There's trouble, *mucho peligro*. I'm going to make an announcement in a moment and when I do –' His wife came out of the kitchen door and bustled over wiping her hands on a tea towel, her expression worried. He spoke to her quickly and softly in Spanish, reassuring but firm. She was to gather up the two girls, pack enough things for a few days and get into Dave's car. They would go over the bridge together. Two cars. She nodded and he turned back to Sophie and Helen. ' – when I do I want you to go straight to the truck and get in it.'

'What's happened?' Sophie asked.

'There's a battle going on five miles up the road. It can only be the Guatemalan army and that means they are coming this way. Maybe I'm being over-cautious but I'm going to encourage as many of you over to the other side of the bridge as I can. We have to move fast. OK?'

'Umm. Yes.' Helen was thinking quickly. 'We've got a jeep.' Pete grinned for a moment. He had seen them in it earlier, gingerly edging it into a parking space. 'OK, but I'll get you a driver. You won't want to be driving, not this time.' He turned the music down and called for silence. 'Can I have everyone's attention please? I have had a phone call. Now this is unsubstantiated, but we believe that there is fighting a few miles up the highway and it's coming this way. I suggest that you make your way back over the river to the eastern side.'

'Fighting? Who?' someone called.

'Up there?' Pete grinned, as if the question was naive in the extreme. 'Who do you think? It can only be the Guats.' There was a babble of talk, and people looked at each other, conferring.

'Can I use the phone?' one woman asked. 'I wanna call the embassy.'

'Do you have CNN?' a man asked. 'They will be there, we can see what's going on.'

'Hey man, that's cool,' another suggested to his friends, 'let's go up there. Check it out, man! It's like, so Central American, man.' He was grooving on it.

'No phone calls, no CNN because they won't bloody be there, and you,' Pete pointed at the long-haired fellow who thought it would be cool to go up and 'check out' the fighting. 'You go up there and you probably won't be coming back.' At that moment the owner of Bel-Brit came in through the door. He grasped the situation in an instant.

'You heard?'

Pete nodded. 'Yeah.'

'What's your feel?'

'It's on. Get across the bridge,' Pete replied plainly. The man nodded, held up his mobile phone and was gone.

'Who made you the fucking sheriff?' the long-haired man said. 'I been in Nicaragua, Salvador. If I wanna go up there I'll go up there.'

'No one made me anything. Do what you fucking like,' Pete said, 'but not here. Eva's is closed. My truck is leaving in one minute, anyone who wants a ride get in. But everyone's out.' He pointed at the door.

'I'm comin',' someone said. Others agreed, and there was a babble of noise, chairs being pushed back.

Sean lifted his bottle to his lips and drank. He looked at Helen. 'You ladies leaving? If you are I'd be happy to see you over the other side,' he drawled.

'Thank you,' Helen replied. 'Our car's just outside.'

'We're staying,' the long-haired man called. 'You can all run, but we're staying. Justa buncha banditos, probably.'

'Not here you're not,' Pete said.

'Oh yeah?'

Helen, Sophie and Sean were walking past at this point and Sean looked back at where Pete was coming out from behind the bar, a determined look on his face.

'Allow me, compadre,' Sean called to Pete. He reached

down and took the troublemaker by his hair, pulled him to his feet and slung him out of the door on to the street in one fluid movement. His two friends ran out after him.

Sean and the girls crossed the street and got into the four-wheel-drive; Sean took the wheel. Pete locked up the bar, and a minute later they were at the roundabout by the petrol station, the bridge just off to the left. The roads were jammed, cars and trucks coming from every direction; the word was out. Sean looked over. The bridge was narrow and passage over it was controlled by traffic lights. A policeman was trying to stop vehicles crossing over when the light was red, but he was being ignored, and people were now choking the entry yelling and screaming; cars were bumping into each other, horns blaring. Panic wasn't far off.

'This is not good,' Sean said.

Suddenly from the right three men appeared, from over the bridge, all in uniform. One, clearly an officer, Sean thought, raised a firearm into the sky and banged off three rounds, and blew on a whistle. The other two men, smaller, slight even, trained their weapons on the nearest cars. The yelling and screaming stopped. The officer jerked his thumb across the bridge and pointed to a car. It began to move forward, then another; suddenly things began to clear, and drivers knew to wait their turn.

'That's more like it,' Sean said. 'That a Brit officer?'

Sophie was looking at him in the headlights, his maroon beret square on his head. She had met him last night – the chap who had been keen on Helen.

'Yes,' she replied. 'C Company of 2 Para.' She surprised herself with the ease of the answer. It was the reply of an insider and when she said it she felt a curious pride.

'Airborne, huh?' Sean nodded. 'Well, they are getting this sorted out.'

'Tim, was it?' Sophie asked, looking over at Helen. She was already feeling better; they were here, Harry's people, British soldiers, and not just Harry's people, but chaps who had stood alongside him last night, friends of his. She suddenly felt very close to him.

'It's Toby,' Helen said, 'Toby Estelle.'

'You two get around,' Sean said drily and inched the car forward.

An American signals clerk had brought the message over, handing it personally to Tyson-Davis upon signature. It was from PJHQ Northwood. Guatemala had invaded the Independent State of Belize, crossing the road border in force at 2103 local time. The message originated forty minutes ago, and orders were to deploy by parachute to support British forces on the ground. The role had changed; this wasn't go and be seen any more, it was lob in and fight.

The pace was now frenetic. Men who had repacked bergens to take simply extra were now ripping the contents out and dumping everything they couldn't eat, drink or shoot at someone. Because they were lobbing in, the bergens were now referred to as containers, and they were stripping out everything. Spare clothing, bivvy bags, hammocks, mosquito nets, personal things all came out and were examined. Did they need this to march and fight? If not it was put to one side.

Corporal 'Elias' Cutter was typical. In customized jungle boots, with the soles from walking boots fitted, DPM trousers and shirt, sleeves rolled down, he was dressed to go. His 'gollock', his machete, was already round his waist and attached to his person, separate from his belt-kit. Also attached were his spoon, a tiny Mag-lite torch, his personal medical kit and his compass. That was in a small pen pocket that he had moved from his left sleeve and re-sewn on the front down his button line, where he could get to it.

His Para helmet was on his container. Light, made of nylon, it was not like the Kevlar ballistic helmets worn by crap-hats, but made for parachute jumping. It would not stop a bullet or shell fragment like a ballistic helmet supposedly could, but they were Para kit, looked the biz, and what's more were visibly different. His SA80 rifle was standard issue. Much lighter than the old 7.62, this weapon fired 5.56 mm rounds and with a thirty-round magazine could, in theory, put out 650 rounds a minute. No one ever did of course; not only would that use the soldier's entire stock of ammunition in under a minute, but that rate of fire would so overheat the barrel that it would warp. Not even their light support automatic weapon could handle that and each of Cutter's two sections had an LSW – sustained fire was for the heavy-barrelled 7.62 GPMG. The SUSAT ×4 sight was left on. It could be removed fairly quickly if they went into the jungle, where they misted up, but for the time being it remained fixed. His rifle, like many of the men's, had a counter attached to the base of the stock where it met the barrel coming up from the working parts. Held on with black insulation tape, the counter, £8.00 in HM Stores, was like those used by people counting heads on nightclub doors, and as the soldier walked he would click it once for every pace, the only way to navigate accurately in the jungle.

He was carrying 200 rounds of link ammunition for the section weapon, a further 200 of bandoleer ammo, this 7.62 for the GPMGs, 220 rounds of his own personal ammunition and 150 rounds for his reserve. He was also carrying one mortar bomb in his container and he would have a 51 mill tube strapped to the side of it as he went out the door, to be dropped and hang below as he descended. He was carrying food for twenty-four hours, one bottle of water, purifying tablets, anti-malarial tablets, two packets of juicy fruit chewing gum, and his luxuries, a small tin of Nescafé Gold Blend and a bottle of tabasco sauce. He was also carrying three packets of Old Holborn. The tobacco wasn't for him, it was for his lads. Three of them smoked, and when they ran out of cigarettes morale in the section took a dip. If and when they ran out of their smokes, they would be pleased with his foresight, even if it was only the makings for roll-ups.

Jonesy had found his two copulating Teletubbies and was now jamming them into his shirt front, their little heads peeking out.

'You taking them?' Cutter asked.

'Course,' the man grinned. '1-800-PARA TUBBY.'

'They wouldn't be left out of this for anything,' Rhah cut

in. 'They are regular airborne psychopaths just like the rest of us.'

Lieutenant Rees was with the CSM working out the jump logistics. They would go back in two aircraft, with four wedges taking in eight tonnes of stores. The chalk and stick sequence was worked out, so as the wedges went out the rear ramp, the men, who had been loaded in jump order with a port or starboard jump number, would go out the side doors, after one door bundle at each door carrying thirty-two motor bombs. The men, wearing parachutes and whatever extra gear they were jumping with strapped to them, more mortar bombs, belt ammo, fifty-calibre barrels, mortar tubes, would lug their 120-lb containers up towards the doors and go in turn.

'I want to go in at first light,' Tyson-Davis said. No one liked night parachute jumps. They were standard operating procedure but they often produced an unacceptable injury rate. Troops were dispersed, it took too long to rendezvous, kit was lost; it was generally a complete cock-up.

'You done?' Tyson-Davis asked.

'Done, checked and checked again,' Rees answered. 'Any sitrep, sir?'

Tyson-Davis shook his head. 'Not in the last few minutes. B Squadron are in. They are out front. The C Coy lads have dug in here,' he jabbed at the map. 'This bridge – hopefully Dickie Fox has got enough of his people up there and Dave Chard will have set up to drop it.'

Around them their hundred or so men were scattered about re-stuffing packs, packing ammunition, loading wedges, the pace frantic. Men from the base, American soldiers, were moving among them; stores people mostly, but some were fighting soldiers, men drawn by the activity, who had heard the news. Special forces stores personnel were issuing equipment, not only the T-10 parachutes they would need for the entry, but virtually anything the Brits wanted. One American handed over a long heavy-bladed fighting knife. 'I can get another,' he said.

There was also a sudden proliferation of sidearms. Soldiers love guns, they are the tools of their trade. Ordinarily access to the standard issue 9 millimetre was limited and the toms put up with it, but now there was a sudden interest in getting hold of handguns. They were freely available in the USA, and most American servicemen had several. For a soldier they weren't much good unless you were very, very close, but in that situation they might make all the difference. Several toms had struck deals with their American benefactors, including Rhah, who had borrowed, against an IOU, a new Browning Hi-Power 9 mill, with a big chunky fifteen-shot magazine. It came with a holster that would clip on to his webbing, two spare mags and a cleaning kit.

'I got a couple of these, so you can borrow one. You clean it, right? I don't want you giving it back covered in mud 'n' shit,' its owner said, the optimism in his voice forced, both of them knowing that many of them wouldn't be coming back.

'I will. Thanks, eh.'

The American put out his hand and Rhah took it. 'You take care now.'

The sniper came back to his kit and found a lump under his smock. Six packets of Remington 7.62 hollow point, six of Remington 7.62 wad cutter soft noses and twelve boxes of full metal jacket made for long-range target shooting, each projectile perfectly weighted and balanced. They were shiny, new, the very best that the US arms industry could produce, but at over $5.00 for each bullet, they should be, he thought. He smiled and called his mates over. It was perfect – now he just needed a Gilly suit.

Sixty feet away Harry Rees looked down at the map in the harsh light of the hangar. San Ignacio – they would hold them at the bridge, the Holdsworthy Bridge. One and a half companies of 2 Para and B Squadron, 22 SAS, two hundred and forty-odd men were going to hold up a divisional-sized mechanized advance until the brigade arrived. Even once the brigade was in they would still be outnumbered three to one. Until then? It didn't bear thinking about. Forty-five to one, fifty maybe? Suddenly he thought about her again; she's still there, in Belize. Christ, I hope she is in Belize City. When did they say they were going up to Xunantunich?

Across the other side of the table Tyson-Davis was looking down at the map, his mind racing, trying to work out what would be happening on the ground. The odds were not good, so what would they do? He had spent two years with the Regiment. If C Coy dug in at the bridge, how many? What would I do? We need to hold the airhead – assume Dickie will have half his force back in Belize holding the airhead, half at the bridge. If two platoons dig in at the bridge, then out ahead, at the line of advance, the Squadron would maul the enemy as they did a fighting withdrawal.

A Sabre Squadron was a formidable fighting machine. The sixty-odd men with the correct weaponry and ordnance could deliver the firepower of a force ten times their size, slow down the enemy till they could bottleneck the advance into San Ignacio. There may be fifteen thousand of them, but they couldn't all fight at once; the bastards would be strewn out along the road back to the border, maybe with half of them still to enter Belize. Their FLOT, front line of troops, might be down to battalion size. Air? When would they have air? If everyone had their shit together Harriers should be preparing to leave now.

0500 BST – Aldershot

At Aldershot, home of the British army, Lieutenant-Colonel Wallace, the commanding officer of 2 Para, was in his office and on the phone. He had advised one person, his 2 i/c, a major, who had a deep instinct for things that could go, as he put it, 'horribly fucking wrong' and had made a couple of phone calls himself. The ripple effect was working. Now trickling in to their lines at Arnhem barracks were the nucleus of the battalion's HQ function. The RSM, the quartermaster and the intelligence officer. The HQ officer, Major Brock, was in Belize with C Coy and some of his assault pioneers, but the signals officer was in and even the padre had arrived. Wallace looked out of the door; OC B Coy was down the block in his office already and 2 i/c of HQ was parking his car downstairs. The news of the invasion had spread like wildfire, and with

C Coy there on the ground the chances they would engage at some point were very high, unless the politicos got something resolved quickly. There was little chance of that and they knew it; an invading force, once in and rolling was committed, politically, militarily, philosophically.

'And what are you lot doing here?'

'I phoned the RSM,' the battalion's XO said. 'I thought we might have some work to do.'

'Aah, I heard the news on the radio,' the padre added. 'They're our chaps. I didn't want to be sitting at home. Is there any news?'

'No,' Wallace answered. 'No news.'

2200 local – Belize International Airport

The fighting had raged, ebbing and flowing along the line, for the better part of thirty minutes now and had tapered off into a lull, with just the odd round fired and sniping from both sides. Fox had expected that; men simply could not sustain the aggression and the energy for longer, and they needed re-supply of ammunition and new tactical orders. How long would the lull last? Five minutes, maybe ten.

This was more than a contact, it was a skirmish, something between a firefight and a full engagement and Major Fox tried for a second or two to find the right word and then abandoned the attempt. He was writing a sitrep, a situation report to be flashed back to Northwood. They had been lucky, but in war, he mused, fortune often favours the bold. They had taken the Guatemalan attack head-on, and dug in deep as they were, they had held the line. His handful of Gurkhas, many unblooded in battle, had fought like tigers, as he knew they would.

Somewhere out behind him in the dark Major Brock and his pioneers were digging trenches at the western end, now the rear. He could hear the JCB working. Corporal Garvey was back there with ten or twelve of his BDF men and they could be supported by the marines if attacked. It was a thousand metres away but the marines had two airport trucks in the shadows of the terminal building and would race to support whoever needed them.

There was a redoubt too, a central position which they could fall back to if it came to that, from where they could put fields of fire right across the airport if they had to. They might lose ground, he acknowledged, but no man would hold it, not under the barrels of their machine guns. The good news was that the mortaring had stopped. The Squadron signals people in their bunker at the camp had taken a message from HMS *Beaufort*. She was now in strike range and her helicopter had already engaged the enemy, knocking out the vessel the mortars had been fired from. Fox grinned; that evened the odds considerably.

He jotted the message, handed it to his radio operator and looked back to his prisoner. The section on the right had cracked it. A Guat patrol looking for a way past had come too close and been seen by the Gurkha soldiers in the sangar; they opened fire, killing three, and they had taken a prisoner. The Guatemalan, dragged across the ground with a kukri at his throat, thought he was going to have his head cut off and was a gibbering wreck by the time he was delivered to the company command post. He talked – the words wouldn't come fast enough. Fox capitalized on his fear and offered him a Mars bar, saying that if he wasn't a good chap and very helpful indeed, then he would be given back to the man with the knife and there would be no questions asked.

The intelligence had been excellent and he waited for Murray the marines' officer to arrive so he could brief him. A few minutes later he slithered into the dugout, his eyes taking in the prisoner, now blindfolded, his ears covered.

'Yes,' Fox beamed, 'he's been rather useful,' his voice low despite his satisfaction. 'From what he tells me – mind you, mine's Benidorm Spanish – they think that the camp is heavily defended, and this is their best route in.' Murray nodded. That made sense. Although they had pounded the camp, they obviously thought it a stronghold because they hadn't come that way.

'How many did he say, sir?'

'Four hundred. There is a second wave, but four hundred in this assault.'

'Well there must be a good fifty wounded or dead out there by now, and we have slotted their boss and at least three other officers,' Murray said. 'My sniper just hit another.'

'We have six wounded and three dead,' Fox said sadly, and then he smiled. 'But we are doing rather well, I think. How's morale with your lads?'

'Very good, sir, all things considered.'

'Good. And there is more good news.' He told Murray about the Royal Navy warship now in helo range and the demise of the mortar barge.

'So now it's just three hundred and fifty of them, with another wave coming,' Murray said drily. 'That makes me feel much better.'

Fox chuckled softly, his moustache creasing as he did so. 'He says he's a marine,' he said, pointing to the Guatemalan. 'So your lads can hold him.'

Murray grimaced slightly and nodded. Three minutes later he was back in his hole where the bulk of his troop were deployed. Four were now forward, one of them with a sniper rifle, doing good work at removing the Guatemalan command structure. He pulled the hapless prisoner into the hole.

'Private Taylor, you have the lingo. Tie this one up, hobble him or something. Tell him to bloody behave himself.' Taylor nodded, and spoke quickly in heavily-accented but effective Spanish. Murray disappeared again to check on his men in their second hole and an animated discussion began, Taylor interpreting for the sergeant.

'And tell him that he is a cunt. A prize cunt! He got caught by fucking Paras. Paras! The scum of the earth! Tell him that he isn't worth a marine's shit!'

'Yeah,' someone else chimed in, 'tell him on behalf of the worldwide brotherhood of marines that he is a fucking failure.'

The Guatemalan was smiling now, feeling a little more secure. He had heard that the British didn't shoot prisoners, but was still wary of being handed back to the others, the ones who looked like Mayans. He wanted to offer something

207

in return. He said something. Taylor looked at him and asked him to say it again.

'What was that?' the sergeant asked.

'He said he hates them too and if we want to shoot some Paras then they are at Belmopan and San Ignacio. Cabils? I think that was what he called them.'

'Get the boss,' the sergeant said softly. 'Ask him how many, and when did they get there?'

There was fast Spanish and Taylor looked up. 'He says they were delayed, that was what he heard. Because of the weather, I guess. His officer was going on about it.'

'How many?'

The Guatemalan understood the question and he realized he had said too much. This wasn't marines with marines stuff anymore, this was more serious. Firing began from the holes to their front, the heavy sustained bursts from a GPMG cutting across every other sound, and the marines stood to. A flare burst overhead illuminating the attacking men and the Gurkha defenders poured fire into them. Behind them they heard the thump of their own mortars leaving the tubes.

San Ignacio

Lieutenant Estelle was still on the western side of the river with his men, who were keeping the traffic moving. The rain had stopped, but that meant little other than improved visibility. His poncho was back over with his bergen and he was drenched to the skin, as were his men. Local police, now in the picture, were helping, but he knew that the moment his men left the scene chaos would return and he wanted as many as possible of the people on the western side evacuated. Only Christ knew what would happen once the Guatemalan advance elements arrived. They could be decent and leave civilians alone, but even if they were disciplined and did just that, the moment the fighting started anyone caught in the middle would be, as the other platoon commander had succinctly put it, 'in really deep shit'.

Estelle looked up the hill. He had aimed his mortars at the

road at the top of the hill, the rise to the left, down which any traffic from the border would need to come. There was another route, round from the north and into the town along the river, but that was a track and in this rain it would be almost impassable. The main advance would come down the hill. His next two tubes were set up to range on the roundabout at the bottom. From their position half a kilometre back the bombs wouldn't be in the air for long. He looked back at the town and the drop down to the riverbank. Somewhere in there were all the mines laid by the Squadron blokes. All exact distances, everything paced out, GPS positions fixed.

Then he heard it, the sounds of the fighting for the first time, over the noise of the traffic. A blast, a mortar bomb perhaps; then another, a mile away, maybe closer. He felt his excitement rising, but liquid fear as well, a weird feeling as adrenaline began to move through his blood. It was time to close the bridge to traffic, get them over on foot now, but he wanted to clear a path for any of the Squadron people who made it back this far. If they were still in the fight they would be the last vehicles down the road before the enemy's lead elements, and if there weren't any, then ... then ... he thought for a moment, just set off the charges and earn his keep. What a fucking disaster, he thought, two platoons against a three-brigade advance. The good news was they couldn't all fight at once; they had to get down the hill first, and then deploy. How many could do that at any one time? The question had been plaguing him for hours now. He looked across the town, what he could see of it, and tried to remember the layout from the maps he had seen. Concentrated fighting? At Arnhem the airborne had ten thousand men concentrated in an incredibly small area. Without air, armour or artillery to hold them back, the Guatemalans could do the same here. You could put two or three battalions into the town and its flanks and have plenty of room to fight and manoeuvre. A small brigade, with bridging equipment and rafts. Four other soldiers arrived, none saluting. They were too well disciplined to identify an officer this close to a potential enemy. 'I want a path cleared through here for Major Chard's men to withdraw with their vehicles. These civilian vehicles,' he pointed, 'in this line cross over. The others stay. People on foot only now. If anyone tries to enter the path and blocks it, stop them. Understood?'

The corporal nodded. 'Yes sir.'

Lieutenant Estelle called to a policeman. It wasn't martial law just yet.

On the other side of the bridge, just over half a mile back from the river, Sophie and Helen were in the garden of the small clapboard house rented by Dave, Pete's assistant. He was inside throwing a few things into a bag. Cassie, Pete's wife was with her two daughters in the small sitting room. Pete himself had put their stuff in his truck and now walked back up the path. It was just them left now; the others from the restaurant who had piled into Pete's truck had gone. He had flagged down a pickup and the owner had agreed to take the tourists to Belize with him.

'I can hear it,' Sophie said.

Pete nodded. 'It's getting closer. Dave is going to take Cassie and the girls up to Spanish Lookout. You're welcome to go with them – I'd advise it.'

'Where are you going?'

Pete grinned. In the soft light, his lean scrawny face lit up, his teeth white. 'Back over to the restaurant.'

'Why? Your wife will want you with her and the children.'

'They will be safe enough. She has family up there, loads of them.'

'But why are you going back? It's madness.'

It's my life, he thought, our future, our place, we've worked too hard to see it looted and trashed. He could have offered this answer, but instead said nothing. He just grinned again.

'How you getting back to the bridge?' Sean the American asked.

'I'll walk. No vehicles are going back over, that's for sure, and I want Cassie and the kids in the truck.'

'If the ladies don't mind,' he pointed at their four-wheel-drive, 'I'll drive you as far as I can.'

'Thanks.' He slipped his mobile phone into his pocket and hefted a small bag he had taken from the truck. 'The road

210

back to Belize City will be mayhem but I suggest you make a move sooner rather than later. If you get there head for the US Embassy. If you don't think you will make it for whatever reason, head into Belmopan. That's only half an hour on a normal day. The British Embassy is there and it's a small town, anyone will be able to direct you.'

'Will they get across the bridge?' Helen asked. 'Didn't you say the army would destroy it?'

'They will have thought of that,' Pete responded. 'They will have boats, engineers with bridging equipment, pontoons.'

'Call us,' Helen said sensibly, 'at least let Cassie know you are back indoors safely.'

St George's Cay

There were now two helicopters on St George's. The Royal Navy Sea King which had prudently headed there after dropping off the marines had been joined by one of the Army Air Corps Gazelles. The AAC flight was now widely dispersed; one machine was up at the SAS forward operating base at the old church hall outside San Ignacio, and one was on St George's Cay. It had been airborne at the time of the attack on the airport; the British adventure training camp on St George's was an emergency alternate and the pilot had headed out there without question. Not only were helicopters a very scarce resource, he didn't fancy being shot at. In the dark there was as much chance of a blue on blue, being hit by friendly fire, as being hit by the enemy.

Airport Camp

The last machine was on the pan outside the bombed hangar at Airport Camp, and it wouldn't be flying anywhere. Shrapnel had hit the fuselage, the canopy was holed, there was puncture damage in the skin around the engine compartment which meant that shrapnel had entered the engine area. The whole thing would have to be stripped down to check

211

hydraulic hoses, couplings, high-speed shafts, and to remove anything that shouldn't be there. FOD, foreign object damage, had downed more than one helicopter. The engineer, the last one alive, although he didn't know it, shone a torch quickly over the machine and shook his head.

'Can you fix it?'

'Mechanics? Assuming we have the spares. In daylight, with twelve hours, maybe. Airframe no, canopy no, electronics and avionics no. You're not going anywhere, sir.'

'OK, get the radio out and any rack mount gear you can shift. Then prepare to really fuck it up. Get something that will go bang, cans of fuel. It's not to fall into enemy hands, OK?'

The engineer nodded. 'Where you off to, sir?' They had been sharing a bunker during the mortar attack and he didn't want to go back there alone. Where were the others, the WO2 and his oppo? Skiving off somewhere, nice and safe.

'I'm on foot now. Better get myself a weapon.' Christ, he thought, I haven't handled a rifle with any interest since basic training, never thought I'd need one again. 'Then I'm gonna have a look around. You see if you can round up your lads, get the aircraft ready to be destroyed. Meet me back here in,' the pilot looked at his watch, 'in twenty minutes.'

'Then what, sir?'

'Then we are infantry.'

St George's Cay

Out on St George's the staff sergeant in charge was having a conversation with three men: the RN officer who was the pilot of the Sea King, his observer, and the army lieutenant who had flown the Gazelle over. Neither of the two pilots were comfortable with the lack of any real defensive capability. Their two aircraft could be critical to the campaign in the coming hours and to lose them could alter events. They knew that the Guatemalans had ships nearby, that they had been hit by the *Beaufort*'s Lynx, and they would know about the small British contingent on the Cay. Tactical or retaliatory in nature, the reason for an attack wouldn't matter. If they arrived here and found two helicopters on the ground they would win this little sideshow with a serious bonus prize.

'HMS *Beaufort* is out there somewhere,' the naval officer said. 'I wonder if she could give us some armed ratings or something?'

'Worth a try,' the army pilot replied. 'The scrotes could be on the Cay before we knew they were here. We could pop up and illuminate, have a look and see if they are coming this way.'

'We can't keep doing that. That would advertise our presence,' the naval man replied. He looked at the staff sergeant. 'How much aviation fuel have you got here?'

'Six drums. That's what; two-fifty gallons?'

'What's its state?' the observer from the Sea King asked.

The staff sergeant bridled slightly. He understood the aviators' concern; contaminated fuel was a real danger, but he was a professional. 'It's locked in the fuel store. Tops are on the drums and they are sealed. Haven't been opened.'

'Top us both up then,' the army pilot said. He wished he had a Lynx, not the Navy's version, but a real Lynx, an AAC ground attack, with rotary cannons, rocket pods and missiles on the hardpoints. Next year, he knew, they were getting Apaches, sixty-seven hardcore, in-your-face armoured gunships, conceived and created to do nothing other than deliver staggering firepower. He had flown in the back of one the year before, when he and another AAC pilot had visited a National Guard base in Arizona – they had Apaches. His mate had looked at one and said, 'Shit, that's not a helicopter. That's a tank with rotors.' A squadron of Apaches could pop up, engage and destroy an entire armoured regiment inside two minutes. Oh to have an Apache, he thought; but no, I'm sitting here on fucking Gilligan's Island while the lads are in the shit and all I've got is a bloody Gazelle without gun mounts. He thought for a second – but then again, maybe not. 'They have small arms on your ships?'

'Yeah. What sort?' the navy man asked.

'If *Beaufort* can support us here, if you go out to her and pick up some lads, can you get me an LSW or something?'

'What's an LSW?'

'A light section weapon, a machine gun.'

'Go one better,' the observer said, 'the *Beaufort* is a Type 23. They carry four GPMGs.'

'Now you're talking, sir,' the staff sergeant muttered.

'What for?' the navy pilot asked.

'Door gun,' the Gazelle pilot replied. 'Sling it in the door and go back and help.'

'I'm your gunner,' the staff sergeant said.

'No. Sorry, you're needed here. Get this place ready to receive blue job fixed-wing. Got someone else?'

'Better raise the *Beaufort* then,' the navy man said

'Try on 248,' the observer offered.

This was going to be interesting, the pilot thought. The frigate would be closed down, at action stations, her systems passive only, in full stealth mode. Her Lynx could communicate, but only with secure comms bursts that were encoded. If he came over open channels there was every chance she wouldn't even respond. Suddenly, there was a flash on the horizon that silhouetted the Sea King as he walked towards it. Lightning again? No, it was lower, on the surface, differing colours. Another – oh Jesus. He counted; one, two, three, four, five, then the low rumble reached him. He knew what it was, he had seen the videos of the Falklands, of a ship dying, hit in the darkness by an Exocet, its main magazines and fuel bunkers going up within seconds of each other. The *Beaufort*'s long-reach weapons platform had struck again. Her Lynx, with ship-killing Sea Skuas on the hardpoints, had made a kill. You take care, boys, he thought. He felt for them, just the two of them out there where it's dark and lonely, as any pilot would, and he felt for the enemy too. They would have heard nothing, seen nothing and now those that survived the missile strikes would have to endure the fires and the secondary explosions. They would be screaming, crying for their mothers. Green water would be rushing into engine spaces – burn or drown or both, poor bastards. He tried to remember who the aviators were on *Beaufort*; he probably knew them. He fired up the power and turned on the radio, selecting 248 megahertz, the air aviation channel most likely to attract a listening watch on *Beaufort*.

'*Beaufort, Beaufort*, this is *Black Rover* helo.' He knew not to even try for a response with a callsign; but they would know that the *Black Rover* was in the area. Shit, he thought, the Blackadder, as the lads called her, was due to refuel and re-supply *Beaufort* in the next two days anyway. If they knew he was from the *Black Rover* he was more likely to get a reply.

'*Beaufort, Beaufort, Black Rover* helo,' he tried again. Then he changed tack. '*Beaufort* helo, *Beaufort* helo, this is Lieutenant Colby in *Black Rover* helo. Talk to me.'

'*Black Rover*, go.'

He smiled. A response, the clipped radio patois of the English military radio operator. Cunning bastards weren't saying who they were, whether they were the Lynx or the ship.

'This is *Black Rover* helo. I need fuel and support. My mummy is a long way away. Can I come home with you, over?'

'Stand by.'

Two minutes later they were back. 'Your last name please, over?'

'Charlie Oscar Lima Bravo Yankee, over.'

'Your last year at Daedalus?'

'Wrong. I was at Yeovil.'

'Your crew chief's name on *Black Rover*, over.'

The pilot told him.

'Good enough, *Black Rover* helo. Advise your fuel status please?'

'I'm on the ground, on a dragon. Delta Romeo Alpha Golf Oscar November. Fifty minutes in the tanks.'

'Stand by. OK, *Black Rover*, can you make . . .' The man on the other end was quick as a flash – he grasped it in seconds. 'Roger, understood. Get airborne and steer zero nine zero and we will find you.'

In the Lynx, the crew were drained, tired, silent. They did their job, did it well, but that didn't mean they had to like it. Neither of them had seen a big one go up before – the barge didn't count. This was a merchantman, maybe 15,000 tons. She must have been loaded to the gunwales with munitions

215

and fuel to have gone up like that. How many men died tonight? How many had their missiles killed?

The observer was feeling slightly sick. Attacking an enemy warship where they had the defensive and offensive systems to make it a fight, where they posed a direct threat to your own safety, to your ship and your shipmates, was one thing, but slamming a pair of Skuas into a virtually defenceless merchantman wasn't what he thought he would ever have to do. The justification was there; it was carrying enemy troops, guns, fuel, ammunition that would be used against British soldiers, but even so. *Beaufort* had issued the challenge. They had heard it clearly.

'This is Her Majesty's warship *Beaufort*, to the six Guatemalan ships approaching Belize City from the south. We believe your intentions are hostile. Turn to seaward or you will be fired upon. I say again, turn to seaward or you will be fired upon. Acknowledge.'

Again and again they tried, over five or six minutes, the last comms from Bennett himself as the Lynx loitered to seaward hidden behind the mangroves growing up out of the swamps of Spanish Cay. Then came the order to go.

The adrenaline had worn off. Now it was just night flying at zero feet, dangerous stuff at the best of times, but this was also E&E, egress and evasion from the attack, and it demanded one hundred per cent concentration from both of them, the pilot to make sure they didn't hit the water and the observer to watch the screens and listen to the passive defence systems. Then came the call from *Black Rover*'s Sea King.

The pilot had met Colby – good man, he said. He was out there, low on fuel, without his deck or support, and couldn't run ashore, not with a battle going on. They would find him, come up fast from his rear, tell him to light up his A/C beacons and get a visual, and then follow them back to *Beaufort*. They would have to come in first, get the rotors folded and their helo pushed into the hangar to make room on the deck for the big Sea King.

The truck came down the hill at speed followed by two Land-Rovers. It slowed at one point, to shove aside an old car that was blocking the road, then ground its way round and into the square with its roundabout. It climbed pavements and shouldered aside a wooden fence and two more cars. People were still in their vehicles, unwilling to leave them to cross the bridge on foot. They stared, sullen, resentful: but no one challenged the occupants of the truck. Tired, filthy, some with light wounds, their eyes were not on the bridge, or the people, but on the road behind them. Everyone knew then – the next vehicles down the hill would be the Guatemalans. People who had stayed with their cars, haranguing the policeman, gathered up their bags and began to run for the bridge; others returned to the town, to their homes, wherever. The truck with its mortars ground its way over the bridge. Major Chard dropped down from the following vehicle and waved it over. The last Land-Rover pulled up.

Lieutenant Estelle walked over to Major Chard, his wide grin expressing his relief at seeing the SAS officer and some of his men and equipment back. So far the whole thing had been surreal, climaxing with a lithe, swarthy-skinned fellow coming back over the bridge and engaging him in a brief conversation in English, his accent from South London.

'I'm Pete Collins. I own a restaurant here and I'm staying on this side. You get your hands on a mobile?'

'I beg your pardon?'

'Can you get your hands on a mobile phone?'

'Why? Corporal!' he shouted, looking away. 'That vehicle there. Get it moved back. Keep these people moving, you chaps.' He turned back to Collins. 'Look, we're busy. Get yourself across the bridge would you, there's a good chap.'

Pete lost his temper. 'Son, don't patronize me. I was in the mob when you were in short fucking pants. I was here with intelligence in the seventies, the last time they looked like doing this. I am staying over here. Now get yourself a mobile,' he held his up, "cos you're going to need to know what the fuck's happening over this side.'

Estelle suddenly understood. 'Oh, I see, yes. You're sure?' He was thinking quickly. He couldn't prevent him staying, and they would need intelligence, but the risks were enormous. 'I don't recommend it.'

'I'm sure.'

'Fair enough. Sorry about that. Give me the number you're on. Hang about.' Estelle was looking over his shoulder at Chard climbing out of his vehicle. 'There's the man you should be talking to.'

A moment or two later there was a small group of men gathered at the western end of the bridge, Chard being briefed by Estelle, Pete Collins waiting impatiently, and two Gurkha soldiers to one side.

'You're not going to believe it, but there's a journalist from ITN over the other side, complete with camera crew.'

'Well, I'm not talking to him, you'll have to manage that. But tell him if he films my blokes his kit will end up in the river, and any cooperation ceases, OK?'

Estelle nodded. 'These two chaps of mine have volunteered to keep people back from the bridge while you do your thing.'

'No,' Chard said. 'Can you swim?' he asked, looking at the two Gurkha soldiers.

One man nodded. Barely, Chard realized, just what the army had taught him. Brave little buggers, with the river this high and this fast. No swimming in the mountains of Nepal. On the other hand, he had men who could swim like fish. 'One of my blokes can do it.' He turned to Pete. 'And you, sir?'

Pete smiled fleetingly – a major calling *him* sir – one of the benefits of civvy street.

'I have a business over here, I'm staying. Get yourself a mobile and I'll help if I can, give you a sitrep every now and then.' That was the giveaway, a civilian wouldn't use that word.

'When were you in?'

'Seventeen years until 1991, most of it here in Belize.'

'Fair enough. You know what will happen if they catch you?'

'Yeah.'

'OK, I'll give you a radio.'

'No, no radio, they'll track it. I'll use a mobile, a digital. There will be dozens in use over here.' He handed over a slip of paper. 'That's my number. I'll turn it on for three minutes at midnight. You call me and give me your number and from there on, I'll call you.'

There was a shout from somewhere, and Chard's radio hissed into life. He listened and then looked at the group around him.

'They're here. Lieutenant, get your people back over the bridge. Mr Collins, we will talk later?' There was a flash of light and a blast from the hilltop, then another – tank rounds. They had learned; they weren't coming over that rise without softening it first. The battle of San Ignacio had begun.

Chapter Eight

The Guatemalan assault began at 4.00 a.m. UK time and even at that unearthly hour, there were those awake for the early news bulletins; inevitably, in a unit as diverse and as disciplined as the Parachute Regiment, some of them heard it. Men from all three battalions, some trailing in bleary-eyed after a night out, some up very early, out training in the dawn light, some on the road travelling, one watching television news in a Heathrow departure lounge. He didn't take his flight; a subaltern in 1 Para, he immediately returned to barracks. Some were off-camp with their families, two were with hired mountain bikes sitting having breakfast in an all-night roadside café, several were hung over in a girl's flat in Farnham.

One was with a girl he had met a few weeks before, lying in the wonderful comfort of her double bed in her flat in Camberley. She had an early shift at the airport, and as she was making some tea and pottering around the kitchen she had turned on the radio.

'And in a breaking news story, British troops have been fired upon in an attack by Guatemala on Belize. Foreign and Commonwealth Office Secretary of State James Hildon said that he is appalled at reports that Guatemala has invaded Belize and that Britain has an obligation under UN mandates to assist Belize in her defence and the actions of British troops in returning fire and engaging were entirely justified. The Prime Minister has called an emergency cabinet meeting for first thing this morning.'

The soldier, a sergeant in B Coy 2 Para, came out of the bedroom, a towel round his waist. She looked at him, surprised he was up, and was about to say something when he held his hand up, his ear cocked to the radio.

'Reports that the Guatemalan army crossed into Belize last night have been confirmed and we take this dispatch from ITN's Leo

Scobey in Belize. The Guatemalan army has invaded Belize. They crossed the border, just a few miles up the road from where I am standing, in strength just minutes after nine p.m. tonight, almost two hours ago. There are reports of an attack on the international airport at Belize City. British troops, just a handful of them, here on a training exercise, have been involved already, something not surprising, given the defence obligation Britain holds for this once-British colony. Guatemala has long held territorial claims to this part of Central America and when British Honduras, as it once was, became the Independent State of Belize the UN put her protection firmly in Britain's hands, till she could learn to defend herself. With a tiny defence force, only six hundred strong, one must wonder if Belize would ever be able to defend herself without assistance from an aggressive Guatemala whose army is 40,000 strong.

During the eighties, when again there was heightened tension along this border area, Britain maintained a garrison here in Belize, a full battalion supported by army helicopters. But defence cuts saw an end to that and now there are never more than a handful of British troops in Belize, normally on jungle training. The Guatemalan army approaches down this road behind me and will be in San Ignacio, the main centre of population in the west of this country, any minute. From here it is only eighty-odd miles through to the coast and Belize City, an hour and a half by car. This is Leo Scobey for ITN in San Ignacio, Belize.'

'Jeeeesus Christ,' he said, thinking fast. The lads – it's the Reg. D are on their way back and C are there now. 'That's the Gurkha lads, C Coy.'

'Oh . . . do you want a cup of tea?' she asked, trying to take it in. She had only been seeing him a few weeks, and many of his expressions were still unfamiliar. But she loved him enough to take pleasure in learning his ways, to find that exciting.

'No. No thanks.'

'Off you go, then.' She kissed him. 'Back to bed with you.'

'Can't,' he replied, thinking aloud, adjusting the towel round his waist, although there was no one there to see him but her. 'Going in.'

'In?' she queried. 'It's five in the morning, in where?'

'Return to barracks.'

'Return?' She was confused.

'Yes, return to barracks. They will be recalling everyone. Umm, I'll see you –'

'Recalling? What? To go somewhere?'

'Yes, probably. That's our lads in the shit there. Not only that, but we are spearhead, and I have got to find my toms.' She still didn't fully understand. 'I'll try and phone you,' he said. 'But I might not be able to.'

'Why, I mean, what's . . .'

He looked at her, taking time to explain it. 'That's our lads in action there. I'm going back to the barracks because they are probably recalling the battalion for deployment. If they do, then we go. We are the . . .' he looked for the words, 'rapid reaction spearhead, the first unit to be sent. OK? I don't know for how long.'

'Oh my God!' she said, the realization hitting her. 'You think you're going to war?'

He nodded.

San Ignacio

Scobey had wanted to say more, to say that all that stood between the invaders and victory was a small band of Paras, but the young 2 Para officer had been adamant. The lessons of the Falklands, where the media were broadcasting tactical details to a listening world and the Argentinians, were imprinted deeply on every army officer, he realized.

'The last time that journalists were with the Paras in action you shafted us, probably cost us lives. Cross the line,' Estelle had said, 'cross the line just once, and you're fucked. Got me? You won't be able to report from here, you will be taken away by the police. You will get no cooperation. I won't have the lives of my men put in jeopardy. Play the game, observe the restrictions, and we will do what we can to allow you to do your job. Have I made myself clear?'

'As crystal,' Scobey had replied. 'Credit me with more intelligence than you do, there's a good chap.'

222

'I'll do that when you have demonstrated it!' Estelle had snapped.

He was watching now, his cameraman taking background shots, catching the Guatemalan advance as they entered the town. You couldn't see vehicles, but there were explosions and fires over the brow of the hill, and now well down in the town as they slowly moved forward. Ahead of him sixty yards away was the eastern end of the bridge, this location chosen by the cameraman as the best they could do. From the window in the now-deserted house they could see across the bridge. It was going to go, and *that* they had to get on tape. It would be dramatic, even if it was only a civilian demolition job; as part of a battle it would be sensational.

'Pity it's fucking dark,' Chubby said. 'Think they will wait till daybreak if we ask them?'

Scobey smiled. 'In your dreams.'

Two men were running back out of the dark across the bridge and as they hit the bank one raised his hand.

The Squadron's demolition expert was a staff sergeant. It was said that he could blow anything up – how big did you want the pieces and how widely scattered? This bridge was a piece of old piss, he thought; in fact, several times in the last ten years he had practised on this very structure and now he was going to get a chance to actually drop it! Outstanding! Elegance. He always wanted elegance. Given enough kit, he always said, anybody could blow something up, but to do it with the minimum of fuss, the minimum of explosives, with the maximum effect – that was elegance. That was what he would say when he saw a decent bit of work from one of his Squadron pupils: 'Very elegant.'

The Holdsworthy Bridge was a centre-span crossing between two buttresses, with a short link span back to the bank either end. Three prime spans supported by two buttresses, that rose up tonight from a fast-flowing, swollen river. He had placed charges to drop the centre and far spans in several pieces. He had seen a bridge once where the central span was dropped and did just that, fell fifteen feet but remained intact. Troops on foot were still able to cross it. Embarrassing, and a tactical cock-up. No, this one would be

223

elegant, a series of small individual explosions within milliseconds of each other would have four sections of centre-span falling. With charges on the suspension cables and on the steelwork itself, they would drop sixty feet to the water within seconds of each other; the river was flowing fast and deep enough to carry the falling steel a few feet, disperse things tidily. The link span on the far side would follow suit.

The two troopers ran past him and Chard tapped him on the shoulder. He blew a whistle, piercingly, a signal to all who heard it, and pressed the electrical detonator sequence switch.

The bridge had lights to illuminate the crossing at night and also for decorative effect. The explosions began at the far end, the flashes and the mini-shockwaves evident. For some reason the lights remained on almost till the last explosions and those watching could actually see the first spans falling amid the dust and flying debris, water splashing up where the heavy steel structures went in. Twenty seconds later it was all over. The dust, minimal because of the rain, had settled and it was dark – very dark, just the swirling floodwaters below.

'Nice one, Ernie. No one is crossing that fucker,' one of the Squadron men said. Either side of him the Gurkhas whose positions were close to the bridge and who had been withdrawn for safety's sake, were scuttling back into their sangars and trenches.

'Yes,' Ernie said with a big grin on his face. 'Elegant, that was, very elegant. Almost dignified.'

5 *Airborne Brigade HQ – Aldershot*

Behind Bruneval barracks, in the small three-storey modern blue-glass and concrete building that housed Brigade's headquarters, the brigadier was in his office where he had been all night.

'We've got one hundred and seventy-odd soldiers holding two fronts against three brigades,' he muttered unhappily. 'What the fuck are they doing?' he snapped, his anger aimed at Whitehall.

The colonel with him, his number two at Brigade, looked

up from the lists he was working on. He had been thinking about little else. 'That's one view, sir. Here's another. B Squadron and C Coy are there now, outnumbered and outgunned, but there and dug in. By morning there we should have Tyson-Davis back in and ten more from A Squadron. They will have plenty of LAWs, Milan and mortars, a fifty-calibre section, two companies from 2 Para, a reinforced Sabre Squadron – probably the best small formation in the entire British army. For that Guatemalan lead element, this is the light infantry of their nightmares.'

The brigadier grunted. 'Bollocks. You can't hold an airfield with two platoons, that's a battalion's job. And you can't hold back a mechanized advance with two platoons and a handful of special forces. Not for long, anyway.'

'He had no choice.'

'I know,' the brigadier muttered miserably. 'Where are we?'

'Wallace is in as you know. OC 1 Para is also in now. Other commanders have been contacted and are on their way –'

There was a brief knock and Colonel Ranulf Wallace, OC 2 Para, strode in.

'Sorry, sir. Any news?'

'Settle down, Colonel,' the brigadier responded. 'It will be through when our lords and masters deem it –'

'Bugger the lords and masters, sir. They're my toms!'

Since the orders had gone out to his lads Wallace had been pacing his office, crossing over to Brigade HQ every hour or so for updates.

'Back off, Colonel. I don't like it any more than you do!'

'Sir, I can have the rest of my battalion mounting in twenty-four hours. Brigade can follow.'

The brigadier was thinking quickly; there was merit in the suggestion. 5 Airborne Brigade were the current JRDF, the joint rapid deployment force, the spearhead. They were to provide a battalion at high readiness to ACE Mobile, and 2 Para was that battalion, the sharp tip of the spearhead brigade. What's the likelihood, he thought? There were only two units set up for a role like this. If there was a response it would be either 3 Commando Brigade or 5 Airborne, both available to 3rd UK Division. The command would come from

Westminster to PJHQ. They would issue orders to UK Land at Wilton, who would assign the task to 3rd UK Div. Although 3 Commando Brigade was available to the Division, it was Royal Navy. Hopefully Division would use its own fast deployment unit, 5 Airborne Brigade, if for no other reason than the initial environment – infiltration to the battle area might require airborne assault. 3 Commando could be air mobile, but they were not trained to be delivered into a theatre by parachute and unless the senior ops people were absolutely sure the airhead was secure this should be 5 Airborne's task.

The Brigade, four infantry battalions, supported by artillery, engineers, logistics and numerous others was usually on seventy-two-hour notice to move. In reality they could get some units away to the air mounting centre quicker, and others would have the inevitable delays.

Ran Wallace had been grinding his people through their paces constantly. If any unit could do it, it was 2 Para. But twenty-four hours? Midweek, they were on three hours' notice to move. That, in real terms, meant that from the recall his soldiers could all be back at 'the Shot' within three hours, but most of them could be ready to personally mount within an hour.

The problem was logistics and supply. They would go in heavy, with enough expendable ordnance to keep the battalion in the fight till the Brigade arrived. Each man would go in with four or five hundred rounds of ammunition, his grenades, a couple of mortar bombs, and other kit. Wedges would have to be prepared and loaded. The only personal stuff would be in their day-bag, a poncho liner, water, food and a toothbrush. They would need to raid ammunition stores across Aldershot to get what they wanted. The brigadier stood and walked to the window, looking out.

'Fair enough, Ran. You'll hear soon enough. UK Land and 3rd Div have had the whisper, they are expecting orders from Northwood any time. We shall,' he paused, looking for the word he wanted, 'anticipate.' He turned and looked back at Colonel Wallace. 'Do it. Recall your people. Assume you will air mount in twenty-four hours unless you get orders to suspend. I'll get on to Div, see if they have heard anything yet. You've only got HQ, support and B. You'll need another rifle company. I'll get you some Gurkhas. If your quartermaster needs help, shout.'

His phone rang. It was 3rd Div at Bulford. UK Land wanted readiness of Brigade as JRDF spearhead for PJHQ and advised that from 0530 hours 5 Airborne Brigade was under the command of CJRDFO at Northwood. Orders would follow on secure comms. The brigadier looked at Colonel Wallace. 'Wait,' he mimed and a moment later he put the phone down and immediately picked it up and dialled a number to talk to the man himself at Northwood.

Within a minute he was raising a thumb at Wallace. 'I understand, sir. I can have 2 Para airborne this time tomorrow. Rest of the Brigade away against . . .' Wallace was going for the stairs at a run and he kept running round the road and across to his offices in the battalion lines. He crashed through the doors where some of his staff had been gathering for the last hour or so.

'Recall everyone! I mean everyone! Scale A! The battalion will air mount in twenty-four hours for offensive ops. I want company commanders, HQ staff here in thirty minutes.'

Battalion G3 reached for a phone. It's on, sweet Mother of Jesus, it's on! Hold on, boys, hold the airhead. Just hold the airhead, we're on our way. We can stop them there and wait for Brigade.

Every soldier had to leave a contact number and it was a cascade effect, each person called would then call others. In theory the entire battalion could be contacted in under an hour but in practice it didn't work that well. There were people away from home, not on the phone, travelling, so there was a back-up comms system that had been used for many years. Local radio stations' news organizations were helpful, dropping the recall on to the end of news bulletins as public service announcements. Railway and bus stations put out blackboard signs, places where the men gathered were telephoned. At Waterloo, the station that serviced the lines down into Surrey and Hampshire, four blackboard signs went up. In addition the large matrix light display between the departure boards made the same announcement. '2 PARA RETURN TO BARRACKS'.

Five soldiers from B Coy up in London for a mate's stag party were entering the station as the signs went up. One was hoping Tie Rack was open, they had some 'wicked' waistcoats. Three of the others just wanted time to grab a cup of coffee before the train. They were due in at work at 0830, so there was plenty of time. As they ambled in, one of them was looking for the fifth of their group, Corporal Tabs Baker, slightly ahead of them leaving the cab.

'Where is he?' he asked.

'Fuckin' 'ell,' one of them muttered, surprised.

'What?'

'Up there,' he pointed, 'the moving sign thing. That's us.'

'Hang on, I want coffee,' one of them who hadn't seen it said.

A piercing whistle cut across the station concourse, echoing around the high roof. It was Tabs, by the entrance to platform thirteen, looking unlike the Tabs who had just been out on the piss with them. This was Corporal Baker, back into work mode. 'MOVE IT!' he shouted.

The four men began to run down the station and Baker went ahead of them and opened a door to a train that was just about to leave, effectively preventing it moving off. The Great Western Trains man on the platform, about to signal the driver that he was clear to move, called down to him, but Baker ignored him, and a moment or two later the four soldiers came on to the platform at a run, piling into the first carriage.

'What's your game?' the conductor called, walking towards Baker. 'Close that door and stand clear!'

'We have to get this train.'

'I beg to differ,' the conductor said pompously, 'this train has officially departed.'

'Now it has,' Baker snapped. The lads were on. He entered and slammed the door behind him.

''Oo do you think you are?' the indignant conductor called after him, knowing the battle was lost.

'Piss off,' Baker muttered. He walked down the train till he

228

found the lads and they predictably wanted to know 'what the fuck was happening'.

'We'll know soon enough,' Baker replied.

At PJHQ Northwood, the J2 Intelligence and J3 ops people had taken a priority signal channelled through Hereford. OC C Coy, officer commanding British forces in the theatre wanted an immediate weather forecast for the Yucatan peninsula, and the area south-west of that, taking in all of Guatemala, with analysis. Intelligence from captured enemy suggested that Guatemalan paratroops had been ready for deployment for air assault on Belmopan and San Ignacio but were delayed by the weather. How long would current conditions hold? The message was relayed to CJRDFO, the Chief of Joint Rapid Deployment Force Operations, Peter Macmillan, a major-general who reported direct through to the boss, the CJO, the Chief of Joint Operations, a three-star general.

From now on everything would go past Major-General Macmillan. Macmillan was young, only forty-eight, a fast-track man, clever, some said even brilliant. He was from the Royal Green Jackets, where they called him 'Mac the knife'. It would be Macmillan's task to command the JRDF from Northwood, rally the specialist support they needed, see it delivered, see them fed, supplied and lead them to achieve their objectives as laid down by Whitehall and the Chief of the Defence Staff through the CJO. At this moment he was ensconced with ACOS J3 Sea, looking at exactly what support HMS *Beaufort* could offer and with what risk profiles. The intelligence about the Guatemalan paratroopers had moved the pace up another notch.

'My problem is this. We have fixed wing VTOL on its way to St George's. I want support for that base, make sure it's still ours when they get there. I also want Fox and Chard to know if they have aircraft inbound, whether that's troop transports or ground attack. The radar at the airport is still operational but no one knows for how long. What can your people help me with?'

ACOS had three of his team there, all Royal Navy, the

duty officer a commander, who pulled a huge chart across from a rack that had appeared from somewhere.

'That's happening already, sir. The *Black Rover*'s budgie was ashore as you know. She then moved on to St George's with one of the Gazelles from the camp. The navy budgie made contact with *Beaufort*'s, followed her home. She is on *Beaufort* now and about to go back to St George's with twenty armed ratings and an extra machine gun for the army lads to mount in their Gazelle. They want to go back and offer what air they can.'

Macmillan was delighted – someone was using their initiative. He expected nothing else, but was always pleased to see such behaviour.

'Commander Bennett has advised that his intent is to get close enough to support St George's with NGS should that be required.'

'Can he get close enough to offer that to the people at the airport?'

'No, sir,' the commander replied. 'Water is generally too shallow and the charts up that way are suspect, but from a position where she can look out over St George's Cay she can put out a radar screen. We will know about any aircraft in the area right up to San Ignacio, but sir,' he paused, 'it will compromise her presence, badly compromise her. Everyone will know exactly where she is.'

Macmillan sat back and thought quickly. Maybe not such a bad thing. HMS *Beaufort* was a brand-new Type 23 frigate. There was nothing that the Guatemalans could throw at her that she couldn't handle. She had more firepower than a Second World War heavy cruiser, radar eyes that could look out the better part of two hundred miles. 'I'd like that – get 'em on the back foot. She is all-powerful in those waters, yes?'

The naval men nodded, but they were uncomfortable with it. You didn't expose stealth ships for the sake of it.

'If it's a choice between keeping her hidden, but with her ability to see out long range hampered by that, and going overt and protecting the lads on the ground with some fore-warning of attack from the air, then I'm afraid the choice is clear. We can balance that by opening Bennett's rules of engagement right out, let him fight as he sees fit.'

Gulf of Mexico

On board *Beaufort* the Lynx was back in her hangar, rotors folded in, and the big Sea King was on the deck. Aviation artificers and armourers were working on the Lynx, getting her prepared for another sortie, and out on the deck, twenty sailors armed with SA80s, now wearing DPM tunics over their blue trousers were waiting for the order to board the Sea King. Two GPMGs and ten cases of ammunition sat on the deck, with medical supplies, and two dozen bacon rolls that the seamen's mess had rustled up. Along with the twenty ratings there was one seaman officer, a watchkeeping lieutenant, and the ship's Chief Petty Officer (Missiles). Chops (M) was the senior non-commissioned person in the ship's offensive complement and he wasn't chuffed with this nonsense. His battle station was down in the Ops room, sitting at his console from where he would launch missiles and personally press the trigger to fire the deck gun. That was where the real action was, not buggering about on some crappy little island with wet feet, midges, chiggers, mosquitoes, sea snakes and fucking green jobs.

Along the ship on the officers' flat the two crew from the Lynx were winding down. They had been quickly debriefed and then allowed to go below, to shower, rest and eat something before they were to be ready to fly again. Both were quiet, absorbed in their thoughts. Bennett knew to expect that; aircrews never had the chance to wind down, to come mentally to grips with the experience. Going in minutes from a combat adrenaline high, missile strikes, exploding targets and dying people, to the comparatively safe cocooned environment of the ship left them disoriented, unsettled, distant. For the sailors no longer were the aviators' WAFUs, the acronym for 'Wet and fucking useless'. They were theirs. The ship was at action stations, they had watched her missiles launch, heard the kill, seen it on their screens, those on deck had seen the flash over the horizon. They felt part of it. The Lynx was theirs, their striking arm, but it wasn't the same as being there, pressing the launch button, flying the budgie that made the attack.

They both walked into the wardroom, their flying suits still on, hair wet with sweat. 'Well done, sirs,' the steward had said. 'Nice to have you back safe.' He saw the look, and was old enough to understand it.

Neither man wanted niceties, to be noticed. The thought of being congratulated was unseemly. They knew that whoever didn't die in the massive secondary explosions would drown. They might have got a boat or two away, maybe a few rafts. The other vessels should have stopped to pick up survivors, but who knew? Maybe they scattered, or were milling about, too frightened to stop, leaving survivors, bleeding and screaming and dying in the water, food for the tiger sharks that prowled here. Strong currents would sweep the men over the reef and out to sea. How many? Hundreds?

The observer poured himself a cup of coffee and lit a cigarette. The wardroom was 'no smoking' till after supper but he didn't care, just lit it and smoked in silence. He looked down and his hand was shaking. A few moments later the steward arrived and put a plate of sandwiches down in front of him.

'Egg mayonnaise, sir, just how you like them,' he said softly. He looked at the pilot. 'And for you, sir, the PO's mulligatawny soup with some chilli wine. Saved you some.'

'Thanks.'

The observer looked at the sandwiches, but instead of taking one he stood up. 'Sorry. Not hungry.' He walked out. He didn't want anyone to see what he was going to do, felt he had to do. Royal Navy lieutenant commanders, grown men, leaders, highly trained to defend the realm and the free world, weren't supposed to want to cry. He went to his cabin, fell to his knees and tried to pray, but nothing came, only tears.

When the pilot came to find him twenty minutes later he was wiping his eyes and mildly embarrassed at being caught in this state.

'Hi.'

'Sorry about that, didn't hear you.'

The pilot nodded, a little smile on his face.

'It was just –'

'I know,' the pilot said, thinking only a sick bastard would not be affected by what we had to do tonight. 'I feel it too. You ready? The other ships have turned southwards so the briefing is for a patrol sortie only.'

On the bridge Bennett was reading new orders from Northwood that had come through on secure comms. He called for the navigator.

San Ignacio

'Pass the word. Tell your men,' Chard said, 'no one is to initiate fire.'

They were in a small hollow, Chard, Estelle, his radio operator, the SSM and the Squadron signaller. Chard quickly outlined where he had deployed his small force for this next phase of the fight.

'When that lead vehicle enters the square we are going to take it out, before it can cross into the side streets. Then we hit whatever's behind it. Once that action has begun your blokes can engage, but I'm not sure many of them will have visual. Our mortars are back there on the rise. They will engage as soon as we have slotted that tank. OK?'

'Fine,' Estelle said. 'How long do you think, sir, before troops on foot make it to the riverbank?'

'Depends who is commanding. A good officer, taking it carefully, but with purpose? No more than twenty minutes I'd say, circle round the back of the town. Could be as little as five if he is a gung-ho dickhead, or an hour if he's finding all our booby-traps. Right, back to your chaps.'

'You staying here, sir?'

'For the moment. If they get through, then as you make for the airhead, we will just melt into the green and do our job. But for now, until the situation stabilizes or changes, I'll have a few bods here.'

At the guest house an ambulance had been and taken away the wounded. They didn't want to take the dead, they knew they would be too busy for that, but Dave the owner slipped them a few US dollars each, just to get them back to the hospital morgue; he didn't want them at the guest house. The American ambassador had been telephoned and at some personal risk – there is no US marine guard detail at the US Embassy in Belize – drove over; the bulk of the guests were Americans. He supported Dave in his request to have the dead removed and the ambulance men agreed to come back.

The police had arrived, four cars of them, followed by the fire brigade, but there was no fire left. Then most of the police suddenly raced back to three cars and roared away, leaving the last four policemen talking to the BDF fellows down on the street, and an officer who had arrived. He wanted to redeploy the men, and there was talk of martial law and a curfew having been imposed, but no one could substantiate that. The bodies of the ill-fated Guatemalan marines were laid out in a row and the British special forces soldier had slipped quietly away from the flashbulbs of the local press.

In the guest house the staff had swept up the glass, cleaned up the blood and dispensed drinks to the survivors, but they did so in a dazed state, still unable to comprehend fully what had happened. Dave had sent two of them home and been on the phone and the manager from the Radisson had responded. Anyone who wanted to move out of the guest house could be accommodated gratis at his hotel just two blocks away. Oddly enough, of the twelve resident guests, only two chose to move, the rest bonded somehow by the experience.

Dion Manuelez had slipped out the back gate and was walking to his car. His girlfriend was getting off her shift at the hotel and he wanted to get her home safe, but he was stopped by a shout from someone who knew him. It was one of the Belize Defence Force guys, still on a high after the contact.

'Dion, need ya, marn.'

'What is it?'

'Come see da boss.'

He was led into the Maritime Wing building to where the SAS soldier was squatting on the ground by his radio, his bergen and kit neatly beside him. He looked up.

'Dis is de marn. Best boatman in da country, sah.'

The soldier looked at Dion. 'You drive that cutter?' He pointed out the open door to where the Maritime Wing's patrol boat was tied up at the wharf. 'We got an engineer, a deck man, but no one who can drive it.'

Dion didn't need to look at it. He had seen it often enough, both here at the wharf and out on the reef. It was two thirds the size of the live-aboard dive boat he had skippered all last year, maybe sixty-five feet long. He knew she had been re-engined, two years before, with a pair of big Detroit diesels.

'Sure,' he shrugged.

'That's good. You happy to help?'

Dion nodded.

At JB's, Sally's roadhouse restaurant and bar on the thirty-two-mile marker, on the western highway out of Belize City and halfway to San Ignacio, things had been quiet most of the evening. Although the invasion had begun two hours before, out where they were it might as well have been in a time warp. Travellers had stopped, eaten, drunk a few beers and moved on. A few of the regulars were in, sitting at the tables by the bar, talking about the early rain, and nothing much seemed to be happening, but now things were going a little goofy. There was traffic flying down the highway, all of it heading east, heavy traffic. She was standing at the restaurant door looking out over the gravel car park and Miss Jenny sidled over.

'This is weird,' Sally said. 'Never seen so much on the road at this hour.'

'Ain't no one stopping either,' Miss Jenny added.

Sally thought about the army trucks she had seen late that afternoon, heading up the highway; they were racing too. And the Land-Rovers? No, that was last night. But – them going up, every man and his banjo coming back?

235

'I'm gonna call some of the boys up at Cayo,' Miss Jenny said.

'Try the Bel-Brit or Pete at Eva's,' Sally advised.

She came back a minute later. 'Phone's dead.'

'What?'

'I said the phone's dead. Maybe the lines are down some-wheres. Could be the rain.'

'Could be,' Sally said, 'but I got a feeling it ain't. Let's see if Mary has her brother's mobile.'

San Ignacio

Chard waited. The SAS were strategic troops, to be deployed against strategic targets, and although the bridge was arguably the most strategic point along the entire advance, this wasn't best use of his people. But they were soldiers first and fore-most, and if they could help the 2 Para lads hold this position then they could halt the entire invasion. If the Guats broke through then they would let the advance roll over them and become stay-behind troops.

The tank inched its way cautiously into the open. Chard watched it through binoculars – he didn't need night-vision kit, the advance had been marked with suppression fire and things were burning in its wake; the streetlights were still on too. He moved the glasses an inch. Infantry were out in front, darting from shadow to shadow. This is more like it, he thought, armour moving up slowly, supported by men on the ground. With sufficient APCs they could have rolled through at speed, but much of their light armour was scattered down the highway back to the border and bogged down on the track through to Negroman. They had a *soldier* in command now, a real one, who used his head. This commander was using what little armour he had left wisely.

The entrances to the bridge and roundabout were clogged with cars that had been deserted. Some civilians were still over there in the square, unwilling to leave their vehicles perhaps, or trying to work out what to do; now they were running from the advancing tank.

The tank would have to move round to the rear. There was only one line of clear sight from their side, the route earlier cleared by Estelle for their egress, but that didn't matter. The tank was high enough that its turret was a clear foot above the cars and the Milan team could target it all the way across. Chard wanted the route blocked. If they hit the tank at the right point then the way round the rear would be closed too. From then on, unless they started moving cars, it would be everyone on foot.

One hundred yards away and below Chard's observation point Estelle was in his command and control position at the rise of the riverbank. Below him to left and right his two platoons of Gurkhas were dug in. They had been working like Trojans all evening and it had paid off. Every section had multiple sangars; communication trenches, just deep enough to slither along, joined many of them. The company command and medics post above them was dug into the vehicle track that led up from the dry-season crossing point to the asphalt road. It was deep enough to sit in, with a berm of logs and earth along the front. Canvas over poles covered it from above, and that in turn was scattered with leaves and earth. It would be safe from anything but a direct hit with a mortar bomb. From here and the fighting holes below Estelle could hold the centre. The other platoon commander was down to the right overlooking the dry-season crossing, the most vulnerable point, and the CSM was on the left flank. But they were pitifully few. The gaps between the defences were more than gaps, he thought, they were measured in tens of yards. The only saving grace was the interlinking arcs of fire for the section weapons.

Some of the Squadron blokes had settled in too. There were teams on the extremes of the flanks, one at the ford where they had laid out their fire-control kit, and one team up on the road with their mortars.

Estelle's mouth was dry, but he felt liquid fear in his guts. It was dark their side, but over the river the town was ablaze with light. From his position he could see nothing of the advance down the hill, and depended on Chard's signaller to keep him informed. They must be down by now, he thought.

The Squadron team at the southern end of the line had their Milan set up at Landy's restaurant, the low building just fifty yards from the entrance to the bridge. Landy's wasn't a restaurant in true terms, it was a flat-roofed shack that dispensed most of its offerings through a hatch. Painted white, its entire frontage was dominated by a huge red and white Coca-Cola sign and below that three men had set up their defensive position. The firing post with two more of the team was above them on the roof. Two missiles, maybe three from here, and when they began to attract return fire, they could drop off the rear and go into cover.

'Got 'im!'

'Hit it!' came the command back.

The missile streaked away across the river, under the Shell sign at the petrol station, over car rooftops, and hit the tank. There was a blinding flash, and a huge blast, secondary explosions ripping the sixty-ton monster to pieces. Debris was falling from the sky, not only pieces of the tank, but of the building behind it, including a sheet of corrugated iron from somewhere. They fired a second missile at a truck that had been nosing its way into the square; when the Milan hit, the driver was trying to get into reverse gear. Over where the tank was on fire the nearest car, its windows shattered by the blast, erupted into flames and soon others began to burn. Small-arms fire was reaching over to them, pinpricks of muzzleflash and tracer in the darkness.

The SAS men dropped down off the roof, the precious Milan post was carefully lowered down by the last man and they moved into their next firing position. Behind them on the flatbed truck the men serving the mortars began their deadly work, targeting over the hill at traffic still entering the town and the road down the slope opposite. Their fire controller was up a hill on the eastern side from where he could look down into the town and even see stretches of the road.

As small-arms fire began to pour over the river from various points, below them, in the jungle along the riverbank, the Gurkhas held their fire, their discipline paramount. There was small-arms fire in the town, too, reconnaissance by fire perhaps, or maybe just edgy, nervous Guatemalans shooting at shadows. All who heard it hoped they weren't targeting civilians.

It was fully twenty minutes before the first Guatemalan infantry patrols made it to where the ground fell away to the water below. These enemy, the first he had seen, were close to what was left of the bridge, but Estelle knew there would be others down the line. Was this recce, patrols to look for his line, seek him out? Or was this the advance proper, men moving forward to set up their positions to fight? Either way he didn't want them settled in there. The corporal looked at him and Estelle nodded.

'Enemy, across the river,' the corporal said, 'two hundred yards, white building right of bridge support.'

The SAW barrel shifted slightly and the rest of the section lined up.

'On the command . . . fire!'

The machine gun opened up, four bursts into the patrol across the river, individual soldiers taking targets either side of its swath of death. To the right a gun opened up, another section automatic weapon. C Company's two platoons didn't have any GPMGs, they had flown out with D Coy, but they had plenty of 5.56 LSWs and one by one they began to fire as gunners found targets. The Squadron did have the heavy-barrelled 7.62 GPMGs, eight of them, and Estelle thought he saw at least five coming back with the teams on the vehicles. Chard had deployed them but they would remain silent until it was time to show their hand. The tactics were simple enough. Mortars provided cover from five thousand metres in to one thousand, the heavy-barrelled machine guns from one thousand metres down to three hundred and then the individual weapon took over. The GPMG was still the queen of any infantry battle, and with a range of a thousand yards, they formed the second line of defence. With interlocking fields of fire they could chop an attacking force to pieces well before they were in range of riflemen.

For now the Squadron's guns were silent, as were the Gurkha positions on the left flank, the extreme southern end, where the CSM, Nandu Goreng, put his hand on his gunner's

239

shoulder and shook his head. They would remain hidden until it was necessary to reveal themselves.

The fire coming back at them was sporadic and this surprised Estelle. Given the size of the Guatemalan force, he expected a sustained volume of heavy fire. His men had engaged the recce patrols using surprise and effectively neutralized them, and what fire was coming back was from the survivors of those patrols as they moved back into cover and tried to organize themselves. He found himself smiling. His own fear had evaporated with the first shots of the engagement, and the nightmare images of thousands of enemy soldiers with fixed bayonets all running at him had dissolved into reality. This I can handle, he thought, this is what I have been trained to do.

He moved out of the hole, his radio operator with him, and scuttled down the line. His lads were fighting by the book – single shots, sometimes the double tap, but no bursts, no full automatic, the classic mistake of green troops the first time they were in action. He dropped into a hole with two of his men.

'All right, Trooper Tan. Norquay?'

'Yes, sir.'

'Remember, pick your targets, conserve your ammunition. OK?'

'Yes, sir.'

'Good lads.' He moved off.

Very soon he was at the ford. This was the critical point, where the river was widest but shallowest. In the dry season you could wade across, or drive a vehicle over. On the opposite side a track led up and to the left, the way into the town. Up there were the bus station and the market, with plenty of cover.

His men were engaging as they saw targets but as he arrived their sergeant called a halt even to that, telling them to wait till they had something decent to aim at. Estelle was pleased with the discipline. Short of ammunition as they were, every shot would have to count. Fire was coming back over, but much of it was high. Again pleasing – the Guatemalans had no idea where they were on this side or the fire would be considerably more accurate. He found the other platoon commander and dropped into his hole. 'How's things?'

'Too bloody quiet.' He was nervous, edgy. 'There's three brigades of them, so why are there only a handful down here?'

'My guess is they are moving down as we speak. These are recce only.'

'What do you think they are going to do?'

Estelle laughed, surprising himself. 'Haven't a clue. If I was them, I'd move some machine guns in, keep us under fire and pinned down. Then mortar us, bomb us. Then, when I figured we had taken a pounding, I'd bring down my rafts and bridging equipment, and roll right through us.'

'Yeah, that's what I thought too. But you know what? These scrotes? They have got as much chance of being able to build a bridge in the dark as my granny does. I reckon that will have to wait till first light.' A burst of fire ripped through the trees above them and both men ducked involuntarily. Then another, a long, sustained burst. 'That's an M60,' he finished. 'You were right.'

Gulf of Mexico

Beaufort was edging into English Cay channel, the main passage into Belize through the reefs, moving slowly, her revolutions right down at fifty a minute. Bennett was going to try and do what Northwood wanted – keep an eye on St George's Cay, but also provide a radar screen for the lads ashore, and all of this without putting the keel aground on the reef. From their position in daylight they would have been able to see Goff's Cay, a ridiculously beautiful little island no bigger than a football field complete with palm trees and a frond-roofed hut. But tonight visibility was bad; it was dark as pitch, and those on the bridge wings could hear the surf breaking on the reefs, not a comforting sound for blue-water sailors.

'Captain, Ops.'

'Ops, Captain, go.'

'Contact, Captain. Surface craft. Small, fast, dead ahead and heading towards us, range nine miles, over.'

241

'Ops, a single target? Over.'

'That's correct, sir, over.'

'Has a vessel broken away from either enemy group on the screens, over?'

'Not that we have seen, sir. This vessel has come out of Belize City area.'

'What speed?'

'Twenty-two knots, Captain.'

Jesus. Twenty-plus knots for a small craft in this weather? So whose is it? If she is enemy, at only nine miles distant he wouldn't need to waste a Harpoon, he could sink her with gunfire; one shell would do it, but that would pinpoint their position. The helo was on its way up to have another look at what remained of the Guatemalan vessels that were off the airport. They were moving southwards now, along with the other flotilla. So who was this?

'Ops, re-task the helo. Call her back and have her stand off the contact to the north. Then we challenge, over.'

The challenge was never issued. Barely twenty seconds after Bennett had issued the re-task order, Ops were back on the intercom.

Captain, Ops, someone is trying to raise us on VHF, over.'

There was no way Ops, taking the comms through the MCO, would respond while the ship was in her stealth mode. This was the boss's call.

'Have they identified themselves?'

'A callsign only, sir.'

'What channel?'

'Thirty-two, sir.'

'Thank you. Get me a comms PO to the bridge.'

Bennett turned on the small bridge VHF radio unit and listened to the repeated call.

'*Beaufort, Beaufort*, this is Bravo Two-Niner.'

The PO arrived up the stairs at a run.

'Listen to this,' Bennett said, turning up the volume on the set.

'I've heard it, sir.'

'Familiar?' Bennett's question was wise; radio operators, even those in secure comms environments, were still radio men. They loved it, they would be ham radio enthusiasts if they could and some were.

'I've heard it before, sir,' he replied. 'It's an army callsign. Sometimes used to get it on the big gear a few years ago.'

'Not any more?' Bennett was suspicious.

'No, sir. These days it's all burst encoded and –'

'Do you know who it might be?' Bennett interrupted.

'Yes, sir. It's army, but we have worked up with their signallers. Good lads,' he grinned. 'It's 22 SAS, sir, 23 use –'

'Thank you, PO.' Bennett took the microphone from the VHF set.

'If I might, sir,' the PO offered, 'ask them to change to another channel. Every man and his dog will be listening to that.'

Bennett nodded. 'Bravo Two-Niner, change to channel 72.'

A moment or two later they were back.

'*Beaufort, Beaufort*, Bravo Two-Niner.'

'Two-Niner, *Beaufort*, identify yourself.'

'*Beaufort*, friendly special forces aboard a Belize Defence Force vessel. Can I speak to your Alpha, over.'

'Two-Niner, turn to starboard now, if you please.'

'Say again, *Beaufort*?'

'Two-Niner, I say turn to starboard, to your right, turn to your right, over.'

Bennett was watching the screens on the bridge now, the small vessel now clear through the storm clutter on the navigation radar. The contact changed direction. Got you, he thought.

'Two-Niner, thank you. Resume your course and state your intent, over.'

'*Beaufort*, Two-Niner, sorry, this is open comms. Need to meet your Alpha.'

'Roger, Two-Niner . . . continue your course and expect a friendly alongside and take instructions, over.'

On board the patrol boat the B Squadron trooper looked across at Dion, who was at the helm. The wheelhouse lights, it wasn't a bridge by any standard, were turned off completely, only the small compass binnacle, the radar screen, and a few engine instruments glowing.

'Get that? Hold your course.'

Dion nodded. He had a fair idea where she might be. His radar showed the mangroves, the tin-roofed fishing huts dotted round the Cays on stilts, and he knew she would be one of those traces, one out there by English Cay light. He had been told by the soldier not to expect to see a full-sized ship on his screen and he had nodded. He knew about stealth, had read about it in boating magazines, seen it on satellite TV. There was only one practical route into Belize through the barrier reef when the tide was this low. He eased off on the power slightly. This was deep water, the main channel. The waves were small, two or three feet, and the big boat powered her way over them at speed. The Robinson Point light was off to the right where it should be and somewhere out over the bows was English Cay lighthouse. He was looking for the light on the sugar ship, a huge swath on the radar; if he hit that at speed it would be no contest. She was too big to enter the port and leave laden, so she anchored as close as she could get, half a mile in from Stake Bank, and lighters took loads of sugar out to her. When she was full she steamed northwards to the rum distillery at Corozal. He had seen her that afternoon. There – a mooring light through the rain. He eased left a touch and moved the power up again. Suddenly the rain cleared and he turned the wipers off and slid the wheelhouse window back on its runners; now he could see properly. It should be clear – any boats in the channel would have lights showing, and all the locals in fishing canoes would have left before dark. The drums of fuel on the back were well lashed. He pushed the throttles forward again and the boat began to fly, dancing over the wave-tops like a ski-boat.

Belize Airport

The C Coy command position was now a medics post – Fox had given it over to that function. It was deep, and safer than all the other positions and at least his wounded would have some respite. Another of his men had been killed in action and there were five dead now, and twelve wounded. He was astonished at their resilience and their courage. Without exception, they bore their pain in silence, helping each other, encouraging each other. Bleeding stopped, saline drips in, condition stabilized, they did what soldiers have always done: smoked, imagined hospital beds with pretty nurses, hot food, home leave, and all the time they loaded loose rounds into magazines.

But three of them bore terrible wounds and the platoon medics did what they could for them, without much long-term hope. Unless they could get to a hospital or a field trauma team their prognosis was grim.

Along the defensive line the fighting was not at the fevered pitch of the first half-hour, but had waned to a steady level. Even that was consuming ammunition at a staggering rate. His men were disciplined, but tracer fire was arcing out from the Guatemalans' positions, and small arms rattled up and down the line, sharp angry firefights in the darkness. One group of Guatemalans, brave or foolhardy, had rushed a foxhole on the left. The four Gurkhas in the hole had fired until the enemy were on them and then it was vicious hand-to-hand fighting, bayonets and kukris wielded and stabbed, slashed and hacked. Two of them were wounded slightly, but had been bandaged and were now back in the fight, buoyant, charged up with adrenaline, yelling obscenities across at the scrotes. Fox was so proud of them he had a lump in his throat.

This was the way it had always been. On the north-west frontier and in every war since the Gurkhas who had taken the King's shilling had never flinched. Even better, they relished it. The gentle, stocky, ever-smiling mountain people were ferocious fighters. They understood and cherished the long tradition of Nepalese service in the British army. This was what they were paid for, were trained for, prepared for, this is what they did. This fight wasn't just for the army or the queen, it was for them, for every Gurkha soldier who ever fought for the empire, for every Victoria Cross holder, for everyone who was there, and for those who would follow them. This was for the Brigade of Gurkhas, the Duke of Edinburgh's Gurkha Rifles, and also, somewhere down the list, for 2 Para, just a recent incarnation.

Fox knew that there were heads over there somewhere. His chaps had fought hand-to-hand with their kukris, and there would be heads separated from bodies. He reminded himself to check that before daybreak, if they were still there; he didn't want any repercussions later. Gurkhas will be Gurkhas, and in the heat of battle old traditions die hard, but there was no way he wanted anything that could later be held against them.

Out on the left he could hear his lads, screaming insults and jibes at the Guatemalans, cries of '*Mamá Puta*' and other things. They had put together a few ripe Spanish insults, but were having trouble with the pronunciation, so they reverted to English and yelled across telling the scrotes that they had fucked their mothers, their sisters and their daughters, then let their dog have a go. 'She love it!' one of them yelled. Fox grinned and moved down the line on his stomach below the fire. Morale was outstanding.

He thought he knew why the pace of the fight had slowed. HMS *Beaufort* had attacked the second wave and now the first Guatemalan force realized they were on their own and might be for some time, and were therefore probably husbanding their ammunition. In addition the loss of their mortar support would have weighed heavily, both in tactical terms and in morale.

The BDF had been unblooded so far, his Gurkhas taking the attacks head-on, and there were still the twenty marines ready to support a breach in the line, but the bad news was that he, C Coy, was down to sixty-nine fit men and twelve mortar bombs.

Over in the camp, the aircraft mechanic had removed what avionics he could, prepared the Gazelle for destruction, and then as the officer had requested him to do, gone off to find his oppo and the WO2. The shooting hadn't moved closer, but he was still shit-scared and wanted his mates. He had been looking for the best part of half an hour, the mortar damage in the camp such that at times he was disoriented. There were buildings blown to bits, rubble, roofing iron everywhere, little bomb craters, and he must have passed the tree twice or three times. On the last time he had the torch at his feet and the beam shone far enough to the right for him to see legs – a pair of legs. Trouble was, that was all. He looked again, unable to take it in, his mind numb. He swung the torch. A body, his mate, up against the tree. He ran the few feet and looked down at him. His face was covered in something sticky. He called his name gently, as though to wake him from a sleep, and then remembered from the movies – pulse, feel for a pulse. Nothing. Jesus, he's dead. Naa can't be, not Davo. Sticky. He wiped his hand on his trousers. No pulse. Dead. He's dead.

'Davo! Jesus! No, Davo, not you, matey . . . please!' He swung the torch. What was the other thing he had seen? There – the bloody stumps of thighs, red flesh, white bone brilliant in the torchlight, trousers and boots still on the legs. What? His brain was reeling. Sticky. He looked down at Dave and then slowly, as in some horror film become reality, he directed the beam up the treetrunk to the fronds above. Gobbets of tissue, wet in the torchlight, bloody mangled viscera, lungs, entrails hanging.

'Ohfuckoogrulshaa . . .' He began to vomit.

Chapter Nine

The Gazelle pilot, Andy Young, was a twenty-eight-year-old lieutenant. He wasn't a veteran of anything other than a few big nights in the mess and as he eased the power up with the twist grip on the collective, he was frightened. He raised it slowly to alter the pitch of the rotors. The aircraft began to hover, climbing up a few feet; he eased the cyclic forward, dropping the disc, and the Gazelle began to move away, gathering height over the sand and palm trees of St George's Cay. This is it he thought, me and my big fucking ideas. Behind him in the open door was one of the lads from St George's, a sailing and diving instructor, a corporal who the sergeant reckoned was good with a gun. Mounted on a hastily fixed door pintle was one of HMS *Beaufort*'s general purpose machine guns, a big heavy-barrelled thing that fired the old NATO 7.62 round. Soldiers liked them because unlike the newer 5.56 mm these big bullets could go through trees and walls. As one of them said as they were fixing it on the pintle arm: '*This* is a gun!'

He turned and headed in towards the coast, the scene even in darkness familiar after so much time spent in the area. Eight months he had been in Belize, and never thought he would be flying over his own base area with a bloody machine gun in the door. He was scared – this was no armoured gunship. Ahead he could see the ground battle, tracer rounds streaking over the terrain, the odd flash of something exploding.

'Three Alpha, Three Alpha, Three Alpha, Foxtrot Two, over.'

'Go, Foxtrot Two.' This wasn't Major Fox, the pilot realized instantly, this was his radio operator. He had met Fox the night before at the barbecue and again several times that day.

'Three Alpha, Alpha actual, please.'

It was a moment or two before another voice came on. 'Alpha actual.'

'Alpha, this is army Gazelle Foxtrot Two. Can you put a flare over the Guat positions? I can offer a little assistance, over.'

Assist, Fox thought? You crazy little bastard. 'Aaah, roger, Foxtrot Two.'

Fox fired off some orders and a few minutes later, the Gazelle inbound, one of the temporary platoon commanders, a sergeant, fired a flare over the Guatemalan positions in the scrub outside the perimeter fence.

The Gazelle came in at one-fifty knots, much slower than it could do, but the pilot knew that a man on a door gun at two-sixty-five knots wouldn't hit jack shit on the ground; fast enough to be difficult to hit, slow enough to let the gunner draw a bead on his targets. Get overhead and do a long lazy turn, disc down to the left, keep the portside door over the target area.

'Get ready!' he yelled. No helmet or internal comms for the gunner, just shouted orders over the engine noise. No lights showing – on *Beaufort* they said they had flash eliminators on the gun muzzle. Bloody better have, because that's all we need, he thought, six feet of bloody muzzleflash lighting us up. The flare went up, blinding everyone; no night sight for anyone on the ground, the whole area bathed in white phos light. 'There. Under the flare!' he yelled.

The gun began to hammer in the door, cartridge cases flying back into the cabin. The corporal was tied in, a climber's harness from the store room on St George's under his belt-kit, hooked into a load ring on the floor with a nylon strop. It was just long enough so he could lean over the gun, even in a tight left turn, the butt into his shoulder, and put sustained bursts down at the enemy rear. These people, two hundred yards back from the forward positions, hadn't been in the fight yet. They had suffered mortar bombs, but that was all and they were being prepared to be moved round to the flank. They were lying huddled in groups in cover from ground fire from the west, where the defenders were, but they had no cover from above. The bullets ripped into them, the Gazelle pilot tightening his turn to leave his gunner over the area as long as he could. Ground fire began then. The gunner, the instructor corporal, flinched once or twice but held the position, exposing himself to fire in order to do his job. In the confusion they had more time than they had expected; the firefight between the two forces was still going on and many of the Guatemalans simply heard another machine gun, or were blinded by the flare. It was some twenty seconds before they realized they were being attacked from above, and began to blast fire back into the sky. They could see nothing, just hear it.

The pilot broke off his run, his attack profile almost classic stuff remembered from training – in low, power up to attack speed, climb to get the gun into position, attack and then drop into a turn and back to treetop height. The machine shot out over the water and the corporal in the back gave a banshee yell of relief, adrenaline coursing through his blood. It had been an astonishing success.

They landed, and while fuel was being pumped into the tanks an aviation artificer, a man from *Beaufort*'s Lynx service crew, gave the little chopper the once over. He found three bullet holes but not much else.

'Looks all right,' he said.

'Right. Then let's go back,' the corporal said quickly. 'Fuck, that was good! Shit! We were pouring it into those cunts.' He was pumped up, excited; delivering the goods on a mission like this, in a hostile tactical environment, was 'doing the business'. 'Can we go in a different way, sir? Scoot down one side maybe?'

The pilot, supervising the fuel transfer, looked at him. It had been a good mission. They had reduced the fighting effectiveness of at least two, maybe three platoons of men. In addition they had opened a new front, got them worried, watching their backs, feeling exposed and vulnerable, and a bunch of them would now be tied up with some sort of air defence requirement. They didn't even have to attack, just fly anywhere near enough to be heard and they would have half the Guatemalans shitting bricks, looking up at the dark sky for them, wondering where they would appear next.

'Can we, sir?' the corporal asked. Jesus, the pilot thought, I was fucking shitting myself. This was a nice diving instructor half an hour ago, now he thinks he's Rambo. 'I want to talk to Charlie Alpha, then one more sortie. Then we evaluate.'

The Lynx led the Belizean patrol boat to the Royal Navy frigate and by the time she came alongside, *Beaufort* had a seaboat in the water. The B Squadron trooper crossed to the seaboat and the coxswain hit the throttles and raced the thirty yards back to the frigate. Three or four minutes later the SAS soldier, Trooper Hagan, was on the bridge. He quickly gave Bennett and two or three of his senior officers a sitrep from Belize City, finishing by saying, 'So, we have the boat. It's got a 12.7 mill weapon and we loaded heaps of fuel. What I want to do, sir, is go up the river.' He produced a map and laid it out on the navigator's chart table. 'From sitreps from the signallers at the camp, 2 Para and lads from the Squadron are holding at the river here. But, if the scrotes have got rafts, and I can't believe they won't have thought of that, then they can move straight down the river, bypass San Ignacio, and if they want to get in behind our lads they could cause all kinds of shit. Boat troop will be on the river – if we can get that gunboat up there, and link up with them, then we can close it off. I'm air troop, sir, boats aren't my thing. Can you supply me with some useful blokes?'

Bennett was thinking fast. 'Who have you got now?'

'Two BDF. One guy who has fired the gun, one engineer, although he says he can't fix the engine, just change oil and stuff.'

'Who was driving?' Bennett asked. Either it was blind foolishness to run a boat out into the reefs at twenty knots plus in the dark, or they had someone who actually knew his stuff.

'A local bloke, sir. Not BDF. This guy is apparently shit-hot, been running big dive boats out here for years,' Hagan replied.

The navigator looked at the captain and raised an eyebrow. 'I'd like to meet him, Captain.'

Bennett nodded. Great minds think alike. 'Lieutenant Lewis, please.'

The officer of the watch went to the main broadcast system

and forty seconds later Lewis was there; lean, young, of middle height, his eyes quick and bright.

'Lieutenant Lewis, get yourself over to that patrol boat. Relieve Mr . . .'

'Dion.'

'Relieve Mr Dion. Offer him my compliments and would he be so kind as to transfer across here please. Maintain station. Do you want a coxswain?'

'No thanks, sir.' He grinned. 'I'll drive.' Bennett smiled. Lewis had been boss on a minesweeper last year, a vessel much nearer the size of the patrol boat than *Beaufort*, where as an officer you had more opportunity to physically drive it yourself, something that never happened on bigger warships.

Fifteen minutes later Dion Manuelez was on the bridge of *Beaufort*.

'Thanks for coming, Mr . . .'

'Manuelez. Dion,' he said. This was bizarre, he was thinking. Here he was in shorts, a T-shirt and a pair of flip-flops in amongst all these guys in flash-hoods and gloves.

'Nick Bennett.' He held out his hand, pulling his hood down so Dion could see his face. 'I'm told you know these waters?'

Dion nodded. 'As well as anyone,' he replied with a shrug that said but they are still a bitch, no one knows them all.

Bennett led them over to the chart table. 'I want to try and get closer to the airport. Is there any deep water outside the channel?' He pointed to the north, the sweep of Cays and white that was the Admiralty chart.

'How close?'

'Seven or eight miles would do.'

'What's your draught?' Dion asked. Bennett told him and he leant over the chart. A little smile crossed his face. 'This is wrong. What year was this chart done?' He reached out and took a pencil and began to make swift annotations.

'Sixty-four.'

Dion's look was one of mild amusement. He had expected the answer, but like the other local boatmen he knew that the charts were incomplete. Not even the British Admiralty had ever charted these waters properly.

'Is there a way to get closer?' Bennett asked.

'At high water, yes, it's possible. But not for long – you would have maybe an hour either side of high water, then you would have to be back out. There are a couple of holes deep enough to anchor, but you would be stuck there till the next tide.'

'Can you mark the way in?' Bennett asked.

'No. I do it, but it's not with charts. It's marks, sightlines.'

Bennett looked over at the SAS soldier who was clearly getting impatient; tough luck, he would have to wait. He looked back at Dion.

'Can you stay aboard? Pilot us in?'

Dion looked at the soldier – this wasn't the plan. Bennett interpreted the look. 'Don't worry about that, I can man the gunboat.'

'Sure,' Dion replied with a shrug, 'but we better get moving. The tide is rising.'

'XO to the bridge,' Bennett said.

Twenty minutes later, *Beaufort* was already underway into the shallows, the gunboat following her. A petty officer was gathering his people; an engineering artificer, a weapons artificer, and three seaman ratings were getting into the seaboat. They wore drab green trousers, their DPM smocks with their kit. The only way for an observer to recognize them as navy was by their blue berets and the blue T-shirts they were wearing. They had kit, weapons, ammunition, lights, tools, a few bits and pieces and were with the SAS trooper Hagan, transferring across to Lieutenant Lewis, who now commanded the gunboat.

'Fuckin' 'ell. Look at it,' the engineering artificer said. 'HMS *Tonka Toy* . . .'

'I'll bet it hasn't even got a head,' someone interrupted.

'And in this, we are going ninety-odd miles up a jungle river in the dark with crocodiles and panthers and shit, to then get attacked by fucking thousands of drug cartel types.'

'That's Colombia, you dickhead,' the petty officer corrected him.

'I was told you were volunteers,' Hagan said. 'I want no one on this boat who isn't here of his own free will.'

'Wouldn't miss it for the world, me old cock,' the PO responded. 'Naa, we likes a little run ashore, we do.' His tone was mildly sarcastic – they had volunteered, down to a man, but they were all now wondering what they had let themselves in for.

Ten miles away at the airport Fox was concerned about his men. He wanted to try something. The AAC lieutenant had arrived back in his Gazelle, all Vietnamized, blasting away with a door gun. No flare this time, so somehow he had got the FLOT right, and came in fast over the trees, no lights, ballsy, very ballsy, the doorman on the gun spraying down his rounds into the Guatemalan positions. Then the chopper disappeared fast and low, tracer searing upward as the Guatemalan troops tried to blast it out of the sky. That was brave or slightly insane, but was he brave enough or mad enough to land? To lift his casualties out, the three lads who needed doctors? The scrotes' fire could hit almost anywhere on the runway or taxiways.

'Foxtrot Two, Three Alpha, that was outstanding, I say again outstanding. Do you copy over?'

'Roger, Alpha, go ahead.'

'Foxtrot, I have three, repeat three casualties. If I can give you a Lima Zulu, can you do a casevac, over?'

'Aah, Three Alpha, roger that,' he replied thinking quickly, where? Where is a safe landing zone? Get in behind a building or something. 'Can you get them to the western end of the terminal, over?'

Sweet Jesus, this is when we will take fire, he thought. Before my strikes I might have got away with a mercy flight, but now they will have every bastard with a gun aimed at me. Where do I take them? He thought about it, the options he had. Clinics? There must be small cottage hospitals outside Belize City. The hospital in town? It wasn't famed for its advanced trauma medicine, but it was a hospital in a country where people had guns and were shot all the time. Where is it? He had never been there, and would probably get fired at trying to land in town, every Belizean with a gun would be looking for something to shoot at. The ship – take 'em out to

254

the ship; clean sheets, sickbay, drugs, a medic. They will know what to do with them. He put the helo into a circle just above the bush, out of range to the north of the airport and thumbed his microphone.

'*Beaufort, Beaufort*, this is Foxtrot Two, Foxtrot Two.'

'Foxtrot Two, identify yourself.' Someone on *Beaufort* was being careful, very careful.

'*Beaufort*, Foxtrot Two, I am an army Gazelle helicopter. Need to run a flight out to you. Can I talk to your medical officer.'

'Stand by.'

Don't piss me about, he was thinking. I am up here, getting shot at, and you want fucking verification checks. The seconds ticked by and it was Major Fox next on the air.

'Foxtrot Two, Three Alpha ready when you are, watch for my Cyalume markers. We will suppress enemy fire as best we can, over.'

'Foxtrot Two, roger that. I am inbound at this time.'

He began his run in, low, fast, disc forward, brushing the treetops. He would bleed speed, flare out, stall her in, just disc back, let off the pitch, but leave the power on, take the wounded lads and lift out again fast and low, hiding all the way out. Terminal ahead – lights still on there. Tracer fire to the left, where the fighting was. Where? No markers yet, over the perimeter fence from the west, there! Cyalume markers, green, waved about by someone. Right a bit, right a bit, fire coming at them now, tracer rounds seeking them out. Flare out, the blade clawing at the sky, down, starboard skid first, green berets, marines, Royal Marines, where the fuck did they come from? One in front, hands out flat, done the helo course, excellent. Wounded coming in both doors, the soldier on the door gun loading them like a pro, hands coming up from the marine in the front, two raised thumbs, you are clear both sides, cyclic up, pitch coarse like a whore's anger, that's my girl, fly now big girl, come on, turning.

'Foxtrot Two, Foxtrot Two, *Beaufort*.'

Just in the hover, a foot above the ground, tail around, lift out and fly straight west to the tree-line, stay below the buildings if I can. Disc down; here we go, gathering speed, height inching up, hold her down, taking fire now, ball ammunition slamming into the fuselage, like a hammer on a drum.

'Foxtrot Two, Foxtrot Two. *Beaufort*.'

'*Beaufort*, stand by, I'm busy here.'

The bush rushed at them, black as pitch, and the pilot had no perspective. Height, we need height now, he thought. There were more hits, and now he felt real fear, and adrenaline raced through his blood. The rotors clawed at the night – forty knots. Come on, baby, he urged, every second you are further away; fifty, we must be clear. More strikes from below, bullets slamming into them, shattering the perspex canopy. The door gun was still hammering away. Clear, are we clear? He looked down at his instruments; no warning lights, no hits in the hydraulics, gearbox or the fuel system. You can still fly, my lovely girl, you are a tough little thing, oh yes! He breathed in, dragging air into his lungs, his heart pounding like a hammer. The gunner tapped on his shoulder, pointing, cool as a cucumber. 'Hit again,' he yelled. Rounds up through the floor had hit one of the wounded lads, poor bastard. We need help now. Where's that fucking ship?

'*Beaufort*, *Beaufort*, *Beaufort*, Foxtrot Two.'

'Foxtrot Two, identify yourself please.'

Don't fuck me around. We've done this shit, you prat.

'Army Gazelle, *Beaufort*, I am an army Gazelle. I need your MO, please.'

'Aah, Foxtrot Two, can you be more specific, over.'

The pilot lost it briefly then: frightened, sweating, limp, tired, his hand shaking, his helicopter damaged by ground fire, comrades dying around him, feeling responsible for them since he was the officer, he let protocol slip.

'Don't fuck me around, you dickhead. I have a casevac from British forces on the ground at the airport. I say again I have a casevac. Figures three, I say figures three wounded. They are dying in the back of my aircraft. I need to take them somewhere. If it's not you then fucking say so, you wankers, and I'll take them somewhere else. Now I need help, *Beaufort*. Do I get it or not?'

'Foxtrot Two.' A new voice. 'We have you on radar, steer . . . stand by . . . one-three-five degrees and be ready to light your A/C beacons on command. We have a clear helo deck and are ready to receive your casualties, over.'

'Thank you.'

The pilot swung his aircraft round, still watching for warning lights, but amazingly his little Gazelle was still seemingly in working order. The wind, cooler from the rain, but still warm was rushing in through the shattered lower windows. His hand was sticky with blood. He looked at it. A nick from something; that would teach him, should have been wearing his gloves. Fuck, that was close, we flew right over them. He suddenly thought and thumbed his microphone button.

'Three Alpha, Three Alpha, Foxtrot Two.'

'Go, Foxtrot.'

'Alpha, I have taken serious ground fire but I am clear of the area. Be advised you have hostiles, I say again you have hostiles to the south-west. Face the west along the runway and in the bush at your eleven o'clock, half a mile from the wire, over.'

'Thank you, Foxtrot. Appreciate your help.'

'I'll be back.'

On *Beaufort*'s bridge Bennett spun a look across at the navigator, who had called the pilot's new course to him, and shook his head. He had caught the tail-end of the conversation with the army pilot and intervened. The comms rating was following procedures but it was an embarrassing incident, lacking any sensitivity or commonsense judgement. The call was genuine, you could hear it in his voice. Bennett looked at the officer of the watch. 'Get on to it please. The surgeon up here to me now.'

'Sir.' The watchkeeper took the main broadcast system microphone. 'Do you hear there, wounded coming aboard, wounded coming aboard. Helo Ops, prepare to receive inbound army helo. I say again army helo. Aft section fire control to provide stretcher parties to the landing deck. Medical officer to the bridge. Sickbay prepare to receive wounded.'

Ordinarily a casualty might have been much better treated ashore at the hospital because of the limited facilities a frigate offered. Usually she only carried a leading medical orderly, but this time it was right and appropriate that they take the wounded, because on this trip she had a doctor aboard, a naval surgeon. He had been deployed with them when Montserrat's volcano had begun to rumble again and *Beaufort*, as West Indies guardship, had been tasked to lend a hand if required. Good job we have him, Bennett thought. He was an odd fish; left-wing, politically correct, dreary, he had asked for the attachment because of the ship's role in the possible evacuation of Montserrat. He wanted to help the developing world, he said. The lads in the wardroom took the piss constantly, but technically he seemed to know his stuff.

At the airport Lieutenant Murray had seen the fire going up at the helicopter and by the time Major Fox had raised him he was already deploying his men. There should have been no enemy this far around and by attacking the helicopter they had betrayed their presence. From here they could make a flank attack, and move round to engage the main defensive position from the rear quickly and under cover. He immediately issued orders and his men, half of the troop, dropped into cover like ghosts. He had left the other half back with Fox, to support a breach in the line, but he needed them here now with the sustained-fire weapon. He looked out at the bush, low-lying, swampy, mosquito-infested Cover was sparse, with gaps between the trees and vegetation. Rifle-grenades, he thought, that's what we need and we don't have them. How many of them would there be? A recce? A section, or maybe a recce in force, a platoon? More, a full monty flank attack? The fire was heavy; it could be a company assault, one hundred to one-twenty men, maybe more. He had twenty.

By the time Fox raised him he knew what he wanted to do. The GPMG, currently in the line with the Gurkha lads, would be hauled out and over to his position. Corporal Garvey, the SAS soldier, was somewhere up the runway; where was he now? The man moved like a will-o'-the-wisp. He would move his own machine gun on to an interlocking arc. Two or three minutes later the rest of his troop skittered round the edge of the terminal building, which was still ablaze with lights.

'Corporal, take your GPMG section in there. Kill the lights, take out a circuit breaker or something. Then get up on the roof. I want a field of fire across sixty degrees through there.' He pointed out into the darkness. 'Engage after I initiate the contact. Goddit?' Murray wiped sweat from his eyes. His face was grimy. They had no cam cream; he had used dirt. The marine nodded. 'Be advised, the Squadron bloke is out there,' he pointed, 'with some of the local lads. Far end of the runway. No blue on blue! Go! Quickly!'

'Three Alpha, Three Alpha, Mike One.'

'Go, Mike.'

Murray looked down at his notes. They were five hundred paces from the command post, paced out that afternoon for just this purpose. 'Three, can you let me have a mortar tube facing my way. Set it up for four hundred metres, on bearing two-six-zero, over.'

'Confirm range figures four-zero-zero on two-six-zero degrees?'

'Roger that.'

Now they waited. He went over his tactical position in his mind. Enemy approaching their front, at their two o'clock the perimeter wire, and the flat open ground through to the hard surface of the runway. Down at the far western end Garvey would be wheeling his position to face the new threat, and behind them the handful of assault pioneers were finished with the JCB and there was a decent set of trenches with a berm that ran between them. With the gimmpy giving cover from above, suppressing the enemy fire, they could fall back to the trenches if it came down to it. He looked across at one of his men, who was lying back under the cover of a concrete bollard beside his mate with an LSW, peeling a banana. Murray looked again. Yes, it was a banana. Where the hell did he get that, he wondered? Mad bastard. He felt a rush of affection for them, pride in his lads. They are coming, we don't know how many of them, but we are Royal Marines, and we are so relaxed we are eating bananas. It was surreal.

Two clicks of someone's fingers. He quickly looked around and the sergeant pointed. Murray followed the finger but saw nothing. That didn't mean they weren't coming, the sergeant had eyes like a cat. At night the human eye distinguishes little, except reflection of light and movement. He slowly scanned across the line of bush in front of him. Move an inch to the left, stop, look, move and inch, stop, look. There! A shape, a man moving round the edge of a big bush. Got you! Another, more; they were moving up, taking it slowly, carefully. Time to do it now, drop bombs into them. If they broke and went to ground out in the bush, then that was fine. They could hold them there, but whoever broke and ran this way, running for the cover of the airport terminal building, would be caught in his arcs of fire like a beaten grouse.

'Three Five, Mike, commence fire on command,' he said and then passed his radio handset over to the marine who had done the MFC training as part of his time on the artillery observers' course with 148 battery.

'Three Five, range four-twenty on two-six-zero degrees, one round fire!'

They didn't hear it leave the tube, the noise from the fighting at the eastern end was too intense, but a few seconds later it landed, a blast two hundred yards out.

'Drop seventy. Fire!' called the marine. The bombs began to come in, the marine directing the fire in a pattern, three, four, then five. Figures burst from the bush, many of them, thirty or forty and an officer on one side.

'Wait for it,' Murray called, 'wait for it . . . Fire!'

The marines across the front opened fire as one, three going for the officer, and above them on the roof, the sustained-fire weapon, the heavy-barrelled belt-fed machine gun opened up, its note deeper, hammering away into the night, ripping a swath through the advancing Guatemalans. It had been a perfectly executed ambush, but now concentrated fire began to pour back at them. The mortaring had stopped; at the start they only had ten bombs left, and this ambush had used up six, so tactically they were down to troop weapons, what they had in their hands.

Murray tried to get a feel for what they were up against. A company at least, maybe a reinforced company, because a heavy-barrelled weapon was firing back at them. It was now a fierce firefight, the darkness lit by muzzleflash; there were cries, shouts, someone was screaming out there. Murray was cool, cooler than he thought he would be. They had been blooded that night, down at the main road. A bullet hit the edge of the concrete culvert he was in, chippings flying off, dust in his eyes. He was aware of movement, a rush from the left. His eyes were watering; he wiped them with a sleeve, lifted his rifle and fired. The attack faltered as other marines turned their fire that way, and suddenly it was dark on that side again, someone crying in pain, calling for his mother. Another scathing burst of fire came from the Guatemalan machine gun. Murray shook the man's cries from his mind – the gun had to be taken out or it would dominate the ground.

'Anyone see that machine gun?'

'On the centre right, sir.'

'Got a tracer?'

'Yes sir,' the marine replied, reaching for a fresh magazine. He had a tracer round in first position and another second to last to let him know that he was one round off an empty magazine.

'Wait for it.' Murray called down the group for the marine sniper who had been so successful that night. Along with his SA80 he had a bolt-action rifle, with a scope mounted on it. He crawled over to Murray and was briefed.

'OK,' the other marine shouted over the noise, 'watch my tracer.'

On HMS *Beaufort*, the army lieutenant, pilot of the Gazelle, was shown into the wardroom, where he could sit down, drink a cup of something and eat some food, while his machine was refuelled. The gunner was taken down to the petty officers' mess and someone found him sandwiches and passed him two ice-cold cans of Coke. He drank them but looked longingly at the beer pumps. 'Go on then, son,' one of the POs said. 'Get a pint in.'

'No thanks,' the soldier replied, 'we're going back. I'll have a half of lager; cold, please.' Someone passed him a can of Red Stripe and he drank it in one long pull, his face a picture of pleasure. One deck above Bennett knocked and walked into the wardroom looking for the army officer, who didn't

261

recognize the three rings so much as his demeanour. He had gravitas, confidence, he was the boss, the captain. The lieutenant stood up and saluted. Bennett quickly returned the salute and then offered his hand to be shaken. 'We are fairly informal here.'

'I gave one of your people a bollocking. Sorry, sir. I lost it there, I'm tired.'

'Not at all. I heard it and I apologize. Your . . . bollocking was well aimed. We feeding you? Looking after you?'

The pilot nodded.

'Good. The MEO has his people looking at your helo, checking your innards for ground-fire damage.'

'Thanks sir. I'll need to go in again.' His tone implied that there would be more casualties tonight.

Bennett nodded. 'You're happy to go back in?' he asked softly

The pilot grimaced slightly. Happy, to fly into that? he marvelled. No, sir, I'm not fucking happy. No one would be, you would need to have a death wish to be happy, but my gunner is prepared to go back and if the toms need us we go. He smiled; 'Not really sir, but no one should have to die in there because it's a hot LZ and a pilot is shitting himself.'

'I don't blame you. I would be,' Bennett replied. He had seen the Gazelle, noted the number of times it had been hit.

'Sir, if we spear in, on the record please – the man on my door gun,' he smiled again, 'actually, *your* gun. I don't know his name, but he is exceptional. Courage under fire. Real courage. I want . . .' He trailed off.

'Consider it done. I shall enter it in the log,' Bennett replied, thinking, and you too young man, and you too. 'Get your hand seen to, won't you. If you need anything my people will see you get it.' With that Bennett left him to it and took the stairs to the bridge two at a time. They were in very shallow water now, and even with a pilot, Dion, the XO, the navigator, and the officer of the watch on the bridge the ship was still his responsibility.

When he got there Dion was standing behind the quartermaster, and the officer of the watch was clearly very uncomfortable. They were trained to navigate the ship on compass bearings, the officer looking through a gyro compass and calling the course to the quartermaster on the little butterfly-shaped wheel. But this pilot wasn't doing that, he was doing it his way, looking out over the bows in the dark, moving round, out on the wing, calling out what he wanted to happen, leaving it to the XO to interpret.

'This isn't working,' Dion said. 'Too slow. Can I?'

The XO nodded.

'What's the slowest speed that you get full bite on the rudders?'

'Thirty revolutions'

'OK. Let's have thirty revolutions. Excuse me . . .' He indicated that the quartermaster should clear the seat at the wheel and then stood beside it, one hand on the wheel, and actually steered the ship. He turned the wheel, watched the bows come round, then back, getting a feel for the ship. This was four times the size of his live-aboard dive boat, so it seemed slow, sluggish, but precise – there was little lag. He looked back at the quartermaster and indicated that he should take his seat again. 'Thanks. Four-zero revolutions,' he called. 'Someone on the bridge wing, please. I want to know when the Fort George light is fair over the port quarter, then as it disappears behind the Ramada Hotel, call out. The Ramada is the big long low building.'

The XO grimaced slightly; they had radar running, navigation radar, defensive, targeting, depth sounders, anti-submarine measures that could read the bottom to the nearest foot, but they were relying on a man looking at some lights on the shore to steer them safely through reefs. Some things hadn't changed since the time of Nelson.

San Ignacio

On the eastern side of the Macal river, the defenders, C Company's two platoons of Gurkhas, were under fire. The Guatemalans had moved down to the buildings nearest the river, some sections forward, nearer the bank; they had dug in, set up their mortars and were fighting. In spite of the earlier setbacks, the loss of the bridge and the non-arrival of the Kaibiles, they were confident, they were strong. This lead brigade, bloodied, angry, wanting some payback, with still two fully intact brigades behind them, was facing just a handful of defenders. They had rafts, engineers and bridging equipment, and until these came forward, they would just pound the Belizeans and their British advisers. They had worked it out now; the one company of British that were normally training must have been in the area, and had been brought into the situation. One company? Against three brigades? They were confident, and when their mortars began to fire, they knew it was only a matter of time. By the time the bridges and the rafts arrived there would be no resistance on the other bank, they would have blasted them into mincemeat. After all, they were what, fifteen minutes or half an hour ahead of them? They were soldiers, they knew that it took many hours to set up proper defences.

Lieutenant Estelle had seen it coming. There was no way that anyone was crossing the river, at least for the next few hours; the water was just too high. Even the worst officer with the most rudimentary training would know just to bring forward mortars, rockets or artillery and pound his position. In simple terms, two platoons could not slug it out with what could be anything up to four battalions across the hundred yards of swollen river.

So he moved his men out; leaving just three positions along the river, each with a section weapon, all volunteers, in the deepest, best-constructed sangars, he was able to move sixty-five of his eighty-odd men back from the bank into the side streets, dispersed and in cover. Estelle stayed with his men. The other platoon commander challenged that decision; it didn't make strategic sense to have half their strength in officers in such a high-risk position. Estelle overruled him. There was no way he was going to ask any of his toms to do this and then go and hide himself somewhere.

The action started, and the tempo quickly built up. Mortar bombs were falling with a rhythm, and although not well directed, with this sort of volume it didn't matter quite so much. Fire returned from the handful of defenders was kept to a minimum because at night even modern flash eliminators will hide only so much muzzleflash, and it simply encouraged response. The Guatemalans forward enough to see his positions, now at the edge of the town along the river, seemed to have not only M60 machine guns, but from the speed at which they were expending them, a plentiful supply of American 66mm high-explosive anti-tank rockets.

The twelve men, in three four-man rifle teams, hunkered down to wait it out, popping up every now and then to fire back. The mortar bombs hit the ground along the river, detonating their warheads, blasting trees and earth, roots and leaves upward. Two of the holes the men would have been in had taken direct hits, and no infantry hole is ever deep enough to survive that. Others had been raked with heavy fire from interlocking sustained-fire weapons. The casualties would have been high, very high, if they had not moved back.

Estelle was squatting, facing across the bunker, still in his maroon beret. Somewhere here in the dark were the four men he shared the hole with. Earlier in the day they had dragged logs and heavy branches over the top and covered those with a lattice of lighter branches; then, covering that with their ponchos, they piled earth on top as protection from falling debris and anything but a direct hit. It was black as pitch down there, just the odd bright white flash of an explosion giving a nanosecond of illumination through the entry hole at the back and the fighting slits round the front.

They were all frightened and the close proximity of the exploding bombs deafened them. Every now and then the bunker took a burst of fire from a machine gun, the rounds hitting the earth bank and log roof. Two of them sat with their hands over their ears, a third kept popping up to look through the slit and the last sat impassive, his eyes closed, shut tight against the dust, his expression a grimace. The soft earth was a blessing; as the bombs dropped they entered the humus-laden, muddy surface which absorbed the force of the explosions. How long can we stand this, Estelle wondered. Men in the First War sat through barrages that lasted for hours, every day for weeks. How did they do it, he wondered. He felt movement. One of them was moving towards the hole.

There was a massive blast, earth, mud and leaves fell in on them through the ponchos, and the ground shook. His heart was pounding. In the flash he saw the Gurkha fellow, crawling over the others' legs, his rifle across his front, exactly as he had been trained to do. The bunker was connected to another by a shallow trench, just deep enough to slither along. Estelle led him out.

Once in the open, although they were below the line of sight, the full Dantean horror was upon them. The whole stretch along the river was being pounded, raked with gunfire, tracer and ball rounds ripping leaves and bark from trees, ploughing up the earth. As he entered the shallow trench he looked back. At the bridge footing there were small bright white glows, white smoke rising. They were using Whisky Peters, white phosphorus, in direct contravention of the Geneva Convention. WP was normally delivered by artillery. Christ, they have artillery? No. Why would you bring heavy guns into a fight that at most could only be against the full BDF, a light battalion of six hundred men? A tank? WP from a tank gun, maybe? He was, like most soldiers, frightened of white phosphorus. It burned through your clothing wherever the drops fell, right through your skin into your flesh, and if you survived it left terrible wounds. He crawled on, the fear returning, the Gurkha soldier following him. The noise was so loud that he could barely think straight, mortar bombs and rockets exploding every few seconds within a hundred yards, and sometimes much, much closer. He looked back. The Gurkha's face was impassive and Estelle was pleased to have him there. Although they had both opted to go out, it was no place to be alone. They slithered twenty-five or thirty yards down the trench and dropped into the next hole. It had been hit, the back had been blown out by the blast and the bottom section of treetrunk now lay over it, its root structure across in the back, the rest of its twelve feet rising out of the hole till its shattered end hung wet and white in the flashes.

Across the river the lights were still on, and smoke rose from the buildings in places. Lower on the other side in front of them a machine gun opened up, its muzzleflash bright flickers, tracer fire moving down the bank away from them.

He wondered quickly how the lads at the far end were doing – to try and get down there would be sure death. So far the British response had been minimal. Chard was holding his small elite unit back, Estelle knew, from anything but harrying fire. He wanted the scrotes moving forward, confident, right up to the river, hoping for dense concentrations of the enemy in pockets where he would get most 'bang for his buck'. Then when they were moving forward, confident in their attack, their bridging gear and rafts in sight and in range, he would act. Estelle wished they would start now, hitting back at the machine guns on the other side, at the mortars which must be at the back of the town somewhere. His eyes just over the lip of the hole, he looked back at the machine gun, its barrel now pointed down the river to their right, the gunner pouring out rounds. Estelle unconsciously evaluated their training and discipline in a heartbeat. There was nothing to shoot at, they were just wasting ammunition, overheating their barrels, betraying their position the way that none of his people would ever do.

It was pointless speaking, he would never be heard, so he touched his soldier's shoulder and pointed across. The man nodded. They both sighted over the river, their SUSAT sights magnifying four times. The Guatemalan gunner had become complacent, or knew no better; he and the other two in his team had set up the gun well above ground level, its tripod legs visible in the flashes of light.

Fuck you, Estelle thought, for putting my toms into this shit. His anger rose like bile, the fear gone. At this 120-yard range he could put a bullet into a teacup ten times out of ten. He sighted on the gunner and fired, a double tap, two rounds away quick, then swung left and hit the man there, two rounds. The private beside him had also gone for the gunner but swung right and poured three rounds into the figure that side.

The barrel jerked up, spraying rounds at the sky, then the firing stopped abruptly and the two British soldiers ducked deep into the hole and scuttled up into the comms trench to get away from the inevitable reaction, crawling away as quickly as they could, the Gurkha's grin beaming widely. A

267

66 mm rocket hit the treetrunk and showered them with bark and debris. They were lucky, the trunk had taken the force of the blast, but Estelle felt something hit his leg, a sharp tug followed by a burning pain. He kept moving, following the soldier. There would be more. His ears were bleeding and ringing, and his eyes were full of dirt and mud, but he crawled as quickly as he could and dropped down into the bunker after his comrade as another rocket slammed into the bank beside the hole they had left.

The sitrep coming through on the little PRC 349 radio was not good. Down at the northern end, away from the bridge, they had casualties; of the four soldiers in the position, two were hurt, one seriously. A piece of shrapnel from a mortar bomb had come through a fighting slit and hit him between the collar and the base of his helmet, slicing through the skin, lifting part of the scalp, and embedding itself in his skull. Incredibly he was still conscious. His comrades left the steel shard in place and dressed the wound to keep it clean, but because it was a head injury there would be no pain relief from morphine – aspirin was the best they could do.

The other soldier had a gunshot wound in the lower leg just above the ankle. Dropping back into the bunker after a little recce down the bank, he had been hit by one of the M60 bursts. They had the wound strapped, bleeding controlled, and the soldier said he could still fight.

Chard wants to hold back while my boys are taking a hammering holding this shithole. Fuck that, Estelle thought.

'Bravo Alpha, Bravo Alpha, Bravo Alpha, Three Two.'

'Three Two, go,' the Squadron signaller came back instantly.

'Bravo, your Alpha actual please.'

Chard responded thirty seconds later and Estelle called for what he wanted.

'Bravo, the fire is intensive. I have two wounded at Blue. I need support. Can you put some fire down on the front positions and do something about the mortars, over?'

Chard didn't hesitate; watching the action from his vantage point he knew the intensity of the fire. There were already civilian dead – a mortar bomb had fallen between two cars just down from the bridge. In one vehicle, four locals, *mestizos*, had been killed, and in the second, a big Toyota Land Cruiser, a white man had died. Chard's blokes had gone in to try and help, but there wasn't much to be done. The *mestizo* family were burned in the wreckage of their pickup truck and behind them the white man's neck had been snapped by the pickup's spare wheel blown backwards through his windscreen by the blast. He was an American. One of the blokes had seen him earlier, parked up on the roadside, waiting to see the bridge go. He'd said he was going to watch history in the making, and then pick up some other tourists, whose car he had borrowed, and head for Belize City.

The bodies were still down there, a stark reminder to any-one that this was no game. He knew that the Para lads only had four men down at Blue, and half were down. That meant that point was weak. He had a B Squadron team on the extreme flank but they were at least two or three hundred yards away, deep in the jungle overlooking the river, not close enough to offer much to help Estelle. He had hoped to give the Guatemalans another hour or so to become over-confident, throw caution to the wind and move units into the range of his weapons, but that was not to be. Oh well, he thought, all good things have to come to an end.

'Roger that, Three Two.'

He issued his orders. His own mortar team on the flatbed were supported by the C Coy mortar team. They had four 81 mm tubes and four 51 mm and the MFC on top of the hill was given his task. The Wolf Land-Rover with the M19 grenade launcher was driven back down the road, towards the smoke and incoming fire, to take up a better position, and four of the troopers would stand ready with LAW missiles. With the missiles' 500-yard capability, they could move along the approach road at will, and still be in range to hit targets on the other side of the river. It was one of the troopers on the Wolf with the grenade launcher who raised Estelle.

'Three Two, Bravo Three Four. Can you correct the fall, over?'

'Roger, Bravo Three,' Estelle replied. His leg was giving him pain, but he ignored it for the moment. He levered himself up the steep face of the bunker to look out of the forward

269

firing slit. A few moments later there were two blasts on the far side, back in the bus park.

'Drop one hundred, Three Two.'

Another brace came in. Much closer.

'Left two hundred. Drop thirty.' Back up the approach road the men on the Wolf ignored the 'drop thirty' part of the call. The M19 wasn't that accurate, not over three or four hundred yards; it was an area defence weapon, designed to saturate a position with grenade fire. They cranked it round to the left and fired again.

'Traverse right. Fire for effect!'

The launcher began to fire a grenade every second. One of the men hunkered down in the Land-Rover, filling circular magazines – they would get through plenty at this rate.

Behind them a mile down the road, the mortar crews serving the 81mm tubes began to fire their bombs, talking to the mortar fire controller in his eyrie on the hill. From his vantage at the slit in the bunker Estelle could see and hear as the mortars fired over the houses and shops landed on the far side of town where the Guatemalans had their mortar positions.

One of the fellows in the bunker with him could see his officer in the flashes of light and didn't like the way he was standing. He edged closer and flicked on his red-filtered torch. Blood ran down the back of Estelle's thigh, black in the red light, and there was a puncture wound high up on the leg. The soldier did what he was trained to do. He opened the wound-dressing pouch on his lieutenant's belt-kit – you never ever used your own – and as another came over to help, went to work. He liked the stoic response from his officer; no whingeing, no complaining, he just put up with it as one of them would have, appropriate behaviour for an officer of Gurkhas. The soldier had been in for eight years, and knew they weren't all like this.

Estelle looked down and then back through the slit. I must be wounded, he thought, properly wounded. He thought he had just bashed it. He felt like fainting for a second or two but shook it off and looked back out of the slit. The grenades were pounding the front positions and from away on the right

270

a rocket streaked across the river and slammed into a small building where machine gun fire had been coming from earlier. This was more like it, he thought. The pain in his leg was considerable now, a deep throbbing ache.

In the house that Pete had taken them to, Helen and Sophie cowered in the bathroom. Nothing had dropped close to them, the nearest explosion had been perhaps two hundred yards away towards the river, but nevertheless they were frightened. The fear wasn't debilitating; there was no panic, nor even a hint of it. They were rational, talking, but nervous and aware of their predicament. They were sorry they hadn't kept driving, and wished they had gone when Pete suggested it. The American guy who had taken their Toyota to give Pete a ride back to the bridge hadn't come back, and they were stuck there.

'They would have blown up the bridge by now, right? So there's no way the Guatemalans could have crossed,' Helen said aloud, more to console herself than anything.

'Mmm.'

'And anyway, we are civilians, tourists, and even if they had crossed we would be well treated.'

'Oh, be bloody realistic!' Sophie said. 'We are in the middle of a bloody war-zone. No one gives a damn whether we are civilians or not, bullets and bombs and things like that don't care. We have to get clear of here. At first light we go, get a car, hitchhike, or something. Pete suggested the embassy, we'll head for there.'

They had chosen the bathroom because it seemed stronger constructed, but the explosions, even at distance, shook the ground and the movement magnified up the pillars into the house; the pot plants shuddered and bottles rattled in the medicine cabinet. Out of the window they could see the glow as fires burned in the town.

'Should we go outside? Would it be safer?' Helen asked.

'Only if there was a bomb shelter or something. Harry would know what to do. I wish . . .' She trailed off. 'He'll be halfway home by now. Seventeen hours, he said.'

*　　*　　*

Across the river in his flat above Eva's Pete Collins was at work; the downstairs wasn't the only place online. He had a fast Dell laptop and he plugged it into his mobile and got himself on to the Internet. The electricity was still on, so the lights were functioning, but he was working by the light of a candle. By the sound of it, there was a major battle going on down by the river and there were Guatemalan troops on the streets, occasionally firing at something. He had heard them earlier, in the building next door, an officer yelling as his men helped themselves to tourist trinkets.

He scrolled down the addresses in his list and selected the one he wanted, a mate of his, Rick, who lived in Luton. They had been in the mob together, but Rick had come off his bike and was run over by a taxi. He was now in a wheelchair; a real Internet junkie, he would be at his keyboard eighteen hours a day. Pete quickly typed in a message and hit 'send'. Then he broke the rig down, remembering to take spare batteries for the mobile phone; the laptop was charged, but he made sure he had the mains adaptor, and dropped it all into a little day-pack, a trendy thing left by a tourist. He went to his wardrobe, opened a locked box at the back and took out a pistol, thought for a moment, shrugged, and took two of the magazines. He figured that if he needed any more than two he was dead anyway. Those he dropped into the bag and then he climbed up into the loft. It ran the length of the building, with two exits, and was full of rats, and where you had rats you had snakes, so he was careful.

He moved down to the end where he could look out over the road through the louvred dormer window feature, a mini-folly by the builder who had developed the row of shops, with flats above, perhaps hoping that one day San Ignacio would be an elegant little town where discerning people lived. The place was crawling with Guatemalans, troops moving on foot. There were buildings on fire over at the southern end of town, flames reaching up into the sky, and with the sound of the fighting just three hundred yards away at the river to keep him focused, he settled down to wait. At midnight he would wait for the call from the SAS major.

From the outside it would have appeared like mayhem, but D Company was working like a well-oiled machine. Everyone was at it, doing their job – and many were coping with two. Lieutenant Harry Rees was working like a Trojan. He had prepared his platoon, kept them briefed, dealt with all the last-minute issues. He still had to work out the jump sequence for two aircraft, allocate chalk numbers left and right, but now he was with the lads on the wedges, making sure they were correct, that the loads were secure. They were using American gear and it was different to their own, so he would have to rely on the American lads to get the parachute attachments right, just give them the once-over with buckets of common sense.

Sophie – he had been thinking about her all day, and he knew he shouldn't. This was serious shit and if he messed up, forgot something, then people, his toms, would be at risk, and that was bloody unprofessional, but she shouldered her way into his thoughts anyway. The look of her, breasts pushing against her too-tight top, heavy golden thighs, the way she smiled, the feel of her arm through his, the way she piled her hair on her head when she was hot, the sun finding strands of copper in the long auburn twirls, slender fingers, the little scar on her hand, the taste of her, the look in her eyes before she laughed. She's still there, he thought, in fucking Belize. The most wonderful woman I have ever met is back there and if the scrotes get her ... Get a grip, Harry, she'll be in Belize City, at the embassy. Bollocks – that's in frigging Belmopan. She'll be safe. Please let her be safe.

'Sir, we got another box of 7.62 link here. Where do we load it?'

'Break it into belts of two hundred. Spread it out with the lads who have only two bombs each.'

'Sir, can't it go on the wedge?' the paratrooper asked. They were already carrying huge loads, and the tab would be a bastard anyway.

'Wedges are full,' Rees replied. 'Get on with it.'

He watched the soldier walk away, finished what he was

doing and moved across to his platoon. Cutter was there, down on his knees helping one of his lads repack his container. The more they stuffed inside it the less they had hanging off the outside, or hanging off them.

'Yowa cunce,' Plonker said, 'yowa cunce think I'm a fookin' wazzak, but I'll fookin' tell yow this for nowt. Newcastle United right, Newcastle United, with Kevin fookin' Keegan – 'ere's Mr Rees, right. We'll fucking ask 'im, right?'

Three or four of them looked at Harry, his size and bulk imposing, the only man in the company taller than Plonker.

'Sir, if Keegan had signed Gazza, we would have thrashed Man U every time, right?'

Rees smiled; the toms, loading live ammo before going into the shit for real, and still on about football.

'Not my game. I play rugby, the real blokes' game.'

There was a chorus of catcalls and groans.

'Aye but . . . but you're a fan right, of some club, right?'

'Yeah, Bath,' Rees replied, knowing it was the wrong answer.

'No sir, I mean football club.'

He smiled enjoying the moment. 'Nooo,' he replied drawing it out. 'Can't say I am.'

'But you see it on the telly, right?' Plonker urged.

'No, but my nephew does. He said that Gazza is the fifth Teletubby.'

There were cheers and laughter from the others and Plonker looked away, hurt by the remark. 'Fookin' 'ell!' he snapped, full of frustration at being with fools who didn't understand the great game like he did.

Rees grinned. 'Those of you with only two bombs, there's another load of link 7.62 that needs a container.' Groans rose up.

'Elias' Cutter looked up. 'How long have we got, sir?'

'Not sure; maybe another hour. Get finished and you blokes eat.'

Maddy Jennings stirred in her sleep and opened an eye. It was raining outside, dark and brooding and instantly she thought about Tom, hoping he was all right. Where are you sleeping? Are you warm? Are you eating? The police said you would be OK. Big, tall, strong lad, streetwise, you may be, but you are still my child, my baby. Please come home. She started to cry and then stopped herself. You'll come back when you are ready. Your dad is home today, please be here when he arrives and make your peace. The phone rang. She didn't look at her watch, just knew it was early, very early in the morning. No one would phone at this time, unless . . . she snatched it up.

'Hello?'

'Maddy, it's Sue. Something's happening.'

'What?' She thought quickly. Sue was a friend and the new wife of one of the platoon sergeants in the company. They had married in the spring.

'Something's happening. Apparently Arnhem is going crazy, someone saw the padre running into the battalion HQ.'

Oh no, please God no. They've gone missing, crashed or something. Please no.

'What else?' She steeled herself. 'What else have you heard?'

'There are people everywhere rushing about and Mary says it's on the radio. They are recalling 2 Para to barracks.'

Maddy breathed a sigh of relief – battalion ops, that's fine, she rationalized. That doesn't mean that anything has happened to them.

'Maddy, they are recalling the battalion. I'm scared. Scale A or something. What does that mean?' Sue began to cry, little sobs down the phone line.

Scale A. Wow! She sat up. Scale A! What does that mean? The last time was the Falklands war. It's serious, this is real, they don't do a Scale A battalion recall for nothing.

'Don't worry, it's probably nothing. I'll find out and call you back,' she said, swinging her legs round and on to the floor.

As the wife of one of the senior NCOs in the battalion, her unofficial role was ill-defined, but real. They were the backbone of the support structure, the link between the families officers, the army welfare people and the wives and families of the serving soldiers. They had no choice. They were usually a bit older than the others, more experienced, with a much clearer understanding of the army and the way it worked. The wives and girlfriends of the more junior ranks relied on them for advice, information, news. She looked up a number and dialled.

Luton

In Luton, in the back room of a redbrick semi, a man called Rick wheeled himself into his tiny kitchen and put the kettle on. He yawned. He usually drank a cup of coffee, caught the early news, had a shower and then started on his PC. He had three but the new one was his favourite; state of the art, a high-speed Pentium MX machine with CD ROM. He had a colour printer, flatbed scanner, and made a bit of a living on his computer as a researcher for a local publisher. This entailed spending all day on the Net, and he loved it.

While the kettle boiled he turned the machine on, logged on, and went into his e-mails. There were nineteen that had been downloaded overnight, the last from his old mate Pete. He turned on the TV for the news and wheeled himself back into the kitchen to make his coffee.

'. . . and we repeat this morning's headline. British troops have come under attack in Belize. That country was invaded by its neighbour Guatemala last night; more on that breaking story in ten minutes.'

Rick turned the chair and looked back at the television from the kitchen door. Fucking hell, he thought, Belize. He knew it well, had spent five years there on and off. So the Guatemalans have finally done it. Pete was still there, with his wife and kids. Shit! Pete! The e-mail! He wheeled himself over to the machine and scrolled down to Pete's message and double-clicked. 'In the shit here. Guats attacked and in the town. Call someone at MoD. I feed int on to Net. Need e address for them. Logging off now. Cunts next door. Will clear box at 0700 Zulu.'

Jesus! Pete's really in the shit. MoD? He wants to feed stuff to the mob? It's six in the morning. Where? Who? Shit man, think! Hereford? No, no way I'll get through there, too many cranks. 3rd UK Div? Northwood? Yeah, Northwood. He dialled directory enquiries, was given the number and dialled again. The call was answered immediately.

'Can you put me through to someone dealing with this Belize scene, please?'

'Who do you want to speak to?'

'Someone dealing with the situation in Belize.'

'I'm sorry. The public relations office doesn't open till nine o'clock.'

'I don't want public relations, I want someone in Operations, please. This is important.'

'Who do you wish to speak to?'

'Someone in Ops!'

'There are a lot of operational people here. I can't help you unless you are more specific.'

'Intelligence then, someone in intelligence. Quickly, please.'

The operator thought he said someone with intelligence and she became a bit shirty. 'There's no need to be like that. I am on the civilian staff but I –'

'No, sorry, you misunderstood me. Someone in the military intelligence team there.'

'Oh . . . hold the line.' There were lots of those, with various acronyms, but she had had enough and there were other lights flashing on her switchboard. She put him through to security where he was given another runaround.

'Listen,' he said finally, 'get an officer to this phone, an army officer preferably. Just fucking do it!'

By now the security system had kicked in, and as with a 999 call, a computer could take the caller's number and throw it up on a screen and match it to an address.

'Lieutenant Connor. How can I help you?'

Jesus, here we go again, Rick thought. 'Listen carefully. Belize – you know it has been invaded?'

277

'Yes, we are aware of that.'

'Right. I have just opened my e-mails. I have a message from a friend in Belize, ex-army. He is in San Ignacio which he says is full of Guatemalans. He wants to help, feed back some int. Are you with me?'

'Yes, I think so,' the young officer replied scribbling San Ignaseo on a pad with a question mark.

'Now to do that on the Net, he needs an e-mail address for someone at your end, or somewhere. Are you people on the Internet?'

'I'm not sure . . .' Fuck me, Rick thought, no wonder the empire is dead. '. . . but hold the line and let me get someone who can help.'

'Well move it along, because he will be clearing his mail box at 0700 our time and I want a response for him.'

The military police officer took his number, name and address, compared it to what was on his screen, and said, 'Someone will call you back.'

Twenty minutes later, a J2 officer on the staff of the CJRDFO called him back and just as his phone rang, there was a knock at the door. It was the police.

'Can you read the message to me, please?' the J2 officer asked.

'I've got police at the door,' Rick said drily.

'Don't worry about them for the moment. Read the message to me, please.'

'Why are they here?'

'Just read the message, please.'

Rick read it.

'Is it genuine, in your view?'

'Absolutely. Pete wouldn't make a joke of this.'

'And he is?'

'An old mate. He did seventeen years in the mob, now owns a restaurant in San Ignacio.'

'If what you say is true, then you can be very helpful. We don't have anyone here on the Net, so to speak. Various individuals with their own e-mail addresses, I'm sure, but nothing official in the building. Question – can you communicate with him from anywhere?'

278

'Yeah, as long as I have a bit of kit; PC, modem.'

'If you are happy to help, they will bring you and your kit in to us here.'

'Hang on,' Rick replied, 'I'll let them in.'

Belize

On the Negroman road the fires still burned. The Guatemalan sergeant who had drawn his men together to wait for daylight hadn't heard sustained firing for the last twenty minutes at least, just the odd shot: that, he knew, was characteristic of nervous, frightened soldiers. The ammunition had all cooked off and now the only sounds were the vehicles that still burned and smouldered, the tortured crackling of heated steel cooling. After the incredible noise of the engagement it seemed there was silence. He knew about ambush; it had happened to him before – guerrillas in the Peten. But nothing like this, never like this – two battalions. Now and then he heard the cries of wounded, moans in the dark. Smoke, heavy and acrid with burnt diesel, paint and oil, billowed slowly, and rose upward on the warm damp air. It was raining again, small drops falling, holding the smell of death. He caught a whiff of cooking meat and gagged, but held it down. He signalled his men to stay put and picking up his rifle he moved back on to the track, ankle-deep in churned-up mud. He moved slowly down the road, stunned by what he was seeing; groups of men huddled together, paralysed by the dark and their terror, unable to move for fear of setting off mines. The dead, were everywhere: on the track, in vehicles; some were burned, some just gruesome bloody remnants of a man. Others, surprisingly, illuminated by the flames, looked to be merely sleeping.

He remembered seeing pictures after the Gulf War of the Iraqi retreat from Kuwait; Death Alley, the mile or so of Iraqi convoy hit by allied aircraft, the lines of burnt-out vehicles and the dead. This was the same. Mother Maria, they said we would be in Belize City in two hours, probably with not a shot fired. He looked down the dark track, at the fires and

279

the smoke and the dead and the wounded. How did they get this so wrong? We can't even control the bandits in the Peten, part of true Guatemala. How would we cope with people who can fight like this? He had travelled into Belize three or four times with his cousin, selling plastic goods from the roadside and he thought about the Belizeans he had met; nice people, laughing, carefree.

There was a flash of white light and a resonant B-L-A-M, like a door slamming, from down the track. He dropped to the ground and as he hit the mud, he heard someone screaming. *Minas!* This was like a nightmare that wouldn't end. He touched something on the ground beside him; wet, fleshy, a part of someone. In the flickering light he could see what it was – a piece of flesh, hair, an eyeball staring at him. He rolled away and was sick, vomiting on to the ground, and wiped his hand where he had touched it, trying to clean it off him, and then pushed himself up. He moved carefully, retracing his steps back to his men, and rejoined them, saying nothing. They were going nowhere till daylight.

Chapter Ten

The Guatemalan captain of engineers was there with his men, looking at a pontoon that had come off the truck that was carrying it. The general was on his way. He had been warned. The old man had left his brigade, the tail-end unit, and was moving forward up the line to try and clear it, get the advance back on the move. Mondragon, the general who crossed over with his second brigade, knew the commander of the lead brigade was dead, and not knowing or trusting that unit's second-in-command, he had absorbed what was left into his own command and was now with the forward elements, at the front, in San Ignacio. The bridge was down and he wanted his bridging equipment and his rafts and where the fuck were they? They are here, the captain thought, because whoever planned the order of march got it wrong; travelling with the second brigade put them miles back down the single road. Keeping them safe was one thing, and he acknowledged that no one had thought they would be needed so soon – maybe by Roaring Creek – because the Kaibiles were supposed to have taken the bridge at San Ignacio; but as usual with the military, it had gone wrong.

He looked down the line. The truck had one front wheel resting in a culvert. Obviously it had been hit, veered to the right, and the tractor unit had left the road. The long, wide trailer was blocking travel in both directions, and the huge, heavy pontoon had snapped its chains and slid off. The crane was half a mile further back. His riggers could get the pontoon on to the trailer, but the truck would need to be retrieved, hauled back on the road, and it had taken a hit so it might not be usable anyway.

'Start the engine, see if it's working,' he said to someone.

Other of the engineering gear had been destroyed, so the colonel had said, much of it stuck here three miles back down a clogged highway. Behind the damaged truck were the rest of the bridging units, and beyond them were other trucks loaded with the boats and rafts. His problem was getting the road cleared, the pontoon on the move.

'Get the crane up here.'

Someone muttered something about soft ground and the risk of it becoming stuck.

'I don't give a shit! Move it round these other vehicles,' he snapped. 'Find a four-wheel-drive recovery vehicle, a couple of tracks to pull it through, but get it here now!'

Bouncing, hooded lights were coming up the field with the familiar whine of a four-wheel-drive transmission and the vehicle suddenly turned and careered in towards him. It could be the general, he realized, the commander of the third brigade stuck behind his trucks, lined up for miles along the road. A figure leapt from the vehicle as it skidded to a halt through the mud, its radio antennae whipping back and forth, and made its way towards him.

'Well?'

It was dark so he couldn't see who it was, but a challenge like that surely indicated that they were senior to him. 'As soon as we can, sir. I have a crane coming forward.'

'How long?'

He thought quickly. Move the pontoon, get the truck back up on the road, fix it. Front axle's gone by the look of it, offside wheel maybe. Reload and secure. They had the gear, welding equipment, mobile workshops.

'Three hours, maybe four.'

'Make it one. General Mondragon wants this equipment in San Ignacio inside an hour and a half and the bridge finished by dawn, and I'm sick of waiting back there like a spare prick at a wedding.'

'Sir, I can only do that if you get me another low-loader, or at least a thirty-five-ton articulated flatbed. Then we can just tow this thing into the field and clear the road. Otherwise it's this truck, recovered back on to the road, towed up to the next lay-by and then fixed. Three hours minimum.' He paused, thinking he might as well tell him. 'I am the bridging officer, sir. I can tell you that there is now no way I can build a bridge by first light. This one is big, very big. We have trained to cross at Roaring Creek – that I can do in under an hour. But at San Ignacio? Once I get there with all my equipment it's a six- or seven-hour job, and after rain like this, and if we are under fire . . .' He trailed off. And anyway, he was thinking, that river, in flood, must be seventy metres across by now. I only have fifty metres of bridge, because that's all I was allowed to bring, and that has a maximum flow tolerance of three knots. The river must be moving at twice that. We will have to wait till the level drops; that might be early tomorrow, so what's the rush?

The general looked away. 'Those the boats back there?'

'Yes sir.'

The general stalked back to his command vehicle and grabbed a map from the hands of his intelligence officer, a major. He grinned – the river was barely half a mile away, and backing up to San Jose, where the chain ferry was, it was right by the road. 'Get Div on the net, I want to talk to them,' he said to his radio operator. 'Juan,' he pointed at the major, 'find out how many boats there are here, how many men they will take, OK?'

San Ignacio

Pete Collins had settled in the roof-space to wait for contact. His phone was on, the little green lights all showing, and as the minutes ticked towards midnight he waited, wondering if the Hereford major had acquired a phone, preferably a digital mobile. He looked out of the louvred dormer window. The town was burning. For a while the shooting had all been outgoing at his lads, but then they began to return fire with some big stuff down by the river, and had put down a mortar bombardment somewhere off to his right, over against the hill at the western end of the town. He had been out once, crossing the rooftops, down towards the roundabout, then doubling back to his hideaway.

Here in the centre of things it looked to be safe for the time being, unless the Guats moved something in to hide in the streets, and his blokes found it. There were troops here, that was for sure; from his position he could see what looked like a battalion command post which meant that around it four or five companies were stretched along the road, hidden in doorways and alleys, hunkered down, waiting to move somewhere. The phone rang.

'Yeah?'

'You said call now. You OK?' Chard asked.

'Yeah. Got a number?'

Chard gave it to him and Pete wrote it on his hand.

'Where are you?'

'In the middle of things,' he said obliquely. 'Your phone digital?'

'Aaah . . . don't know.'

'Get one. Right, listen carefully. Southern end of Burns Street a battalion command post – careful when you hit that. Get me?'

'Yes, I copy that.'

'Further down, behind the gas station, there's a track, loads of aerials and comms shit.'

'Right behind the gas station?'

Pete was looking out of the louvres. There was movement. 'Yeah. Thirty feet back out of your line of sight. Gotta go, I'll call you later. Get a digital. I'll only call this number once again.'

'Thanks, thanks very much.'

Fifteen minutes later the signallers had taken from Northwood the details of the man on the other side. He was kosher, and they were now preparing to talk to him on the Internet.

Belize Airport

West of the passenger terminal, the fighting was still fierce, but the Royal Marines were still where they had first met the Guatemalan flank attack, and holding. The long scything bursts of fire had petered out and Lieutenant Murray thought it was to conserve their ammunition. That was fine with him;

284

he had the same re-supply problem, and every bullet not fired was one saved for when they would need them. This was now a stalemate, his small unit holding a strong defensive position against a larger force, but strategically it had its implications. While the Guats pinned down his troop here they were not available to support the Gurkhas' main line at the eastern end.

The GPMG on the roof fired again. The marines up there had moved the gun three times along the rooftop, and in this last position, behind a full water tank, they had managed to protect themselves. The tank had taken hits and water was now running out, so how much longer it would stop a bullet no one knew, but it was as good as it was going to get for the time being.

They had a second wounded man; the first, offered a place on the helo, had said no, and morale was good. Murray looked across at him, wishing for a second he had ordered him to go. The wound was now giving the marine some trouble and he was unable to lie prone, but the bleeding seemed to have stopped. The second man had his forearm unzipped by a bullet that ran the length of his arm under the skin before exiting at the elbow. Luckily no bones were hit.

'Marines,' someone called, 'they aren't fucking marines.' Murray looked down the line at the speaker. It was a private, a fellow from Falmouth, hard as nails, tattooed, with enough holes in his ears for four earrings each side. He had said once to Murray, when drunk as a skunk, that the Royal Marines had been the making of him. If he had failed selection, he had said, he would have ended up inside for GBH or something. 'They are crap,' he finished. A burst of fire came over their heads.

'I think they heard you,' someone said.

'Fuck 'em,' he replied. He rose up an inch or two to yell over the bollard. 'HEY, YOU CUNTS! I WILL KILL YOU AND THEN I WILL FUCK YOUR MOTHER.' Clearly, Murray realized, he had been impressed with the Gurkhas' yelled insults. The shout carried, and seemed to be understood on the other side because three or four rifles opened up and the marine dropped back down again.

'Ooooh, scratchy, aren't they.'

The gun team on the roof had obviously seen the muzzle-flash because there was a burst of fire from them, and across on the other side the bullets had found their target because someone began to scream.

'You see,' the Falmouth lad said with a grin, 'no fucking discipline and look what it cost them. Marines? Are they shit! It's disgraceful.'

More fire slammed into the concrete they crouched behind, chipping off bits that flew through the air, the bullets ricocheting away like angry bees, and they returned fire as targets presented themselves.

On the Belize River

The patrol boat, christened HMS *Tonka Toy* in conformity with the sailor's first rather disparaging remark, was now on the river. Lieutenant Lewis had crept in at the mouth, eased up towards the road bridge and then, unsure of exactly where the Guatemalans were, he gunned the boat up under the bridge and on to the fast-flowing waters on the other side, pushing up the throttles. The river was wide, in flood, and the risk of hitting the bottom was minimal, but ramming something drifting was a real danger: a log, an uprooted tree, flood debris. The moment he was clear of the airport – off to the right they could hear the fighting – he slowed down and had the electrical artificer break out the lights. Two halogen lamps, one for a seaboat, and one spare for the Lynx, were mounted on the wheelhouse combing. One pointed ahead and the other was on a swivel. The foredeck, dominated by the 12.7 mm cannon, had no space to set up the GPMG so they put the lighter gun, provided by *Beaufort*'s armoury, aft of the wheel and high up in the position originally designed for a light weapon by the boat's builders. Even the pedestal was there, but Belize didn't have enough machine guns and luckily the fitment had never been removed. With a bit of ingenuity and a piece of two-inch piping, two of the sailors mounted the gun fairly quickly, both aware that within four feet of its position were six forty-four-gallon drums of fuel lashed to the deck.

Trooper Hagan, the B Squadron man, was up at the forrard gunwale, with the Belizean fellow who had fired the cannon before, familiarizing himself as best he could. This was not ideal; in fact, it was dangerous. In the Regiment they trained with a variety of weapons, over and over again; hours and hours of practice in every scenario meant they could hit the target in their sleep. If they were a bit rusty they had a special-ist, a weapons man who could retrain them, show them the little idiosyncrasies of each type, how to get the best out of it, in whatever conditions they were likely to be in. But Hagan had never been near a 12.7mm before.

He told the Belizean fellow to show him again. He knew that before they approached the battle he would have to strip the gun, rebuild it, strip it again, try to understand the mech-anism, fire it, feel the recoil, the speed of the action, fire it again at various distances. They had plenty of ammo, but even so he could afford to let go only fifty rounds tonight and he hoped it would be enough. Back at Hereford or on work-up for an operation they would have fired hundreds, thousands of rounds from each weapon they would use.

At the wheel Lewis was concentrating hard. He had the boat running at near top speed, one spotlight fixed on the water in front, another being directed by the PO, round the next bend, at the banks, sweeping back and forth over the brown foamy rushing waters. This was risky, but if they arrived early enough to make a difference, and if the Guate-malans did use boats then the risk was worth it. They were moving at times at thirty-two knots, but speed over land was only twenty-six or seven. At that pace hitting a log or some-thing swept up by the floodwaters could drive a hole into the hull and sink them, so he was being careful, very careful indeed, powering off whenever he was unsure, running up the engines again when they were clear.

On *Beaufort* their shipmates were about to go to work, to do what they had done since before Napoleonic times. The role was naval gunfire support – fight the ship against shore targets, stand off the coastline and use their guns as artillery to support an action ashore by either marines or army. The ship ceased to be a moving, living thing, master of the seas. It became little more than an artillery battery. It was called the gunline.

It was also high risk. In the modern era of high-speed sea-skimming anti-shipping missiles, even with equally up-to-date defence systems, putting your ship so close to a hostile environment was dangerous because when a threat became apparent the time available for your defences to react was so much shorter. If Commander Bennett had thought or even suspected that the enemy had weapons capable of hitting his ship from the shore, he would never have moved in so close, certainly not into reefs and shallows, where his manoeuvrability was severely limited. He had forty minutes.

'The hole is just ahead,' Dion said. 'Two hundred metres or so.'

Bennett looked across at the depth. The tide was still rising and water under the keel was nine feet.

'Stop both!' Dion called.

'Stop both, aye aye,' from the quartermaster. He rang down and in the mechanical control room the petty officer sitting at the engine stations pulled back the power completely. The ship ghosted forward; Bennett, aware that the moment the power came off the drift would increase, waited for a few seconds as she lost headway, but he didn't need to say anything. The Belizean boatman was on to it.

'Wheel ten to starboard.'

The QM repeated the order back to him. The silence was palpable.

'Water under my keel?'

'Three metres, sir . . . three and a half, four, five.'

The hole. They were in it.

'Slow astern both.'

'Slow astern both.'

'Stop both.'

'Stop both.'

Dion looked at Bennett. 'Well, I got you here. How long you stay here is up to you. You have half an hour or so before we ought to be moving.'

'If we stay will the hole take us?' the navigator asked.

'No problem. Anchors will hold, and with a short line, dead centre, she will swing through with the tide.'

No, Bennett thought. Come daylight, they may throw air at me and I want to be out in the blue water where I can move and fight. His three command imperatives were float, fight, move. In here he could float, he could fight, but he couldn't move and any decision that affected a command imperative needed a compelling reason.

'Thank you, Dion. Pilot, hold us over this point, please. Thirty minutes, gentlemen, let's make them count.'

They were ready. The load ring was full, the racks were loaded, the hoist down to the main magazine was open. The 4.5 inch fast-firing Vickers Mark IIX would be aiming at map coordinates, then controlled, they hoped, by an FAO ashore, a forward artillery observer. Northwood had come through. One of the marines at the airport had done the course with 148 battery, and if he was out of the frame then the B Squadron soldier or one of the Para officers would have to step into the role. Bennett walked over to where the Clansman radio was in its normal position with the other handhelds by the starboard comms station.

'Three Alpha, Three Alpha, Three Alpha, *Beaufort*, over.'

'This is Three Alpha – say again your callsign, please?'

'Three Alpha, *Beaufort*, *Beaufort*, this is Her Majesty's warship *Beaufort*. Your Alpha actual, please.'

Twenty seconds later Fox was on the air, down in the dugout on his knees, holding the radio handset with one hand, the other covering his other ear, so he could hear over the firing. He wasn't the carefully groomed officer and gentleman of the barbecue the night before. His clothing was filthy, torn, his normally carefully twirled moustache, one of his little eccentricities, was matted with dirt. He was grimy, sweating, his maroon beret caked in dried blood from when he had carried one of his wounded toms back into the bunker over his shoulder.

'Go, *Beaufort*.' In the background they could hear the battle, the sounds of small arms coming through the transmission.

'Alpha, can offer November Golf Sierra for limited time. Do you copy, over?'

Up at the terminal, Murray, who was listening to the conversation, was wondering if Fox knew what the naval captain was on about, but back in the command dugout, the response was swift. Fox raised a thumb at one of the wounded fellows with a big grin on his face.

'Roger, *Beaufort*, delighted to hear that. How soon, how soon? Over.'

'Alpha, a Romeo Mike at your location,' Bennett spelt the marine's name, 'is a Foxtrot Alpha Oscar. Can you get him ready, over?'

Murray, in anticipation, was already calling the man's name. He was seven down the line of men to his right, where he had been since guiding in the mortar rounds.

'Roger, *Beaufort*. Stand by. Mike One, Mike One, did you copy that? Over.'

'Roger, Three, he is on his way down to you now, over.'

A couple of minutes later he was in the command bunker.

'*Beaufort, Beaufort, Beaufort*, Foxtrot Alpha Oscar, requesting November Golf Sierra at this time, over.'

'Go, Oscar.'

'Coordinates are . . .' He read them out, repeated them, heard them back, and then said, 'Roger, confirm that loc, one round Hotel Echo, please.'

On the bridge a comms rating had the link so that the FAO could talk directly to the officer deep in the Ops room down in the bowels of the ship. Here in the dingy half-light, flash-hooded figures bent over radar screens, plotting desks, consoles of every description. From here they fought the ship, scanning the skies, the surface or the depths below them for the threat; then, using Harpoons, Sea Wolf systems, torpedoes, the attack helo, or the radar and laser controlled main armament, they engaged and destroyed the enemy.

'Coordinates in, sir.'

'Thank you.'

'Gunbay, Ops.'

'Ops, gunbay.'

'Gunbay, you ready?'

'Gunbay ready!'

'One round HE, fire!'

The controller at his console in the top right corner of the Ops room, standing in for the CPO(M), who was ashore on St George's, pressed the button. Up on the main deck the gun, its trajectory computer compensating for the roll of the ship, fired, a whiplash CRACK, the barrel slamming back into the turret, belching smoke. In the next second, the automated system opened the breech, ejected the shell casing, scooped up another from the hoist, loaded it, closed the breech and was ready to fire again before the first projectile had landed.

Belize Airport

Ashore they heard it coming, the roaring, whistling sound that preceded artillery shells, made grown men wet themselves, and drove others into panic. Many of the Guatemalans didn't really know what it was. The 4.5 inch shell hit and exploded three hundred yards out, a flash of white-orange light and a massive blast that they could feel, both in a concussion wave through the air, and in the ground beneath them.

'Add one hundred! Fire for effect!'

The next round dropped right on the Guatemalan offensive line.

'Left fifty, two rounds HE each call, *Beaufort*, I say again two rounds on each call!'

Each call preceded shells landing and the ground shook, the explosive delivered by the naval gun like nothing the engagement had seen this night, blasts that left huge craters in the earth, blew men to pieces, deafened those up too close, left ears bleeding. The whole area was engulfed now, in flames, flying mud and debris, branches, shrapnel, secondary explosions as stores of ammunition went up. It was an inferno, a vision of hell.

'Right fifty! Drop one hundred.' He beat an area through the enemy's rear, pulverizing the earth, shattering trees and shrubs, blasting great craters, and in the process taking out whoever was in there.

'Stop! Stop! Stop! Cease fire, *Beaufort*. Now coordinates are . . . Stand by.' The marine was scrabbling with the map, Fox helping him, then they were ready. The marine grabbed the Clansman radio and took off out of the bunker, running back through the now-reduced fire towards the terminal. He needed to see it, had to see it to do his job. He dropped to the ground, the bushline in view, his own comrades seventy yards out ahead of him. Please God don't let me fuck up. He called the coordinates and heard them back.

'Roger that loc, *Beaufort*. One round HE.'

It roared in over his head like a train in a tunnel, landing back in the bush and too far to the right, almost on the airport fence. Thank you, Lord, I love you.

'*Left two hundred, left two hundred, left two hundred, one round HE.*'

It hit. Dead centre. Fuck, I'm good.

'Two rounds HE! Fire for effect!'

Minutes later, the area was devastated – no holes, no dug-outs, no trenches. Anyone left alive in there was probably wounded, terrified, with perforated eardrums, weeping, traumatized. They would have no fight left, for the time being anyway. Let them withdraw, care for their wounded.

'Stop! Stop! Stop! Cease fire, *Beaufort*, I say cease fire. We thank you. I say again we thank you, over.'

On *Beaufort*, Bennett was pleased to hear the cease-fire called. Not only because they had been able to help – he wondered how long the barrel of the gun could take that rate of fire without overheating. He took up the handpiece from the Clansman radio.

'Three, pleased to have been able to help. Your Alpha, please?'

'Stand by.'

Bennett looked across at the XO. 'See how much HE we have left, please?'

'Sixteen, sir,' he replied. 'I was counting.'

England

At Aldershot, the home of the British army, 5 Airborne Brigade was on the move. The whole town was bustling. Major arterial routes that passed the various gates of the camp had been closed off to civilian traffic; military police were directing and marshalling the many drab green and disruptive-pattern painted vehicles that were grinding about, trucks laden with stores and equipment. 5 A/B was four infantry battalions with HQ and support units, some 5,000 personnel, and huge resources were being deployed to get them away in record time, the muscle and organizational expertise of the UK 3rd Division thrown at the effort. Other units were stripped of equipment, stores and skills. Every detail was in the plans somewhere, every roll of toilet paper, every round of ammunition, every hexy block, every floppy disk, every spare part and every eventual letter home.

The first unit away would be 2 Para, and the instructions and mood were clear. They were to have everything they wanted, both in matériel and assistance, and people were either to help or just to get out of the bloody way.

JRDF planners were moving at an extraordinary pace, dusting off contingency plans in a dozen formats across three services. Aircraft, the prime uplift, were being marshalled on airfields, scheduled ops abandoned. Every refuelling tanker on the active list was made available, two due for certificate of airworthiness tests pulled back on to the flight line. France came through with two tankers, the Americans with as many as Britain wanted. This operation could involve the largest mid air refuelling exercise ever undertaken by Great Britain. The Harriers, now within two hours of departing, would be the first to snuggle up to the huge tankers over the Atlantic, to take on board thousands of pounds of precious fuel. The

C-130s carrying 2 Para would be next, and within forty-eight hours, the first transports with the rest of 5 A/B.

The first Harrier flight crews, ground crews and stores were airborne already, and bound for Pensacola Naval Air Station in Florida. For the first time in history, a mainland US military base would accommodate the strike power of a friendly nation on active service. Britain had made its airfields available to the US often enough, almost continuously since the Second World War. Now the Prime Minister had called in the debt. Until the forward elements of the RAF package could get themselves sorted out on St George's, or on the long hard runway at the international airport, the Harriers would fly ground attack and air defence sorties from Pensacola.

Belize Airport

Corporal Garvey, who had spent the bulk of the battle up at the far end of the runway, made his way back down the airport until he could call to Murray. He spoke for a few minutes and then the two men moved down to the command dugout where Fox was waiting for them.

'I'm going to go out, get behind them,' Garvey said. 'This is our last chance before daylight. I want to evaluate positions, the extent of their lines around the southern edge, see how much that NGS hurt them. Then if I can unnerve them I will, open fire from their rear. After that they will need to watch from the back as well. They will be nervous, seeing threats in every shadow.'

'That's fucking dangerous,' Murray said in reply.

'I know.'

It broke every rule in the book. Recce was just that, it was intelligence-gathering. The SAS were opportunists, but in principle you never combined covert reconnaissance with an attack. You went in quiet, you came out quiet. The enemy never knew you were there; if they knew they had been looked over, they would change positions, deployments, move, reinforce.

Also, depending on the objectives, an attack required a core critical mass and with enemy in numbers, anything under patrol strength, with supporting fire from grenade launchers, the interlocking fire of the patrol members from various positions, wasn't likely to achieve much. In this instance Murray and Fox had to agree; having the Guatemalans edgy and using resources to protect their rear was worth the tactical risk, but they didn't have enough men to send out a patrol and Garvey had volunteered.

'But I'll move quickly. I'm fast, and if I'm alone, anything that moves is the enemy. I'll be back in before first light.'

That would be the scary part. Where to re-enter? The chances of blue on blue were high, so he wanted to come back in at one of the places that were undefended, even if it took much longer to work his way round.

'If we agree a time and place, I'll move forward and expect a challenge.'

'My sector,' Murray said. 'You can probably move back in through the car park to the terminal. I have one rifle there, covering that ground. He'll be waiting for you. I'll have my blokes on the gun further along the roof cover you. What time?'

Garvey looked at his watch. Three hours – he would need at least three hours, maybe four.

'First try between 0330 and 0332, then an hour later. If I'm not in at the first window then I will be in at O430. Can you put someone with my lads? They need someone steady, or they will be firing at shadows.'

Murray nodded. 'My sergeant. Happy, sir?' He looked at Major Fox, who nodded. 'Carry on.'

When Murray returned to his troop, the news was bad. In his absence one of his men had been hit and killed by a bullet.

Garvey was ready and had prepared his equipment before going down to talk to Major Fox. He had stripped everything down and would go out with just his belt-kit. He had a side-arm, a 9mm pistol, four hand-grenades, six rifle-grenades. He would take his own 203, primarily for its ability to fire rifle-grenades, and he had swapped the heavy 7.62 machine gun he had been carrying all night with the marines, for a smaller section automatic weapon, what the Squadron called a minimi. It was lighter, effective and wouldn't slow him down when he had to move. In his belt-kit he had a small handheld radio, a water bottle, miniature survival gear, medical equipment and magazines for his weapons. The grenades and some flares he carried in a small day-pack. He crossed the wire out in front of his BDF position, and melted into the dark like a chimera, moving slowly and carefully until well out in the bush, beyond where any Guatemalan recce patrol would have positioned themselves. A kilometre out he began to swing south to come in directly behind the Guatemalan positions facing the small band of Royal Marines by the terminal.

San Ignacio

At the house on the eastern side, back from the river where the fighting raged, the girls were still indoors but no longer in the bathroom. They had become used to the sounds of the battle and the explosions near to them seemed to have stopped. Twice they had ventured out into the garden, and once Sophie had stepped out on to the road to look up towards the main highway, hoping to see their vehicle returning. Over to the west, just a mile away, they could see the glow of flames against the clouds, and odd swirling skeins of darkness that could only be smoke rising from the ground. The firing was still intense.

'Do you think something's happened to him?' Helen asked.

'Maybe, or maybe he just drove off in it,' Sophie said bleakly.

'No, he wouldn't do that. He was a gentleman.'

'So where is he? God, he was only going to drive down to the bridge and back again. That's a ten-minute journey at the most and that was what? Nearly two hours ago now. Bastard! He probably dropped Pete, and turned round and just kept driving.'

'No,' Helen responded. 'I am a good judge of men. God knows, I have known enough of them,' she said with a little smile, 'and he wasn't that type. Something has happened to him.'

They went back inside the little house and rummaged round in the kitchen till they found some instant coffee – there was no tea. They boiled water on the stove and talked through their options and as Sophie filled their cups, she looked over at Helen. Well, she thought, then we are here without transport. The fighting hasn't come any closer, but we need to make a plan.

'It'll be OK. Let's try and sleep. We wait here till it gets light and then we go out and try and find someone, hitch a lift, hire something.'

Suddenly the lights went out. Both looked out of the windows – the few lights that had been on in houses nearby had gone off too.

'Oh no,' Helen moaned. 'That's all we bloody need. I hate the dark. I hate it!' She began to cry. Sophie pushed a long hank of her hair back behind her ear, rubbed some dirt from her hands on to her jeans and then hugged Helen. 'It's all right. We're OK, it's just a power failure. We were lucky to have had lights this long. We'll be fine.'

'I'm scared, Soph.'

I am too, Sophie thought, I am too. 'Silly old thing. We'll be OK. That's Harry's unit down there remember, the berets we saw, 2 Para. It will be light in a few hours and then we'll go. Drink your coffee.' She wished he was here. He would know what to do.

A mile away Eddie Sanchez, the taxi driver, helped his sister's husband carry the last load out to the truck and tie it down. There were clothes, bedding, two mattresses, some food from the fridge, an electric fan, some utensils, all piled on the bed of the truck. They were moving out, taking the six kids and heading for relatives near Orange Walk, but by the back way, through Gallon Jug. His sister was crying, standing in the dark kitchen, trying to empty the contents of the fridge into a blue plastic bucket, saying it would spoil, trying to appear normal and steady in front of the kids. But they knew it was bad; the sounds of the fighting carried the two miles and the eldest, at sixteen, wanted to ride his bike over there to get a closer look and she lashed out and hit him, something she had never done. That stunned everyone, and now they finished loading in silence.

'Das da lot,' the brother-in-law said. 'You kids geddena tra.' He looked at Eddie. 'What you gonna do, man?'

'I'll wait,' Eddie said. His sister was coming out now, the blue bucket heavy in her hand, locking the door as though it might stop anyone looting. 'Let the road clear a bee. You go' ena petral?'

'Extra ten gallun. Shoo' be nuf. You ta' care, man.'

'You too.'

He watched them leave and then walked to his car. Wait till daylight, he thought, give the road through to town a chance to clear, maybe get a fare. Normal price was somewhere between seventy and a hundred US, but he could get double that tomorrow.

Half a mile away Major Chard looked across the river and raised the binoculars to his eyes. Over the bridge buttresses, the Shell station was in sight, but he couldn't see the tracked vehicle. The man said it was there and he must assume it was. He glanced across at the soldier to his right, who had the radio command detonators for the explosives they had set in the southern end of the town. They had just destroyed the generator station – why give the Guats the luxury of light? The place was now in darkness, except where flames from fires illuminated the signs above the forecourt. Well, he thought, if there is a C&C vehicle there, then let's have the bastard.

'OK,' he said. 'Blow the fucker. Let 'er rip.'

The soldier pressed the keypad.

There were three flat cracks they could hear on this side, and then the big one. A delivery was due the following morning and the underground storage tanks were almost empty; a thousand gallons of leaded and just over that in unleaded. The diesel tank was the one they really wanted, you didn't give an enemy fuel, not ever, not if you were hitting his comms lines, but they had rigged all three tanks to go. The safety measures, escape valves to bleed off explosive vapours, were not totally effective. The valves gunged up over time; instead of letting the vapours go, they allowed them to build up to a level that, while not dangerous enough to trigger the warning lights in the office, if they ever worked, would certainly make any ignition of the vapours a major explosion, spectacular in the extreme – it was.

After the third small explosion, a nanosecond later a massive blast shook the ground, smashed windows, ripped roofs from nearby houses. A blue-white fireball expanded upwards, like a transparent cloud, and died in a second, and then the remaining fuel caught, huge orange flames leaping. Debris was landing on this side of the river, and when Chard looked back over, the petrol station forecourt was still there, but the roof, the office and lube bay had gone, flames reaching sixty feet upwards from the tank.

'Fuckin' 'ell,' the man beside him said. 'Fuel vapour. The escape valve must have been dicky, boss.' Like it needed an explanation. There was cheering, a few whistles and a burst of spontaneous applause from some of the lads nearby, but Chard wasn't impressed.

Two miles away, up the road to the border, the captain of engineers saw the flash in the sky and heard the dull whump. Some of the men nearby cheered, thinking that General Mondragon and his brigade had delivered another mighty blow, but the captain knew otherwise. He looked back down at the job; the crane was there, towed alongside the clogged road through the mud by an eight-wheel-drive recovery truck. They had strops under the bridge section and were ready to lift.

Further back, a convoy of four-wheel-drive vehicles pulled from the stalled line of advance were now awaiting the boats that were being unloaded. Some were rigid inflatables, others big aluminium flat-bottomed skiffs, but they were all light enough to be manhandled across to the vehicles facing the other way for the mile-long journey back to the chain ferry, the nearest point where the riverbank and the road came together. With the eighteen boats divided into three flotillas of six they could move 230 men and their equipment, plenty, the general knew, to work a flank attack.

Major Tyson-Davis looked up. Across one end of the hangar a kitchen had been set up and base personnel were serving food. He smiled briefly, amazed again at the sheer resource and organizational skills of the Americans. In the Paras, before they lobbed in or fought, a huge grill plate was laid out and the men could amble over when they were ready and cook themselves a couple of fried eggs and jam them between two slices of bread – the ubiquitous egg banjos. That was the joke; if you didn't like the idea of a punch-up and you saw them bringing out eggs and bread for a DIY egg banjo then you knew it was going down and it was time to shit yourself. But here there was even a choice of food, a blackboard with the menu. Cajun chicken, burgers, a pasta dish, sandwiches, ice-cream, sodas, coffee. Someone with some foresight who knew British tastes had scrawled 'and tea!' at the bottom.

Atlee arrived with Harry Rees and the CSM. 'Wedges are loaded. Stores issue is complete.'

'Almost everyone is packed, sir,' Jennings reported. 'Another five minutes and we'll be there.'

'You happy?' Tyson-Davis asked. It had been decided that CSM Jennings would remain in charge of support platoon and Atlee would command the smaller but highly specialized patrols, a small force but potent if used properly.

'Got everything we need,' Atlee responded.

Tyson-Davis looked at his watch. They were on track. 'Right, you two eat. Then we'll brief and mount immediately.'

Fifteen minutes later the toms stood round in a semicircle and Tyson-Davis prepared to give the briefing of his lifetime. He began with what he knew, without all the detail he had been given, but enough so they knew the task ahead of them, where they were going, why and what they were facing. He then covered the plan: entry, DZ, rendezvous, route of march, rules of engagement. That over, he paused and then began to speak again.

'C Coy are there now, and as you know, they have engaged. What you don't know is, B Squadron is in. They got there this morning and have spent the day ensuring that the scrotes have a few surprises in store.' There was a ripple of laughter. The men were excited, the adrenaline beginning to flow. 'At Arnhem, Brigade will be waiting for the go and, I don't have to tell you, the Reg will be straining at the bit. If the rest of 2 Para are not loading wedges as we speak then this isn't the best bloody company in the airborne. Yes?' There were positive murmurs. Tyson-Davis began to move among them, lifting his hand to his ear. 'I must be going deaf! I said the best bloody company in the airborne. Yes?' There was a trickle of laughter and louder words of approval.

'Are you 2 Para?'

'Yes!' Louder now.

'Are you D Coy, spearhead company, spearhead battalion, Five Airborne Brigade?'

'YES!'

'The best company, in the best unit, in the best bloody standing army in the world!'

'YES!'

'Is there anything the scrotes have got that can match us?'

'NO!'

'Are you the best trained, best motivated, best equipped, most fearsome bunch of bastards that ever lobbed out?'

'YES!'

'OK, lads.' He dropped his voice a level, matey now. 'This is it. C Coy are in the shit and under fire.' Louder then, 'I'm going back to Belize . . .' softer now, a dangerous low tone that the men had to strain to hear, '. . . and I'm going to lob out and show those bastards that you don't fuck with Paras. Are you coming with me?'

'YES!' came the roar.

Tyson-Davis turned to the CSM. 'Sar' Major. The company will air mount.' As the toms gathered their parachutes and containers Tyson-Davis went to find the man who had prepared everything for them.

General MacLennan was in an office at the back of the hangar with the supply colonel and a woman, too old to be active, wearing civilian gear. The general had witnessed the briefing and had been impressed. The young major was a

301

natural leader and obviously extremely popular with his men. For MacLennan, who had been in Vietnam where officers were fragged by their own troops, it was something he knew he would remember for a long time.

'I must thank you, sir. Your people really turned out for us.'

'Don't mention it, son. Least we can do,' MacLennan said, rising to his feet. He indicated the woman. 'My wife, Tricia. Never very good with off-limits areas,' he said gruffly.

'How do you do?' Tyson-Davis held out his hand to take hers and nodded briefly, ever the gentleman.

She stepped closer. 'I heard you didn't eat,' she said, as if talking to one of her sons. 'Sam never did either. I scooted home. It's just a BLT, some cold chicken, a slice of pie and some cookies. You'll be hungry before dawn.'

He smiled, touched at the gesture. 'Thank you.'

'You're welcome,' she said. 'Come home safe now.' Home, here, England – anywhere but where they were going. Home for soldiers was where they didn't have to fight, where their families were, where there were people who cared about them, where they were among friends.

Aldershot

Local radio stations were broadcasting the announcement every few minutes and at railway and bus stations across Hampshire and Surrey, the boards were out. 2 PARA RETURN TO BARRACKS.

At Aldershot station local people knew. Army vehicles were leaving every few minutes to take men back to the camp. Two fellows came off one train, missed the green Land-Rover and ran to the taxi rank. They didn't have to queue, people motioned for them to go to the head of the line, and one man waiting for a cab who stepped back to let them through mildly surprised himself by calling a soft 'good luck, lads' as the taxi drove away.

Around the camp the military police had closed off the roads, only allowing through army vehicles and those with official identification. Inevitably gawkers had begun to arrive, the plain curious, the mawkish and the military anoraks. At the gate, reserves who had heard of the Scale A recall had begun to arrive, crowding round the guards: ex-Paras, those who had left the Regiment, gone into civvy street but still had a defence commitment, one or two who had been retired for health reasons, and one, incredibly, with only one leg. 'Here to make up numbers, sir,' he said to an arriving officer. The officer didn't have the heart to tell him he had no chance, just nodded and moved on, both amused and strengthened by the innocence, the optimism and the esprit de corps – once a Para, always a Para. Active soldiers were now arriving every minute, pouring through the gate, the guards waving them through with the lightweight vehicles, trucks grinding in with supplies. Maddy Jennings had finally tracked down a families officer attached to 2 Para. He was working flat out with his small support team, but agreed that he would meet her with as many of the D Coy wives as she could gather at 1000 hours at the NAAFI rec room. After that he was back to back till midnight, dealing with the groups of other battalion wives and families.

US Airspace

They were somewhere over Florida, Cutter knew, heading southwards, or maybe they had even begun to swing south-west. The platoon were all around him, their stick numbers determining where they sat. The boss, Ted, would be out first, followed by his radio operator, but he was in the other aircraft. On this plane the CSM would lob out first, Big Harry behind him and then the platoon, as the wedges were going out the back of the ramp. The others would follow them. Plonker was quiet at last, dozing a few feet down. Spud and Rhah were on his right and Jonesy on his left, his Teletubbies' heads sticking out of his shirt. He looked round at Elias.

'You all right?' Elias asked over the engine noise.

'Me?' Jonesy grinned weakly. 'Like everyone else. Dial 1-800-CRAPPING.'

Elias smiled, tried to ease himself into a more comfortable position and looked back down at his weapon. He could smell it, the oil. He ran his hand over its familiar contours, like a man might do with his lover. You and me, my girl, you take care of me and I'll take care of you.

He thought about what Jonesy had said. Everyone seemed calm enough, but he knew that like him each would be in his own private turmoil. They were going into action he thought – live ammunition, real bullets, thousands of enemies in brigade-sized formations with armour and tracks, trying to kill them. No air, no artillery, no support and outnumbered sixty-five to one. What a fuck-up.

Chapter Eleven

In Belize the main landline phone system had gone down, the work of Guatemalan saboteurs, but in real terms it didn't make a huge difference because much of the country had been without telephones until the recent introduction of a satellite network for mobile phones. People all over Belize who owned mobiles were still talking, looking for news and information. The government, in a naive attempt to restore calm, had reported that there was simply tension on the border, and in a pre-emptive move they had declared martial law and imposed a curfew. But anyone with a mobile phone knew the truth, and thousands of people, now refugees, were streaming eastwards along the highway from Cayo district. To add to the surreal situation, many of the country's people who had satellite television dishes were watching Leo Scobey's reports from San Ignacio, now syndicated and flashed live to CNN and the Sky Network. Although there was a satellite dish on the house they were in, Sophie and Helen didn't know, so they sheltered as best they could, unaware of much of what was going on. For others watching, the reports were urgent and dramatic. In the background of the live sequences there was heavy, sustained weapons fire, and much of the town on the western side of the river seemed to be ablaze, the flames from the Shell station at the roundabout, a place everyone knew and recognized, forming a most spectacular backdrop.

Out of camera shot of this latest report and half a mile nearer the flames, the B Squadron troopers were still laying down their specialist fire, seeking targets of opportunity, neutralizing automatic weapons as they identified their positions, with Milan and LAW rockets. Their mortar teams were slowing their rate of fire now, the job of taking out the Guatemalan mortars behind the town seemingly done as they had fallen silent.

Below them Lieutenant Estelle was still down in his defensive positions on the riverbank. He had rotated his men, bringing down fresh troops, and doubling up on the original number. Now with over half a platoon down there he was better positioned, and he still had a fresh platoon back from the line, to move down as the day dawned, or the river dropped, whichever came first. The Squadron soldiers were impressed with the Gurkhas. Their stoic strength, their steadfastness under intense fire were exemplary, but in truth they had expected nothing else.

Belize Airport

Corporal Garvey was now behind the Guatemalan positions on the southern flank. He had travelled the last quarter of a mile very slowly indeed. The sounds of the battle would mask much, but somewhere back here he knew there would be people, the rearmost positions, official or otherwise. This was a company at least so there might be a first-aid post, a command post or mortar position perhaps, or even a small bunch of Guatemalans not so keen on getting too close to the fighting. He loaded the 203 with a rifle-grenade, slung it over his shoulder, checked the minimi for the umpteenth time and began to move forward, a little at a time, slowly, from shadow to shadow. It was low stunted bush, short stubby fan palms, swampy and wet underfoot. This was dodgy stuff. In theory a patrol moving out to establish where the enemy lay was meat and drink for soldiers. For the Special Air Service intelligence-gathering was a prime function, but nevertheless, going forward alone, on foot, into unknown enemy positions was highly dangerous. There was no support structure, none of the lads to come powering in if he was compromised, or was hit. And he was going to stir them up, attack from their rear, force them to turn some of their resources his way. By definition that was no longer covert recce, he would be under fire. Mustn't fuck up, he thought; do this properly. He had to determine the time and the place, get his egress route sorted, hit fast and hard, and then disappear. Move along, hit them again from another point. He could hear voices now, speaking Spanish. They must be fifty yards ahead, he thought, maybe sixty.

He moved forward and found himself in a shallow depression, a long dip in the contours of the ground, that seemed to run east to west. At its lowest point there was running water. He smiled; undulating ground, depressions and outcrops were the infantryman's friend. Thank you, whoever is up there, thank you. He turned to his right to follow the gully, to see how far it ran, and almost walked into them, but heard just in time the scrape of a bayonet coming out of a sheath. He froze and waited. There, faintly visible, were three of them, sitting in the shallow gully, their feet just above the water, below the line of sight from the north. They were silent, avoiding talking, and Garvey thought they might be temporary deserters. If so they would sneak back up when the fighting died down, but for now they were safer back here and they knew it. One of them was trying to open a tin with a bayonet, the point held downwards, the palm of his other hand hammering down on the hilt.

Garvey knew that he could take them, but that would compromise his position. He wanted to fight from this gully, it was perfect – but how many more of them were back here? Just these three, or another ten, twelve, or fifteen scattered along the length of the gully? He stood absolutely still, assessing the situation, then very slowly settled down on to one knee, ready to let rip with the minimi if they turned round and saw him. His heart was pounding, and he began to move slowly backward. There was a bush that he could settle behind, still only fifteen feet from them, but it was cover. One of the Guatemalans lit a cigarette, the flare of the match bright in the darkness and Garvey immediately felt better; not only had they slipped off from the fighting line but other poor discipline was showing through.

Too far to go back, he thought. I can engage from here, move, engage again, just make these three sorry bastards my first attack. He rose, edged round the bush and leaving the three men in the gully he advanced slowly to establish where the bulk of the Guatemalans were. Twenty yards on he stopped. He could see their rear now, maybe thirty yards ahead, a hooded torchbeam, the glow of cigarettes. There was a circular depression in front of him and he realized that it must be a crater, made by the naval rounds coming in. He looked back up. The torchbeam was moving again and he saw the pale flash of a map being turned in the light – an officer – good enough. He took a sighting, lining up the trees on the other side and moved slowly back to the gully, knowing what he had to do. Once there he marked the spot on the gully bank and took out three hand-grenades.

OK boy, just fucking do it! I'm tired and hungry and they are really beginning to piss me off! He was spooling himself up, getting the adrenaline moving in his blood. The first grenade, fused for five seconds, went at the three men hiding in the gully. He counted to three and lobbed it into them, ducking down and bringing the minimi up to his shoulder as it went off with a nasty flat crack. He let rip a burst at the place the officer had been, and threw the next two grenades in quick succession at the same spot, before turning the minimi on the survivors in the gully, one of whom was now up, screaming in pain. He fired a burst into them, put another over the top at the Guats' rear, sprang up and moved west-wards along the gully, running flat out. There was shouting, fire coming back his way, tracers reaching at the sky. He dropped, fired again and then reached for the 203 with the rifle-grenade already mounted. He lined up and fired at its minimum seventy-yard range, then let go a second. He scooped up the minimi and ran on again, cutting upwards now and much closer. A figure moved in the dark and he fired a burst into it. A fleeting shadow in the darkness, firing at whatever moved, he ran through their rear, the minimi tearing bullets into whoever he encountered. The Guate-malans, most of whom never even saw him, were firing blindly, and when he returned to the gully, his heart was pounding. He moved again, away from their men firing into the darkness, hitting each other, perhaps; from the shouting it seemed there were officers trying to gain control. It was mayhem, hundreds of rounds being fired off into the darkness.

The chances that they were shooting their own people in the confusion were very high indeed.

He stopped one hundred yards away, loaded a grenade and fired back into their lines and ran on before settling again to check himself over, to make sure he hadn't been hit. Sometimes, he knew, with adrenaline and fear in the blood, you could be hit and not feel it for a while. He was OK; his heart was pounding but he was unhurt.

San Ignacio

Pete Collins had surprised himself. After seventeen years in the British army he had long been a proponent of the 'never volunteer' school of thought. Volunteering for anything was likely to involve risk, work, dirt, sweat, maybe blood – not good for a bloke who just wanted the easy life. But without being asked, and before the next scheduled download on to the Net or contact with the Hereford major on the eastern side of the river, he left his roof-space hideyhole and went out to do a recce. He put the phone into the day-bag with the laptop, emptied his pockets of anything that could identify him and checked his clothing. It was all available in Belize, except his underpants, which he had bought at Marks & Spencer on a recent trip home. He took them off, put them in the bag, dressed again, and cocking the 9mm pistol he eased the hammer forward, put it on half-cock and slipped it into his waistband under his shirt. If he was seen and stopped he would have to make a decision. He could bin the weapon and trust in his flawless local-accented Spanish, or speak English in the patois, concoct some bullshit but believable story, and hope to get away with it; or if there were only one or two of them and he thought he could use the gun and get away, he would.

He briefly tried to rationalize why he was doing this. He had been up here in the seventies when the Guat scrotes had rolled a tank or two on transports up to the border, in what turned out to be a bit of old-fashioned bullying. There was a Brit presence, and the Guatemalans were simply saying, we know you are there, we are watching you. Back here in San Ignacio the support units, a couple of companies of the lads and HQ facility had arrived from Airport Camp, to sit it out and be there in case things got nasty. There was a field kitchen and the media had arrived, filming the lads looking warlike, drinking tea and powering through scoff. He had come back down for water and compos and as he had driven discreetly away from the attention, he looked across at the lads posing for the cameras and one or two looked back at him a little sheepishly. It was Collins and his three oppos up at the wire with fuck-all but a radio and small arms, looking at among other things two tanks, while they were back here playing at heroes.

It had been tense for a while, the situation made worse by the rumour, never substantiated, that a few days before the body of one of the Hereford blokes had been pulled from the river. Apparently they had cut off his head and he had been tortured, but Pete never knew whether to believe that or not. So, he thought, I've been here before, waited for this before, and it seems right to help again. He was also pissed off. He was a Brit, always would be, but he had married a local girl, had two little toffee-coloured angels, his darling girls, born in Belize. He had a business here now. It was a good place, a sleepy town, but the people were laid-back and life was good and now these Guats were fucking it all up. Reason enough, he said to himself – bollocks, the other half of his brain said, sentimental romantic shit. It's hairy; armed troops, scrotes, trigger-happy and power-mad, their nose bleeding already, would probably shoot on sight anything they didn't like the look of. Let someone else sort it. But there is no one else, the pro side said, so do it.

'Fuck it,' he said aloud. 'I hate this shit.'

He slipped out of an inspection hatch and in the flickering light of the flames, he made his way along the rooftops.

The ship had finished her NGS mission and was forced back into the deeper water of the main channel by the retreating tide; Commander Bennett had put her in the best position to provide a multi-role capability. Sliding silently through the water, barely underway, but with her engines ready to run up to full power, she patrolled up and down the channel. From here she could protect the coastline of the city, sweep her radar out to scan the skies, launch anti-aircraft missiles, offer cover to St George's, and prevent any re-supply or reinforcement of the Guatemalans still attacking the airport.

He and Major Fox had jointly vetoed the army lieutenant's offer to go back in on a second medevac mission. There was no way the helo could get in anywhere close enough to lift out the wounded without coming under intensive ground fire. They had agreed a second option; that the helo would fly back in, but to some point north-west of the airport, and take the ship's doctor ashore. If they couldn't move the wounded, then he would have to get to them. He had batched up drugs, equipment, saline drips, the limited blood plasma he had from the ship's medical stores and was ready to go when they had worked out where to put him. The wounded already on the ship would be cared for by the LMO until he was back, and there was apparently an air-mobile field surgical team on its way from the UK. They would take over ashore and allow him back to his patients aboard ship sometime the next day.

Belize River

Lieutenant Lewis was driving the patrol boat hard and running through the possibility of fighting the boat in four or five hours. In the Royal Navy sailors don't fight, the ship fights. They speak of 'fighting the ship', because individually no one can achieve anything, and the entire ethos is one of teamwork and using the ship, enabling her systems to do what they were designed for.

If they arrived in time, and there were enemy on the water then they would have to fight the boat. He looked down the deck of the little patrol craft as the light from the lamp swung over her bows, and wished she was externally equipped more like the same boats used as training vessels by the Royal Navy, which were provided with a 20 mill gun. They only had this odd-looking belt-fed 12.7 mm. Still, it was bigger and better than the GPMG from *Beaufort*'s arsenal. The good news was that with her upgraded engines she was faster than any of the RN boats and the Belizean crewman had explained the reason for the upgrades. Bought as an anti-drugs patrol vessel, her draught was in fact too deep to follow her targets into the shallows, so she was re-engined to give her greater speed to catch them before they got that far in.

'Caught any?' Lewis asked, his eyes on the water ahead illuminated by the spotlight.

'Two boats,' the man yelled back proudly, then shrugged. 'But it was just ganja.'

Lewis nodded and looked down at the small mobile-phone-sized sat-nav system that the SAS soldier had passed him – the coordinates put them nearly one third of the way there. Just ahead the river forked, with Labouring Creek to the right. They must take the left, and try to maintain the fast pace even as the river narrowed. It would be dawn in five hours. He signalled to two of the lads to transfer fuel from the drums into the tanks. He wanted all the fuel currently in drums pumped into the tanks, deep below the waterline, by the time they arrived, and the drums refilled. If they had time they would stop somewhere and fill them with earth, mud from the riverbank; if not, with river water. They would be heavy, but make bloody good shields for the men to hide behind. The SAS bloke was still on the weapons. He had finished with the 12.7, and was now aft, stripping the 7.62 machine gun. He clearly didn't trust sailors and as weapons were his thing, Lewis just let him get on with it. Someone, just visible as a hand in the dark, put something wrapped in tin foil on the top of the instrument panel. Food – he looked at it for a second or two, suddenly realized he was hungry and looked up again, and saw something in the lights, in the foam and rush of the waters. He swung the boat and a huge log came surging past them. Jesus! Nearly hit that bastard. Concentrate man!

San Jose Soccoths

The Guatemalan soldiers had been forced to unload the boats from the vehicles and reload them three times already. There were points where the terrain narrowed right up to the road and there was no way past except to inch vehicles backwards and forwards so they were literally touching bumpers for three hundred yards each side, to make enough room to get the convoy moving westwards back up on to the road, through the choke-point and back off again. There were places where not even this was possible, and they had carried the boats on their shoulders, and commandeered other vehicles on the other side. It had taken them all this time to move half a mile and the colonel in charge of the job looked at his watch. At this rate they would be lucky to have the boats in the water by 0400, but he acknowledged that even that would suffice. Once on the water they could move quite quickly and have a flank attacking force in place by first light. They could take out the small group of defenders and by the time the bridge was ready to bear traffic, they would hold the eastern bank.

England

The separate elements of the situation were being closely monitored by command and JRDF at Northwood. The SAS signallers in their bunker at Airport Camp and their two colleagues up at the forward base camp near San Ignacio kept a steady flow of information moving up the link. As their efforts temporarily failed due to atmospherics, communications were channelled through the MCO on HMS *Beaufort*. The RAF detachments were airborne, six Harrier GR7s and their entire

313

support system en route to Pensacola in Florida. They would be on the ground there by 0800 local, and refuelled and armed they could, weather permitting, sortie within two hours. Also airborne were the ten members of A Squadron's air troop, and travelling with them were members of the 359 air-mobile field surgical team. They were air-mobile, not necessarily parachute trained, so they would be jumping in with the air troop men on tandem chutes. The drop would test the parachute entry skills the air troop men possessed, because they would also be going out with massive amounts of stores and equipment, medical and otherwise. At Aldershot the apparent mayhem that was 5 Airborne's departure preparations was on track.

An RAF Hercules, chosen for this mission because of the aircraft's STOL capabilities, was airborne and en route to Ambergris Cay. Ambergris was twenty-five miles north of St George's and the decision had been made that if the C-130 could land on the civil airfield at Ambergris then she would disgorge her load, a company of the RAF Regiment, who with a Rapier missile system would secure the airfield. This would be the first alternate British airhead and if the international airport fell, then operations would proceed through Ambergris Cay. It would certainly be an operational base for the GR7s, if nothing else, to refuel them, and with a runway allowing the Harriers a run-up it provided a better option than St George's, which although twenty-five miles closer to the battlefield would only allow VTOL operations.

Elements of the fleet had been re-tasked and turned westwards. HMS *Invincible* and two Type 42 destroyers, HMS *Nottingham* and HMS *Southampton*, were powering their way southwards from Gibraltar where they had been allowing their people some shore time on their way home from a NATO peacekeeping role in the Balkans.

Deep in the main facility, with a temporary security pass round his neck, Rick, Pete Collins' wheelchair-bound friend was found a desk where his computer was set up. The intelligence team were now sitting alongside the JRDF planners and command, some tables pulled round so they could all see the wall chart and the projection screen. There were now fifty people at Northwood, directly involved in the JRDF deployment, and they were taking over desks, space and resources as needed. Comms coming in from *Beaufort* or Hereford were decoded by the computer and projected on to the screen as they came through and were printed out.

'He's our only asset that side until first light and we can get a downward look at what's happening,' the officer said to Rick. He was a major, intelligence type, lean, and, Rick noticed, not wearing regulation shoes, but a pair of suede brothel-creepers. 'So the moment you get something from him, shout. I'll be here in a wink, OK?' Rick nodded without looking up from his screen; tapping keys, he logged himself on to the Net.

'Pete, me old cock. Got your note. Where are you? Waiting for news. I'm with friends. Everyone is very, very interested.' He hit 'send'.

Buena Vista

The eight boat troop men were six hundred yards upstream from Buena Vista. They had seen scrotes on the riverbank earlier, a patrol, but had not engaged them. They were hidden in the overhanging vegetation at the river's edge, at the start of their command detonated minefield, in two boats. One, a big Rib, a rigid inflatable boat with an eighty horsepower Evinrude they had purloined from a river tour operator, the other also a Rib, but much smaller; with four men and their equipment there wasn't much room.

Upriver it was very hairy – a sequence of mines laid earlier ensured that. Suspended in the trees on the bank, and initiated by whatever crossed a laser beam, they would be the first thing any scrotes came across – and hopefully the last. The mines were sequential; a Claymore mine set into the trees was the first explosive to go, followed a few seconds later by floaters, what the lads called 'bubbles', anti-boat mines. These were anchored to the bottom with a ten-pound lead sinker and activated by a signal triggered by the same laser beam that set off the Claymore. The 'bubble' unhooked itself from the sinker, floated upward and when on the surface exploded, firing two hundred fléchettes designed to rip inflatable hulls and sink the boats. Any person that happened to get in the way would have a very unpleasant experience. There were three of the sequenced mines on the stretch of river above them.

They waited in silence, the branches above their heads dripping with water. The bows of the boats had been covered in camo netting, engines had been muffled down with wadding and shirts. Weapons were checked and rechecked, faces and bare skin were creamed to prevent reflection, everything was ready.

'Time?' one of them asked.

Someone lifted the cover on his watch face. '0430.'

'If they are coming, they better shift it. Light in an hour and a half.'

Fifteen minutes later they heard it, the flat BLAM of a Claymore mine, followed by three lighter cracks half a second apart.

'Showtime,' someone muttered.

'Thank fuck for that,' another whispered.

'For what?'

'They went off. I have never trusted them.'

'Two to go,' the sergeant said, thinking they will be slow now, taking it very carefully – hope it was them and not some Mayan bloke in his fishing canoe. He looked back at the troop commander, a captain, but the officer was head down over a radio, calling it in.

Three minutes later came the second, and then fairly quickly the third.

The other boat came up alongside. 'That was too fast. They must have floated an empty down to see what it triggered,' the captain said. 'Let's go.'

They went to points Alpha and Bravo. They had sectioned off the river into fighting zones from various points of cover. Alpha was the first, round the bend; from a vantage point they could hit boats from the bank, jump back in the inflatable and egress the area, leapfrog past Bravo and on to Charlie. At each point was a discrete minefield, a set of mines dug into the bank, attached to trees or a rock, with command switches. There would be no more remote detonations.

The boat eased into position Alpha, a steep bank that jutted out into the river on the bend, a rock and a massive tree root having prevented the river from eroding it to the same level as the rest. A perfect ambush point, if a little obvious. The captain slithered up the bank with three LAW rockets and his 203 and looked over at the stretch of river they had just navigated. Two others joined him, one with a GPMG and the other with the remote arming/detonation devices and his personal weapon, also a 203 with a grenade already mounted; the fourth trooper remained with the boat, the engine burbling softly under the sound dampeners.

The captain watched through an image intensifier and up ahead on the black river the enemy boats came into a hazy green view. It wasn't as good as the big infra-red sight on the new Milan mounts but it was better than the naked eye. They were being cautious. The lead boat was empty, and seemed to be keeping exact pace with the two following, in which he could see figures huddled low. He swung the sight. In the one on the right a machine gun was set up in the bows. They had attached the empty boat to those two to stop it drifting into the bank.

He looked further back; more boats behind them, he could see three, but there would be more moving in groups, maybe with a minute or two between them. No one, not even the Guatemalans, who had so far proved themselves to be tactically inept, would risk every boat in the same time and place. He looked at the two troopers, the one with the GPMG, settling the bipod legs into the soft muddy humus and earth of the bank, below a thick, curling tree root exposed by rain and time. 'After the mines, Pete, with the gimmpy, take the right boat. Then elevate and go for the three out the back. I'll take the one on the left with a LAW. Den, initiate the Claymore then try and put a grenade into the centre-back boat. OK?'

They nodded and the captain passed Pete the sight and quickly opened up the LAW rockets, fully extending two, but leaving the third.

'Boss?'

He looked up. Pete, now peering through the sight, was pointing. The captain held out his hand for the sight and quickly looked through it. The second wave of boats was in sight, six or so it seemed. Fuck it! He quickly ran through his options. They could engage both, hit the first bunch and then move their fire up the river – the second bunch would be in range, no problem, but they could also escape to the bank. They could let the first boats through, use the mines to hit the bigger group, and then take the first wave as they came past the ambush point, or even leave them to the second team at point Bravo. Skoshey. His force was split as it was, he didn't want enemy between them.

'Right, Den, save the mines for the next group.' He was extending the tube on the third LAW rocket as he was speaking. 'Pete, you hit the inflatable on the far side as they come past. Den and I'll take the near boat. Then we take the others. They should be almost on the minefield by then and won't be expecting that. If any boats look like making the bank try and drill 'em. Sink the fuckers. I will initiate the contact.' As he finished Pete was swinging the GPMG around to give it the new arc of fire.

Fifty seconds later, as the empty boat drifted past them ahead of the two boats loaded down with armed soldiers, he sighted on the nearside boat, a flat-bottomed skiff, and fired. The rocket hit on the waterline, exploding and punching a hole through the bottom of the aluminium hull. Two of the figures in the boat were thrown out by the blast, a third nearest the impact point was blown to pieces. As the hull settled back on to the surface, water began pouring in the huge hole. The captain snatched up the second rocket; the machine gun was firing beside him, bullets ripping into the inflatable boat on the far side. He turned and found another target, some seventy yards away, the men in the boat scrabbling to bring their weapons to bear on something. He fired again, watching the yellow-white trail of sparks from the rocket motor as it seared away through the dark. Fire was coming back at them now, from boats up the river, bullets hitting the bank they were sheltering behind, mud, leaves and bits of bark thrown up by the impacts. The soldier with the arming devices was waiting, cool as could be, watching the boats approach the optimum effective area for the mines. The fire from the boats was heavy now, three of them advancing down the river, others steering in towards the banks. Tracer rounds were cutting through the dark, men were screaming and there was a flash of sparks darting in at them. 'Sixty incoming!' someone yelled, and a massive blast on the bank below shook the ground and left mud and leaves and debris falling back down on them. The captain's ears were ringing; that was close, he thought; they have 66s. The American lightweight disposable anti-tank rockets were similar to the LAW and standard issue in the Regiment.

'Stand by . . . now!' The trooper hit the clackers, three fast presses and the Claymore mines exploded, convex baseplates the size of a breadboard with seven hundred ball-bearings set into military high-explosive.

There were three of them, set diagonally on the riverbank, two one side and a third between them in the opposite bank. The arc of fire covered one hundred and fifty yards of the river and anyone who had more than half their body above the sides of the boat was hit, at least once. The only people who escaped the terrible swath were those lying low in the boats, and by the time the firing had stopped and attackers had escaped, the Guatemalan commander of the first two flotillas of boats had strived to regain some order. On the southern bank, his men in the jungle along the water's edge in huddles, he took stock. Of the seventy-six men in his detachment he had thirteen men dead, five missing, and over half the remainder wounded, some of them seriously. The inflatables were in tatters, and only five of the aluminium boats were still serviceable. The major looked across at his radio operator. The young man had two wounds, one shoulder, the other thigh, where the ball had come right through the inflatable wall of the boat. He talked to the colonel who was back at the embarkation point with the general and then looked back at two of his junior officers who were now with him.

'The next wave is to come through and take the point. We

319

have five boats. We tuck in behind them and go on, only eight men per boat. Get their kit packed round the sides, everyone down low. The seriously wounded stay here. Get your men sorted out.' I should have thought of that, he was thinking, I should have expected mines along the bank.

'Sir,' one of the lieutenants said, 'they knew we were coming. They had time to set the mines. There may be –'

'We go on,' the major snapped. 'It will be light in an hour. We must be past the fork by then! Get going!' His wound was troubling him. He had taken shrapnel high in the left arm, and blood was seeping round the dressing. He shook his head. It was throbbing, the pain a steady beating rhythm that was beginning to dull his thinking. They would have to unload later anyway, get round the falls. There was a path for that, but it would take time.

Two miles away down the river, McKay and his patrol, exhausted now in their third night without sleep, held the northern flank on the British side, where the two rivers met. McKay rubbed his grainy eyes and looked out at the water below them. To their left was the Gurkhas' position, and they had taken a real pounding for most of the night, but this far along the bank, they had so far been ignored, but only, he knew, because the scrotes didn't know they were here. They were in range and only needed fire aimed their way to take the shit like the Paras had done. Somewhere up the river were the two boat troop patrols. McKay was awake. Dozy was asleep over the butt of the minimi, Boyce asleep too. Gibbo, the jungle man, was out on the right, down by the water watching their backs, on stag. They were tired, bone tired. They had been at it since their first contact three days ago, moving, watching, preparing, fighting on the Negroman road before cutting back through the jungle to the river and making their way back to the Squadron at San Ignacio.

Each had managed snatches of sleep, but this was modern combat, where the fittest men survive because they can stay awake longer. He let the two men sleep, every minute valuable, recharging batteries; the rain ran down Dozy's face, his cheek pressed into the minimi, but his hands were on the grip, his finger hooked on the trigger. McKay knew he could be awake and fighting in seconds, but now he was in deep sleep, REM sleep, the best kind. They hadn't come through the night entirely unscathed. It was one of those things – in the move from one fighting position to another at the Negroman road ambush, Boyce had missed his footing in the dark and slipped down a twelve-foot bank, catching his left foot at the bottom, his bodyweight crashing down on the trapped lower limb. He had damaged his knee, which was ballooned out with fluid now, swollen like a ball, and he was in pain, even when not moving; but he had kept up with them on the march out, limping heavily, and although he hadn't complained, McKay knew that he was suffering cruelly. He suspected the knee might have momentarily dislocated in the fall, or perhaps the ligaments were torn. Dozy had been hit by something; perhaps someone down on the road below had a shotgun, or a Claymore mine they were transporting had cooked off, because Dozy had what looked like entry wounds for three big shotgun pellets in his right thigh. Bigger than bird shot, not quite number nine shot, Gibbo had said.

The rain was falling again, but nothing like earlier in the night, and the water level was dropping. He watched out over the water, comfortable with Gibbo out on the right; nothing would get past him. Not even Snowy, who moved like a big black panther through the bush, could get close to Gibbo, so the right was secure, as long as he could stay awake. Upriver he could hear fighting; the sound, coming in snatches, was further away than the firefight still raging down the bank nearer the bridge. That was, he knew, the boat troop lads getting stuck in, because there was no one else out there, no friendlies anyway.

Up the river the boat troop were in some trouble. The lead boat had hit a stump or a log in the water. The hull had ripped open, with one side wall in tatters, and water was pouring in. Both boats were racing back to position Delta, the boss's Rib in front, when it hit the submerged obstacle. All four men had been thrown out, and as the other inflatable turned back, three were striking out for the bank with what gear they could swim with. By the time the second inflatable was back, the last man, the boss, troop commander Captain Ericson had disappeared from sight. They quickly searched the water with a torch, but the Guatemalans were not far behind them and they knew that if he was conscious then he could make it to the bank like the others – he was boat troop, and they all swam like fish. If he wasn't, if he had hit his head on something, then they were unlikely to find him. One of them pressed the mark button on a GPS, so they could come back to the point later and pick him up, and they checked over the gear they had salvaged as they surged downriver. Delta was just ahead and there were at least a dozen fully-loaded Guat boats just behind them.

0600 – Day 2

The boat troop had attacked again. They had set up a position on the bank, triggering their fixed command-detonated mine and pouring fire into the Guatemalans, then went back to the boat, fighting on the move, but in the contact their inflatable took four hits, puncturing the sidewall aft on the port side. On the bank further up two of the soldiers from the sunken Rib turned east, running downriver, to try and get to their last position in time to get set up. Their oppo and the boss would have to catch up. Those in the damaged boat were moving downriver as fast as they could. They had to get there, because they knew that opposite that position on the other bank was McKay's air troop patrol. With luck they could hold there, set up interlocking fields of fire, but they had to get there and water was swamping over the gunwales now, and the boat, heavy with equipment, was filling faster than the bungs could cope. The Guatemalans could smell blood. The boats that had survived the last attack were surging after them; gunfire slapped the water around them, throwing up little splashes, the sound of bullets passing them like angry bees.

'How far?'

'Quarter of a mile.'

They couldn't move a gimmpy back to return fire; it was too heavy. One of the lads down by the helmsman was passing gear forward to get the weight away from the ruptured side-wall, the other two were firing back with their 203s. Dawn was approaching, the sky pink ahead of them. The cloak of darkness was being withdrawn along with their boatspeed and mobility. They could try for the bank and leave the last defensive position unmanned, or go for it. The bank, brutally steep in places, would mean slowing so much, that the chasing boats would be on them and with the weight of fire the Guate-malans could bring to bear they would be up shit creek. They had to follow the plan and under the cover of McKay's rifles, get set up to fight from something stable.

The nearest scrote boats were just a hundred yards behind them now.

HMS *Tonka Toy* was powering her way up the river, the pink light of the dawn tinting the foaming water surface. Lieuten-ant Lewis was steering; he had handed over twice during the hours of darkness, to take a break, but was now back at the wheel. The fuel had all been transferred into her main tanks, and the drums were now filled with water, and standing upright around the rear gun position.

Hagan of the SAS was beside him, holding a map and his GPS. 'Next bend. It must be,' he said. Lewis nodded; he had been thinking that for the last mile or so. He powered back so they could listen – gunfire, a big contact up ahead some-where. They were close, very close. Hagan dragged up the Clansman and tried to raise the Squadron FOB, but the radio wasn't cutting it, there were too many hills between them. Suddenly they had voice from someone, fast comms between a team on the water, and another nearby. The lads in the boats were in trouble. Hagan looked up again, jabbing a finger at the river ahead. 'Go for it!' He ran forward to the 12.7.

'On your feet!' Lewis yelled, pushing the throttles forward all the way. 'Action stations! Prepare to engage enemy boats!'

Men were scuttling to their stations, rehearsed several times in the night, and when Lewis looked back the white ensign was now trailing out, not from the staff at the stern, but from the radar mast just behind him – it was now a battle ensign. They rounded the bend, the boat doing twenty-nine knots, twin engines roaring, her bow-wave curling out. He could hear the battle now over the engines, and in the dawn light he could see smoke rising. They rounded the next bend and there suddenly on the left was the wide, brown, swiftly flowing mouth of the eastern branch. We're here, he realized. We're fucking here! Suddenly the gun began to hammer; Hagan, leaning into the butt, was firing bursts dead ahead. Lewis looked out past him. There on the water was something with men in it; it was moving, but sluggishly, an inflatable he realized but deflating by the minute, the sides loose like a hovercraft's skirt. Behind it the river seemed alive with small boats, a whole armada, everyone shooting guns. Friendlies, he realized, the first boat is ours. He pushed up the throttles. Hagan's gun was firing long sustained bursts, the bullets going over the first sinking craft and hitting the water and boats at the back, and he flicked a look behind him. 'First boat is friendly!' he shouted. The chief nodded and raised a thumb. 'Ready aft. Fire as you bear! Chief, drop a raft!'

In the sinking inflatable the four boat troop men were so busy that only the helmsman noticed them come round the bend. His first thought was that they had been outflanked, that somehow the Guats had got past them and were now coming back, huge and noisy and fast and wanting revenge. One of the lads firing back at the ever-nearer Guats saw the look on his face and turned and swung his rifle, prepared to fight to the finish, letting the big boat get close enough to try and slot the man on the bows. Then the heavy machine gun opened up, the bullets going over them, and they both realized that the firing was aimed at the scrotes. The patrol boat roared past them, someone yelling an excited obscenity, the bow-waves and the wake rolling at them like surf on a beach, a white drum coming off the back. 'It's Hagan!' someone yelled and the wave hit them, coming right in over the side and swamping the boat.

Lewis knew in a millisecond what he had to do. He had forty tons of boat moving at nearly thirty knots. Up on the plane she had a fairly respectable turning circle and he swung to the right and aimed at the Guatemalan boat nearest the bank. 'Prepare to ram!' he shouted. 'Ramming!'

He ploughed it under his heavy bows, turning as he did so, lining up to ram, run over, sink and damage as many boats as he could. They hit the second, this one a light aluminium flat-bottomed punt, men and weapons and kit flying everywhere; ahead in the next boat in his line-up the soldiers were already jumping into the water. The small inflatables and flat-bottomed river punts never stood a chance and by the time Lewis whipped the wheel over again, thankful that his props were recessed, he had trampled five under his keel and the river was alive with struggling, swimming men, bodies, floating kit and overturned boats. The aft gun had opened up now, the GPMG crewed by one of *Beaufort*'s ratings, raking the boats further up the river. Soldiers who had watched their comrades being run down by the big gunboat were now jumping into the water from the second wave of boats, their yellow life-jackets bright on the brown foaming water. Hagan was on the foredeck, still firing the big 12.7 mill gun, and the GPMG was firing off the sides and back, the gunner behind Lewis screaming like an ancient berserker Viking, the adrenaline coursing through his blood. Other ratings were firing their SA80s, and the chief was lobbing markers on to the water, purple, orange and green swirls of smoke clouding their wake.

Enough, he thought. If they went too far up their withdrawal might be jeopardized, and besides, they were beaten; what few boats still floated were racing for the banks, some sluggish, swamped by the huge wake of the gunboat's passing. He turned and ran back downstream, through the rainbow of smoke, the gunners still responding when fired upon; but they tired of it, sickened by people dying, drowning, their last gasps pretty mauve, tangerine or green smoke.

Hagan pointed, waving his hands down parallel to the deck – slow down, power off. The Brit lads in the water were holding on to the raft they had heaved over; Lewis stopped both engines, the ladder dropped and hands reached out for them. When they were safely aboard Lewis began to run back downriver, the ensign snapping out behind them, holed by shot, but still flying. His heartbeat was slowing. Jesus! They had done it, got here in time and closed the river. Yes! Now what? Patrol? Damage assessment; tie up somewhere and let the lads get some rack time. No, they had no racks. Let 'em rest a bit, do some repairs, grab some food from somewhere. Then let's fight the boat, fight HMS *Tonka Toy*. Lewis was confident – up here she was queen, a dinky little coastal patrol craft no longer, sixty-five feet of armed gunboat that could outrun and outgun anything else on the water.

'Mr Hagan, if your lads are all aboard, let's get sorted. See if you can raise your signals people ashore. I'd like orders from *Beaufort*.'

One of the SAS men pulled from the water came forward. 'Thanks,' he grinned. 'We were in the shit a bit there.'

'Pleasure. Welcome aboard what the lads have christened HMS *Tonka Toy*. The Senior Service aims to please. Only the four of you?'

The man nodded but the smile had gone.

A mile away up the eastern branch at the bridge defence, below the rolling hills, first light was breaking after a bad night for the small band of 2 Para Gurkhas. Of the original defenders down near the river holding the bank, four were dead and nine wounded, four seriously. Estelle had rotated them as best he could, and now he had some fresh men. More importantly, the support from his mortars and the Squadron's more specialist skills had made a huge difference. The Guatemalans had been finding the mines left by the Squadron the hard way and whole stretches of the town side of the riverbank were no-go areas.

In addition they had taken out almost every machine gun that had exposed itself during the hours of darkness. Defensive positions and trenches developed by the enemy were targeted with focused high explosive from LAW and Milan missiles. The dreadful firepower that had rained down on the small band of Gurkha defenders early in the attack had petered out as the Guatemalans realized that they could attempt to bomb the defenders out, but they would get it back in spades, and the Guatemalan troops on the other bank were now lying low with considerably more respect for their opponents. As the rate of fire of incoming slowed, Estelle moved more of his men into their former positions and by first light he had just over half of his force back in the line; the others, some wounded, some who had been fighting all night, were resting. They had no body-bags, but he wasn't leaving his dead to be flyblown. They were moved back on to the track down to the river, and placed in black bin-liners. The water level was much lower than nine hours earlier. He looked up at the sky where the first tinges of light were appearing from behind them; soon now, he thought.

By first light at the airport it was as bad. There were nine dead and sixteen injured Gurkhas. Garvey had come back into the line just before dawn, later than he had intended, having spent four hours roaming the rear of the Guatemalan lines causing mayhem. Down to one magazine for the minimi, and half a mag left in his 203, it was time to withdraw, his night's action over. The battle that had ebbed and flowed through the darkness slowed with the light, Murray's marines still holding the southern line. He now had two dead and three injured, one seriously. There would be no helo evacuation now, not in daylight, and plans were afoot on *Beaufort* to move their doctor ashore. The Gazelle would carry him in and drop him in the bush at a rendezvous to the north-west where the B Squadron soldier would go out to bring him in.

Fox, like the rest of his battered, beleaguered little command, was grainy-eyed and tired, but holding them together. It was going to be a long hot day, exposed to the sun. Without the cover of darkness, they would not be able to move as they had the night before. He had foreseen this; water and ammunition had been resupplied to his men in the holes that could not be reached from a shallows comms trench, and now they would have to sit it out and wait, fight when they could, but wait.

The RAF VC10 made a long, lazy turn and flew down the border, low and slow. The huge engines were powered back, the doors were opened; the first detachment from A Squadron was about to come out with tons of equipment, stores, and the handful of medics from the 359 air-mobile field surgical team in tandem chutes. The DZ was two miles back from the river, and two B Squadron men were there with smoke markers in the field they had selected. They had found a local man with a tractor and trailer and he was there waiting to help move the gear forward. The big jet came through, low enough to be out of sight of the enemy on the riverbank at San Ignacio and the mini-pallet loads came out of the doors in rapid succession, followed by the ten A Squadron air troop men, eight of them with a medic hooked on to their larger parachutes. One of the B Squadron reception committee would lead them forward and the other would stay at the field. Thirty minutes out behind the VC10 was D Coy 2 Para in two C-130s.

In the lead aircraft Major Tyson-Davis, Alpha, was sitting on the jumpseat between the two pilots. From here he could see out ahead, and be in touch with Brigade command via the secure comms panels. His laptop was out and open, and maps were unfolded on the engineer's station. He was still working; he had wolfed down the food given to him by the American general's wife, and was now hard at it again. In 2 Para's command structure, officer commanding D Coy was senior to OC of C Coy, and although 22 SAS had a major on the ground, he had his own role. Upon arrival, Tyson-Davis would be in command of British forces in the theatre.

At the back of the second aircraft half a mile behind, Lieutenant Harry Rees's platoon were now all awake. Some had dozed fitfully, or tried to. They were nervous, scared; the Falklands had been one thing, the whole brigade going in, with air and ships and reasonable odds: but this?

'Elias' Cutter felt a nudge on his shoulder and looked over.

Plonker had Spud's Buzz Lightyear toy and had made a little parachute out of a face veil.

'To Belize and beyond! I reckon, right, I reckon we should let this fooker lob out wi' us.' He shook it in front of Spud's nose, hoping to elicit some reaction, but Spud seemed lost in his own thoughts. Rhah saw this. He knew how important the little toy was to Spud, and if he didn't try to get it back it was because something more immediate was bothering him; Rhah suspected he knew what. He moved to take the toy but Plonker pulled his arm away. 'Fook off!'

'Give it back to him,' Rhah said.

'Fook off!'

'Give it back, Plonker. I'll not tell you again.'

'Oh aye, and what are you gonna –'

Elias had felt it building, the tension, and turned to manage it but was too late. Rhah's hand flashed out like a viper and snatched the leather thong from Plonker's neck, on which was hung the former girlfriend's suspender clip.

'Fookin' hell, mun!'

'Good, I have got your attention,' Rhah said, his voice barely audible over the drone of the engines. 'Give 'im the toy, or I'll fucking smack you one. Understand? And something else, don't start on Jonesy, right?'

This was a threat to be taken seriously. Rhah rarely became involved with violence, unlike Plonker, who was so insensitive and abrasive that he was invariably caught up in something at least once a week. But when Rhah, their philosopher, turned to street fighting, it was short and brutal. He was smaller than any of them, but he made up for it by being lightning-fast: he was wiry and tough like steel rope, with sharp-knuckled fists that cut on every blow.

'Plonker, give it back. Rhah, you settle down.' Elias raised his voice so all the section could hear it. 'Save it, right? Save it for the fucking scrotes!'

Jonesy woke up then. Somehow he had managed to slip off into sleep, real sleep. 'What?'

'Never mind,' Elias snapped.

'Oooh. It's dial 1-800-CRANKY.'

A few minutes later, the pilot turned the lead aircraft to

starboard, giving the airport and the hostile forces on the ground a wide berth. This would be a tactical approach, one that assumed the enemy were near enough to shoot at the aircraft, but there was sufficient cloud-cover; they could just drop down through it, and then climb back into it and out of sight.

Above the hills the wind was swirling and gusting, and heavy rainclouds were moving in from the west, but there were breaks; the pilot could see them on his weather radar. Five minutes later he looked back at Tyson-Davis and pointed out the front.

'There be dragons.'

Tyson-Davis stood up to see better. Ahead beneath the cloud where the forested hills rose upward from the dry plains, where the jungle began, from a fold in the earth a pall of black smoke was rising. Swirling, smudgy, coming up from what seemed a variety of points into one lazy wreath over the land. He looked at the pilot who nodded, taking in his first view of the battlefield.

'We start our approach now, get down to jump height,' the pilot said. 'Red on in fifteen minutes.'

Tyson-Davis nodded and unplugged his headset, still looking out of the front windscreen, unable to draw his eyes away.

On the ground at the LZ the A Squadron troopers were in with their cargo, human and otherwise. The two B Squadron men there to meet them were helping them load the vital stores on to the trailer towed round by the tractor, stopping at each pallet. On the other side of the hill, the newcomers could see the rising smoke and hear the exchanges of fire, the odd heavier beat of a belt-fed weapon in the background. The medical team were helping and their boss was trying to ensure that his kit was loaded at one end so none of it was separated, never to be seen again, something that invariably happened whenever soldiers came across his stuff. It was flashy, expensive, and deserved guarding from anyone and everyone.

'We've found you a spot, well, two really, half a mile back.

One's concrete, a bit smelly, but safe – an old pump station. The other is next to it, a house, four bedrooms.'

'Airy? Clean? Natural light?' the senior surgeon asked. He was mid-forties, brisk, efficient, and wearing the insignia of a colonel.

'Yeah,' the SAS man answered. The colonel didn't notice the casual response as a line officer might. They were both specialists and neither took much notice of protocol.

'We'll take the house.'

'Thought you might. We have rounded up about half a dozen local BDF people who reported offering to help during the night. They are happy to work with you, fetching and carrying. One's sister works at the local clinic. She knows where others live, so they have gone off to see who is still here. Most people took the smart option and buggered off last night, but if she can find some help it's yours.'

'Fine. Where are my patients? Have you got a triage set up?'

'They are there now. You've got thirteen; nine Paras, four of those serious, and four of ours. Our bloke has got 'em all stabilized as best he can.'

A few minutes later the trooper watched the tractor drive away, and settled down to wait for the next drop, three orange smoke markers ready.

Estelle the C Company lieutenant, had no idea that D Coy were due in. His last face-to-face with Chard had been late the night before, and the arrival time of reinforcements wasn't the sort of thing that you broadcast over VHF. Chard had overlooked it too; he had other things to worry about, but if he had remembered it he would have sent word with some-one, but for some reason he assumed that Estelle would know. After all, it was his unit coming in. Down at the river the young lieutenant was in his platoon command dugout. This hole didn't qualify for the word 'sangar' anymore. It had been hit twice in the night, once by a mortar bomb and once by a 66, blowing the log and dirt roof off, but it was still central and still deep. Sporadic fire was coming in, slashing into the trees behind him, and somewhere over the other side was a sniper. He was keeping low, and in the growing daylight he would be a problem. But they had held, made it through the night. The first phase was over; now the real shit began. In the dark, at range, you could hide, dig deep; darkness was a great leveller if the attacking forces were not sure what they were facing, but now they had twelve hours of daylight. He thought of what his unit could do in that time – plenty. Even for these pricks it was long enough, sufficient time for the scrotes to do a full quick evaluation, see they were only up against two platoons and then just throw up the bridge and roll through.

'Charlie, Charlie, Bravo Alpha.' This wasn't Chard but his signaller. They had dispensed with full callsigns during the night.

'Go, Alpha.'

'Charlie, be advised your wounded are now with field surgical, over.'

They knew he would want to spread the word. It would be good for morale if his toms knew that they now had expert medical help in the area. 'Aah, thanks, Bravo.'

He had reinforced the bank, but was thinking about moving some men back again to form a sizeable reaction group. He wanted to be able to throw force at any given point, but as the water level dropped back to normal, there was more chance of a rush across the river by men on foot. He knew that by lunchtime it could be low enough to drive across, little more than calf-deep at the ford. He had left men overlooking that point, sixty yards away to his right and down the track.

'Sir,' his radio operator called to him. 'I heard aeroplane, sir.'

Estelle looked at him and smiled. This wasn't his usual radio operator; he had been killed the night before. This was the most junior man in the company, whose radio English was very good, above standard for Gurkha regiments, but for some reason when he spoke it face-to-face he dropped words. I wish, pal, I wish you did – they will be hours away yet. He knew that D Coy were being turned, but when would they be back? Later today with luck; to be out and back inside twenty-four hours would take some doing.

'I heard it, sir. Hercs.' The fellow had taken his headphones from round his neck; his head was canted up to the right, listening. 'They come to help us, sir.'

'I don't think so,' Estelle replied and dropped into Gurkhali. 'Too soon, my friend. Later, they will come later.' He was wrong.

The C-130s dropped out of the cloud and fifteen seconds later were over the DZ barely a mile away. It was a masterful piece of tactical navigation, the red light on, aft ramp down, loaders already preparing to run wedges back to the edge as they cleared the cloud and levelled out over the DZ. The loaders had been along the aircraft checking every man's static line on the cable and in addition each man checked his own and his mates' either side.

On the lead aircraft Tyson-Davis was in the port door. He would be first out. CSM 'Robo' Jennings was opposite him in the starboard door, Ted's radio operator and others from support company lined up behind them. Tyson-Davis was watching the lights, the sergeant air-loader standing between him and Jennings, the doors open and the wind and noise rushing in. The lights came on.

'Red on . . . green on . . . number ones go!' The despatchers pointed at Tyson-Davis and at Jennings on the other side. They kicked out the door bundles and jumped, their static lines trailing out behind them along the aircraft.

'Number twos go!'

At the back the first wedges were going out off the ramp.

'Number threes go!'

'Fours!'

'Fives!' They had the rhythm now: men with incredible loads in their containers, with mortar tubes, fifty-calibre barrels and GPMGs strapped to themselves, shuffled forward and finally put their hands over their reserve chutes, kicked the containers out and followed them. The second aircraft was running in, doors open, ramp down.

On the ground, the SAS trooper ran over to Tyson-Davis, indicated the road out and then moved on to the next man he saw. He pointed out their boss, and as the command element assembled, he made his way back to the egress point. The 2

Para major had his bergen on and was already moving. This was now a well-oiled machine, the post-drop routine well practised; soldiers landed and the moment they were down and had their bergens on, they hoisted their loads, some carrying more than 120 pounds, and did what made them famous – they tabbed. They claimed they could carry more, further, faster than any other green army unit in the world and they set out to prove it every time. But tabbing was one thing, knowing where to go was another. At points on the edge of the DZ non-coms waited to direct them. The standard instruction was which way to march and how far the unit was ahead, and when Cutter and his section made it to the edge of the field where Lieutenant Rees was waiting for them, the support company corporal was also positioned up by the road.

'Along there,' he pointed, 'turn right at the T-junction, then straight on. Head for the smoke.' He looked at his watch. 'Company is three minutes ahead of you.'

They hefted their loads and moved off. Someone had used their initiative because there was a tractor and trailer heading back towards them. It soon passed them and standing behind the driver, a local wearing a straw hat, was the support company sergeant, obviously heading back for the wedges.

'Fookin' 'ell it's 'ot, I'm sweating like a fookin' pig already,' Plonker grumbled. He had taken off his helmet, attached it to his bergen, and was already wearing a floppy bush hat.

'That's 'cos you are a pig, you fat bastid,' Spud responded. There was chorused agreement from the section.

'Yowall cunce, yowa lot.'

Estelle was forward, down in a hole with his lads, fire ripping over their heads, preparing to hit a new Guat position they had spotted, when one of his men tapped him on the shoulder. He was wanted back in the command hole. He nodded. It was a long crawl and his wound was giving him trouble; he had blacked out twice in the night, the pain intense, when something had bumped the back of his leg.

He crawled back out below the line of fire. This hole had a comms trench, nothing more than a shallow scrape but deep enough to slither along, and he moved up it to the track, where he could crawl along to his command hole. His radio man was in there and there was someone with him. Estelle thought he was one of the Squadron people for a second until he saw the 2 Para flash on his arm.

'Morning, sir. I'm with D Coy. We're up there. If you could –'

'Where the fuck did you come from?' Estelle didn't even try to hide the delight in his voice.

The soldier smiled. 'We are up there. Ted – the OC,' he corrected, 'would like a word, sir.'

'You're here? D Company?'

'Yes sir.'

'All of you?'

'Yes, sir. All of us, the whole company.'

Estelle was stunned for a second, then the relief washed over him. 'Very good. Yes . . . pleased to see you.' The radio man was right, he realized, he had heard them. He looked across at the little fellow still leaning over the radio. He had a smile that beamed from ear to ear. Christ, they must have moved, he thought, they only left at three yesterday, sixteen hours ago. Later the D Coy man repeated the story to his mates and finished by saying, horrified, 'I fort for a minute 'ewa gonna plant a kiss on me cheek.'

'Lead on,' Estelle said. He followed the soldier out of the back of the hole and up the track, staying low. When he had trouble keeping up the soldier looked back and then waited. Not far now – thirty yards or so.

'You all right, sir?'

Estelle nodded and kept crawling but as he passed the soldier noticed the dressing on the back of his thigh. It was bleeding, fresh blood over the dried, blackened crust that had seeped from the dressing for what looked like hours now.

'Hang on, sir,' he said. 'Wait here.'

'I'm all right.'

'No, you're not, sir. Wait here.' He was back a minute later with another bloke and taking the lieutenant's chest webbing, they hoisted him off the ground and ran doubled over the last thirty yards over the lip and on to the road.

'Get a medic here.'

'Where's your OC?' Estelle asked.

'Over there, sir.'

Estelle stood up shakily and began to walk that way, the fresh clean D Company men making a path for him as he limped through, his DPM trouser leg black and red with blood, his clothing filthy and torn where it wasn't bloody. He was still wearing his maroon beret, the crossed kukris cap badge of his Ghurkha roots over the Para cap badge. He found Tyson-Davis, who was with Major Chard; he had arrived from his FOB, and his platoon commanders had gathered round. They all looked up.

'Sir,' he saluted, 'we met the night before last. Toby Estelle, C Coy.' He looked round at them. 'Very pleased to see you all here.' Then his eyes misted over and he began to fall forward. Chard and Harry Rees caught him but he came to again as quickly and tried to stand up. 'Sorry about that.'

'Get him seated,' Tyson-Davis said quickly, 'and get a medic here.'

'I'm OK.' He wiped a hand over his eyes. 'Right, here's the sitrep,' he began.

A few minutes later a medic arrived but Estelle was in full swing, still on his feet so he could point out things on the blown-up aerial photos spread out on the car bonnet they were standing around. The medic asked him to lie down so he could examine the leg. Estelle ignored him and continued with his report. The medic insisted and the young lieutenant finally turned and looked at him.

'I'm tired, I'm hungry, I've had a bad day and you're beginning to piss me off. Let me do my job, OK? You can do yours when I have finished.' The medic looked at Tyson-Davis, who nodded, and he stepped back. Another twenty minutes and it was done.

Tyson-Davis asked his final question and then said, 'Outstanding job, Lieutenant, outstanding. Well done – anytime you want a job working with me you've got it. I'm going to pull your men out for some rest. You will now allow the medic to treat you and that's an order. OK?'

Estelle nodded and a few minutes later, a belt of morphine

holding the pain at bay, and with a mug of tea, the British toms' answer to everything, in his hand, he finally gave in to the medic and dropped his trousers, while Tyson-Davis assessed the situation.

'Oh, there's a boat too,' Chard offered.

'Say again?'

'We have a boat. An RN crew from *Beaufort* came upriver last night, in a BDF patrol boat. They picked up some of my blokes on the water and broke that flank advance. They are moored just downstream awaiting orders. The stretch of river opposite us is still navigable but it narrows bloody quickly under and past the bridge. It couldn't turn up there so it's not much use, but it's here and available on the right.' Suddenly and with almost comic timing a mobile phone went off, a tiny little synthesized warble playing 'Camptown Races'. 'Excuse me,' Chard said, reaching into his pocket.

Tyson-Davis grimaced slightly – he hated mobile phones – and turned back to the task. He concurred with Chard's and Estelle's assessment. The main attack had to come soon, and as the river level fell it became more and more feasible.

'Right, gentlemen. Orders.'

By the time D Company's platoons were ready to deploy, the A Squadron troopers were settled in and waiting. They had two man-portable Javelin missiles set up and had handed over the Milan and LAW missiles they had brought with them, and when the Paras made their way down the track to relieve their Gurkha colleagues they were passing new Milan positions that looked out of the trees straight over the river into the town.

The company of three rifle platoons and a support platoon was oversized because they also had the patrols. This gave Tyson-Davis the opportunity to replace the Gurkhas with a force twice the size without anyone knowing. The Guats didn't necessarily know they had even arrived so he would hold two fresh platoons and the Gurkhas in reserve over the lip of the rise, near enough to support the line, but out of sight. In the meantime the reserve platoon were to help support company to unload and issue the stores that had come in on the wedges and get the fifties set up. Rees would see his platoon settled in and then throw his personal skills behind the logistics effort back on the road.

Pete Collins had tapped the message out on his PC, sent it, and then phoned the Hereford major. He wasn't an engineer but he knew bridging gear when he saw it. He had been watching the petrol station roundabout from the roof of a cheap hotel he sometimes sent guests to, his vantage allowing him to see up the hill and down the road into town from the west. It had taken him half an hour to get back to his lair in the pre-dawn light and he knew that by now the heavy trailers would be in the town somewhere. There were only four roads loads that wide could take, so finding the trailers wouldn't be difficult. The town was full of Guatemalan troops, more had been arriving in the darkness, and from the look of them there was more than one brigade in the town. Fires still burned, smoke rising, the worst of it on the far side of town where the lads had dropped their mortar bombs. The petrol station had burned itself out, but was still smoking, and the ruins of the forecourt superheated by the fire were still hot.

There had been looting, but thankfully not yet at Eva's; the plain exterior and shuttered windows had obviously helped to make the place look uninviting. If the scrotes knew there was a fully stocked bar in there, tables, chairs, food, they would have been helping themselves, he knew. He had seen evidence of the brutality of war, atrocities committed by frightened, ill-disciplined troops: smashed windows, bodies of people shot on the pavements and in their cars. A child, a boy of maybe fifteen, lying half in and half out of a car. A woman, big, heavy with the years, dead in her doorway, her skirts lifted and thighs splayed by someone after death. A donkey lying dead – why would anyone shoot a donkey? He had seen them shooting at a stray dog, not because they thought it dangerous, or were panicked by a movement in the dark, but firing at an animal they had clearly seen – bastards.

There was shouting on the street and he carefully moved over to the slatted dormer window and looked out. Troops on foot, a company, maybe more, carrying assault kit and heading for the river. There was another unit behind them; they were moving up. He dialled the number again.

Chard had been hard at it when the second call came through, trying to get the civvy specialists with the RA officer moving back at the FOB. If his source over the river had seen the bridging gear arrive then he wanted to know where it was and it was now light enough to fly the remote surveillance drone. If they found the trucks they could pound them with mortar bombs.

The Gurkhas were relieved hole by hole, section by section, the D Company men settling in, twice the number that were there before, moving down the muddy, slippery comms trenches into the sangars and holes with ammunition cases, grenades and LAW missiles and helping the Gurkhas out, some of them wounded, all of them tired and hungry after a night of fighting.

Elias Cutter's section of two fire teams were in adjoining holes directly opposite the ford. They had approached gingerly, nervous, hearing shots fired in anger for the first time, but the training came through and they just did what they were trained to do. Robo, the CSM, hard as nails, the only veteran in the company, having been at Goose Green and on the march to Stanley, had steadying words for them in his own manner. As Elias's first fire team moved down he looked at them. 'Do your job like you were taught and you'll be fine. Fuck-up and I'll scrape the scrotes off you and fucking drop you myself.'

As sections they moved forward. The sangar had been hit in the night, the original pole roof blown away, so they dragged it back and began piling up the earth again, rebuilding the defence; bullets were whizzing past them, the odd one hitting a nearby treetrunk with a 'thock!'.

Plonker, brutally powerful with a trenching tool, was digging out a firing step and a base for the LSW bipod, constantly interrupted by fire from the far bank. When he was finished, he settled back; Spud and Rhah moved up to the forward aspect, and looked back at Elias, who was pleased. They had occupied their holes, strengthened them, seen the lay of the land, been shot at, and were now ready. This had been a gentle introduction.

'Can we shoot back?' Spud asked.

It was Lieutenant Rees who answered. He appeared suddenly, his huge bulk completely filling the comms trench. 'Yeah, but only if there's something to aim at. Don't be a dickhead and waste your ammo. One of you keep watch at all times – any movement of more than a couple of them, call it out.'

They began returning fire as targets presented themselves; the sensation of actually firing at a live enemy was weird. Plonker sat back and like an old trench warfare expert from another war long ago, he began to sharpen his trench tool, a collapsible spade, honing the edges. Swung, it would cut like an axe. The individualism was now apparent; Rhah was wearing the pistol the American had lent him in a shoulder-holster that he had fixed to his chest webbing. Gollocks, the heavy jungle knives, were varied, but everyone wore one and each man would sharpen his and his bayonet again as the opportunities presented themselves, as Plonker was doing now. Four or five bullets suddenly ploughed into the earthen wall they had built up, and as Spud ducked down, closing his eyes, Rhah let go two rounds.

'Did you get 'im?' Spud asked.

Rhah shrugged. 'Dunno. He dropped out of sight.'

'The cunt,' Spud said angrily. They all looked at him. He never showed anger, never, not about anything.

'What?' asked Jonesy, who was sitting at the back of the hole, minding his own business. He was unpacking ammunition, and brewing up on a little burner.

'That cunt fucking shot at me,' Spud answered indignantly. 'He's never even met me!' Rhah looked at him incredulously, and Plonker burst out laughing.

'O aye. Yowa cunce want to be fookin' introduced do yowa?' He stood up, all six-feet-three of him, at least one third above the level of the hole and bellowed across the river. 'Oi! YOWA DAGO CUNCE! This is Spud!' he roared, jabbing a finger downward into the hole. 'Now ya can fookin' shoot!' He ducked down and dropped back into the hole as three or four rifles opened up on him.

Elias shook his head. What had he done to get lumbered with bastards like this? This was the Paras, for fuck's sake, professional soldiers, the best of the best. He wondered quickly whether to give Plonker a beasting but decided not to. Morale was high and he didn't want that damaged. They were all laughing and from somewhere in Spud's day-bag came 'To infinity and beyond' as his Buzz Lightyear doll suddenly sprang to life.

'Fucking hell,' he said softly. 'You cunts are gonna wear me out.'

'I could fookin' murder a beer,' Plonker muttered.

'Movement.' Rhah was looking out the front. 'I have movement.'

Elias moved forward. 'Where?'

'Dial 1-800-FUCK THIS,' Jonesy muttered, leaning over to protect his brew from the big feet that were scrabbling and sliding round in the mud at the bottom of the hole. Elias looked out across the brown water. The waterline was only twenty feet below him, the river maybe fifty yards wide and still flowing quickly, but the level had dropped six feet by the look of the debris on the far bank. The track down to the river from the other side was visible now. In the briefing they had been told it was covered. The water level was falling, bloody quickly by the look of it. On the other side there was movement, occasional glimpses of a head or shoulder above the cover, perhaps a patrol moving down nearer the water's edge.

'How many, ja reckon?' Rhah asked.

'Dunno. Half a dozen maybe.'

'There's more,' Spud said. He was looking through small binoculars. 'To the right. Bushes, maybe twenty yards, up a bit from the bushes in line with the yellow building. There's more of 'em. Maybe a platoon.'

'I see 'em.'

'Fuck! They have a gun, an M60. They're setting it up.'

Elias grabbed the binoculars. 'Sure?'

'Saw it.'

341

'Jonesy, get over to the platoon CP. Let Big Harry know they are moving up.'

'What was that?' Jonesy said, looking up.

'What?'

'I 'eard summat.'

'What?'

'There again . . . aircraft,' Jonesy muttered.

'Hope they're fookin' ours. Can't see piss-all up through this shite,' Plonker muttered, looking up at the dark green canopy above them and then back at Elias. The look on Elias's face said it all. They weren't – not this soon.

'Bollocks 'n' shite,' the big northerner said. He had stopped honing his spade and was looking up again. 'That's all we fookin' need.'

Gulf of Mexico

On HMS *Beaufort*, her radars cranked out to the maximum range, they saw the two contacts approaching Belize from the south-west. They were slow but close together and could only be military. The contacts popped up into radar view, high enough to be seen over the hills and the earth's curvature and then dropped down again. Then they were back, illuminated and with the ship's targeting systems designating a contact number and tracking them. The ship, already at action stations, was given the word by the main broadcast system and tired sailors sat upright at their posts. It was the Ops officer who called it. 'Sir, maybe they aren't coming at us. Maybe it's a ground strike.'

'Bugger it,' said Commander Bennett. 'Advise both Major Fox and who is the . . . ?'

'Major Tyson-Davis.'

'. . . Tyson-Davis that there are aircraft inbound. Target unknown, suggest air defence posture. They're slow. What are they?'

The Ops officer answered. 'Sir, they have eight twin Cessnas fitted out for COIN ops, and eight PC-7s.'

'What are they?'

'Says here twin tandem seater turboprop training aircraft,' he replied looking at *Jane's*. 'I think they are built by Pilatus . . . and ah, yeah, here we go. Has hardpoints for underwing stores. Sir, all modern trainers are multi-role. These could be fitted out for COIN ops, ground attack. They could have mounted cannons or bombs on those hardpoints. Could also be helos, sir. They are slow enough.'

'Thank you,' Bennett responded.

San Ignacio

Harry Rees was back up on the road and supervising the unloading of the first wedges when the Guatemalan aircraft came over for its first pass. There was a gap in the cloud, not for long, but enough for the sun to break through, moisture rising from the wet jungle and sodden ground the moment warmth hit it.

The PC-7 came over the hills and the jungle from the south, low and fast. It began its strafing run, in the classic attack posture: in low over the terrain, pull up, find the target, drop down firing and then turn and evade. The heavy 20 mill cannon ripped through the buildings by the bridge just yards from where he was standing, and then cut down into the trees and jungle along the bank. Some fire was coming back up at it, but most of the lads down in the holes, beneath the canopy of trees, had little sight of the sky and could not do much. As it passed two of the B Squadron men were tracking it with a GPMG and down on the right the 2 Para support company blokes attached to D Coy had one of their fifty-calibres up and firing, its big hammering report rolling across the valley.

In the hole everybody except Jonesy did what they were trained to do. If you can't see it to return fire, then get under cover until you can. While everyone went for the bottom of the hole, Jonesy waited till the rounds churning up the rise passed by, then took up the LSW and let rip as the shadow crossed over them. The second aircraft was close behind on the same run and by now many more of the defenders were ready, including half a mile away the Royal Navy crew on board the gunboat now moored on the river. Hidden as she was under a leafy overhang, Lewis knew that if she fired she might well compromise her hideyhole, but he gave the command to fire anyway. Hagan and another of the boat troop men, who would have engaged even without Lewis calling the command, loosed off with the 12.7 mill and the GPMG but didn't think they had hit anything.

Back in the hole Plonker, who had forgotten his introduction of the Guatemalans to Spud, looked at Jonesy who was changing the mag on the section weapon. 'Dumb cunt,' he said. 'Yowa'l git fookin' slotted like that.'

'Na,' Jonesy said, 'once the rounds have gone past they can't shoot backwards, can they? The rounds have gone past but they haven't. Just got to pop up and fire at the fuckers and hope you hit something.' He grinned, 'Dial 1-800-GROUND FIRE.'

'What was it?'

'Scrote crabs.'

'Was that a 20 mill or what? Look at that tree.' He was pointing out behind them where a small tree, maybe six inches thick in the trunk had been snapped off six feet above the ground by one exploding round.

'Dunno but if we shoot him down I'm gonna give 'im a right fookin' beasting,' Plonker promised.

'Me too,' Jonesy said, ''Cos some bastard's knocked my fucking tea over.'

Rhah, long appreciative of Jonesy's dry humour, was chuckling, but Elias was at the front wall looking out. 'Cut the cackle and get stood to, something's happening over there. Jonesy, keep an ear open for that plane again, eh? And get over to Big Harry.'

'Been here half an hour, just half an hour,' Spud said, 'and in that time I've been shot at and fucking strafed. This is going to be a bad day. I can feel it.'

'It's gonna get worse,' Elias called. On the far side there were men moving forward to the bank of the river, on to ground where six hours before the floodwaters had flowed. If they became established there, well dug in, they would be a bastard to winkle out again and from there to the ford was only twenty yards. 'Stand to! Don't let 'em get established on the bank. Hit 'em!'

Chapter Twelve

On the far side there were enemy troops running forward, out of the low bush into the more open, undulating ground, a plateau of maybe four acres that had been under water an hour ago. That level area dropped away to the river, with low concrete walls six inches high in a grid pattern, built to prevent erosion. The natural undulations of the ground provided enough cover for infantry, allowing them to get close. Too bloody close, Elias thought; where are their guns? No one advances like this without machine gun support.

'Hit 'em!'

The section opened fire, Spud on the LSW targeting groups and hitting them with measured bursts, the others rapid-firing their SA80s. The sections either side of them had opened up too, pouring fire across the river into the advancing Guatemalans. Suddenly their machine guns opened up, heavy fire reaching across towards them, bullets slamming into the front of the sangar hole, churning up mud and leaves. There were two explosions over there, each a millisecond of flash and white smoke and dust and shock wave, men going down. Someone was firing rifle grenades, Elias thought. On the left the rush was faltering, but in the centre and on the right they were dropping into cover. The shooting settled into a steady fusillade, as the Paras slowed their rate of fire as targets dropped from sight. There were dead and wounded on the ground over which they had rushed, at least twenty men, some still, others moving, and on the eastern bank the Paras could hear the wounded calling out, the sounds of men in pain, dying.

Spud had ceased firing, and was looking out of the slit under the log at the men he had fired at. He looked away and closed his eyes for a second.

'Fuck it,' Rhah snapped. 'They will get settled in there. This river is dropping like someone pulled the plug. When it's low enough, they will come at us. There must be 'a hundred of them – we have to get them out of there.'

'Who fired the grenades?' Jonesy asked, thinking that's minimum range, that's good shooting, whoever it was. He was the best grenade shot in the platoon. He looked down – his hand was shaking.

Suddenly there was another blast on the other side and Elias and Plonker realized it at the same moment – the surprises left by the B Squadron blokes. They had mined the bank, but it was Plonker who articulated it. He grinned, a beaming, slightly menacing, toothless apparition. 'That was a fookin' mine!' he said. 'The cunce have run into a fookin' minefield.'

'Grenades, give 'em to Jonesy,' Elias said, looking at him; Po's head, sticking out of his shirt, was now muddy. 'You take your time. I want you putting grenades into them, get them moving. Let them think they are sighted and they have to move position.'

'Force them on to the mines?' Spud queried.

'Just give Jonesy your grenades,' Elias snapped.

'You're a hard bastard,' Spud muttered.

'Fucking do it! Give Jonesy your grenades. If they consolidate there we are fucked. Goddit?'

''Ere, I'll fookin' do it,' Plonker shouted. He turned from the front of the hole and flicked a look at Spud. 'Ya woose.' Spud, who had just shot and killed four or five men and didn't like it, just looked away and sighted down the barrel of the LSW. The fire was intensifying again, tracer rounds streaking past them to hit the earth of the rise with a dull thumpthumpthump.

'I saw Cap't Atlee loading an automatic grenade launcher thingy back at Bragg. Let's see if we can get that?' Rhah suggested, lifting the handset on the Clansman.

'Two fookin' chances, son,' Plonker advised, as he dropped down to wipe dirt from his eyes. 'None and fook-all.' He changed magazines on his rifle and stood up, leaning against the front wall, his weapon out of the firing slit, and looked for a target.

'I can hear a helicopter,' Jonesy said.

347

Up on the bank hidden in a shed, Chard was at his vehicle. He had the surveillance camera airborne and was waiting for news from the FOB, and while he wanted to have a quick, fairly one-sided conversation with the two A Squadron blokes with the Javelin, for security reasons he couldn't do that over the net.

The next time the enemy aircraft came back they were ready, but it wasn't the PC-7s that had appeared the first time. It was a helicopter, one of a pair of Bell 212s and they had rocket pods. The first appeared over the hills from the west, fast and low, over the town, coming directly at the river, letting his first pod of twelve rockets go the moment he had visual on the far bank. This time they were visible to the Paras on the ground and furious fire began reaching up and then died abruptly as everyone saw the smoke from the side pods and ducked deep into their holes. The two A Squadron men were up on the hillside to the south of the bridge, overlooking the entire battlefield, and the helo's egress route would take it past the hill left to right.

With an attacking enemy aircraft, as long as it was under 3,000 feet, Javelin could put 2.7 kilos of high explosive accelerating up past Mach 1.5 straight up the jet pipe with its SACLOS guidance system. SACLOS was simple – as long as the operator could see the jet through his viewfinder all he had to do was keep it there and the electronics did the rest. With a turboprop or a helicopter it was not substantially different; if anything it was easier, providing the chopper pilot didn't know he was being targeted and suddenly lose enough height to drop out of the sight. As long as he was in the sight SACLOS would do its job.

The trooper sighted on the helo still coming in over the town. He didn't want to wait, in case he needed time for a second shot. 'Got it,' he murmured and fired. The missile seared away, white-hot smoke in a tail behind it and a few seconds later it hit. There was a blinding microsecond flash, and the helicopter exploded, fuel and ordnance going up, in a brilliant orange ball of flame.

The trooper grinned and looked at his mate. 'You know when you've been Tangoed.' He had done it before; he had shot down an Argentinian Pucará in the Falklands in his first year with the Reg.

'Tango that fucker, then,' his oppo said pointing. It was the second 212, this one coming from the north to run parallel to the river. He had obviously seen his wingman get hit because he was jinking left and right, but committed to his attack. The trooper held off – if he hit the helo it would fall directly on to the men dug in below it along the riverbank. By the time it was clear it was flashing overhead and hidden behind the hill before he could sight on it.

'Next time, you scrote cunt,' he muttered, 'next time.'

Down on the riverbank there was cheering and yelling from the Paras in the holes. The Guat helo had been slotted right in front of them and they had watched it explode and fall to the ground just two hundred yards away, on top of the scrotes' positions opposite. They had taken casualties. The salvo of rockets had been slightly high, the first hitting the trees on the rise above and just behind the D Company positions and the rest staggered out behind, some of them hitting and exploding in the area where the tired Gurkhas had settled to eat and rest. A rocket hit the ground beside the Toyota pickup that Estelle had commandeered to get some rations into his people. He was there, limping along, making sure they ate and drank, changed their socks, did the things soldiers do, in the brief snatches of sanity in battle and he took the blast along with one of his corporals. The corporal was killed outright and Lieutenant Estelle's right leg was blown off below the knee. When he came to moments later he pulled himself away from the vehicle, his lads running over. He was aware, alert, but going into shock, holding his leg up in the air, his trousers torn and tattered round a shattered stump, a shard of bone, yellow-white, sticking out of the end. He had other wounds, burns and punctures from shrapnel. He was tourniqueted, hit with a syrette, bundled back into the pickup, now with no windscreen, with two lightly-wounded men, and driven away to look for the field surgical team.

Harry Rees was on the road with the wedges, almost finished, when the vehicle raced up to him, past the BDF roadblock, looking for directions. He flicked a look into the back where three very concerned Gurkhas were holding on to their officer. He almost didn't recognize him, covered in blood as he was. He had seen him only fifteen minutes before when he had handed over the scoff from the wedges. Oh Jesus, he thought, it's Tobes.

'Down the road, second right turn, six houses along. Repeat.' The driver repeated it and Rees nodded. 'Go!'

He turned back to his task, thinking about what he had just seen. Toby Estelle. Played centre in the battalion's rugby team, ran like a greyhound; saw him outrun Jeremy Guscott once at a charity game. No leg. Jesus, Tobes. He looked at his watch. He wanted to get back; his platoon sergeant was a solid bloke, but his place was with his toms, down in the shit. He watched the last stores on to the trailer, and then a movement caught his eye. Two people were coming up the side road opposite him. He just caught them out of the corner of his eye and he knew, something triggered in his brain. He looked up; they were a hundred yards away and coming up slowly towards the main road. Sophie. Sophie and Helen. Naaa, can't be, it just looks like them – the walk. He looked again.

'Corp, secure here and get back. I'm behind you in this,' he said, and jumped into another of the four vehicles they had the use of. He started it, and drove down the road towards the two figures, his SA80 on the seat beside him. They had disappeared again, and he slowed down – there, movement behind a big flowering bougainvillaea. He pulled up, climbed out and walked forward, his rifle in his hand, crossing silently round behind the bush like a big cat, suddenly looming up over two figures. It was them, the two girls, squatting down looking the other way, hiding like a couple of kids.

'Hi,' he said.

There was a pair of shrieks, his surprise complete; one of them, Helen, frightened, was coming up at him with a big stick, her eyes wild.

'Whooa!' he said, stepping back. 'It's me! Harry!' He realized that they had never seen him in DPMs and certainly not with his face cam-creamed up. 'It's me! Calm down.'

Helen dropped the stick and walked towards him; Sophie came up off the ground, disbelieving what she was seeing.

Helen took three steps, put her hand out and burst into tears. 'I thought you were them. I thought you were . . .' She buried her face in his chest, sobbing. With the other arm he took Sophie and pulled her close too, his rifle still in his hand round her back.

'Sssh. Don't worry, it's going to be OK.' He looked down at Sophie who was gazing up at him, rubbing her hand up and down his shoulder, trying to reassure herself he was there, that it was really him. She reached up to kiss him, and smiled.

'I've never been so pleased to see anyone.'

'Me too, but I wish it was somewhere else. What the fu . . . what on earth are you doing here?'

She began to tell him the story, and while she did he eased Helen back and pointed them both at the old GMC pickup. 'I want you two out of here. I will organize something.'

'I thought you were back in England by now. Have you been here all along?'

'No,' he replied, 'we left. We were turned around in mid-air, got back in just after seven this morning.'

'Are they winning?' Helen asked, wiping a tear away.

'No. But it's daylight, they have bridging gear coming forward, and they will try and get through. There is going to be a hell of a punch-up, and it will stretch well back from the river, both sides. There's nowhere safe here.'

'You're back,' Sophie said softly, still looking at him. 'I prayed.'

He pulled over at the BDF roadblock where the three soldiers and a policeman were stopping anyone going towards the town and the river. They were talking to another man, a local fellow, standing beside his car and all looking back at the smoke billowing up where the chopper had gone down, one gesticulating with his hand, explaining how the other flew across in front of them. Rees got out of the truck and the men all turned round; the civilian stared at the two girls. It was Eddie Sanchez, taxi driver, guide, Lothario and man-about-Belize, and he recognized them from the guest house.

'Hey, wa' you two doin' 'ere?'

Rees glared at him and the look must have been menacing because Eddie grinned. 'I know them, man. Saw them at the guest house.'

'Who are you?' Rees asked.

'Eddie. Dis is my cab. Got air-con.'

'Taxi?'

'Yeah, marn,' Eddie said proudly.

'You going back to Belize? Can you take them?'

'No way, man. Road's blocked, these guys tell me. How about JB's? Can get them that far?'

'That'll do. You get them to Sally, OK?' Rees had only ever met her once, but she was an institution in Belize. Straight as a die was Sally at JB's, every squaddie who had ever been in Belize rated her. Rees stepped closer. 'You get them there safely and I'll pay you. If you don't . . .' His voice dropped; funny things happened in wars, normally decent people did odd things so it was time to make himself clear. '. . . Central America ain't big enough for you to hide from me. They are my women – understand?'

Eddie did. He was also a pro, and there was no way he was going to do anything other than his job, especially for a man doing the business for Belize. 'Don' worry, man, I'm going back anyhow. I don' wan' yo' money.' He jerked a thumb back at the smoke billowing up from the town and the sounds of the battle. 'You takin' cara us. I'll take cara dem.'

Rees walked back to the truck. 'Recognize him?'

'He's the taxi guy from the guest house,' Helen replied.

'Right. Belize is closed off. He's gonna take you as far as Sally at JB's. Sally's a wild American woman, great fun. Stick with her. By tomorrow, that ground there will probably be an FOB for Harriers, and there will be RAF Regiment and dashing chaps in G-suits wandering round throwing their white scarves back everywhere. You'll be safe, OK?' he finished, hoping he was right.

They nodded, both of them smiling now.

'Good. I'll see you soon and if you move on, leave word, OK?'

They nodded again.

'I have to go.' He kissed his finger and reached out and ran it down Sophie's nose, and she turned her face and lifted her lips to kiss it.

'Please be careful,' she whispered. 'I just found you. I don't want to –' He covered her lips with his finger, bent and kissed her quickly and straightened up.

'Eddie,' he called. 'On your way.'

Twenty minutes later Rees was down on the track, crawling forward below the lip to the shallow comms trench that led to his platoon CP and a few minutes later he slithered into it.

'Right, Sarn't. How we doing?'

He was quickly given the sitrep for his sector, the four sections in eight holes along the riverbank. He knew that up behind them, thirty metres back, was a B Squadron position, two troopers with the clackers and arming devices for the mines they had set on the far side the night before. Smoke billowed over from the still-smouldering remnants of the helicopter, mixing with paler smoke from the town. Red and green tracer arced overhead, highlighting the classic mistake of the green rifleman, aiming too high, but there was someone on the other side with an M60 who knew his stuff because every now and then bullets churned into the sangar, ripped bark from trees, and tore up the ground. Below him in the section sangars and holes his toms were returning fire and the sergeant pointed across.

'Over there, sir, opposite Cutter's section, we had an advance towards the water, company-size movement. We met it. They ended up on that piece of what looks like flat ground there, but it's undulating and there is cover. The Regiment lads mined it last night, and a few went off as they moved down, so I think they are wondering what to do now. Cutter dropped some grenades on to them, but they haven't moved. Digging in, I reckon.'

'Shit.' He didn't want that; the river level was still dropping and this was the ford, that was why they were moving down, had to be. Sooner or later it would be shallow enough, knee-deep, to rush across. 'Get on to company,' Rees said to the radio operator. 'Request mortars. They have the GPS coordinates.' He pulled out a hand-drawn map, looked at it and handed it to the radio operator. 'This grid here, F9. God-dit? Just say grid F9.'

'Yes sir.'

'I'm down with Corp'l Cutter.'

Up at the company position Major Tyson-Davis had maps spread over a trestle-table made from the bonnet of a car on two sawhorses. The company CP was in the concrete-walled remnants of what had been a car repair workshop. It had been hit during the night, so most of one side was gone, but the bulk of the roof was still in place which kept it dry, and the concrete walls would offer protection from anything other than a direct hit.

Tyson-Davis was conferring with Atlee. Behind them against one wall was his radio man, now the critical link with the mortar crews, the air defence team, the boat and the other various elements of the command, and he had been supplemented by the SAS major who had moved one of his two signallers into the CP to ensure there was sufficient resource. At the table the two officers were looking at the map and aerial photos, and comparing them with the voice link information coming back in from the FOB and the Royal Artillery lieutenant studying the images coming back from the surveillance drone that was flying over the town. Even at altitude, dropping down through the scudding clouds, it was attracting ground fire.

'It must be in there,' Atlee said, pointing at a spot on a large photo.

'Major,' said the SAS signaller, 'bridge gear is on the move.' He was on the link back to the FOB.

'Sir,' the company radio man called, 'Lieutenant Rees requesting mortars on F9.'

'Advise. Mortars are committed,' Tyson-Davis replied. 'No, wait.' He was thinking quickly. It could be a diversion, but it might be more than that. 'Get a sitrep from twelve platoon. Then from ten and eleven.'

He looked up, considering. They had plenty of mortars. C Coy had four from support company, big 81 mm and their own two 51s. D Coy had their two 51s and four 81s borrowed from the Americans at Fort Bragg. Chard's people had six 81s. They had in effect the mortar strength that would normally be enough to support two battalions. Suddenly Chard walked into the CP. It was an odd position he was in; rarely did 22 SAS fight alongside the green army. Their role was different, normally they were either covert or deployed separately, but for the time being, he would allow his men to support the Paras. What was the 2 Para major's expectation? Tyson-Davis looked at him. 'Good. I was about to raise you. They will support the bridge approach with troops, move them forward. I want to split the fire; your tubes and two of mine on the approach road, the others as fire support.' Chard was listening, evaluating him. He knew Tyson-Davis had done a tour in the Reg. He was rated highly. Focus, was what everyone said, and Chard could see it now, complete focus. Tyson-Davis saw nothing but the task, the objective. 'The bridge – can I leave that with you?' Chard nodded. Bridges were strategic targets, this was what his people did – a good decision. He was pleased, he could work with this guy.

The sitreps were coming in now, Tyson-Davis listening with half an ear as they did so. It was building, there was movement all along the bank. A minute later he issued fire orders against grid squares and a mile back the bombs began leaving the tubes, Rees calling corrections from Cutter's sangar, now under intensive fire from the far bank. This was part of the enemy's larger strategy. The bridging equipment was coming up, but the defenders had to be suppressed while the engineers did their work, or they would be picked off like flies. This was suppression by fire, the volume staggering. In the hole Plonker and Jonesy were at the slits in the front, returning fire, while Rhah and Spud were shovelling earth into sandbags that had finally made their way down to them from the wedges, in a frantic race to strengthen the sangar. They had five up already, each lifted and pushed outwards so the loose earth was piled up against the front. That had two benefits. First it disguised the sangar, the earth in front of the sandbags the same red as everything else; nothing would attract attention and fire like a row of fawn-coloured sandbags. Second, every inch of earth slowed down anything hitting them. Another one full; Spud called to Plonker who stood back for a second while the sixth bag was hefted up and placed in front of him.

Spud dropped suddenly. 'Down! Incoming!' he yelled.

Everyone dropped into the mud as a 66 mill rocket streaked inches over the log that formed the top of the fortification and hit the bank behind them with a huge explosion. Jonesy was still going down and took some of the blast. It threw him bodily up and back against the sangar wall, winding him, knocking him out and leaving him in a heap in the mud, his ears bleeding. Everyone was shouting, they were all deafened by the blast, and it was Spud who pulled his face clear of the water in the bottom of the hole. Jonesy was gasping and then took a huge draught of air. 'He's breathing.'

More 66s began hitting along the bank, the Guats targeting the holes they had found, and then bigger incoming started, mortar rounds. Rees looked back at Jonesy; Elias had him up out of the water and was checking him for wounds. He was still unconscious, but he was breathing and they hadn't found traumatic bleeding anywhere. Rees pulled himself up and went back to his task of spotting for their mortars. Where did that rocket come from? Where's the possie? There! Another one away, this time at nine platoon's sector.

'Plonker, on the gun!' he called. 'In the trees to the right of the bus station. One, two, three trees along. The base of that tree, back ten feet. See it?' A burst stitched its way across in front of them, throwing clods up in the air, some bullets ricocheting upward, buzzing past.

'Aye.'

'Hit 'em!' Rees snapped. Jennings, the CSM, in his role as OC support platoon was up with the mortar teams and Rees went for his callsign. Three-Three, Three-Three, Four-Two, one bomb, right one hundred, right one hundred, over!'

Jonesy's eyes were open now and he was still gasping for breath, but Elias knew he would be all right and stood to, at the front. 'You two get back on filling bags,' he shouted to Rhah and Spud. 'This is just starting.'

Plonker had ranged and let rip with the LSW, both sides of the river now under a mortar barrage. Anyone out of a hole now would be in real trouble: burning hot shrapnel

356

peppered the air, white cordite smoke curled in wreaths over the ground, tracer fire from the Guatemalan side cutting through it like a flash from a child's laser pen. The bomb fell just to the left of the position where the rockets were coming from. 'Three-Three, Four-Two, four rounds, fire for effect!'

Belize Airport

Major Fox was waiting for the big one. It was broad daylight now, and his positions were in clear view. They were under fire, constant small arms, and the odd burst from something in a sustained-fire role, but the lads were in deep.

You didn't have to be a tactical genius to see that he only covered the eastern end of the runway and the approach road and that his holes were widely spaced. For him the defensive issue was simple. What's their strength? They took a pounding last night; from my positions, from the air and then the NGS. How many of them are still fighting fit? What's their officer cadre like? How much expendable ordnance do they have left? What's morale like over there? They had expected to take the airport without a fight; their reinforcements had not only failed to arrive, they would know they had been interdicted en route and taken out. They were short on ammo and had no fire support now the barge had been sunk. They know we have a helo and they know we have NGS, but must have figured that it is dependent on the tides. How would they be feeling now? Like shit, exposed, cut off, running out of ammunition, wounded still on the ground. What's their reaction, their plan? How much punishment will they mete out before they figure they can't take the airhead and decide it's time to try a withdrawal? Then where to? They have to fight, have to win this. Well, so do we. He looked back behind him quickly; his own dead were lined up in three sad little rows behind the trenches. He had moved them back because by nightfall, in these temperatures, decomposition would have begun and they would start to smell.

They will know we are 2 Para and they will have identified us as Gurkhas. This is the airhead, the most strategic objective in the theatre. He looked at his men deployed out in front. My lads – he felt a rush of fondness for them, for their loyalty, and immense pride in their courage. We have never run from a battle yet and certainly never from an airhead. They know they have a fight on their hands, so what will they do? There's nowhere for them to go. They must be worrying about their rear too, from the road in both directions. If the BDF have got their act together then they could attack them from the south, up the road from the city. What chance of that, a flank attack by the BDF? I must find out what's going on, he thought. *Beaufort* must know. Four hundred last night – must have taken down, killed or wounded at least eighty or ninety; let's be optimistic and say one hundred. Three hundred left. If we could flank them they would have to turn to face it, and that would take the pressure off here.

'Raise HMS *Beaufort*,' he said to his radio operator. Ten minutes later he was none the wiser. *Beaufort* had had no comms with anyone ashore and no one knew where the BDF were except for reports that they had closed the city from the north and the west with roadblocks. That had been on the radio. Garvey, he thought.

Ten minutes later the SAS trooper had skittered through the concrete bollards and trenches into the rear of the CP hole and Fox was quizzing him.

'Don't think so,' Garvey replied. 'They will have closed Haulover Bridge, that's the one going back into town, the northern highway, and the toll bridge, that's the western highway. That will have closed off Belize City. That will be the priority, for both BDF and civil police. They won't have thought to have a go at these bastards if they are outside that ring.'

'Could they be encouraged to advance past the bridge to support us? We won't need much, just enough to turn some of this strength their way, and keep it facing that way till dark falls again.'

Garvey looked at the 2 Para officer. He was sweating already in the humid heat, his face grimy, his eyes red-rimmed, his smock stained with blood and red mud. He didn't envy him his job. Command here? Command what? They were still outnumbered at least four to one and it was going to be a long hot day, fighting under the beating sun, without cover or shade and for the lads in the forward holes, limited water. It would be at least another twenty-four hours before they could expect relief to arrive. Levelling the odds was his job, but soldiers were dying here, and when the Guats realized how small a force they were, it would all happen. It was a pretty fair guess that they would be overrun. Even someone with an optimistic view would estimate that by nightfall half of them would be dead, and whatever he did some armchair commentator back home, some wanker retired colonel would be on television, miles from the action, a critic of the tactics, virtually as they were happening.

'Maybe . . . depends who does the convincing.'

'You said you had one of their officers.'

Garvey grinned. 'This is Belize, Major. My bloke is a lieutenant, a nobody. It will be fucking chaos in the city. Even if he finds someone . . .' He trailed off. 'I'll go.'

'Absolutely not,' Fox snapped. 'I need you here. Ask your lieutenant to join me here, please. We can but ask – it's his bloody country, after all.'

'OK, sir, but not alone. I'll get a three-man patrol together, the best three. It's only a couple of miles back to the bridge.' A burst of fire ripped past them, chippings flying off the concrete bollards.

San Ignacio

The ITN journalist Leo Scobey and his camera crew were settled in. They had been down to the hospital and shot some footage, being careful not to show faces of anyone but cheerful smiling men, these all Gurkhas, raising thumbs and grinning at the camera. Chubby hadn't filmed anyone badly hurt, least of all the young officer who arrived in the pickup truck, his shattered stump up in the air, his face a mask of pain. The surgeon had whisked him in; his team were still treating the overnight casualties, but he pulled some off those who were stable to work on him.

They had then moved back towards the front line again and found themselves a position on a hill overlooking the river and the fighting, the Paras below them, the Guatemalans on the far side of the narrow band of brown water. From there they could record the action from a wide angle, getting lots of good background footage of smoke rising, and the battle on the river below them. Fate, planning and experience had put them in place to record a spectacular sequence of events because below them heavy trucks had begun to move forward, infantrymen, shielded by the vehicles, running down on the far side.

'I have visual!' the B Squadron trooper reported. 'One truck coming into view. Bridge section, bridge section on the back.'

'Got that, Bravo Three-One?'

'Roger. We have the target.'

'Track it only. Fire on command.'

Chard was watching, personally taking control of this attack. There would be a minimum of three bridge sections required and before he hit any of them, he wanted as many as possible of them in the open, the Milan teams going for the tractor units, the mortars for more general damage. He had three Milan teams, with three missiles each, ready to go. At £10,500 each time they pulled the trigger this was big bucks, but they were worth every penny. He didn't just want to stop the bridge gear getting into a position where it could be lifted off and floated out, he wanted to destroy it, remove it as a tactical and strategic option.

The first truck and trailer were moving down the track, escorted by an armoured tracked vehicle, towards the ford, where there was a stable expanse of water with access both sides for vehicles. He didn't want them getting too close to the ford because once the trucks were knocked out they would provide cover for the troops to advance behind. There was a fearsome battle going on across the water, heavy fire from the Guatemalan side as they tried to suppress any attack on the bridge unit transports. Mortars were falling across the front and 66 mm rockets were searing across, leaving white smoke trails, while machine guns hammered out their tattoo

360

of death. A second, then a third rig rumbled into view, each escorted by an APC, running alongside the lightly armoured cab of the truck. It all seemed terribly one-sided and it appeared that the mighty trucks would roll down to the water's edge unchallenged because nothing could raise its head on the far side.

'Stand by! Hit 'em! Mortars, fire for effect!'

All hell broke loose. It was awesome, terrifying, a focused, concentrated attack by the combined heavy weapons of a Sabre Squadron on a series of targets grouped together. In the next five seconds all three trucks were hit by Milan missiles, LAW rockets and 50-calibre fire from the 2 Para support elements. 40 mm grenades fired from an M19 were falling every second, and by the time the second salvo of Milans was away, this time aimed at the escorts, the trucks hauling the heavy trailers were on fire. The advancing men broke and ran for cover through the grenade blasts in the trees and bush off to their right, leaving behind many of their comrades, and by the time the first mortar bombs began to land the task was half done – they had been stopped. Now Chard's mortars would pound the bridge sections, blowing holes through the heavy steel pontoons that needed to be watertight to float and carry the weight of vehicles. Two minutes later the mortar barrage stopped. This bridge was going no further and with each of the sections now damaged beyond immediate repair, the task was complete. As fast as the Squadron had engaged, they disengaged; the whole area fell quiet, as even the small arms battle one hundred yards off at the ford died away. Then ammunition in one of the tracks began to cook off and smoke was climbing into the low clouds.

The Guatemalan officer of engineers, the captain who had spent most of the hours of darkness repairing the lead truck, was still alive, but barely. He had argued against this, as best he could. He wanted to wait till the water dropped and save his equipment for the one section of the river where there was no ford, at Roaring Creek. He was demolition-trained and the moment he saw what was left of the bridge he knew who had done it – British special forces. That meant they had also planned the defence of the ford; this wasn't a couple of companies of the Belizean Defence Force. Then he requested to deploy just one vehicle at a time. He could handle losing one, but to put all their equipment in one mad dash for the water was, he said, too risky. He was told to shut up and get his gear down and build a bridge. There would be support, four companies of infantry, armoured vehicles, suppression fire.

As he lay bleeding to death on the ground beside the lead vehicle's cab where he had been blown outward by the blast, his body covered in flash burns, he wondered about the futility of it all and who would love his children now.

From his vantage Tyson-Davis looked down. The next assault would be on foot, or in vehicles over the ford, but the water level had to drop first. They might even wait till tonight, he thought. I would. Then come across the ford the old-fashioned way, behind armour. Three brigades; fifteen thousand men. The Reg people carved up two battalions last night and we've bloodied one down here. That's a brigade just about buggered in terms of morale, wounded and attrition of non-replaceable equipment. Just two more, fresh and raring to go and prove their Latin machismo. But, and he grinned wolfishly, we have bought ourselves a few hours. The cloud was rolling through, low and dark and 'pregnant with potential precipitation', as one met-man used to say. Come on, you bugger, he thought, open up, rain, pour down. With the bridges gone and heavy rain they could hold, maybe even until spearhead, the rest of the battalion, lobbed in.

Down in the twelve platoon positions, Elias Cutter's fire teams were now in a rhythm. In their hole the sandbags were up and they had reinforced it as best they could. Two men, currently Rhah and Plonker, were at the front, firing as and when targets presented themselves; Spud was scraping the comms trench out the back deeper and Jonesy was taking a breather and trying to get a brew going. Cutter and Rees were pleased. The main attack with the bridge sections had been beaten by fire support, every infantryman's dream, and they had settled as a platoon and as fire teams, their first blooding complete. Knowing they were going to be here for a while, they were into basic stuff; dig deeper, move ammo up, and drink tea. The Paras' motto – if in doubt, brew up.

Jonesy had dispensed with a hexy block and was using his prize possession, a small camping-gas stove, which could heat each man's cup of water much faster. He also carried tubes of sweetened condensed milk, a real luxury and when Plonker looked back he had it out, ready to dispense in a thick yellow-white worm into stewed strong tea. If you couldn't have a beer then this was it – bliss.

It was stinking hot and humid under the cloud layer. They were all sweating, filthy, Spud most of all as he shovelled earth off the floor of the comms trench into sandbags to lie along the top. If they needed to get out quickly they wanted to be able to do it below the line of sight and with some element of protection back to the track. Elias slithered back in past Spud. He had been over to his other fire team in their hole, where one of them had been wounded, hit with a ricochet, and two support platoon guys were pulling him back to the medics with a sucking chest wound.

'Torpy has caught one,' he said. There was other bad news. A bloke in eleven platoon had been wounded by shrapnel from a 66 millimetre rocket, and a mortar had hit very close to a hole down by the bridge support. There was rumour of someone dead. Rhah just looked at him, his expression one of shock. Torpy was a mate. 'Is it bad?' he asked.

'Chest is always bad,' Spud said.

Elias nodded. 'He's back with the medics now, so cross fingers.' He wiped the sweat from his face. 'There's ammo coming down. What do you need?'

'Box for the LSW,' Rhah said softly, too softly for Elias to hear over the noise around them.

'What?'

Rhah looked down and kicked an ammo box for the section weapon. Elias nodded. Jonesy didn't answer, bent over down in the mud, protecting the single contoured tin cup on the small gas burner. They had dug a hole in the side of the sangar forming an alcove out of the way, big enough for a metal ammo box to be wedged into it. The little burner sat inside the box. Plonker had stopped firing as things quietened down; then, remembering he had unopened letters in his pocket, delivered the day before at the camp, he pulled them out and began to open them.

Suddenly fire ripped over their heads and behind them up in the trees three mortar bombs came in. The blasts shook the ground and showered them with clods of dirt and leaves, the smell of the explosives drifting over them. Jonesy ducked his head, along with the others, and put a hand over the cup on the stove.

'This place,' Plonker said, 'is a fookin' shithole. Elias mate, if you want out after this I don't blame yer.' Rhah looked out. It is now, he thought, just ten hours of fighting and look at it. Burning buildings, death, smoke, wrecked vehicles, old trees, rain-forest trees along the riverbank blown apart. People are dying here. He was scared, they all were. Then what Plonker had said sank in. Elias, out? Jacking in the mob and going for civvy street? Rounds stitched their way up towards the sand-bags at the front of the sangar and he and Plonker dropped down into cover. They were getting good at anticipating this.

Rhah looked back at Elias. 'You jacking in? Can't think why,' he said drily.

'I'll fookin' tell ya why,' Plonker said, ''cos he has to work with yowa cunce.' He looked down at the contents of an envelope.

'He goes, I go,' Rhah said with some finality.

'I think I will too,' Spud said, winking at Rhah. 'Let's take our ball and go home.'

'Yeah, why not,' Jonesy chimed in. 'Fuck 'em. Let's call a cab. I'm 1-800-PISSED OFF.'

'Fook off!' Plonker yelled, aghast at the thought. 'We've fookin' trained for years, taking a hundred beastings, tabbed for hundreds of miles, thousands probly and now we get to do it for real and yowa pooftas want to fookin' jack in. Ain't that booger boiled yet, Jonesy, ya cunt?' This from Plonker, who had never brewed up for anyone other than himself in his life. 'Anyway, Elias ain't jacking nowt in. Are yer?' He looked at Cutter. Rhah was grinning, and mimed winding in a fishing reel – Plonker had taken the bait again. Suddenly Lieutenant Rees's head appeared down the comms trench. 'Everything OK, Corporal?'

'Oh aye, ask them, sir!' Plonker was in full flow – it was a sight to behold and the others were enjoying it immensely. 'These fookin' pansy cunce will never be Oor Kare! What about me? I'm the only fookin' real grunt in this 'ole, I am. Don't worry about me, oh no. Tell ya wa', I'll get me own fookin' 'ole . . .' The others were in stitches now, openly laughing at him. 'Ooh, big fookin' joke now, is it! I fookin' tell yowa cunce, and fookin' Barclaycard, right. Those bastards,' he waved the letter, 'they're telling me my fookin' card hasn't been fookin' paid. Well fook yowa lot and fook them 'n' all.'

'Plonker!' Rees interrupted.

'Sir?'

'Shut the fuck up.'

'Aye, sir.' There was mild applause from the others. The moment had provided some respite and they were all smiling, three of the five with brews in their hands.

'Nothing wrong with morale in here,' Rees muttered. 'Got everything you need?'

'Yes sir.'

'Good.' He crawled in and moved up to the front of the sangar. 'You see that stick poking up from the water over there, on an angle. That branch?'

'Yes sir,' Elias replied.

'There's a white tape marker on it. Squadron blokes think there's about a foot to go but it may be less. When you can see the marker, let me know. That means the level is waist-deep. Any time after that and they could try for it.'

'Waist-deep? Are they that crazy, sir?'

'They won't know it's waist-deep, they might think it's shallow enough. I suggest you get some scoff down your necks now. The good news is that air has arrived. The bad news is that they can't fly in this shit.' He pointed upward. There were groans from the team.

'So much for our much-vaunted all-weather day and night NATO multi-role mission capability,' Rhah commented.

'Air force, Barclaycard, Guatemalans. All coonts,' Plonker muttered, like it was a grand conspiracy against him.

Florida

At Pensacola the Harriers had arrived. The ferry pilots were exhausted. They had flown the first 3,300 miles, the limit of their ferry range, with four drop tanks, then ditched them and snuggled up to a tanker in turn, two at a time, to suck on board thousands of pounds of fuel, enough to get them on to the next point. Ten hours, it had taken them.

The other lads who had come down in the VC10s were in, the aircraft parked down at the far end of the airbase away from prying eyes. Tents were erected, service areas laid out, the crews who would fly the first sorties were resting. Again the Americans had come through. Portakabins had been placed in their area, mess tents and facilities for the team of US navy cooks who were going to feed the visitors. The crew who had come over on the big jets had been given sleeping pills and slept most of the way across, and now it was tactical decision time, preparing the plans for the first strikes.

US personnel on the base had trickled down to have a looksee, interested in the GR7s. Their marines had a variant of the Harrier, but this was the newest version and armed for bear. No one had ever flown an armed mission for real from Pensacola, not if you discounted recon over Cuba, and this created a buzz of interest, mostly in the absolute simplicity and almost minimalist approach to warfare of their allies. If this was an American op there would be many squadrons of carrier-borne aircraft thrown at it: ELINT missions, top cover supported by AWACs, A-10 Warthogs, Apache attack helos, the works. These guys had pitched up with six, count 'em, just six aircraft, a handful of support people on the ground, and seemed incredibly lightly equipped.

Int coming out of the theatre was that the Guatemalans had air. The green jobs had been attacked twice so far, when breaks in the weather allowed, and A Squadron had splashed an armed helo with a Javelin shoulder-launched missile. The

RAF people knew that the Guats would now be very careful. Scooting in fast and going out low, dropping below the hills, so the SACLOS sights wouldn't function.

As soon as the weather cleared the first package would sortie, five ground-attack GR7s and one fitted out for air-to-air. He would go in first, fully loaded with Sidewinders on the pylons, and a full load for his Aden 30 millimetre guns. They wanted air superiority, and right now the Guats had the upper hand. That would alter as they arrived but what resistance could they expect? The enemy had no jets, but you didn't need a jet to mount modern missiles. You could put them on turboprops, helos, pickup trucks, even carry them. What chance that either the Guats' turboprops or helos were fitted with air-to-air missiles? No one knew, but they were trained by the Israelis, some of the most innovative, practical people in the world; it would surprise no one if they had something slung on a hardpoint. They knew the PC-7 had cannons and that the helo had ground-attack rocket pods. They could try and draw the Guatemalan aircraft out and deal with them to clear the way for the ground-attack sorties following them ten minutes later.

But how to draw them out? They didn't have long loiter capability, not with these weapon loads, they would need refuelling as it was. Or they could just haul in, do the mish, and if they were attacked, deal with it. As someone said, you would have to be certifiable as a pilot in a turboprop or a helo to take on fast jets entering a theatre with unknown weapons configurations – your chances of surviving the encounter were slim indeed.

'What's the met?' someone asked as they gathered for the briefing. It wasn't good; the cloud was low, very low. They couldn't operate ground-support sorties if they couldn't see the ground. The only good news for the lads down there was that the Guatemalan aircraft wouldn't be back anyway, not with visibility this bad. At about this time, they knew, an RAF C-130 Hercules was about to land on Ambergris Cay. They had spoken to the ground people, friendlies, a seaboat full of sailors from HMS *Beaufort*. She had been busy overnight and had raced up to Ambergris, only twenty-five miles away from

St George's, and put a seaboat ashore, with ten armed ratings and an officer. No enemy there. The strip was open and functional, if a little wet from the rain. On board the Herc were RAF Regiment to secure the airfield. The Herc would drop them with their anti-aircraft detachment and immediately fly back up to Pensacola and uplift ground crews, ordnance, stores, equipment and fuel. If all things ran to plan the Harriers would not return to Pensacola unless one of them was damaged. The US station would be a staging post for logistics. The next FOB, forward operating base, for the VTOLs had been selected and the ops planners had been looking at two sites. One the grass strip at Belmopan and the second at the thirty-two-mile marker, at JB's restaurant. The advantage of the JB's site was hard cover on the ground, necessary for all-weather flight ops if it kept raining, and it also had electricity, lights, buildings, things that made life easier for the ground crews to work twenty-four hours a day.

Belize

At JB's Eddie Sanchez had dropped the two girls and not really knowing where to go, he had turned the engine off and wandered in to sit down. Sally hadn't even enquired who they were, just sat them down, produced coffee in a pot, asked the early shift in the kitchen to fix them something and sat down with them to hear the news.

Sophie told her all she could and finished with Harry's instructions. 'He said you were a wild woman but straight as a die,' she said with a smile, 'and we would be safe here.'

'Don't think I remember him,' Sally said with a chuckle, 'but hell, there have been thousands of them through here over the last few years. Well, you're welcome here as long as you like. And he's right; this is as safe as anywhere for the time being. There's fighting at the airport too, so Belize City is closed off.' A woman walked over and Sally introduced her. 'My friend, Miss Jenny. They have a business and she is with me visiting while her husband is up in St Louis buying some equipment.'

'He's gonna be real worried,' Miss Jenny said drily and dragged up another chair and helped herself to coffee. 'You girls just come down from Cayo, I hear?'

'Cayo?'

'The west. San Ignacio. You see any of the boys last night, the guys from the Bel-Brit or Eva's? I tried calling, but nothing.'

'Yes, we were at Eva's last night. Pete got us across the bridge,' Helen replied.

'Jeez, I'm pleased to hear that. He OK?'

'I don't know. He took his wife and daughters across and then went back over the other side.'

Sally didn't seem surprised. 'How was it?'

'Dreadful,' Sophie responded, sipping her coffee, holding the cup in both hands as if it were warming her, 'last night the whole place seemed to be burning. There are bombs and things going off and you can hear shooting. There are bodies lying around. The bridge is down. The boys . . .' She smiled at her own use of the word; they were hers, British, and what's more they were Harry's unit, her boys, '. . . the boys blew it up last night, but Harry said there is going to be fighting there. They will try and cross with rafts and they can build a new bridge apparently.'

'They won't need to, sweetie,' Miss Jenny said, 'I have driven across the Macal many times. There's a ford.' She pointed up at the clouds. 'Just pray for rain, girls, pray for rain.'

Belize Airport

At the airport Garvey's three-man patrol had gone out. He had chosen the best two blokes he could think of to accompany the officer. A rock-hard corporal, not bright but brave and more cunning than most, and a young kid from the hamlet at Ladyville, the small group of houses where the airport road met the main highway, where the marines had first engaged. The kid, only nineteen, was keen as mustard and grew up playing in the bush round the airport. He knew the area well and would guide them back out to the road and down to Haulover Bridge, he said, without being seen.

They had been gone an hour now and Fox tried to put them to the back of his mind and concentrate on the task. The attacks by HMS *Beaufort* and the helo had served as lessons because the Guatemalans had used the darkness to dig themselves in. There were two hundred yards between his positions and the nearest enemy foxholes at the edge of the dry, scrubby bush, and thankfully the battle had dropped back into small-arms fire only. It seemed they had either run out of mortar bombs and 66 mill rockets or were holding them in reserve for something because there hadn't been any incoming since just after daybreak. Over at the terminal the marines had held their position. There had been three rushes during the night, one straight at them and two round to the right but each time the marines had repulsed the attackers, and over where they were the fighting had subsided to odd shots as both sides tried to conserve ammunition and think up the next tactical move.

It suited Fox; they had only three bombs left and he wasn't expecting HMS *Beaufort* back in near enough for support fire until about noon. He looked at his watch: 1000 hours.

San Ignacio

Down in the sangar it was Spud and Jonesy at the firing line and the battle had dropped into a curious rhythm. The small-arms fire was constant in that never a minute went by without someone shooting, but there were periods of silence. But every now and then a 66 mill rocket would be fired, or the big 50-cals would open up, or mortar bombs would come in. The fire up till now had been erratic, some bombs dropping along the riverbank, some out behind up to half a mile back, one memorable one in the river itself downstream of the battle.

The D Coy guys had infinite respect for their mortarmen. Part of support company, the men serving the big 81 mill tubes were hard. They tabbed with huge loads, moving up behind the fighting almost as fast as the rifle platoons, and would fight absolutely exposed if that was unavoidable. In the Falklands, 2 Para mortarmen supporting their comrades, faced with baseplates that were sinking into the mud at odd angles, stood on them as they fired to keep them level in the full knowledge that the exploding charge to force the bomb out of the tube would break bones in their feet. They did it, broke bones, and then carried on.

In comparison the Guatemalan mortarmen were novices worse than any crap-hat the D Coy toms had ever seen, but eventually they would get the picture, and they did. Three bombs came in, ten seconds apart, being controlled back down towards the water. They knew instantly; this at last was someone who knew what they were doing. The third bomb landed on the edge of the track, blowing away the lip that had protected soldiers moving up and down from the fighting positions and the road above them to the left. Two more came in, one to the left and one to the right and when Elias looked back out his heart sank; he realized the Guatemalans had at last got a decent MFC. Their mortar fire controller had perfectly ranged on the gap in the track and he held the tubes' elevation and bearing on that spot, because another round came in, and then a third, this time anti-personnel, not HE, shrapnel cutting out through the trees. The smoke drifted back towards him, its taste acrid in the back of his throat. Someone had once described it as how you would imagine birdshit tasting. There was now a fifty-yard stretch with no lip, no protection at all, and the Guat gunners on the other side could see anyone coming down the track. The jungle in behind was too thick to allow much movement and anyway all they had to do was increase elevation and blast that to shit as well. As he thought it, they proved they could do it, a white phos bomb exploding in the trees and an M60 blasting an arc of fire across the gap.

Twelve platoon, half of eleven, and the Reg blokes out wherever they were on the flank, were now cut off from the road, company and any support or re-supply till nightfall and even then if the scrotes had flares that fifty yards would be lethal. Now they were in the shit – deep shit.

Cutter looked across at eleven platoon to his left. They were at the base of that mortar's line of fire, directly below the section of the track that was gone. The Guats must have identified their hole. As holes went it was deep but no sangar, not like this one with some fortifications around the top.

Rhah, up from his turn at defending the way out, was peering that way too. 'Jock and Stan an' those lads are gonna be right in it,' he shouted. A good hole could sustain a hit almost directly on top of it, on the lip at least, and still save the soldiers inside, but they had to get a direct hit sooner or later.

Smoke, Elias thought, we will need smoke to move. They can't draw a bead through smoke, but they can saturate the place with fire. What's worse? It hasn't been used yet, so they may not be ready for it; we may be able to get those lads out of there. Jonesy liked anything you could fire off the front of your weapon; he would tab with shit on the off-chance. Jonesy had picked up smoke at Bragg; Cutter had seen him.

'Jonesy!'

The soldier looked back at him and then ducked as another mortar round came in, showering them with dirt, leaves and clods of earth.

'How much smoke have you got?'

'Two.'

'Let's have 'em.' As Jonesy went into his day-pack, Elias popped his head over the top to look at the eleven platoon hole thirty yards away. 'Stan! Jock!' he yelled. 'You guys get the fuck out of there!'

'Yeah,' came the shouted response. 'How? You gonna beam us up?'

Rhah chuckled and Elias grinned, ignoring the Clansman that was going off, someone wanting sitreps. This was shit – there was nowhere on the bank that was safe, but eleven's hole had to be the worst.

'We'll pop smoke. Come this way.'

'Never make it,' came the yelled response. 'We'll sit this –'

'Get out of there,' Elias yelled. 'We can give you smoke!' As he said the last word, he saw something falling, a blur. The blast blew him backwards into the hole and when he

372

struggled up, the acrid smell of the HE in his nostrils and the birdshit taste in his throat, smoke was trailing away on the whispers of breeze. The hole had taken almost a direct hit; there was a huge crater in the ground beside it.

'Fuck! Rhah, get on to Big Harry. Fire support, vector that fucking mortar. I'm going –' But suddenly Spud was up and moving, out of the hole like a rabbit and running across the gap. An M60 on the other side opened up, and at the slit, Jonesy was joined by Plonker and then Rhah, pouring fire across towards where the M60 was located, adrenaline coursing through their bloodstreams.

'He's in,' Elias shouted, picking up one of the two smoke grenades. 'Ready for suppression fire!' On the right in the other section hole beside them, they were following the drama, Elias knew, because he could hear Scruffy, the lancejack over there, calling directions to put their LSW on to the M60, and the gunner calling for 'box'. It was pointless however; the 60 was well back, three hundred metres, carefully positioned to cover just that gap, almost out of range for an SA80, and hidden as it was, getting it would be a bitch.

'Spud!'

'I've got one,' he yelled back. 'Gimme smoke!'

'Wait for it!' someone yelled and what looked like a bundle of rags came slithering into their sangar from the back. It was one of the patrols blokes in a Gilly suit; in his hand was a Remington 3006 with a telescopic sight. A sniper, the new rifle courtesy of the stores at Bragg. He had spent an hour that morning sighting the scope and he was now happy. 'Tell him to wait. Where's the 60?' he asked, coming to his feet, his expression calm.

Rhah pointed to it, and the man moved forward. 'Right of the green building in the bushes there, maybe two-fifty yards back. See it?'

He peered through his scope for a full thirty seconds. 'Goddim,' he muttered. 'After my first shot throw your smoke.' He worked the bolt action and leant forward. This was child's play – three hundred metres with a ten-power Unertl scope and he could put bullets into a matchbox. The gunner was well concealed, but watching the movement through the sight he worked out that he was looking at part of his shoulder and neck. That was enough. He sighted and fired; in a blur his hand worked the bolt and before the smoke grenade had hit the ground he fired again, and then a third shot. As the smoke billowed slowly across, Spud came up out of the hole, a man across his shoulders. The M60 was silent, but other odd shots rang out, the scrotes shooting into the smoke. Spud was still moving, his rifle and the wounded man's in his hands. Suddenly he stumbled, falling forward and then dragged himself and his burden the last few feet and into the sangar and fell into Elias's and Rhah's arms. Elias took the casualty and laid him down on his side in the back of the hole. It was Jock, a mate of the lads. He had a huge back wound, the whole thing open, his spine and internal organs visible through the blood and torn muscle tissues.

'Well done, Spud. Fucking ballsy, mate,' Rhah said. Spud was looking at him, taking great heaving breaths, his face pale, and then he settled to one knee and then the other.

'You OK?' Rhah asked.

'They're dead. All dead,' Spud said.

'Are you OK?' Rhah asked again, thinking, fuck, he's going into shock, he's been hit.

'I don't think so,' Spud said. 'I feel like shit.'

Rhah took him and eased him backwards. 'Where are you hurt?'

'Others are dead,' Spud said. 'All dead.' His eyes rolled back and his breathing was ragged.

'Fuck it,' Rhah muttered and he began pulling Spud's chest webbing away. 'Stay with me! Spud!' There was blood underneath, plenty of it. He looked up. Elias was busy with Jock. 'Somebody give me a hand.'

Elias looked over. 'Jonesy,' he said, 'get on the net, get a medic down here.' Jonesy bent for the radio and the sniper put his rifle down and dropped down on one knee to help. At the slit Plonker had ceased firing and was just standing looking down at the activity at his feet, his expression blank, stunned, disbelieving. Rhah had found an entry wound and a very large exit hole, big enough to put a fist into. A bullet had hit Spud low in the right chest. He took a shell dressing from Spud's belt-kit to cover the exit wound where most of the blood was coming from. Another dressing landed at Rhah's feet. He looked up. Plonker had thrown it. Each man carried a dressing or two to be used on himself and you never used your own for another's wound in case you were next, then your mates always knew that the nearest dressings were in your own belt-kit. Rhah didn't throw it back but ripped the cover off and used it, the sniper holding the dressing on the back wound. 'You'll be fine, mate,' the sniper was saying. 'Just get you patched up.' He looked back down at the large wound his hand was covering, his expression angry, his eyes hard.

Plonker was still standing looking down at Spud's face; drawn, pale, his breath rasping, his eyes tightly closed in pain, as Rhah taped the dressings in place. 'Give 'im something for the pain, mun.'

'No,' Elias said, looking up from Jock, 'can't. Morph slows the respiratory system.'

'Get down here and hold him,' the sniper said, coming up and reaching for his rifle. Plonker put his weapon down and stepped over the tangle of legs and people in the mud at the bottom of the hole.

'Where's the medic?' Elias yelled looking at Jonesy.

'Up at the road,' Jonesy said, putting the radio handset down. 'He was taking someone out when those bombs came in.' They were on their own – no medic.

'Fuck it!' Elias snapped. Plonker settled down beside him and took Spud in his arms, his expression still one of shock. The sniper was on his feet now, reaching into his pocket, taking out big shiny bullets. He had emptied the magazine on his rifle and was reloading with what looked to Elias like hunting rounds.

'Big Harry's coming over,' Jonesy said.

'I wouldn't let him see those,' Elias said to the sniper, nodding at the bullets he was loading.

'Fuck 'em,' the sniper muttered. 'What do you think did that?' He nodded down at Spud.

'What the fook are you saying, mun?'

Elias, still with Jock, was watching Plonker. He was gutted;

375

the big, insensitive, rock-hard Geordie had tears running down his cheeks.

'The exit wound. Some bastard over there is using hollow points.'

'Fook, mun.' It was a little cry of despair as Plonker looked down and held Spud closer. He must have nudged something in Spud's pocket, because a little synthesized voice said, 'To infinity and beyond.'

Chapter Thirteen

Big Harry slithered in from the comms trench. He was filthy, his shirt torn, his eyes taking it all in. Standard for combat, he was no longer wearing any badges of rank and his radio operator had coiled the Clansman radio aerial down into a low loop round his back. Nothing attracted fire like an aerial sticking up in the air. Platoon CP was now with Big Harry, wherever he happened to be.

'How are they?'

'Not good, sir,' Elias answered, looking up. 'Jock's dead. So are the other three in that hole. Spud was hit in the chest carrying him in. Sir, we need to get him out of here, back to field surgical.'

'We're cut off. Just do the best you can – company are going to cut a way through the "J" behind us here, and then start a diagonal trench. That will take a few hours. Right, the sitrep.' He lit a smoke. Elias noticed that – Big Harry didn't smoke. Other than that, he seemed to have it all together, to be in his element, even.

'Sar' Norris is dead. Corp'l Cutter, you are now acting platoon sergeant. Stay down this end of the line. This hole and three down to the CP. I'll take the far end. Lance-Corp'l Bundy?' Rhah looked over at him. 'This is now your section. We're on our tod till nightfall. As I said, company have rounded up some locals and some ten blokes to come through the trees behind us there, cut a new way in, but for now the strip between us is a killing ground, as is the track. They have cut us off and that means they are going to come across here, and now they are going to soften us. Dig deeper. The good news is we have fire support and plenty of ammunition.' He took a drag on his smoke. 'The Squadron lads in the position above us have got the Shrike pads and clackers for a whole shitload of mines in the shallows here. Patrols lads are up there already with a pair of fifty-cals and a gimmpy and I'm going to ask for some mortars to be zeroed on the same area, and get some people with LAWs and an M19 up on that rise – but we fight as if they aren't there, OK?'

Elias and Rhah nodded.

'Plonker?' Rees asked. 'You OK?'

The big Geordie nodded his head. 'Aye, sir, fookin' magic,' he said with bitter sarcasm.

Rees gave Elias a look that said keep an eye on him, and then moved back out of the sangar into the comms trench and Elias turned back to his lads. Rhah and Jonesy were controlled, but he had never seen Plonker like this.

'Have to get him back up to the medics,' Plonker said. 'I'll take him.'

'No. You'll never make it, either of you. He's better off here till nightfall. We'll take care of him as best we can, OK?'

Plonker looked up. 'He won't fookin' make nightfall. 'E's got one chance and that's if we fookin' get 'im out of 'ere now.'

'No!'

Spud weakly opened his eyes then. 'I'm ... O ... K,' but as he finished saying it he coughed blood. Rhah wasn't so sure and looked away. Jock, Stan the man, Stevie and Dave Cosby – all dead. And now Spud, with a hole in him, coughing blood and dying down in the mud and the cartridge casings.

Rees slithered down into his own central hole and sat back to take stock. His sergeant, Norris, was dead. He looked out of the back of the hole to where the body lay, covered by his own poncho. Killed by shrapnel, it was mercifully very quick. Like most of them, he had never really got to know Norris, but he was an effective sergeant and popular with the lads who had known him before he did his training stint. He had let Tyson-Davis know and it had been his call who to put into that role. Any of the corporals could do it, but he had gone for Cutter. Elias Cutter was young, only twenty-six, but he was stable, experienced, respected and in the shit that would count for more than classroom scores, time served or who could brown-nose better, and this was the shit, no doubt about that. Not since the Falklands, and maybe not even then, had a British army platoon taken so much sustained fire in such a short time. This was it, what they were paid for, trained for.

Fox looked up at the sky. It was hot, but thankfully the cloud had rolled through again, so instead of beating sun, it was just humidity, stinking, close, sweat in your eyes, dripping perspiration. He had got water out to his lads before dawn and he hoped it would be enough. Rehydration was critical to fighting effectiveness; heatstroke in tired men set in quickly. Thank God they weren't tabbing, he thought. The doctor from *Beaufort* was methodically working his way through the wounded. He had done a triage, stabilized three, then on Fox's insistence, looked at the lighter wounded so they could return to the line. The doctor wasn't impressed. 'None of these men should be going anywhere but a hospital.'

'I'm sorry, Doctor, I need them doing their jobs.'

'They should be relieved.'

'There's no one else. If they can pull a trigger, or load loose into magazines they go back into the line.'

'Can't you reorganize or something? I mean, it's hardly our fight, let alone theirs.'

'I won't tell you how to do your job – don't tell me how to do mine, and let's leave the morals for another time,' Fox replied frostily, his eyes red-rimmed, grainy. 'Get those men treated and ready to go back to work.'

On the southern edge of the airfield, Murray of the marines was hunkered down out of the line of fire. Most of the lads were doing the same, some snatching a little sleep. They had three blokes on stag, one at the centre and one at each flank, standing to, weapons at the ready in case the scrotes rushed them, but the intensity seemed to have tapered off in the last few hours, desultory shots being exchanged but not much more. They must be as tired as we are, he thought. Tired, short of ammo, hot and wishing like hell they were somewhere else, just like us.

'Siesta time, I think,' one of the lads muttered. 'Dago cunts. Middle of the day and everyone stops to go to sleep.'

'Fire a grenade over there, get 'em up and doing the macarena,' said the marine on the other side, singing the last word.

'Waddya reckon, sir?' one of them asked. 'They gonna come again?'

Murray looked at him. Honesty always, he thought, never bullshit the lads, they can see through it a mile away and will never trust you again. 'Difficult to say. Depends on how they were going to be extracted if it all went pear-shaped. They may have been so confident they hadn't planned on ever needing to get out again. If that's the case, then it's desperation time, their officer will try and get 'em moving. My bet? They don't have it in them. If we go at them, they will defend like lions, they will have to. But have they got the stomach to try another attack in daylight? I doubt it; they must know we can't be supported for at least another day or so. If I had that shower of shit, I'd wait till dark and come round the top end there.'

'They could walk through the camp, sir.'

'They don't know that,' Murray replied, wiping his face veil across his forehead. 'They will have assumed it's heavily defended.'

He looked across at his wounded. They were bearing it with stoic courage. The doctor from *Beaufort* was down in the CP; Garvey had met the helo and guided him into the enclave, and he had treated them and three of them were now back. Two would remain down there, quite badly wounded, and two were dead, over by the terminal wall, their green berets laid over their faces. Out of his twenty-man detachment, seven had been wounded or killed and he was down to thirteen fully fit, with three others able to load, fire, fight, but not yomp or carry loads.

It was an hour later, when the doctor had finished and crawled back up from the depths of the sangar to look out, he found himself alongside the major and another officer. Fox looked across at him and passed him a water bottle.

'You need to understand something, Doctor. Believe me, I'm not that big a bastard. I don't want anyone having to return to the line, I don't want any of my chaps having to fight at all. But this is the airhead, and this is their job. If they believe they can go on, then they must be allowed to do it.'

'With due respect, Major, that's crap. In my opinion –' But Fox was tired, and didn't like his men being patronized. He interrupted.

'You didn't try and stop the marines going back to their positions, did you?'

'No. I knew –'

'So why my men? Political correctness, no doubt. You're defending the downtrodden people of the developing world who are so poor they have to join the belligerent fighting forces of a nasty old nationalistic nation, clinging to the last vestiges of empire, to put food on the table? And here they are in someone else's war. Ever been to Nepal, ever commanded Nepalese troops? Speak Gurkhali?' He jerked a thumb at their line. 'They are Gurkhas, enormously proud people, with a long tradition to live up to. I speak their language, I know Nepal and I have immersed myself in their culture and I am very honoured to command such men. So let me tell you, you hold one of these chaps back, when he and his mates know he could be with them, alongside them, you are working directly against them. With Gurkhas that's a mistake. It's detrimental to morale, to standard operating procedures, and to the mindsets and attitudes of the men. So watch my lips, you patronizing little prick; when I want any opinion other than a clinical one, I'll ask you for it. Until then let my blokes do what they do, their way! Have I made myself clear, Doctor?'

'You have, sir.'

'Very good. Carry on.'

Fox slithered away down the comms trench towards the nearest hole. Captain Brock, who had spent the night digging revetments, foxholes and sangars with his assault pioneers, looked across at the naval surgeon.

'Never mind, Doc. That was what civvies call "assistance in realigning thinking".' He grinned. 'We call it a beasting. Fox,' he nodded after the man crawling away, 'he's a good man, and there's not an officer in the brigade who cares more about his toms.'

The company command post was empty except for a support platoon fellow directing anyone looking for Tyson-Davis to where he was, at the rear of the twelve platoon position. 'Robo' Jennings was with him, and ten toms from thirteen platoon were hacking their way through the thick scrub and secondary growth, supported by a gang of local men, BDF, who had reported to help. One of them had come with his brother, a logger, in his truck. On the back was the equipment he used and now the chainsaws were running. It was gruelling work – years of slashing and cutting had resulted in thorn, wait-a-bit bush, young saplings so thick you couldn't see more than a foot in front. The creepers clogged the chainsaws, gave under axes and bounced back. To compound the problems the slope was steep, wet from the rain, and the men were sliding around.

'How long?' Tyson-Davis asked.

'He reckons three hours, sir,' Jennings responded. 'There's only room for one man at the front with a saw, the rest clearing up what he cuts. Trouble is, every time a mortar comes in, work stops.'

'Make it two hours, do whatever you need to do. I want another way in there and support for twelve before dark. Get them going and meet me back at eleven's hole under the bridge.' Jennings nodded; from there you could see along the bend in the river to the beleaguered twelve platoon position and the track.

Over the rise on the riverbank the battle ebbed and flowed, the Guatemalans trying to soften the positions overlooking the ford, tire them out, wear them down the old-fashioned way, by attrition. Jonesy and Rhah were at the front of the sangar, not firing back but conserving ammunition. Plonker was down with Spud; he looked up at Cutter.

'Elias, mate, we have to get him out, mun. I'll take him.'

'No. You'll never get there, and neither will he.'

'Let me try.'

'No.'

He looked up again. 'Fook you, Elias. He's my mate, you know. My mate.' He looked down and when he looked up again, there was anger in his eyes and through the anger the tears were welling up. 'You're all my mates. I never had mates, never had fookin' no one. Fookin' orphanage, fookin' care, fookin' social services, I never had no one till now. I'm not leaving 'im to die down 'ere.'

'We're doing our best for him; you're doing your best for him.' He looked round, then up at Rhah. 'Right. I'm next door.'

Plonker watched him go and quickly stripped off Spud's belt-kit and gollock. He peeped over the left lip of the sangar – fifty yards. They see me, fire a mortar bomb and I'll be across by the time it hits. 'Come on then, you fat scouse git,' he said softly. He hefted Spud's limp form over his shoulder, and with his rifle in one hand and the other holding his wounded comrade across his shoulders, he climbed out of the sangar and began the run up to the track. Rhah saw him move from the corner of his eye, and he knew what Plonker was going to try and do.

'Fuck! Cover him!' he yelled, sweeping the LSW back and forth. Jonesy was firing too and the patrols soldier entered the fray. In the hole alongside they heard it, and began shooting too, pouring out suppression fire as fast as they could. The toms were yelling now, screaming encouragement. 'Go! Go! Go! Run! Go Plonker!' Above them the B Squadron team with the command mine Shrike pads could stay silent no longer; their two GPMGs opened up, and LAW rockets seared outwards.

Everyone watched Plonker make the track, run, stumble, gather himself like a racehorse, willing him on. Fire was reaching out at him, bullets plucking at his clothing and webbing, on the killing ground of the exposed section of the track. He stumbled again but ran on, bullets hitting the ground at his feet and up the bank behind him. A 66 mill rocket streaked past his front and then another behind him, exploding as they hit the rise of the ground, and he kept going, Spud over his shoulder. 'Go! Go! Go! Go!' yelled everyone watching him, and cries of 'Come on! Keep going!' came from the lads on the other side. Suddenly he was there, falling to his knees, two ten platoon toms taking Spud from him, dragging great draughts of air into his lungs.

'OK, relax, we got 'im,' their sergeant said. 'Stretcher, someone! Corp Davis, get this man up to the field surgical team.'

'Yowa cunce tek carra 'im, eh! He's a mate,' Plonker spluttered, through his gasping. Sixty yards away across at the beleaguered twelve platoon position the lads were cheering and clapping, chanting and whistling.

'We will,' the sergeant said.

'Fookin' 'ell, I'm knackered,' Plonker said. 'You take care o' Spud! Ya promise, mun!'

'We will. Stretcher is coming down,' the sergeant promised.

A minute later Plonker watched Spud carried away. 'Well, gotta go.' He stood up, hitched his belt-kit tighter and slipped the safety off his rifle, his face wreathed in his maniacal grin, the gap in his teeth showing through.

'You stay here,' the sergeant growled. 'You're going fucking nowhere.'

'Na' Plonker said, his face a mask of concern. 'Canna stay 'ere, mun.'

'Why not?'

Grinning, he told them, 'Yowa ten coonce are a bunch of pooftas,' and with that he went out of the hole and on to the track, running back through the exposed ground the way he had come. The enemy gunners, caught out by the speed of his return, or maybe thinking that no one could be that crazy, missed the first twenty yards but then opened fire with a vengeance. The toms were screaming like it was the closing seconds of a cup final match as Plonker pounded towards them, his knees pumping, a rocket streaking past him, bullets tearing up the ground around him, and then he dived the last few feet into the hole.

The toms were ecstatic, clapping, cheering, whistling. The firing had stopped on both sides; the only noise was the raucous chanting coming from twelve platoon. Along the river they could hear it, up at the eleven position under the bridge support where Tyson-Davis and Robo Jennings were, the chant drifting up from the twelve platoon position – Ooo-Aaa, Plon-Kaa, Ooo-Aaa, Plon-Kaa.

'Plonker Smith. He never was the sharpest tool in the kit, but my God, there's no doubting his courage,' Jennings said softly.

'Airborne,' Tyson-Davis said softly. 'Outstanding.' He paused, thinking there's nothing wrong with morale down there and that act has done nothing but strengthen it. He felt immense pride in the toms chanting and cheering down on the bank by the ford, and he felt honoured to lead them. 'His chances of surviving that were just about nil. That was the bravest and the most stupid thing I have ever seen. I'm going to put him in for a gong. You, on the other hand, will give him the beasting of his career.' Jennings nodded.

Down in the sangar Rhah, then Elias and finally Big Harry all gave Plonker a bollocking, but it was difficult to sustain any seriousness when the other blokes in the platoon were still on such a high. Plonker, on a roll, had listened and nodded to Big Harry's beasting and then as the lieutenant crawled away, he reached down and tripped the recording on Spud's Buzz Lightyear, the little voice carrying over to the next hole. His final act of defiance was to take the letter from Barclaycard, the one telling him that his card had been suspended. He pinned it to a stick and then waved it over his head. The Guatemalans acted predictably and it was soon hit by several bullets.

'Ya see,' he said, 'they reckon Barclaycard are cunts too.'

By four o'clock the track through the dense secondary growth from the rear had been finished. The men who had cut their way through, exhausted, dripping in sweat, their kit torn and filthy, stood back to allow others to pass carrying trenching tools, spades, mattocks, short-handled digging implements rounded up by the Belize Defence Force people. These fresh men would now begin cutting a diagonal trench through the soft earth, down past where the B Squadron team were positioned, past the open strip towards the lower level where Rees's twelve platoon were on the ford. The trench had only to be a channel, twelve to eighteen inches deep, no deeper than a drainage ditch beside a road; with the earth removed piled up on the river side it would be deep enough for a man to crawl along, unseen and out of the line of fire. Behind them ammunition boxes were moved up. Every foot dug was a foot closer and when the river dropped enough and the main attack came, as they all knew it must, every foot they weren't exposed to the withering fire was a bonus.

England

At Aldershot the pace was frantic. Vehicles already loaded were formed into convoys and two had left, under military and civilian police escort, for the short drive to an RAF base near Alton. Colonel Wallace, OC 2 Para, was driving his people at maximum speed. It was just after 2300 Zulu; the schedule was that air mounting would take place at 0500, and by Christ that would happen. The twelve-man detachment from 216 Parachute Signals Squadron had reported in ready to go, the field ambulance and a small unit of air-mobile field hospital were due through the gate by midnight. The embuggerance was the extra rifle company – half the Gurkhas coming over from 1 Para had arrived, with typical army efficiency, to find their bergens hadn't. The truck on which they were loaded, which only had to travel a third of a mile, was now parked somewhere in a sea of green trucks, senior NCOs trying to sort out the mayhem. The Gurkhas' company commander had sent his own men out to find it, in patrols of two, reporting back to the CSM every half-hour. He had already made his decision; if they didn't find the bergens, then they would load stores into whatever they could find and just go with belt-kits. The bergens could follow, his own included – there was no way his blokes were going to be left out of this one.

'Don't worry about us,' the major said to Wallace. 'We're here. We have weapons and belt-kits and enough containers for ammunition. Either way, we'll be ready.'

Colonel Wallace nodded and took a message slip from someone who had run to find him. He looked at his 2 i/c and passed him the flimsy, a huge grin on his face. 'The Foreign and Commonwealth Office have come through. If Fox can hold another couple of hours he'll have some help and we will have an airhead.'

Away from the frenzied preparations at Arnhem lines, down in the sleepy married quarters the mood was one of apprehension. The streets were quiet, tense, just the occasional person out with small children, who oblivious to what was happening were still playing normally. Almost everyone was indoors, watching their televisions as the reports came through. Maddy Jennings, like many other D Coy wives, had a house full of people. The hardcore centre position was in the small sitting room, a dozen wives and girlfriends clustered round the television, the channel selector moving between ITN, BBC, and on the satellite channels, Sky and CNN. The kids were mostly next door, or upstairs.

As the 2 Para padre was at Bruneval getting ready to go with the battalion, another padre attached to 5 Airborne Brigade had been round with a families officer to see if everyone was all right, but when the wives realized they had no news they were given short shrift and everyone turned back to the TV.

People had brought food and there was a team in the kitchen getting ready to feed everyone; Maddy popped through every now and then to see if they could find everything. She was back in the sitting room when the front door silently opened and a tall, slim, good-looking teenager quietly entered the house. Uncharacteristically, he took off his baseball cap – his father had asked once if it was permanently attached – and dropped it on the stairs, and slipped into the sitting room. Everyone was watching the television screen, a report from CNN showing satellite images released by the Pentagon of the three Guatemalan brigades hours before the invasion, and library footage of RAF Harriers in the Falklands, the reporters saying that the White House had announced that the Royal Air Force was now for the first time operating from a mainland US military facility. There was no report of the strength of the force that had arrived, just some hazy long-range shots from the nearest point that the outside broadcast vehicle could get to the 'British air force' encampment. The reporter then said that their analysts had predicted that the weather would not allow operations for at least the next twelve hours.

'But,' said one of the wives, a Merseyside lass, her voice near to cracking, 'there's only a blurry river between 'em. What's to stop them dropping their bombs on our lads?' A woman breezed past the teenager in the door. 'Hello, Tom,' she said with false brightness.

'They will mark their line,' Tom said. His mother, hearing his name, had whipped her head around and just looked at him, tears rising in her eyes. She had told no one he had gone. 'It's called the FLOT,' he explained, 'front line of troops. The aircraft then come in very low, in daylight, parallel to the FLOT, so there's no chance of a mistake.' He looked at his mother, a half-smile on his face. 'Our pilots are very good, the best in the world. Dad slags them off, but he wouldn't have any other flying close battlefield support.' She was fighting back the tears. Thank you, Lord, you have brought my baby home.

'You sure?' the lass challenged. He nodded. 'Blurry hell, someone who knows sooming at last. Come 'ere, chuck. Get your bum down here and interpret what these wallies are saying. Is 'e one of yours, Maddy? Oh, don't you look like your dad, eh? Come on, come 'ere.' She moved a few inches and patted the sofa beside her.

On the floor against the wall a woman sat with a small child on her lap. 'Where's Belee, Mum?' the child asked.

'A long way away, pet. A long way away.' She held the child closer and watched the television, unable not to. Her man was in there somewhere, her life. Suddenly, the rows, the shortage of money didn't matter, the arguments after separations for deployments and training seemed insignificant. She just wanted him home safely.

It was twenty-past-five local when HMS *Beaufort* contacted Fox. The comms link had been running all day, the relationship between Fox and Bennett, *Beaufort*'s captain, deepening. They were to expect friendly aircraft overhead in twenty minutes but few details were given. Fox looked up; the weather over the airport was clearish, a gap in the shitty stuff, low cloud but operable. If we can get air then they can, he thought. So who will get here first?

He quickly called Murray, Brock, Garvey and two of the sergeants in holes close enough. Garvey was concerned; his three-man patrol sent out to contact the BDF at the bridge had either thought better of it and gone home or had been unable to convince anyone to advance. Perhaps they had run into a Guat patrol – there had been no word or activity suggesting they had got through.

'It's good news, gentlemen,' Fox informed them. 'It's about time we had some. Expect air overhead and parachute entry, friendlies, out from Guyana. A company of 2 REP, the 2nd Battalion, the French Foreign Legion. Best bloody paratroops in the business, after us of course.' His smile widened. 'Now, if we can drop people in, the enemy can, so be alert. This airhead isn't secure yet.'

'Major,' Murray said, 'the Guats – if they grab this chance to jump in through cloud we have no way of identifying who they are till they hit the ground.'

'The friendlies are *la Légion étrangère*. They will have thought of that. We will have VHF comms by the time they are on the run in and that by my watch is in about ten minutes. Get back to your positions and prepare to lay down suppression fire. Corp Garvey, can you mark a DZ somewhere out at the far end?' The SAS soldier nodded. 'The further from this area they come in the better. Good, on your way all of you, you have done good work, excellent work.'

Fox was five minutes out and as the two French C-130s called in, they were advised to drop on the markers north-west of the airport. Garvey didn't have smoke and so lit three small fires, sweating, having run most of the way to the DZ, with a gallon of diesel taken from the JCB digger. The smoke curled up black as pitch, a marker for the parachutists to aim at as they broke through the cloud.

The Guatemalans saw them at the same moment that the defenders did, and the fire reaching up at the 2 REP soldiers was proof enough that these weren't enemy paratroops. They landed with precision, coming in towards the smoke, the lead jumper with a French *tricolore* attached to his feet on a weighted line. Several of them touched down east of the LZ on the airport itself, dropping straight to the ground facing the threat and waiting for their colleagues to move forward past them. Garvey stood in the open, his rifle in the air above his head, calling to them in very bad French, lest he be mistaken for an enemy, and as their OC landed a dark-skinned soldier pointed him out. As he arrived the major was getting a report and Garvey understood enough French to take it in. Two of the *légionnaires* had been hit by small-arms fire on the descent and Garvey grimaced slightly – these were Foreign Legion. When he was a Para, other than the Regiment these were the only bastards they respected; hardcore, iron-disciplined, extremely well-trained, extremely well-motivated fighting men. You don't shoot at these men while they were in parachutes and expect any quarter once they hit the ground. The major wasn't wearing a helmet, but his green beret, and below it his skull was shaven down to the skin. He was mahogany brown from the sun, and had a knife-scar that ran the length of his cheek.

'Corporal Garvey, 22 SAS. *Moi france est merde*, aaah . . .' Another officer dropped down beside them.

'Jean-Luc Pascale,' the Frenchman said. 'This is Captain Du Preis.'

'Howzit,' the other man said, extending his hand. 'Fire away. The major's English is pretty good, better than mine.' His accent was South African or maybe Zimbabwean, Garvey thought, and his face betrayed his excitement.

'Good.' He drew on the ground. 'Main line at the eastern end, Major Fox is down there with two platoons of Gurkha 2 Para opposing we think maybe 250 Guatemalan marines. Here,' he drew another box, 'is the terminal. We have a Royal

Marines troop, half-platoon strength, facing another force, maybe a company. Up this end are my Belize people. Fifty of them. No enemy up here as yet.'

The major nodded. 'Weapons?'

'They have mortars but we think they have run out of bombs. There have been none for several hours now. M60s, some 66 mill rockets, and infantry weapons. We had gunfire support from HMS *Beaufort* last night and again at noon today, with the tide, but the ship has now run out of HE. Apparently there is more coming down from the US, but we aren't sure when that will be.' He shrugged.

'Your view?'

They are stranded, Garvey thought, they have to fight. But I think their morale is shit and deep down they know they have given this their best shot and failed. Having said that, they still outnumber us four to one. If they knew that, they would have kept coming, but they didn't. Your arrival has just tipped the balance in our favour. They have gone from four to one to two to one, Third World army against 2 Para and 2 REP. No way, José! I think they have lost this one.

'My view, Major? They have no support or re-supply, they have many wounded. They could have won this last night, or at dawn, but they didn't. It's too late now, they are fucked,' he said with a grin.

Ten minutes later the two parachute majors from different armies shook hands.

'Very pleased to see you,' Fox said in flawless French.

'There are French nationals here, I believe,' Pascale said drily, playing the political game. 'My task is to secure this area so they may be evacuated if that becomes necessary.'

'Quite,' Fox replied wearily, playing along. His exhaustion was now apparent to the French officer. The bond and the mutual respect between the two airborne units was strong. In any major conflict involving NATO it was likely that they would be working together and they had trained together many times in that role, swapping parachutes and equipment, learning from each other.

'OK. I have said the official bullshit. Unofficially my orders are to assist you in any capacity within the airport perimeter and immediate area. Don't worry, *mon ami*,' the 2 REP officer declared with a smile, 'we shall hold your airhead. You may rally to your colour. Leave your wounded with me. We 'ave a field surgical team with us.'

There was a rolling burst of fire from somewhere down the road.

'Very well,' Fox said. He looked across at his radio operator. 'Platoon commanders to the CP.'

A hundred yards away a bizarre meeting was taking place. Three of the *légionnaires* dropped into a Gurkha sangar they had been allocated to relieve. The first one in was a Laotian, who spoke his own language and French, meeting a Nepalese who spoke only Gurkhali and English. They grinned, shook hands and did what soldiers have always done – swapped cigarettes. Other trading would take place later; 2 Para wings were very *de rigueur* in 2 REP and if someone could spare the crossed kukris that they wore beneath their wings, they would be lifelong buddies – but with rifle fire snapping past over their heads, that could wait.

San Ignacio

It was dark, black as pitch, the only illumination coming from tracer rounds and muzzleflash, until the cloud cover broke and then moonlight bathed the battlefield. Driven by Robo, the lads digging down to twelve platoon had come through, at least near enough to support the line. There was a ten-foot gap as night began to fall, but Tyson-Davis had been on it and behind the diggers were ammunition boxes, more soldiers with LAWs, flares, extra Claymore mines. When they got to ten feet they began passing supplies forward, fire ripping above them, men skittering across the last few feet using the cover of darkness to get forward and into the comms trench and down to the sangars.

The holes prepared the night before by the Gurkhas were staggered and at no time till now were all the holes occupied. As the rested Gurkhas moved down, Rees's platoon were moved fifteen feet back into the second line of holes. The hole had a clear arc of fire, but for now they could relax. This would be as near to relief as twelve platoon would get for the time being, and back in their new hole, with the luxury of comrades in front of them, they could for the first time all settle in the bottom of the hole at the same time, rip open their vacuum-sealed rations and get some scoff in them, brew up, and rest, without one of them always at the front standing to, or actually fighting. Big Harry had no rest – this was Estelle's platoon, without their officer, so he absorbed them into his own, and personally positioned the Claymore that had come down, checked each section and fire team. Any time now they would come.

An hour before, down on HMS *Tonka Toy*, still moored up under a leafy overhang, the boat troop lads had a quick Chinese parliament with Lieutenant Lewis. The boat was here, but wasn't much use unless the scrotes came down the river again. They agreed what they wanted to do and swung it by Chard. He approved; HMS *Tonka Toy* would move the quarter-mile up to the confluence so she commanded that stretch of water, and the river approach downstream. The boat troop lads would move off, link up with McKay's team and they would all tab back down the track to defensive positions at the ford.

By dark they were there and had dug themselves into a position where they could fight on the right flank, Gibbo moving down to find the 2 Para 'Rupert', to let him know they were there. For Big Harry, delighted as he was to have a Squadron fighting patrol on his flank, this was not an ideal command structure. He had his platoon, some Gurkha reinforcements without their officer, and now men from another unit on his flank.

He slithered into Elias's hole. Elias, now acting platoon sergeant, had this end of the line.

'All right?' Elias nodded. Big Harry passed him three parachute flares and a green. 'This is it then, lads,' Rees said, looking round the men in the hole. 'The water level is down. There is movement over there, they are moving down. They will try tonight. The good news is that the Reg is air mounting in about two hours and so will be here late tomorrow afternoon. Brigade follows. All we have to do is hold them for another twenty hours and we will have some help. The weather is clearing and the met people say that by first light it will be good enough for air. The other good news is that 2 REP have lobbed in to the airport. Looks like we still have an airhead.' There were some smiles and a fist punched at the air from Rhah.

'2 REP. Fookin' 'ell, wellard they are, 'ow come they got here so soon?' Plonker asked.

'They came out of Guyana,' Rees answered.

Plonker was none the wiser.

'What, in Africa?' Jonesy asked.

'That's Guinea, you dumb cunt,' Rhah enlightened him. 'French Guyana. South America, above Brazil.'

'Sir, any news on Spud?' Plonker asked, the geography lesson already boring him.

'No . . . but no news is good news,' Rees said, getting to his knees.

They talked for a few minutes after Big Harry had left, having eaten, sipping mugs of tea, satisfied as much as they were going to be. Suddenly the lads in the hole to the right and front of them opened fire at something with their LSW. Elias didn't wait. He dropped his tea and fired a parachute flare as weapons in other holes opened up and suddenly all hell broke loose. As the flare burst into light, there across a forty-yard front at the ford Guatemalan infantry were in the water and wading, running across where they could. There seemed to be hundreds of them. As they were fired upon, any attempt at surprise gone, they opened up, supported by fire from the far bank. Behind them a tracked vehicle, an APC, had burst out of the bush and was nosing its way down towards the water, then another. The B Squadron team, positioned above the Para line with their Shrike pads and electronic detonation kit let rip, and mines began to go off, along the far bank and in the water, the whole dreadful horror illuminated by muzzleflash, high-explosive detonations and the flare that swung merrily under its little parachute above them.

Rhah had their LSW up and was firing, Plonker and Jonesy

either side of him, Elias on the radio calling for fire support, shouting into the microphone to make himself heard. Down in the water the APCs were moving, troops behind them, and they had something else; rafts loaded with sandbags, that soldiers were pushing in front of them and sheltering behind. A LAW rocket streaked out from the right followed by another. The second must have hit the engine or transmission of an APC, and as Rhah watched, it ground to a halt, smoke pouring from its rear. He knew the men inside would be piling out of the back. Elias was going at the clackers, trying to initiate the Claymore, but nothing was happening. Suddenly the first of them were out of the water and Rhah swung the gun barrel. The sangar to their front right, their hole two hours before, was about to be overrun, one of the Gurkhas up stabbing with a bayonet, as figures rushed at them.

Plonker let out a scream of rage, and was scrabbling to his feet and they followed, moving as one, Rhah firing the LSW from the hip as they crossed the ten or so feet. Plonker, his magazine now empty, was swinging his trenching tool like a battle-axe, hacking into them, muzzleflash and screams in the dark. Mortars were now coming in on the water and the GPMGs from both ends had command. As the attack faltered the final horrific scene in Rhah's mind was Plonker, in the rage of a berserker, hacking into a Guatemalan soldier with his spade, the scene lit by burning white phosphorus. They settled down into the sangar with the Gurkhas; two of them were badly wounded. Elias skittered in from the back, thinking this should not have happened, they should never have got this far; his men were dragging in great panting breaths, their eyes wild. Plonker was covered in blood, his trenching tool in his hand, like something out of a horror movie. One of the Gurkhas was sheathing his kukri, the blood on the blade reflecting back light in a dull way. Elias stepped on something and flicked his hooded red-lensed torch downward. He bent, hauled up a dead Guatemalan and shoved him bodily out of the front of the hole. 'Right, listen up. Stay in here,' he said, 'guns up, get box loaded, move it! Jonesy, get that fucking Claymore in here and get a new set of wires on the terminals.'

There were still Guatemalans in the river sheltering behind the two APCs, and there were rafts, plenty of them, some forty or fifty feet away, some closer. A wounded man just on the edge of the hole was crying and whimpering, holding his stomach, his face a mass of blood. Another still alive moaned nearby. Someone fired another flare and Elias looked around in the eerie, harsh, swinging light. The shadows in the bottom of the hole were dark as pitch. Rhah was down there with a Gurkha tending to one of the wounded and his expression said it all. He seemed aged by it, older, saddened by his own brutality and that around him. Jonesy was twisting new wires on to the contacts on the Claymore that had failed to go off; the old wire had been cut in two by something. He seemed under control, the same old dependable fellow, and Plonker was up loading boxes of ammunition on to the two LSWs they now had in the sangar. He was filthy, covered in mud and blood, his hair matted with leaves and dirt and somehow he had lost his shirt and was stripped to the waist, wearing just his belt-kit and chest webbing above his trousers. He had been wounded in the struggle; something, a bullet maybe, had gone through the fleshy part of his lower back above the hip. Jonesy stopped him long enough to get a dressing on it and Plonker carried on.

He finished on the section weapons and then began changing magazines on the various SA80s around the sangar. That done he flicked a look back into the hole. For once he seemed to have nothing to say to anyone. He took up one of the LSWs, stood to and began to fire it, looking for targets in the water, where mortar bombs were still falling, forcing men into the open. It was brutal. As they broke or tried to go for new cover, they were cut down. One man, obviously completely traumatized by it all, got up and began to walk back to the other bank, dropping his rifle in the water, and for a few seconds sanity reigned and for the length of the Paras' line no one shot at him. There was a collective understanding – this man was no longer a threat to anyone and he was just doing what deep down they all wanted to do.

An hour after the 2 REP landing Fox led his column out of the enclave, the area round the road cleared by an aggressive two-platoon sweep by the *légionnaires*. Chances were they would have a contact or two before making the bridge and picking up the western highway; the most likely place was the intersection with the road, but there were 2 REP patrols out there already. When the Paras were clear, they would return to the defensive positions. In front was a big American pickup truck. Some of his blokes had sandbagged the roof and mounted a GPMG. Travelling in the two trucks were fifty-one remaining members of the original seventy-nine Gurkhas, Murray and his Royal Marines and Garvey with half of his BDF people. The remainder stayed at the airport to work with the *légionnaires* and a very pissed-off marine, the man trained to call NGS, in case *Beaufort* was re-supplied with shells for her gun and the 2 REP people needed to call it in. One of Garvey's blokes with a mobile phone had called ahead.

At JB's Sally had taken the call and immediately stirred her people into action and by the time the convoy pulled up on the road, JB's staff were waiting for them with food. The highway was still busy with people running east away from the fighting, but not clogged like the day before. When the trucks halted, burger buns with fillings, sandwiches and bottles of water were passed up in big plastic sacks. The men were ravenous and ate like wolves. They were filthy dirty, some with bloodstained bandages, exhausted, loading loose rounds into magazines, tending wounds, but still managed to look cheerful as the food was passed up.

'Oi, Sally! Got any beers?' one of the marines yelled from the back of the truck.

She stood back, her hand on her hip, a raunchy parody of some southern roadhouse girl and replied, 'I got the beers, sweetheart, you got the time?'

The lads loved it, but Murray thought he'd better bring this exchange to a halt. 'No,' he responded for them all. 'Thanks anyway.'

A very pretty girl was passing up food and she looked at Murray. 'Do me a favour?'

'Anything for you, darlin',' one of the marines responded.

Murray smiled at her, his smile saying forgive them – they are basic, but they're mine. 'Sure,' he said.

'My name's Sophie. When you get there – Lieutenant Rees, D Company; tell him we are here and safe, OK? Sophie and Helen.'

'No problem.'

The trucks began to move. 'Take care,' she called quickly, waving to them as they drove off into the darkness.

A few minutes later they were sitting looking at each other. It was just past eight o'clock and JB's was quiet as a grave. The four of them sat at a table, Sally the most affected by what she had seen. Her eyes were moist and she rubbed her hand across them, images of the British soldiers in her mind. The bandages, the walking wounded still prepared to go on and fight again.

'Dammit,' she said. 'They are fighting and dying up there.' She thought for a moment, then she lifted her head and her shoulders squared. 'But there are things we can do.' She looked up and into the kitchen. 'Chloe, get John and Paulo. Saddle up.' She clapped her hands together. 'I want the eight-burner and the paraffin fridge on the truck. Gas bottles, some workbenches from the kitchen. I want every burger roll we have, then get that damned baker out of bed. I want another five hundred rolls by midnight, another load by first light. Lemme have three hundred pounds of steak mince, two sacks of onions, two boxes of tomatoes, two cases of lettuces, oregano and burger seasoning. I want ten dozen hot dogs, all the fruit we have, thirty sacks of oranges. Get some people up here picking them. A case of ketchup and another of mustard, twenty cases of soda, twenty cases of water –' She stopped and smiled. 'Twenty cases of beer. I want coffee, tea, all the milk we have. Got any chickens? Lemme have twenty now and fifty later. Rice – what do those Gurkhas eat? Have to be basmati, we don't have anything else. Chilli sauce, curry powder. Big pots.'

'We'll help,' Helen offered.

*   *   *

398

The Harriers were on the move. Not wanting to waste the hours of darkness when the whole detachment could be moving forward, the heavy aircraft were repacked, ordnance taken off the hardpoints and the whole operation began the move to Ambergris Cay, twenty-five miles north of St George's, the biggest of the Cays and the only one with a viable runway.

RAF Regiment had secured the airfield, fuel had been lifted in and they were ready. The objective was to move to the first FOB and be operational with aircraft ready for sorties by first light. Everybody was excited with the pace of events, although some were dismayed to be leaving behind the wonderful facilities provided by the US personnel at Pensacola. Portable showers, latrines, canvas mess halls and air-conditioned Portakabins were paradise to what they were going into.

In the UK there were already 2 Para elements at RAF Brize Norton awaiting their orders to air mount. This had been achieved in record time; B Coy and HQ Coy were there already with Support Coy and the Gurkha Coy from 1 Para about to leave Aldershot in a convoy escorted by civilian police. Well-wishers, families and friends lined the road waiting to wave them off, many frightened and tearful.

The brigade commander was delighted and when Colonel Wallace, OC 2 Para reported his final elements were ready to leave the garrison, he telephoned Northwood with some pride to advise that 2 Para, as JRDF spearhead, going to war for real, had been able to air mount in under twenty-four hours, an astonishing achievement.

San Ignacio

The fighting had abated, and there was now a lull in the battle. A Squadron team was still pounding the far side with an automatic grenade launcher, wearing them down, making any advance by a fresh unit hazardous. The river flowed past the burnt-out APCs in the ford, washing the bodies of the dead away downstream, and although there had been a second attack, it had failed. There were still a few men clinging to the rafts, but they too had floated away.

Rees thought they were pulling back the unit who had attacked to make room for fresh troops to come forward, and for now it was quiet along the front. Squadron had moved a big thermal-imaging night-sight taken from a Milan down to the forward position and now two of their blokes took it in turns to watch the far side, every now and then calling for the grenade launcher to cease firing. If they didn't the flashes from the explosions made the electronic optics flare and it was useless. They had treated the wounded Guatemalans and had them removed along with their own casualties for treatment by the surgical team. Plonker had refused to go and see the medics. Down in the hole one of the Gurkha lads was standing to; Rhah, Plonker and Jonesy were down in the mud, sweating, trying to rest, talking softly. Rhah was deep in thought, silent but for the odd comment. The philosopher was still there, but something else had come through – disgust. The conversations in fighting holes were muted, soft with a particular etiquette. Rhah had told them that on a racing yacht, whatever was said on the rail late at night stayed there. Whatever was said in a hole stayed there too. It was too personal a time, with too much honesty to feel that anything you said was ever to be repeated. It was at this time that Plonker began to talk, going deeper into his past, explaining the things he had said to Elias when he wanted to get Spud away.

'O aye, fookin' care workers, homes. There were abuse too an' all. I were only a little lad then. This bastard, Dennis, he used to mek us. There were a bloke like Spud there, older than us, but just like him. He tried to protect us young ones from . . .' He trailed off. ''E told someone; 'e got sent away, no one believed him. The day he left he winked at us like, and said, "All ya got is your mates." I were up there beginning of last year. Last time I was there,' he looked at Rhah, who nodded, 'I found him, Dennis. Allas said I would, one day. Well I did. 'E were coming outa Boots. Yowa know how yowa never really know what yowa gonna do like? Well, I fookin' knew. I followed 'im. Down past the chipper and he took a short cut. I slotted the coont.' Jonesy looked up, but said nothing. 'I kept thinking that's for all the times you hurt us, and for all the times you hurt the others, and all the poor wee bastards yet to come and I kicked the fuck out of him and kept kicking till 'e were dead.' There was silence for a moment, no one saying anything until Plonker spoke again. 'I 'ad to get rid of me trainers and jeans, right, they were covered in blood, so I did that. Tha's why I ain't bin back there.'

'Jesus,' Jonesy uttered softly.

''E were right. All ya got is your mates. Yowa gotta take care of your mates.'

What they didn't know was their mate had just died, and so had another comrade. Within five minutes of each other, Private Spud Murphy, D Company, and Lieutenant Toby Estelle, C Company, both succumbed to their wounds. Estelle had always been touch and go, listed critical since arrival at the field surgical unit, but Murphy's deteriorating condition concerned them, and without X-rays they had to do it the hard way, invasive investigative surgery. They found that the bullet had fragmented and a piece of it, breaking off at a bone, had travelled downwards into his kidney. They couldn't save him and he died of acute renal failure.

Behind them the Gurkhas not in the line had been digging like Trojans down the comms trench from the rise and now it ran all the way to the twelve platoon positions. Eleven platoon, to their left and upstream to the bridge were holding and all of ten were now on the right, moved over to help defend the ford. Support platoon up on the road were ready to give fire support with the fifty-cals and their mortars and they waited. Tyson-Davis was now down in the shit with the lads from twelve, moving from position to position, sangar to sangar. It was nine-thirty when Fox's odd little mixed column drew up. There were raucous cheers from the support platoon blokes on the road, especially when they saw the handful of Royal Marines, one of whom couldn't resist saying, 'Relax, scumbags. The Royals are here!'

Several of the Paras looked through the darkness and then one finally identified the marines through the mass of milling men debussing from the transport.

'Fucking crap-hats!' he called. 'Where the fuck have you been then? Yomping on the beach?'

'Doing your job and holding your fucking airhead, you wanker!' came the response. There was some laughter that died as Tyson-Davis loomed out from the darkness and took Fox's offered hand.

'Welcome and well done, Dickie. Outstanding job your people did. Have your blokes move back down to the junction and then go left. Rest up for a couple of hours, get some scoff in them. I want them back up here to relieve twelve and your nine lads for an hour or so at midnight, so they can eat. When they're ready to go back I want to re-position things. It's a bugger's muddle down there with Harry Rees looking after his own lads, what's left of nine and half of eleven. Your blokes have taken a hammering, and I'm afraid Toby Estelle was killed.'

'Bugger,' Fox said softly. 'He was a fine young man. We had high hopes for him.'

'He fulfilled them – his command and his conduct were exemplary. Get your men settled, then come back up here and I'll give you the detailed sitrep.'

'You said my blokes have taken a hammering and you said, "what's left of nine"?' Fox stiffened slightly. 'What is,' he asked slowly, 'left of nine?'

'Half, Dickie, there's only half of them left,' Tyson-Davis answered.

'And eight?'

'Not quite as bad; they have been deployed here by the bridge, but they are down to twenty-seven fighting fit.'

Fox turned and looked back at the remnants of the other half of his company still coming off the trucks and the bus, some bandaged, limping, men who refused the option to remain with the 2 REP medics back at the airport. He had brought a reinforced company, one hundred and twenty men with some assault pioneers to Belize only forty-eight hours ago, for a training exercise. There were less than seventy left, many of those wounded.

'Dear God,' he uttered.

'They fought like lions,' Tyson-Davis said, like that was all that mattered, like that should be enough, and he regretted it immediately because Fox turned back to him.

'I never doubted they would, and you shouldn't have either. But they shouldn't have had to. They should not have had to fight here, alone and unsupported. Two platoons and a Sabre squadron? This was a disaster, a monumental fuck-up by someone that has cost my men their lives. How did this happen? How did they get three brigades up to the border before anyone noticed? It's the Falklands all over again. Someone knew and took no notice, or someone should have known, and Peter, don't lecture me on fate, limited resources or peace dividends. I'm too fucking tired.' He squared his beret and walked off.

Two hundred yards away, on the extreme left flank, Company Sergeant Major Nandu Goreng turned his eyes and ears to the left, the jungle. They had so far been out of the battle. The odd stray burst had come their way, a few mortar bombs, but the fighting had been downstream of his flank; he knew that couldn't last. The enemy had been held down there. Here at his position the river narrowed in places and even more so further up. If it were us he thought, we would have put patrols across the river, to probe, recce, harry the flank. He looked out at the jungle, pitch-black, the trees thick. There was a track along the bank, he knew; they would come that way. The patrols people had been out there twice during the day, he with them the last time. Lazy, tired men took the line of least resistance, and if the options were trying to move through the jungle at night or along the track, even the prospect of it being mined might be ignored.

They had set up two Claymores earlier in the day, but that was an area defence weapon, only of use if they actually got this far, and then it could be too late. He wanted to go out and recce. He had done it in daylight, paced the track with his counter: twenty-two paces, then it curved right around a big tree, then thirty paces, a steep climb of nine or ten feet, then down a spur, round to the left, forty-four paces, and so on. No one moved in the jungle at night. The chances of getting lost or injured were simply too high, and the noise movement made was astonishing, but he knew he could do it and quietly – if there was a Guatemalan patrol that had crossed the river he would find them.

He was thinking it through when there was a soft call from behind them and a big figure slithered down the slope into their sangar. It was the company commander, Major Fox, and the two men shook hands and exchanged genuinely warm greetings, Fox speaking in fluent Gurkhali. They hadn't seen each other since the previous day and much had happened in that time.

'Sar' Major, I want you to hand over here to the marines. At midnight we are going to re-form the company down by the ford.'

'Very good, sir, but, sir, before I go, I want to do a patrol, make sure they haven't crossed the river up round the bend. The water shallows there, maybe half a mile up, and there are rapids. If they have put a patrol across, then . . . I paced it this afternoon.'

Fox looked out at the inky blackness and a creeping flicker of fear went through him. He wasn't suited to the jungle, he hated it. He was too big and clumsy. But Goreng was good in it; he had passed out top of his course in jungle warfare, the SAS instructors remarking that he moved like a cat.

'All right. Take two men.'

'Better alone, sir.'

'Very well. I'll wait here with your chaps. When you come back, make the call of a male goat,' Fox said with a smile. The sar' major nodded. He was the best mimic in the company. He spoke quickly to the other men and then slipped over the lip and left the hole silently.

He moved along the track, counting his footsteps, quickly for the first thirty or forty yards and then slowing till his pace was that of a stalking tiger. Heel first, toe slowly forward, feeling for anything that would snap or make a noise. His night-sight was good, the moonlight breaking through the clouds and the trees and he made steady progress. He was half an hour out from the sangar, maybe one hundred and twenty metres, when he smelt them. Not tobacco smoke, but the smell of a man who smoked; chilli, toothpaste and, oddly, he thought he could smell aftershave lotion. The wind was blowing downstream towards him. He stopped and stood absolutely still for a full two minutes and listened. There were voices, up ahead somewhere. He was holding his rifle in both hands, but now he took the weight in his left and with his right he drew his kukri slowly out of the oiled, silent sheath, and began to move, as stealthily as before. It took him twenty minutes to move up on them and when finally he was able to see them, ahead in a clearing on the track, what he saw pleased him. It was only a patrol, seven or eight men.

They were sitting on the track in the clearing, resting, one of them squatting down beside their radio, another standing over him. Goreng watched from the edge of the clearing, taking it all in; they could be a recce party for a larger advance. They were sloppy, tired, apathetic; one of them lit a cigarette, his lighter flicking twice before the flame caught and there was a sudden snapped admonishment from the man standing by the radio – their officer, Goreng realized. The officer muttered something else and then began to walk towards the place where Goreng was hiding, his figure dark, but his hand movements unmistakable. He was undoing his fly buttons, coming over to relieve himself. The Gurkha sank down on to his knees and incredibly the man came closer and closer until he finally stood over him, separated by just a foot of undergrowth, and began to urinate in a steady stream. The aftershave, Goreng realized; up this close the smell was strong, as strong as the urine. Some splattered on to his knee and up he came. The opportunity was too good, to take out their officer.

The Guatemalan, Capitano José Biente, the man who had been in this forest a week ago, looking out over this very river, and just wanted to get back to the city, back to his girlfriend and the plaza, felt or saw something; he turned his face to the shadow and took the first blow from Goreng's kukri, a downward chop cleaving open his cheek and separating his lower jaw-bone from his skull. He had no time to cry out; the blow dulled his senses and he never heard or felt the second, the one that took his head from his shoulders, left it hanging by some skin, a fountain of blood shooting upward. Goreng lowered the body, cut the final strip of skin holding the head on and looked up at the group in the clearing, one or two of whom were now turning his way. He swung the head by the hair and let it go, scooping up his rifle as he did so. The head arced through the air and landed with a wet thump amongst them, actually in the lap of one of the soldiers. The man looked down, touched it, recoiled and someone flicked on a torch. He let out a blood-curdling scream and a second later the lone Gurkha opened fire, a hammering burst into them on full automatic, then another. He dropped as fire reached back, moved twenty feet, threw a first, then a second grenade, and slipped round to the right, firing from each new position.

Downstream they heard the scream and the shooting and the Gurkhas in the hole grinned at each other and stood to. They knew the Guatemalans had just met their CSM. Fox looked back at his radio man and signalled for the handset. They had enemy on the flank.

Sally's driver had simply stopped at the roadblock, chatted for a few moments and was then waved through. They found a spot back from the bridge, at an intersection where men were moving around and he pulled the truck over on to the wide roadside verge. 'This'll do,' Sally said. 'We can run a hose out of that house. Let's go!'

In twenty minutes the eight-burner was running and a big portable gas barbecue was lit. Stainless-steel work tables were out on the ground and they were hard at it, the regular staff dropping into a smooth rhythm. A curry mix begun back at JB's was loaded into pots, water was boiling for rice, burger rolls were split and buttered by the dozen. Salad to go with the burgers was already in bowls and hot dogs went into water to heat.

A generator in the truck gave them lights, and the kerosene fridges in the truck were running. They had been working almost unnoticed until a Chevy pickup roared to a halt.

'You shouldn't be here!' a civilian policeman called, stepping from the cab. Sally was about to reply when another vehicle pulled up, this one an army Land-Rover.

'Hello, boys!' she called. 'Anyone hungry? How about a famous JB's cheeseburger and a cold Coke? On the house.'

The four B Squadron blokes piled out and walked over, two of them recognizing Sally, and the thought of hot fresh food was too much for them.

'I could bloody murder one,' the first said.

'They shouldn't be here,' the policeman protested.

'Piss off,' one of the men muttered. 'I'm hungry.' He took the policeman to one side and said something and he drove away, two cold Cokes on the seat beside him. Support company men were next and the word spread like wildfire, and within half an hour, a tired medical orderly turned up and asked for food to take to the field surgical people. He left laden and was told to come back if they wanted more. The staff from JB's were now supplemented by other people who arrived from nowhere, Paulo and Chloe showing them what to do. Then even they were gently nudged aside by two men, both normally employed as short-order cooks at the Bel-Brit across the river, professionals who just dropped into the rhythm.

Men were lining up, Paulo and Chloe emptying great steaming ladles of rice with chicken and shrimp on to paper plates that buckled under the weight. Suddenly, alongside Sally and Sophie a man appeared, ramrod straight, his maroon beret squared perfectly on his head. Sophie recognized him immediately, as did Helen – Harry's boss.

'Good evening, ladies. Where did you all spring from?'

'Major,' Helen said. 'Major Peter Tyson-Davis, meet Sally Moretto.'

'Hi. I'm Sally, I've got a restaurant down the highway, JB's. I've come to feed my boys.'

'Well, you are doing that,' he began, smiling. He knew JB's. He wanted his men fed, but he was slightly embarrassed. He stepped forward so his conversation would not be overheard by the men lining up for food. 'This is a delightful surprise. We can sort something out later with money. I have two hundred and thirty-odd of my people and some BDF. How many can –'

'We'll keep cooking as long as they keep coming. I have some more supplies on the way, if you could advise the roadblock.'

'No problem.'

'And Major,' Sally added, 'I don't want your boys' money. Right now they are all that stands between here and JB's becoming an all-Spanish-menu part of Greater Guatemala.'

'Thank you.'

'No problem,' she smiled.

Sophie reached over and passed him a plate with a huge hamburger on it and a small bottle of cold mineral water. 'Handmade by me.'

'I will, but after my men have eaten.'

'Eat, Major!' Sally said. 'There's plenty!'

He took the plate and looked up at Sophie, seeing the question in her eyes, knowing what she wanted to ask. Sally turned away and as she did so he passed the burger to one of the hungry waiting men. He looked back at Sophie. 'He's fine,' he said, and as she smiled in delight he ripped the top off the bottle and drank deeply.

Lieutenant Murray slithered down the bank, his men following, and found Major Fox in the big sangar at the base of the shallow trench.

'We're to report to you, sir.'

'Very civil of you. Your blokes eaten? Watered?' Fox replied. He was pleased – the marines could hold this side and allow him to regroup his company.

'Yes, sir.'

'Right, let's get you briefed. This flank is now yours. You have two Claymores out there already, one at thirty metres by that tree,' he pointed, 'and one at fifty in a direct line. There's three more down there.' He nodded down into the sangar. 'My CSM is out there; he has had a contact so it's confirmed they have crossed the river. This is the only track downstream. I'll leave one of my blokes here for now and this fellow will know the password when the CSM comes in. When he's back get a sitrep and send them on, if you would. Your call, Lieutenant, but as soon as CSM Goreng returns I'd get some mortar fire in while you can. Things are likely to get a bit busy later.'

Murray nodded. His lads had been re-supplied and were

now packing plenty of box for the section weapons, link for the GPMG, rifle-grenades and LAW rockets. They had eaten, drank vast amounts of fluids, some had even slept on the way up in the trucks. They were ready.

'Right, listen up,' Elias said. He had appeared through the back a few moments before, from the adjacent hole. There had been another two attacks since the first major assault after dark, but these were still probes, the enemy commander trying to find the weak point at the ford. 'Relief is coming down. When they are in, get yourselves back up to the cutting. Have a bit of a break – there's hot scoff up back there somewhere. OK?'

They nodded and within five minutes they were on the move, back up through the comms trench. Tyson-Davis was at the top, chatting to each man as he came to his feet, directing them to the cutting through the undergrowth. Big Harry was at the rear, following the last of his platoon out, and when he reached the OC, Ted helped him to his feet. He was, like all of them, covered in mud, filthy dirty, tired, but so far unhurt.

'Well done, Harry. Your people have done an outstanding job. Get 'em fed and then, in an hour, back down here to this position. Oh . . . I just saw your young lady.'

'Sorry, sir?' He had got the message from the marines, passed down the line with some smirking and nudging – they were safe and well at JB's.

'Your young lady from the other night. Sophie, wasn't it?'

'Yes.'

'Well, I just saw her. She made me a burger – very nice it was too.'

The position on the intersection where Sally had set up now had all the appearance of a marshalling and rest area; harsh generator-powered lights under a canvas awning, huge jungle insects hovering in from the dark. There were men moving past, some sitting and eating, a few catching some sleep in their hour out of the line, Squadron vehicles, one or two refuelling, while the crews ate. Twelve's sections moved up in turns, just two men ahead of them for food. Rhah's section was in the middle of the line and when Plonker reached the front he ordered ninety-six cheeseburgers and offered his Barclaycard in payment. There was some laughter and Sally caught on immediately. She met him head on with a laugh and as they started on each other, Sophie looked round to the side, where someone had loomed up.

'Hello, you,' he said.

She wiped her hands and threw herself at him. He gave her a quick kiss and pushed her back as a chorus of whistles and cheers rolled towards them. 'Don't make your mind up yet, chuck,' someone yelled, imitating Cilla Black on *Blind Date*, 'here's our Graham!'

She blushed furiously.

Plonker, grinning from ear to ear with some food and cold drinks in his hands eased back from the table and was walking away when Robo Jennings appeared from the dark. Company Sergeant Major Jennings, the man responsible for discipline, had been waiting for Plonker to appear.

'PRIVATE SMITH!' he bellowed.

Chapter Fourteen

'Private fucking Smith! You long fucking streak of pig-shit thickness. Get here!' Robo, because there were ladies present, stepped behind a shed. Plonker rolled his eyes and turned towards the outburst and followed.

'What the fuck was that I saw earlier?'

'I dunno, Sar' Major. What was it yowa saw earlier?'

'Don't get lippy with me or I'll fucking drop you! I saw, I'll fucking tell you what I saw, I saw the most stupid fucking thing I have ever seen anyone in this regiment do.' The bellowing was so loud it carried past the shed, past the cooking area, and out to the twelve platoon lads, who fell silent. This was a classic, the mother of all verbal beastings. 'Once we are back at Arnhem you are in shit so deep you are fucking drowning in it! Bad enough you run across once, but then you do it again! Then what the fuck was it you were waving at them? You attract fire like shit attracts flies! And don't fucking eat when I am talking to you!' They didn't hear Plonker's response, but they heard Robo's next bellow, like a maddened bull.

'Barclaycard! Your fucking Barclaycard letter!'

The lads were laughing now; even Sally had dropped her head and was trying to stifle a giggle. A few moments later Jennings stormed off and Plonker appeared from behind the shed, a grin still on his face.

'That's you, Plonker,' Jonesy said. 'Dial 1-800-IN THE SHIT.'

'Fookin' 'ell,' Plonker replied, finishing his burger, his huge mouth opening like a maw. 'I'll drop you,' he mimicked. 'Like to see him try. Fookin' 'ell,' he said brightening up, 'tha's good.' He looked at Sally. 'Can I 'ave anootha, please?' Rhah looked at him, marvelling; it was like water off a duck's back. Plonker came across with another burger and sat down with them, now with a can of soft drink.

411

'Wait till them lasses see me stripped down, with me Diet Coke. They'll be lining up at fookin' windows like in that fookin' advert. I-just-wanna-make-lerve-to-you.' He began to sing the song from the commercial, imagining a crowd of lovely office girls watching him drink his Coke, stripped to the waist.

His people fed, Big Harry took a burger from Sophie, and was biting into it when he heard a familiar voice – ''Tis a wonder to behold.' It was Captain Atlee, and Rees grinned around his mouthful. Atlee had been off with his patrols people and Rees hadn't seen him since they had lobbed in that morning. 'Every time I see you, you are at a barbecue with a very pretty young lady.'

They spoke for a few minutes before Atlee, food in hand, turned and looked back at the bridge supports, silhouetted in the light of flames. He was acting oddly and Harry was wondering about the reason. 'Well, must away,' Atlee said. 'I'm taking my chaps down to the left flank. We are going for a wander up that track. The worry is that down there it's marines.'

'Be gentle with them,' Harry said, 'they are only crap-hats.'

Suddenly and uncharacteristically Atlee put his hand out. 'Been a pleasure, Harry.' He passed Rees a letter with the other hand. 'For Beth,' he said awkwardly. 'Do the biz for me.'

'Bollocks. You tell her –'

'No. Not this time. Please?'

He took the proffered hand and the letter. 'Of course. You can have it back in the morning.' Atlee nodded weakly and walked away, and Harry remembered he had another job to do. He walked over to Rhah's section and squatted down beside them; Rhah, Elias, Plonker and Jonesy. When they saw the look on his face they knew before he said it. 'I'm sorry, lads. Spud – he didn't make it.'

They took the news in stunned silence, Plonker's head dropping, half of the second burger falling uneaten to the ground.

'Fuck it. Fuck everyone,' Rhah muttered.

Plonker looked up and saw Robo Jennings crossing back over towards some men by the feeding station. He put down

412

his rifle, stood up and moved towards him, but Big Harry was there and physically turned him round. He said nothing, just looked Plonker in the eye for a second or two, the only man in the company tall enough to do that.

'Sit down,' he said softly. 'Come on.'

'He said he would drop me. Let him try.'

'He always says that,' Rees countered, 'and he never does it. So back off.'

Elias was there too then and together they prevented Plonker committing a court-martial offence.

Twenty minutes later they were moving back down the cutting and into the sangar. Twelve platoon was now concentrated at their end and for the first time since they had left the holes in the second row and moved forward to support the Gurkha lads at the time of the first major attack those holes were now occupied. They set up their LSWs, and replaced the men at the front one by one, the thirteen blokes moving out to re-form further down. Extra Claymores had gone in, three of them across their sector. For the first time that night, Tyson-Davis had D Coy's entire strength on the ford, support platoon included, with C Coy to the right. C Coy's support platoon were now up on the road serving the mortars, but Tyson-Davis had moved four of support company detachment's fifty-cals down as well. Sometime before dawn they would come again, and this one would be the all-out effort.

Down at the junction of the two rivers, barely a mile away, on a request from the petty officer, Lewis pulled the lads together in the wheelhouse of the patrol boat. It was just them now, the SAS people all having gone ashore. They had been stooging up and down, aware that this far away they could do little to support the people at San Ignacio; the lads, still high on their earlier success, were keen to get stuck in again after a whole day of being tied up.

'Sir, we want to get closer, to where we can be of some use,' the PO said.

'All of you?' Lewis asked, looking round at them in the darkness.

There was a chorus of approval. One or two were not quite so vocal but they didn't challenge the majority.

'They are defending at a natural ford. I'm not sure how deep the water is,' Lewis countered.

'Just near enough to use the gun, sir. We can be two hundred yards downstream from the ford, and still be of use,' one of the lads said. Lewis looked at him in the dark. It was Forrester, a weapons artificer.

'We'll take fire from the shore, you all know that. This is very dangerous.'

'Yes, sir, we know that.'

'Very well. Get those drums round the guns filled up.' Christ, he was thinking, why am I doing this? These lads are my responsibility. That branch of the river is narrow, maybe even too narrow to turn the boat.

Murray's men out on the left flank were silent. The patrols group had gone out, a recce, to try and establish where the Guatemalans were and how many had crossed the river. Murray didn't know much about patrols, only that they were the nearest thing to special forces actually in the Parachute Regiment. Using many patrol skills developed by the SAS, they were the only maroon berets trained to operate in anything other than the usual fire team, section, platoon structure. There were four soldiers on this mission, led by their officer, the last two, the snipers, left back at the main effort. They were going out this way, but they would egress by a different route, tab through the 'J' and then round the back. The reason was out there in the dark now – two B Squadron troopers, booby-trapping the track. They didn't have any more Claymores, just the three set up earlier. Their entire stock of those was now down at the ford, but they were able to rig up a few nasties that would slow down the enemy and, more importantly, give the defending marines warning.

Their GPMG was in the main sangar, the hole big enough that they could turn and look out of the left-hand side to face the track. The problem was that when the Gurkhas had prepared the position they had designed it to fight across the river and prevent a crossing below them, not to defend the track, so the other marines had been digging like fiends, excavating two new holes, one above and one below, facing south.

They were ready now. One of them, settled in alongside the gunner, boxes of link ammunition at his feet, looked out at the inky blackness of the jungle, the only light from the occasional glow of a flare out behind them.

'Remember before that final battle in *Platoon*? When they are getting dug in and that patrol goes out? The bloke watching them go out says, "The beast is out there, and he is hungry tonight." That's what this feels like.'

'Yeah, well, they were septic pongos,' the other replied dismissively. 'Fucking wankers.'

They dropped into silence as one of the lads appeared round the front of the sangar clutching eight or nine long poles, each with a sharpened tip. He began to work them into the earth so the points jutted outwards, looking up every now and then to make sure the machine gun had a clear sweep for its barrel. They had no wire, so this would have to do, a defensive technique as old as war itself – anyone running into these would impale themselves mid-thigh. The gaps between the three holes were spiked as well, and the makeshift defences extended out about twenty feet down the track. The last stakes went in and the lads moved quickly back into their holes. Murray had called in mortar fire earlier, on the spot the C Coy CSM had marked on the map. His briefing had been short and to the point; what he had encountered was a recce group for a larger formation, maybe a company, perhaps more. Murray knew when they would attack; around the same time that they had a go down at the ford. Either one could be a diversion for the other, or it could be a full two-pronged assault.

The two SAS men appeared down the track and softly gave the password. A marine called them in and as they dropped into the sangar one of them pointed out at the stakes. 'Fucking 'ell! Nearly skewered me self. Where are we? Fucking Agincourt? Got yer archers, have ya?'

The marine gave him the traditional archer's two-fingered salute. 'That's the whole idea, dickhead. So where are you two off to now then? Why don't you go and abseil down that house over there, with your Heckler and Koch? Give us a bit of a floor show.'

The trooper grinned. 'We're going nowhere, sunshine. We're staying here with you because we love crap-hat marines. Don't you want us, then?'

'Stuck in a hole with a couple of squaddies? I'd rather have fucking syphilis,' the marine replied. The troopers grinned; the inter-service rivalry was always good sport. At that point Murray slithered back in and peered through the darkness to identify the two men. 'Ah, good. You guys finished then?'

One of the troopers quickly briefed him on what they had arrayed and he had barely finished when a furious contact broke out somewhere down the track. They all stopped to listen, trying to identify the weaponry and who might be involved. There was ferocious small-arms fire, grenades going off, and when a machine gun, an M60, opened up, followed by a second, it became obvious. The patrols guys had either been ambushed or had a contact with at least a two-platoon-sized formation. The fire was intense for about a minute and a half and then petered out to nothing, an M60 having the last word. The marine who had been ribbing the SAS guys looked down and muttered two words.

'Poor bastids.'

This was the one place the scrotes might some experi-ence – on a jungle path, classic COIN-type ops. Some of the lads might have escaped, but either way this wasn't good. The patrol's mission was reconnaissance, not fighting.

'Jesus. Now what?' someone asked.

'Now we fight,' one of the B Squadron guys said.

On the other side of the bridge Elias was in and out, moving up and down the two sections of the platoon at his end, and down in their sangar at the ford Jonesy, Plonker and Rhah were standing to.

'She were a real bushpig that one,' Plonker said. 'She had a face like a bulldog licking piss off a nettle. I'll bet she's a great shag though. Nature, ya know . . .' He trailed off. 'Wha's tha' word?' he asked Rhah.

'Compensating?' Rhah responded.

'Aye. Compensation.'

Rhah smiled – this was as deep as Plonker's thinking ever got. They heard the contact start, down beyond the bridge, the rolling, hammering echo of a firefight some way away to the left.

'O aye, that's the crap-hats over there, innit?'

'Yeah,' Rhah said. 'Looks like they are in for a snotty.'

'Aye, like fookin' uz.'

'That means they are across the river up there,' Jonesy said.

''Ere,' Plonker said; moving to the side of the hole, he put Spud's Buzz Lightyear doll up on the lip. 'I'll stick old Buzz up there. If the crap-hats let 'em through, then he can sort the fookers.' Suddenly a single mortar bomb came in, off to the left, and then another behind them.

'Here we go,' Rhah said.

The battle started at the marines' position. The first mortar bombs began to fall and the men dropped down into their holes and trenches, settled in the bottom, and covered their heads. Any attack would only come after the bombs had stopped. The marines had no helmets; most were wearing floppy jungle hats or indeed, like Murray, just berets. Leaves, mud, clods of earth, bits of wood and stones thrown up by the blasts were showering down on them. Murray was trying to work out the direction of the fire. Was it coming in from the town, or down the river from somewhere along the track? Either way they had someone controlling because the ranging was accurate. A couple of bombs dropped on the roadway up behind them. He lifted his head and looked out at the track. They would be moving up now, under the cover of their mortar fire. He looked at one of the two SAS men and raised his thumb and the man quickly spoke into the radio, calling in support fire from the M19 up on the road. The 40 mill grenades began landing out along the track and in the jungle either side and a few moments later a flare burst into life as someone ran into a trip-wire.

'Sixty metres!' the SAS man yelled. Murray nodded and as he did so the mortar fire stopped. The other Squadron guy came up to his feet, pulled the pin from a white phosphorus grenade and threw it. It exploded, the night turning into day. Murray yelled, 'Hit 'em!' and from all three holes the marines poured fire into the attackers, now visible in the white glow, running forward, dropping into cover, some firing from the hip. As the glow from the phosphorus died, the scene was lit by nanoseconds of muzzleflash and there seemed to be dozens of them, coming down the track and through the trees and bush each side. The two section weapons, their own and the minimi being fired by one of the SAS, supported the heavier GPMG. The three weapons, concentrated as they were, all within thirty feet of each other, formed a devastating defensive arc of fire – until the GPMG jammed.

'Stoppage!' the gunner screamed. He whipped the gun open and scrabbled at the jammed link, trying to get it cleared and suddenly they were at the stakes. One Guatemalan soldier, brave but night-blind after the phosphorus ran straight into one and was impaled screaming, the sharpened end in his groin. The marine beside the gunner was firing his SA80; he changed mags, fumbled, dropped the fresh magazine, and suddenly a figure was looming over him, falling into the sangar. He swung his bayonet up, plunging it into the attacker's stomach and as the Guatemalan fell in on top of them, he pulled it out, went for another mag. More figures appeared above him, and one of the Squadron blokes did a quarter-turn and from somewhere produced a pump-action shotgun and took out another attacker, knocking him backwards. The gunner had got his weapon cleared and link in and the gun started up again, sweeping its murderous fire into the fight. There was hand-to-hand on both sides of the main sangar now, vicious fighting, gollocks, bayonets, trenching tools, gunfire at point-blank range.

Down at the ford they were charging across, but not just men on foot. They had followed the old Red Army doctrine – if you threw enough at an objective, something would get through. A line of trucks poured down the side road approaching the ford. They could hear the engines, and someone fired a flare, and the sight was awesome. The Guatemalan engineers had been busy all day – the trucks had steel skirts welded on to their sides and cabs as blast shields, light armour-plating, at odd angles. Bullets and even some missiles might glance off. There were men in the backs of the trucks, and they would shield others moving on the far side. Another flare went up, followed by a pair of LAW rockets. A Milan streaked in from the bridge and hit the lead truck, but instead of just grinding to a halt, it careered off to the right down the steep five feet of bank and rolled over. The vehicle behind accelerated and right down the Paras' front they began to open fire with everything they had, as soldiers rose up from their holes and positions on the far bank. Fifty-cals blasted away, their note heavier and slower than the page-ripping sound of the fire of the LSWs. Jesus, Elias thought; images of old footage of the Korean War filled his mind, hordes of men running towards you. Come on, come on, where the fuck, CRUMP, the first mortar round hit, the toms in the hole were pouring fire out; something caught his eye off to the right. No, couldn't be. A boat down the river, a gun on the bows, a big fucker like a fifty hammering away at the trucks. From that angle they could hit the cabs, he realized.

On board HMS *Tonka Toy*, the PO was on the 12.7 mm hammering rounds out. 'Go for the drivers,' Lewis yelled. He was slowing the boat, the ford maybe one hundred yards ahead of them. This was far enough; time to get her head around again. Bullets were slamming into the boat, thunks on the hull like hammer-strikes. He jammed the throttles into reverse and swung the wheel over. The killing ahead of them was lit by parachute flares, flames, the flash of explosions; it was like something from a nightmare. He was concentrating now – one mistake and they would run aground, and be torn to pieces by gunfire at leisure. The gunner on the stern with the GPMG was swearing as he had to cease firing. Power up, bows round, one more swing and he could egress; a bit more, both guns bearing now, bullets ripping them, windows gone, glass, shards of aluminium, blood, blood, running down his arm. The PO had hit the lead truck on the ford now; it slewed right and into the deeper water and he raked the back with his gun, then swung to take the next truck. Lewis waited till he had got two good bursts away, and using one hand, the other didn't seem to function, hit the power and spun the wheel, his vision bad, tunnelling for some reason. Three hundred yards downstream, as the jubilant PO crashed into the wheelhouse, Lewis fell forward on to the wheel before standing again. He had been wounded. Down aft, the gunner on the GPMG had also been hit, two bullets going through his right thigh and lodging in his left. The BDF Maritime Wing man was dead, killed as he carried a box of link ammunition back to the gun.

Elias saw the truck slew off the ford, hit by gunfire from the patrol boat. The ford wasn't wide enough for two big trucks and when the second stopped, hit by a Milan missile and by the boat's guns, he knew that the men would be pouring round the trucks to run the last thirty yards. A phalanx of the enemy was coming across in front of Rhah's section. This hole was overstrength, eight men, but he knew that Rhah's two holes were undermanned. He grabbed a soldier, yelled at him to follow, and jumped across into the comms trench and raced down it as fast as he could as bullets whipped over their heads.

They were just in time. Plonker had the LSW up, and was shooting not out at the water, but at the men coming at the sangar. As the box emptied he dropped the weapon, snatched up his trenching tool and rose to meet them. The position was being overrun. Rhah was up shooting his SA80 with one hand, and firing the pistol he had borrowed back at Bragg with the other, both at men no more than six feet away. Jonesy was still shooting outward, leaving his comrades to handle those in close but then as he changed magazines they were on him too. He lunged with a bayonet, managed to get a mag in, and Elias put a burst into the mêlée above him.

Plonker was up out of the hole, on the lip, fighting hand-to-hand, hacking at men with his sharpened spade, swinging it like an axe, slashing with his gollock, a Gurkha kukri, in the other hand. There were grunts, screams, splattered blood, the terror of close-quarter fighting in the harsh white light and exaggerated shadows of parachute flares. Elias and Rhah were firing continuously, short bursts, and a few seconds later they had the upper hand but Plonker, his blood up, wasn't finished. From his vantage standing over the sangar he could see the lads in the other section hole in real trouble and he charged, a fearsome sight. Stripped from the waist up, covered in blood and dirt, the spade swinging back in one hand, the kukri in the other he crossed the few yards like a berserker, his eyes red and flecked like a madman. Screaming a battle cry he hacked his way into the attackers, the sheer momentum of his run bowling three of them over. Caught up in the frenzy, Jonesy snatched up the LSW, rammed on a fresh box and followed, bursts of fire and the sharp edge of the spade doing equal damage. This gave the toms in the bottom of the hole a chance and they rose up too. The Guatemalans never stood a chance and a few seconds later it was all over. There were bodies everywhere; everyone was back in the hole, panting, adrenaline racing through them. Plonker, splattered in blood, turned to face the ford, holding the spade aloft over his head, and like a victorious animal he let out a roar.

Of the original eight soldiers, two were dead and two wounded. Jonesy took command; he put the remaining four men back into the battle and called for help. Elias barrelled over the edge, and took in the situation at a glance. One of the dead was the section corporal.

'You two back with Rhah,' he yelled. Plonker and Jonesy took off back to their sangar where Rhah was on his own, leaving Elias there. Up their end the main attack had faltered, but there was still fierce fighting further down, but even that began to ebb, the murderous intensity of the battle consuming men and energy and life-force like the flames of a flash fire. A minute later it was over, and other than the odd gunshots, the only residuals were smoke and smells, and the cries of the wounded and dying. One man – no one was sure whose side he was on – was so confused, dazed, stunned, that he was sobbing.

Robo dropped into the sangar. He was panting but his eyes were focused, calm, deadly. 'You bastards all right?'

Rhah looked at him and nodded. 'Yeah.'

'Box and mags coming down.' He looked round. Jonesy was bent over Plonker's leg, putting another dressing on a second wound, this one a bayonet stab in his upper thigh, and Robo shook his head with a grin. 'Get yourself back to a medic.'

'No,' Plonker responded. 'Time for that tomorra. It's not bad. Wha' yowa gonna do? Drop me?'

421

Robo just grinned and gave a short laugh that came out like a bark. 'You're a mad cunt,' he said, 'but there's hope for you yet!'

As Robo left the hole, Plonker reached into his trouser pocket and pulled out his morphine syrette and while no one was looking he jabbed it into his thigh. The relief was instantaneous.

Up at the marines' position they had held the first attack and the second. The ground in front of them was littered with dead and wounded. One of the attackers was badly hurt and crying in pain, asking for his mother. Taylor, the marine who spoke Spanish, without conferring with Murray, shouted to the Guatemalans, saying that he was coming out to help their man and not to fire on him. Still shouting, he crawled out of the hole and moved forward, everyone trying to call him back. He ignored them. They watched, fingers on triggers. If the scrotes fired on their mate while he was committing a humanitarian act, then all hell was going to break loose. Perhaps the Guatemalans heard and understood. Perhaps they were as tired and sickened by it all as this *inglés*, but he wasn't fired upon. He reached the wounded kid, bound a dressing on a stomach wound, and dragged him back to their hole, talking to him all the while. A few seconds later a voice called out from the Guatemalan side.

'*Señor!*'

'*Sí,*' he yelled back.

'*Gracias.*'

Murray called across. 'Tell them they have five minutes. Two men can come forward, unarmed, to care for their wounded.'

'We'll all be singing silent fucking night next,' someone muttered. 'Fuck 'em. They started it, let them wait.'

'Shut the fuck up,' someone told him.

The marine called out the offer and it was accepted. Murray's motives were chiefly humanitarian, but there were also tactical benefits. Every wounded man needs others to care for him, who would otherwise have been fighting. In his own position he had four of his able-bodied marines caring for wounded. He looked around; by any orderly appraisal he no longer had an effective fighting force. All of his original twenty men were hurt in some way or other, several of them seriously. Three had gunshot or fragmentation wounds that had received first aid, been bound, and they were still there and willing. Classified as walking wounded, they would fight on. The brief pause in hostilities gave them a reprieve too, and several of the lads had hexy blocks out and were brewing up.

One of the SAS blokes, who had slithered out of the hole at the start of the truce, reappeared with a crate of bottled water, and a comprehensive medics kit from one of their Land-Rovers. He passed the kit to one of the marines treating the wounded at the back of the hole, ripped the top off a bottle and drank deeply, passing others around. One marine began to throw them across to the other holes.

'Don't give him any,' he said pointing to the Guatemalan. 'Not with a stomach wound.' He looked at Murray.

'That's it then, I reckon,' he said.

'What?'

'They won't be back tonight. Oh, they'll snipe, take pot-shots. But they won't attack again, they'll wait till daylight tomorrow.'

He was right. On both fronts the Guatemalans had learned that a small but well-motivated group of defenders with enough critical mass at a choke-point could hold back a much larger force, and their tacticians were flummoxed. They had thrown fresh troops at the ford, supported them and been turned back. They had done the same with a full company crossing the river upstream, trying for a flank attack and failed again to breach the defensive line. For the rest of the night they probed and harried, looking for a weak point.

The PO on HMS *Tonka Toy* had found an overhang, and drawing in, put the lads ashore to carry their wounded down the track towards the ground forces and whatever medical attention they could find. Lieutenant Lewis and the gunner, LWA Forrester, were carried in makeshift litters, leaving just the PO on the boat. It was an A Squadron team who found them, and called down some help to carry the men out.

*   *   *

Just before dawn, the RAF leapfrogged the main airhead, still the scene of some enemy activity according to 2 REP, to move on to the next FOB. Ahead of the strike aircraft, four heavy-lift USAF Chinooks lifted off to begin shuttling RAF Regiment people, technicians, fuel and ordnance on to the forward operating base on the hard at the thirty-two-mile marker, the site of JB's. Two of the Chinooks were specialist aircraft, without a fuselage, and could be lowered over a jeep, truck, field gun, or fuel tank to lift it with special wire strops. The Harriers, when they took off from Ambergris Cay, as when they left Pensacola, would not be returning.

The RAF were determined to deliver maximum support from their small detachment and the closer they could get to the action meant less fuel was needed, and that in turn allowed bigger bombloads. As the sky turned pink behind them the six Harriers lifted off, every hardpoint carrying rockets or cluster bombs. The leg into the mission was covered at low level, the aircraft in three pairs streaking in at five hundred knots over the bush to the north of the main western highway, and as they passed above Spanish Lookout, the power came off and they did a lazy left turn and dropped still lower. The pilots had been studying aerial photos of San Ignacio at length, and when the first pair came hurtling in over the hills from the north and dropped into their attack run they knew what they were looking for – the mortar positions and rear marshalling areas at the western end of the town. But they wanted the comfort of knowing where their people were. They called up the SAS signallers and requested that the forward positions mark FLOT, the front line of troops.

All the lads on the ground saw was Robo throwing two smoke markers by hand, one left and one right. Then two jets came searing in from the north. The lead aircraft lined up and attacked, the pilot pickled and dropped two cluster bombs. The containers fell away from the hardpoints and opened up, spreading the smaller bombs. The ground shook as they hit, half a second apart. The Paras watching from half a mile away were shouting, cheering, chanting, dancing in their holes, whooping and clapping.

The second jet followed but dropped no bombs. Instead,

rockets streaked out from its hardpoints, and then it began a sharp left turn, coming round to run down the river.

'Oh fuck,' someone muttered.

'Cover!' someone else yelled. Everyone who had been chanting and enjoying the action suddenly dropped down into the bottom, the very bottom of their holes. This was going to be close.

The pilot, a thirty-nine-year-old squadron leader, an ex-instructor from the Weapons School back when it was at RAF Brawdy, was arguably the best ground-attack pilot on Harriers. He lined up, poured the power on as he came out of his turn and aware that there were friendlies not seventy yards away on the far side of the river, he did what he did best. With icy, surgical precision he dropped two cluster bombs on the Guatemalans dug in amongst the bush back from the river. The bomblets that fell from the falling containers, each powerful enough to kill tanks, did their job, and as the jet climbed out from the theatre the Paras came up from the bottom of their holes and looked out. The scene was appalling – smoke and dust rose from the other side but it was omin-ously silent.

'Fuck me,' someone muttered.

The other four jets came in from the west, their mission to strike at the line of vehicles and men strung out along the road as far back as the border. They each dropped two cluster bombs on the crowded road, working from the border east-wards into Belize. Then with full rocket pods and 30 mill cannons, they returned, seeking other targets, where indi-vidual commanders had sensibly left the road and hidden their troops. Trained to do just this, a squadron of Harriers with an FOB close to the forward battle area could pin down and destroy a division over the course of a day. This six-ship detachment, half a squadron, had cut off the Guatemalans from both re-supply and retreat; the first mile of road into Belize now just a line of burning, smoking wrecks. Back in San Ignacio they could hear the attack, and see the smoke rising and four minutes later, the six jets were egressing the battlefield area, one dropping low to do a roll over the beleaguered men on the ground. They loved it, hooting and cheering and waving as the Harrier roared past. This was the only time they had any respect for the blue jobs. It was love or hate, and as dawn broke over San Ignacio the bloodied Paras loved them.

They returned half an hour later, two jets, and from then on with fast turnarounds the only limitation was pilot fatigue. Changing crews, they were able to keep two aircraft constantly over the battlefield. Closer to the fighting and needing less fuel they could now carry four cluster bombs and rocket pods, firing at troops they could see in San Ignacio and attacking the stalled Guatemalan line of advance. By nine a.m. they had stabilized things enough that the next sortie was east again, to support the French at the airport, where they dropped four cluster bombs into the bush where the Guatemalan marines were still holding on. Their mission was to force them further back, out of range of the runways, so that by the time the spearhead arrived they could actually land the aircraft.

Down on the riverbank morale soared. The Guatemalans hadn't gone away, but they were keeping a very low profile. The sound of a fast-attack jet, one of theirs, constantly in the skies above them gave the exhausted defenders a fillip. They brewed up, slept, took it in turns to ease back out up to the road where Sally, Sophie, Helen and the people from JB's were still turning out the food. Well set up now, they had curries cooking, barbecued chicken and chilli beef on the go for lunch, and they were frying bacon and eggs by the dozen and handing them out in sandwiches as the tired men arrived. A local woman had turned up to help, bringing three huge fire-blackened kettles. There was no room on the gas burners so she built a fire and brewed tea the colour of creosote and the toms just loved it. Other locals, sensing that the tide of the battle had turned, were coming forward to help. They brought fruit by the basketful and the local Coca-Cola distributor sent a truckful of his stock in the old-fashioned bottles. The hospital was full of Mennonites; the men were dour and bearded, and the womenfolk were dressed in bonnets and long, full skirts. They were pacifists, but they had walked or ridden in their horsedrawn gigs from Spanish Lookout, to do the Lord's work. This relieved the field medics who had been down in the line and were now treating men at the feeding station. Tyson-Davis would allow no one out of the line if they could still fight, and the medics knew that hot tea and a decent doorstep-sized egg and bacon sarnie were worth any amount of medical treatment for those lightly wounded. The esprit de corps was pervasive – wounded men swallowed powerful analgesics or took a shot of morphine and chose to return to the line where their mates were.

Big Harry Rees had seen Sophie twice since midnight, each time her smile giving him the strength to go on. On his first visit since the massed attack, so relieved was she to see him that she had clung to him for a full twenty seconds and this time he didn't care about the watching toms. They in turn made no cat-calls, no ribald remarks, each thinking about their own families, or pleased that if this gorgeous angel had a bloke, at least he was a Para. That gave them part ownership, in particular the twelve platoon toms, and they were territorial in the extreme. One of the field medics made some boorish remark about the size of her bust and there was a low growl from the nearest lads. He got the message.

Fed and back down in their sangar, Rhah, Jonesy and Plonker took turns to stand to, the other two dozing. It was stinking hot in the bright sunlight and they were dripping sweat; Plonker, who was covered in dried blood, had tried washing some of it off before going up to the feeding station, but all he had managed to do was smear it everywhere. Rhah looked across at him as he dozed and turned away, gagging for a moment. The big Geordie, sleeping the sleep of the innocent, had bits of what looked like dried body tissue in his hair. The corpses down at the water's edge were beginning to bloat and swell, the smell wafting back up to them on the slight breeze, flies buzzing around. He gagged again, swallowed, forced it down. Jonesy was standing to, facing out at the river and Plonker was still asleep, and for the first time in thirty hours he was alone with his thoughts. His head lowered, he tried to control himself but couldn't, and he began to cry silently, great tears rolling down his cheeks.

*   *   *

Over the river in San Ignacio Pete Collins was up in his roof-space. He had been feeding back int all day, but now the batteries in both his mobile and his PC were running low so he was off the air. His final e-mail to Northwood had been at 0400 and he was now dozing fitfully, hoping his hideyhole wasn't going to attract the attention of the attacking jets. The Guats had been in the shop below, smashing through it and looting and at one point he had heard footsteps on the first floor just below him.

At 1700 hours, after a day of sniping and odd exchanges of fire, repairing sangars and digging the comms trenches deeper, Ted had them stand to. Darkness wasn't far off. In the distance behind the town the smoke was still rising from places on the road through to Benque and the border. The vehicles may have been hit, but there were still thousands of Guatemalans and they would know, as the Paras did, that the Harriers were not equipped for battlefield support at night. They would be preparing to come out of cover and move down the moment it became too dark to fly.

Seventy-three miles away at the international airport the 2 REP officer was looking up at the sky. The lone British signaller still at the camp had sent the message over fifteen minutes ago. There, to the north-east – the C-130s had been airborne seventeen hours, re-fuelled in mid-air by RAF tankers. The first was on long finals, and looking for his flare, the green that indicated the airhead was secure for a landing. He raised his arm and fired, the flare shooting upwards before exploding in the sky. The Hercules immediately dropped its undercarriage and flaps, the note changing as the propellers changed their pitch for a short field tactical landing, the second immediately behind it. Four others were circling over St George's in the protective screen of HMS *Beaufort*'s air defence systems, awaiting the go to their alternate destination, the short grass strip at Belmopan via the LZ at San Ignacio. The Gurkha rifle company on attachment from 1 Para would take over the defence of the airhead. The remaining three companies, Support, Headquarters and B Coy would, on the signal that the long hard runway was secure, fly on to San Ignacio. The three companies would lob out and the aircraft would turn round and fly to the airstrip at Belmopan and off-load the medical teams, support equipment, supplies, extra ordnance and vehicles. There were no enemy reported at Belmopan and from there it was just thirty miles to San Ignacio, so it was too good an opportunity to miss. RAF Regiment had driven up from their FOB, and now six of them were on the ground to meet the aircraft. They had been brought by a local taxi driver who claimed he was mates with the guys at San Ignacio. 'Lieutenant Rees, he's my buddy. Ask anyone,' he said. 'The name's Eddie. I'm trusted, marn. Took Lieutenant Rees's girlfriend down to JB's just yesterday!' He had then gone into Belmopan to round up some trucks.

San Ignacio

'Hear the one about King Harold, his last words? He said, "Watch that bastard with the bow and arrow. If he's not careful, he'll have some bugger's eye out with that." Aye? Good joke that.' A medic had slipped him three syrettes of morphine; the pain was under control, and Plonker was on form. What's more, he had even got the king's name right; the last time he had told that joke, he had said it was King Arthur.

Rhah looked at his watch and then at the sky. The sun was now down behind the hill across the river. Darkness fell very quickly here and he knew that in ten or fifteen minutes night would be upon them. The sky was clear; there would be a moon, maybe, and stars. He looked up and tried to imagine himself somewhere else, anywhere but this.

'Aircraft,' Jonesy said. He was listening, his head canted to the right.

'Been there all fookin' day, mun,' Plonker responded irritably. No one had laughed at his joke.

'Turboprop,' Jonesy said.

'Fookin' 'ell. Our boys are in their kip for the night and theirs come back. Fookin' great.'

'No,' Jonesy said, 'Hercs. Listen.'

'I hear it,' Rhah said. It was getting closer and closer, more

429

than one, he thought. The sound was clear now, familiar to any paratrooper; C-130s over a DZ.

'It's the lads,' he said. 'Spearhead.' Then, as if not believing it himself, he said, 'The battalion is lobbing in.'

'So Rabid Ran finally got his shite together. About fookin' time,' Plonker muttered. The remark was unfair and Rhah smiled. Aldershot must have been bedlam, getting them away so fast.

'Just in fucking time, more like it,' Jonesy said, but he was smiling. It was getting darker by the minute and the shit was about to start up again, but the effect on the men was dramatic. Hearing their Hercs coming in, knowing that the boys, friendlies, maybe even the rest of the battalion would be lobbing out to support them was all they needed, and morale soared. The whole of 2 Para? They could hold the scrotes here no matter what, and with Brigade somewhere out behind them? If the scrotes wanted a fight then they had one now. A shot rang out from the far side, then another.

'O aye, ya scrote bastard, Plonker muttered, 'want some more, do ya?' He levelled his rifle through the slit between the sandbags and the log and waited, looking for muzzleflash to betray the enemy soldier's position. 'Canna see fook-all.' He rose up further, put a foot on the firing step and looked over the top of the log.

'Geddown!' Rhah snapped.

Plonker ignored him. There was another shot and from behind it somewhere an M60 opened up. 'Gotcha, bastid,' he said softly. He was bringing his rifle up when the 60 fired again. Bark, sand and mud chipped off the log by bullets flew back into the sangar and Plonker's body jerked twice and he fell backwards. Jonesy and Rhah taped dressings on, called for a medic, but by the time Elias had crossed from three holes up, Plonker, hit twice in the chest, was dead.

The fighting intensified suddenly, as word whipped down the line that another of the lads had bought it, and the mood changed. Plonker's towering presence, his courage, his wonderful foolhardiness had welded them together. Everybody looked for something to aim at and let rip.

*   *   *

Colonel Wallace left the recently-arrived half of his battalion to sort itself out and tab up to the river, and jumped on the back of an SAS Land-Rover with the battalion number two and a radio operator. A few minutes later he was walking through drying, claggy mud down towards where Major Tyson-Davis had set up his command post just over the rise from the ford.

Major Fox, OC C Coy, was there waiting for him with Ted. Both of his officers were exhausted, filthy, bloodied. He was briefed and then took command, taking Tyson-Davis's advice and reinforcing the marines on the left flank with support company.

'Captain Atlee and four of his patrols team are missing, believed dead. They went out to patrol the left flank. If they were alive we'd know by now. The marine lads, they have taken a real hiding. There were only about seventeen of them to start with. Fought a Guatemalan company into the ground. There were nine still fighting fit at last sitrep,' the Para major said. 'C Coy have been in it longer than us. They fought like Trojans but they are dead on their feet. My ten is on its chinstraps, and so is Harry's mob, but they can go on.' Wallace nodded. He had too much respect for his company commanders to ignore this advice and he ordered his fresh B Coy into the line and pulled C Coy back for some rest. Through the night the fighting ebbed and flowed, but the Guatemalans didn't try to cross again.

At dawn the next morning at the same time as the first two Harriers were lifting off from JB's, an SAS signaller took an encoded burst from Northwood for OC 'Long Reach' British Forces Belize.

The Guatemalans were prepared to discuss terms for a withdrawal. While talks went on there was to be a cease-fire commencing immediately, but there was to be no direct communication until authorized. It came very quickly; at 7.16 a.m. local time, Wallace took a second message. The Guatemalans would be permitted to withdraw with whatever equipment they could move back to their own border. Wallace grinned and passed the note to Tyson-Davis. They had just been looking at recon footage from the remote camera that Chard had kept flying. Chard knew what the terms would be – it was his people supplying the int back to Hereford that had allowed the negotiators to argue from a position of strength. They knew more about what would be moving back to Guatemala than the Guatemalans did. There was no way matériel in any quantity would be going back – the road was clogged, the last mile into Guatemala completely blocked. They were walking back.

In his hidden command post, Chard looked down at the little mobile phone and checked for the tenth time that it was on. He was concerned; he had heard nothing from his asset, Pete Collins, across on the other side for many hours now and he feared the worst. The ex-soldier's contribution had been excellent, the flow of intelligence solid stuff, almost every hour on the hour, but now it seemed it had cost him dearly.

Big Harry was standing up at the feeding station, looking for Sophie. The team from JB's had stood down now, cooks from the battalion having taken over their facilities. He found her behind the truck, sitting in a folding chair, talking to Helen about whether they should stay on and finish the holiday, go out to Cay Caulker, or go home. Helen wanted to stay, but Sophie said she couldn't possibly lie on a beach in public view. 'I'm fat,' she said.

He grinned and crossed the last few feet. 'No you're not.'

She spun her head, looking up at him, smiling, and then burst out laughing. 'Oh, Harry. Is it true? It's over?'

He nodded. 'Yeah.'

Two hundred feet away Leo Scobey, the ITN correspondent, still the only foreign broadcast journalist inside Belize, was doing a piece to camera. 'Not since the Welsh 24th Regiment of Foot met the impis of the Zulu King Cetewayo at Rorke's Drift in 1879, when a company of that regiment held off four or five thousand Zulus, has there been such a feat of arms in British military history. There the ratio was fifty to one. Here it was more like seventy-five to one. There are similarities – in both battles the British were defending, in both they had limited time to prepare, and because the defensive area was so small, at no time could the enemy bring their entire might to bear. The weather worked for the British; they used the geography wisely, they channelled and harried and then bottled up the advance here where the rain-swollen rivers meet at San Ignacio, this picturesque hill town. The bulk of the Guatemalan army were still strung out behind their lead elements on the road with nowhere to advance to. There is no doubt that the Guatemalan tactics were flawed, but even when pushed into going against the weather because they had been compromised, and then coming up against, not the small Belize Defence Force, but the men they met here, all the money would have been on them making their objective, Belize City, if not the first night, certainly by yesterday lunchtime.

'Regardless of their tactics it has been a victory, an astonishing one. Two hundred and forty-odd men of 2 Para, and obviously some Special Air Service as you would expect, held three brigades here, that's fifteen thousand enemy, for thirty hours until the first air support arrived and a further twelve hours till the lead elements of 5 Airborne could get here, vindication if ever it was required of the need for airborne forces in today's world. The Royal Marines were here too, a detachment of twenty men who defended the airport, then raced up here to hold the left flank, where some of the fiercest fighting took place. Those marines, like the Paras at the ford fought their attackers to a standstill, and when dawn broke, not one of them was unwounded. Bloody, but unbeaten . . .'

Captain Bonner, who had spent the last thirty-odd hours behind Guatemalan lines, made his way down to the river with Major Chard. McKay and his team, part of his air troop, were down there somewhere. The Squadron people had tasks to do, standard stuff, but he was going to leave them for a few hours, crash out, get some kip, and he wanted to walk the battlefield, check each team that was still in situ.

Boyce was down with the Paras, sitting smoking in silence. He had cadged a smoke and sat down with them, his knee strapped up with bandages, no one saying anything. Finally he stood up. 'That was a hell of a fight you guys put up.'

Elias, shirtless, filthy dirty, bandaged in two places, nodded, accepting the compliment, and threw Boyce a packet of Old Holborn roll-up tobacco and some papers from his day-bag. Rhah looked up at Boyce, the expression in his eyes one of sadness, as if he didn't want to be congratulated, didn't want to be even identified with what had taken place, like the whole thing had sickened him. As the SAS trooper limped away Elias looked across at him. He knew Rhah – the move to Sandhurst was a non-starter. There was no way Rhah was going to stay in the mob, go on to be a retread. Behind them in the trees a bird cried and then another.

'It's so quiet,' Elias said. 'Have you noticed?'

Rhah nodded and smiled for the first time in hours. 'Nice, isn't it. Peaceful. Never appreciated that word before.'

'You've decided, haven't you?'

Rhah nodded.

'What are you going to do?'

'Dunno,' he replied. 'Do some sailing, maybe.'

Jonesy, brewing up, passed Rhah his cup, and had just put Elias's on the flame when a woman started walking towards them across the river, past burnt-out vehicles. In her fifties maybe, she was slender, tired-looking, her skin the coppery tones of the local Mayan people. She had something in her hands, a small cooking pot perhaps. She was taking a risk, walking through the ford. After the mines and all the fighting it would need clearing, but Elias put the thought from his mind.

'And after that?'

Rhah shrugged.

The woman walked up out of the water and approached them, stopping by Elias, who looked up. She held out her hands, offering the cooking pot.

'Take it,' Rhah said softly. Elias took the pot and looked into it. Rice and beans, and meat of some kind. As he looked up she took a crucifix from around her neck and placed it over his head. The three soldiers sat in silence, no one sure what to say, the poignancy of the situation affecting all of them.

'Thank you,' she said. 'You save us. God sent you.'

She turned to walk back across the river, and it was Rhah who spoke.

'*Madre?*' he called softly. She turned back. 'Go in peace,' he said. She smiled and nodded and moved away.

Robo strode up. He looked as bad as any of them, his short hair dark with dried blood, and behind him Elias could see some support company blokes moving the dead. The Paras were put into body-bags and carried up to the road, but they were laying out the Guatemalans in rows, their shirts pulled over their faces. It was not a pleasant job; some had been there over a day and in the tropical heat nature was taking its course. Robo sat down beside them.

'Wanna brew, Sar' Major?' Jonesy asked.

Robo nodded. 'Please. Elias, when you have finished your tea, secure down here. B Coy will relieve us.'

Two of the support blokes walked over and looked down at Plonker's body, one of them unzipping a bag. Jonesy looked up from his little gas burner. 'Leave him. We'll take him up.'

'Got orders,' came the reply. One of them bent down and took Plonker's arms.

'I said we'll take him, he was a mate. We're gonna take care of him. Now fuck off!' Jonesy snarled. One of them brushed the remark aside.

'We're doing the others. So what makes –'

Robo looked up. 'You heard him. Fuck off or I'll drop you.'

Maybe the man didn't recognize him, or perhaps he was tired after the long flight from the UK, but it came out anyway; 'Piss off,' he muttered.

Robo came up off the ground like a coiled spring, his weight behind the punch, and his fist flashed out and took the big soldier full in the face. He went down as if pole-axed and lay there stunned for a few seconds; then he shook his head and looked up at Jennings, who pointed down at Plonker's body. 'That's the bravest man you'll ever see.'

The soldier got to his feet, and his oppo, finally noticing the leather strap and crown on Jennings' wrist, pulled him back and they warily moved away, on to the next hole. Another figure was crossing the river, this one a man; lean, swarthy, tanned and heavily tattooed, carrying a box on each shoulder.

He waded out of the stream and sat himself down with the twelve platoon toms. 'Anyone fancy a cold one?' he asked in an English accent, ripping the top off a case of Belikin beer.

'Where the fuck did you come from?' Robo asked.

'Over there,' Collins said with a grin, nodding back across the river, handing out beers to outstretched hands. 'I've got a restaurant; Eva's.'

'You been there all through this shit?' Jonesy asked.

'Yeah. Fucking stupid, eh?' Collins replied. He looked down the river a few yards and recognized someone. He smiled and reached into his pocket; he had changed batteries on the phone, and he dialled a number. Ten or twelve feet away Chard's phone rang in his pocket. He snatched it out.

'Hello?'

'Fancy a cold beer?'

'Christ, am I glad to hear your voice. Thought you had been caught! I'd love a drink sometime. We'll be over later this afternoon.'

'I meant now,' Collins said, grinning and pointing out the SAS officer, leaning over the tiny telephone, to the toms around him. Even Robo was smiling.

'Now?'

'Yeah, now, dickhead. Turn around.' There was a burst of laughter from the toms which told Chard where to look and he ambled over, grinning like a kid.

A few minutes later a corporal from B Coy strolled up, his rifle over his shoulder. 'Fucking hell, party time. Where's Elias? Oh sorry, didn't recognize you. Right hole, anyway.' He dropped to his haunches and then sat down. 'Gentlemen, you are relieved.'

Someone passed him a beer.

Epilogue

First attempts to find any survivors or trace of Captain Atlee's small patrols team failed and the next day a Mayan tracker went out to where they had disappeared. He was able to look at the ground and follow what had happened. He showed them where the firefight began, where more than a hundred enemy had been, and they found the first body quite quickly. They smelled it before they saw it. He then followed the tracks of the rolling firefight for another hundred yards, then cut deep into the jungle and found the second body. Atlee and the third were wedged into a fighting position up a bank – both were dead. The tracker pointed out blood trails, showed the deep indentations of one man carrying another. Atlee, hit several times in the torso, had been carried by one of his men, until he also was hit. They holed up, all of them mortally wounded. The fourth soldier had crawled away for help, but had also died of his wounds. They found his body fifty yards from the others in the direction of the bridge. Captain Ericson, the B Squadron boat troop commander was never found but the missing private, the last man unaccounted for from the sunken SAS boat, was. His body was wedged under a tree root, where wounded he had made his stand and had his last contact. His ammunition was all expended and he had finally died from multiple gunshot wounds.

It was three days before a mixed Mexican and US army unit arrived wearing blue UN helmets and body-armour as a security force to oversee the end of the Guatemalan withdrawal. 2 Para were moved back to Airport Camp; they cleaned themselves up, their gear was stowed and palleted, and they flew home, the wounded having gone on ahead. The airlift was large, with refuelling at Miami and then again at the NATO base at Gander. As it turned out C and D Coys, with the remaining seven Royal Marines were in the last two aircraft, which took off an hour after the rest of the battalion; there was a reason, but none of them knew it.

When they landed at RAF Brize Norton their families were there to greet them, with many of the wounded, released from hospital to be there, the media, hundreds of wellwishers, dignitaries and the band of the Parachute Regiment. They played the Regiment's quick march as the men disembarked. Families were held back for a few minutes. This was a chance for the military to honour their own. After their last campaign, the Falklands, many of 2 Para were flown home, landing at dark airports, unnoticed, forgotten, because the main body arrived by sea and all the attention was there. They hadn't felt valued, nor appreciated as returning warriors should be. Wallace was determined it would not happen again.

The two companies were lined up, the small group of marines to one side. The rest of the battalion, who had arrived as planned an hour earlier, and an honour guard made up from the remainder of 5 Airborne Brigade then formed up opposite them. As the quick march came to a close the 2 Para RSM gave the command and the representative companies of 5 Airborne presented arms across the oily pan to their comrades, the survivors of the battle of San Ignacio. Within a unit, there is no higher honour.

That done, the barriers were dropped and the families and girlfriends were allowed to move forward to greet their men in the harsh lights of the television crews, the eyes of the world upon them. The marines were honoured six weeks later, as was their way, when the handful of survivors attended a drumhead ceremony where, in front of the entire Comacchio Group, the band of the Royal Marines beat the retreat, the time-honoured recall to marines in action ashore – 'You may disengage and return to the ship.'

Lieutenant Harry Oliver Rees and Major Peter Tyson-Davis of the 2nd Battalion the Parachute Regiment were both awarded the Military Cross for leadership. Lieutenant Toby James Estelle also of 2 Para, posthumously received the same award for conspicuous gallantry in the face of the enemy.

Major Fox, also of 2 Para, Lieutenant James Murray RM and Major David Chard 22 SAS were all awarded the Military Medal for leadership. For his courage in carrying a wounded comrade to safety under intense fire and for three other separate incidents where he left the safety of his position to go to the aid of his comrades, each time exposing himself to intense danger, and twice being wounded, Private Rodney Desmond Smith, D Company, 2nd Battalion, the Parachute Regiment, posthumously received the Victoria Cross.

There were nine other awards for conspicuous gallantry above and beyond what is expected of a British soldier in the face of the enemy at the battle for San Ignacio.

Harry Rees was promoted captain and went on to a tour in a training establishment. He and Sophie were married the summer following the training deployment in Belize. David Chard, his tour with 22 SAS over, impressed with what he had seen, transferred from his parent regiment across to 2 Para and went on to command the battalion. McKay, Boyce, Gibbo and Dozy Tupping, the air troop patrol members who first encountered the Guatemalans on their patrol all returned safely to Hereford but sadly Paul Gibson was killed in a training accident two months after their return. Pete Collins asked for his role in the affair to remain unknown. He had to live in San Ignacio and if what he did became public knowledge then one day he knew some disgruntled Guatemalan would have a go at him, and he just wanted the peaceful life. He was however on the New Year's Honours list, receiving the OBE for his services to his country as the honorary British Consul in San Ignacio, and it occurred to no one to ask why he was given the award after only nine months' service.

Rhah Bundy never did go to Sandhurst. Appalled by what he had witnessed during those days and nights, he left the army, never collected the MM he was awarded and took a job delivering yachts and working as a sailing instructor.

Elias Cutter stayed in. He applied to the Royal Military Academy and was instantly accepted. There were many that said he should have been decorated, both for valour and leadership, but he wasn't – such is the way of things. There is no doubt that the selection board at Sandhurst knew of his role in the battle; they had taken no less than five telephone calls from very senior people, one of them from the CJRDF at Northwood, Major General Macmillan, after a request from Colonel Wallace, CO 2 Para.

2 Para have a new battle honour. The words San Ignacio now sit below Falkland Islands and it is their intent, each year from now on, to have a dinner in the various messes sometime between the twentieth and twenty-second of June, when the VC awarded to Private Rodney 'Plonker' Smith is taken from the Airborne Museum and placed in its glass case on the table. An officer from 2 REP attends to represent his battalion. It has also been decided that on that night, when the officers of the battalion are in full mess kit, the junior subalterns of D and C Coy will wear DPM into the mess. They will receive a toast, retire early and join their companies for a less formal celebration where no badges of rank are worn, outside in the open air where the food is barbecued.

There is only one alcoholic beverage – beer, almost entirely Belikin beer provided each year by the Belize Defence Force, three hundred cases of it. But as someone pointed out, that wasn't a 'decent pint, mun', so there was always a barrel of real ale. The first year there were fifteen gatecrashers, led in by Lieutenant Murray. On that night the toms new to the companies since the last San Ignacio night are presented with a lapel badge. In silver, it has two little stumps rising from airborne wings, representing the two buttresses of the Holdsworthy Bridge. Set into the top of the wings like gemstones are grains of sand, taken from the bed of the Macal river. That first year, the fifteen surviving Royal Marines were presented with badges, but with the little silver Para wings clipped because after all they were only crap-hats. Dilwyn Jones stayed in the Reg, went on to do the corporal's course and on the mantelpiece over the gas fire in his quarters is a Buzz Lightyear doll, very grubby with dark, stained fingerprints and a cracked helmet. His kids sometimes ask why they can't play with it, and he tells them that one day he will explain it to them.

Glossary

AAC Army Air Corps

Addermine An anti-vehicle leave-behind mine using an *LAW*, light anti-tank weapon

APC Armoured personnel carrier

Basha A soldier's personal bivouac area. May be a poncho 'bivvy' cover under which he sleeps or in tropical conditions a hammock with a mosquito net

BDF Belize Defence Force

C-130 Lockheed Hercules, heavy-lift, short-field, turbo-prop, transport aircraft in common use with the military worldwide

Claymore Convex-shaped anti-personnel mine containing 700+ ball bearings. A defensive-position weapon

CO Commanding Officer, only used to describe the battalion commander. Anyone below that level is described as OC, Officer Commanding

COIN Counterinsurgency operations

CSM Company Sergeant Major

Cyalume A brand name of 'lightstick' – a cylindrical plastic tube the thickness of a cigar which when bent in the middle and 'snapped' allows two chemicals to meet, making a luminous green, red or yellow light, enough to read by, or signal with, for up to twelve hours

FCO	Foreign and Commonwealth Office
FLOT	Front line of troop. Used to work out the limit of friendly forces
FOB	Forward operating base
Gimmpy	See *GPMG*
Gollock	The common-use term for machete or heavy-bladed jungle knife
GPMG	General-purpose machine gun. Fires heavy 7.62 round and can be used in a sustained fire role. Infantryman's heavy section weapon. Also called *Gimmpy*
GPS	Global positioning system, now a hand-held device
Green army	Term normally used by special forces to describe their conventional army colleagues
HAHO	High altitude high opening – a parachute entry technique. With modern high-performance canopies troops can exit the aircraft many miles from the drop zone and, by steering their chutes, fly in silently
HALO	High altitude low opening – a parachute entry technique, used when troops are dropped directly over the drop zone
Head shed	Senior officers – origin Malaya, from water-shed, where the flow comes from
Hum-int	Human intelligence, as opposed to satellite, code-breaking or other forms
JRDF	Joint Rapid Deployment Force
LAW	Light anti-tank weapon, one-use throwaways
Loggies	Members of the Royal Logistics Corps
LUP	Lying-up point. Rest area where soldiers may

	or may not erect a *basha* depending on routine
LZ	Landing Zone
M-8	Armoured recce vehicle
M16	Assault rifle, standard issue to American forces
M-41 A3	US-built medium tank
M60	American machine gun, a sustained fire platoon weapon
M-113	Armoured personnel carrier
M203	M16 with rifle grenade launcher attached
MFC	Mortar fire controller
Milan	Second-generation anti-tank weapon – a missile, wire guided, fired from a launching post
Minimi	Heavy-barrelled with a bipod, it is the fully automatic version of the 5.56 mm SA80. In infantry it is the fire team's light automatic weapon
Mk19	Rapid-fire grenade launcher, can deliver grenades over 1000 metres
MO	Medical Officer
MoD	Ministry of Defence
Northwood	The tri-service Permanent Joint Headquarters at Northwood in Middlesex
P1	Pilot in command
PNG	Passive night-vision equipment
Recce	Reconnaissance
REME	Royal Mechanical and Electrical Engineers
RLC	Royal Logistics Corps
ROE	Rules of Engagement

R V	A rendezvous point
S A 80	Standard British Army infantryman's weapon. 5.56 compact 'bullpup' design
Scaleys	Special-forces term for communications people
Stag	Sentry or sentry duty
SUSAT	Four-power telescopic sight mounted on the standard *SA80*
T-10	Parachute favoured by US forces
VTOL	Vertical take-off and landing. Describes the Harrier's capability
Wolf	Latest version of British Army Land-Rover, equipped with a built-in mounting for a Milan-missile firing post
WP	White phosphorus. Designed as an illumination device, but the particles cause terrible burns if they come into contact with flesh
XO	The executive officer, the First Lieutenant. On a British frigate, normally a Lt Commander
66	Disposable anti-tank rocket

King's Shilling

Mike Lunnon-Wood

King's Shilling is an explosive novel of action and character, pitching the men and women of a British warship into a nail-biting race against time to evacuate civilians from the bloody cauldron of an African civil war.

With the country suddenly plunged into political chaos, and insurgents only a few miles from the capital, the Western powers need to get their people out of Liberia. HMS *Beaufort* is diverted to make the pick-up.

It soon becomes clear that even in the age of smart weaponry and sophisticated geopolitical planning, the modern naval commander must still rely on courage, ingenuity and guts to survive.

King's Shilling is a superb portrait of the modern navy, and thrillingly describes how a brilliantly drawn cast of characters reacts to a life-or-death situation.

ISBN 0 00 651162 7

Angel Seven

Mike Lunnon-Wood

Angel Seven is a high-tech, high-drama, high-emotion ride to the brink of the end of the world in an aircraft built at the edge of today's technology.

Global nuclear disarmament. So many people have dreamed of it, so many more have dismissed it as an impossible dream. One such is Peter Carson, a former RAF pilot, whiling away his premature retirement in the Caribbean.

As a new Middle East crisis threatens to plunge the world into conflagration, Carson is approached by a clandestine organization with an apparently preposterous idea: they want him to fly an aircraft they have developed that is faster and more lethally effective than any the world has seen and they want him to use it as the spearhead of their plan to create world peace.

Carson is an unlikely knight in shining armour, and the team that wants him is pitted against unimaginably powerful forces. Can they succeed?

A superbly orchestrated narrative of worldwide action and suspense, *Angel Seven* is a thriller of the future that could be happening now.

ISBN 0 00 649979 1